To Race the Wild Wind

Dianna (JOBI) Esquibel

Table of Contents

To Race the Wild Wind Ch. 1

Talon Templer Constantine eased his powerful cycle off of the almost deserted street and into the shade cast by a small, well cared for Inn. Dark eyes noted the simple sign displaying the ancient gnarled tree that gave the place its name. Thin lips quirked in a small one sided smile as the man shut down his machine. The name was appropriate. Ironwood was one of the few trees able to survive the harsh, poisoned climate of the Western Waste. Where a grove stood, water could be found. Whether you dared drink it or not... well, that was a different story!

A deep rumble drew the man's attention away from the Inn to the creature tethered to its hitching rail. He was careful to leave plenty of distance between it and his bio-machine. Destria often trashed objects that for reasons known only to themselves, the beasts deemed offensive. This one's smooth, long legged lines screamed quality. Its owner would be VERY unhappy if Templer killed the pricey racer while defending a machine he parked too close. Large nostrils flared as the beast caught his scent when he strode by. It chortled another nervous snort. The deceptively soft lips lifted to expose long black fangs as it pulled away as far as the tied reins would permit.

Ignoring the stallion's nervous antics, the man glided by well out of its reach and slipped through the Inn's heavy wooden door. He paused just inside, giving his vision a moment to adjust from the bright sunlight outside to the cooler dimness within the small establishment. Templer blinked and knew his dark eyes brightened as his outrider stirred in reaction to its vessel's surprise. The man expected to step into the usual booze smelling hole that was the standard venue of these small border towns. The arrogant creature he played Host to HATED these places with a passion that bordered on rabid. This was one of reasons Templer looked for them. To avoid the unpleasant PHYSICAL sensations rife in the seedier parts of civilization, the demon would bury itself deep within his Psyche. This act left its partner's mind blessedly quiet until the man chose to leave, or its particular set of skills was needed. Something that Constantine doubted would happen any time soon. Again, one corner of the man's thin lips quirked up. If the Reaper was hoping for some death, blood and mayhem... it would be going hungry. His superiors made it clear in no uncertain terms they had been sent to Edgewater to give the human half of their "partnership" a chance to rest and recuperate. For the next week, this particular Talon was out of circulation.

Constantine felt his outrider stir as he scanned the bar with an assassin's unconscious attention to detail. Although small, the common room was very clean. Heavy wood tables gleamed in the faint light coming through the still open door. Templer's sensitive nose picked up the faint scent of good quality alcohol and some very interesting smells emanating from a door he presumed lead to the kitchen. The man ruthlessly stomped on the sudden desire to stay here. If he wanted any peace of mind in the next week, he would have to find another Inn. An echoing growl of displeasure followed by a sudden pain behind his right eye let the man know what his companion thought of this decision. The man rode the wave of agony, trying to outlast it. When the sight in the affected eye wavered, he resorted to dirty tactics!

"If you don't back off... Azra... we will spend the next week in a brothel!"
The pain disappeared, leaving in its place an echoing silence. Templer blinked to clear his vision while savoring his small victory. Rarely did the man come out on top when his symbiont disagreed with his actions.

The day was young, the bar still empty. No one noticed his slight hesitation. No one except a burly man standing behind the curved ironwood bar. This individual paused in the act of polishing a glass when Constantine stopped just inside the door. Light brown eyes set in a pleasant face studied the ebony wrapped stranger as he approached the bar. Those wise eyes widened as a swing of the approaching man's dusty black cloak revealed its deep crimson lining. This motion also exposed the telltale triple barreled gun that rode the holster tied low on his leather clad thigh.

"Do you serve Benedictine Stout?"
Templer kept his words soft, uncomfortable with the other man's sharp assessing look. Damned if it did not feel as if the big man was cataloging every weapon visible or not tucked on and around his tall slender frame. With one last narrow eyed glance at The Trinity, the Bartender seemed to reach a decision. Those large hands set the glass and towel down.

"No Padre... That one is hard to come by out here. We have a comparable home brew if you are interested?"

Padre... he had not heard that title in a while. Priest was most common. Reaper, hellhound and other names not as nice were more the norm. At his slight nod, the man expertly filled a tall glass from the tap. As he did this, he glanced again at the big gun.

"You aren't planning on starting any trouble with that, are you?"

"Hnn... It's TALON Constantine, not Padre." Templer answered. The other's face paled as the man realized what the rank paired with a Trinity meant.

"And No, I don't make a habit of STARTING trouble." (Although, he thought as he accepted the dark foamy beer, his kind had no problem at all with FINISHING it!)

Talons held a unique position within the Order's complicated hierarchy. Only those with the rank of Talon, Inquisitor or one of the Fist killed with impunity. The Fist consisted of soldiers, masters of the blade and bow. People feared and respected them for the usual reasons. Talons, were recruited at birth. Tortured and genetically modified, those that survived the long years of brutal training were bonded to an elemental slave when they took their vows... and received a Trinity. Talons were the elite of the Hand's killers. Priest, mage, assassin, judge and executioner, all rolled together into one gun-slinging package. Citizen's called them hell hounds for a reason. If one was set on your trail, there was little chance of escape. You could not bribe a Talon... you could not sway him from his assigned task. Death would come for you be it by blade, hot lead or on a demon's shadowed wings. The public feared the Fist... the WICKED feared the Reaper!

Constantine carried his drink to a back table, settling into a chair with his back to the wall.

From here, the priest could view the common room, all the doors, and a darkened stairwell leading to the upstairs. This habit had saved his ass many times. Being on vacation was no excuse to change it. A slight smile stirred his lips when he sipped the cold brew. The beer's quality had not been exaggerated.

Templer rolled his shoulders, wincing as tight muscles protested. No one needed to fear the gun slinging priest THIS week! It was evident that his mind and body had reached their limits. For two long years they had been denied entrance to the Holy cities. The creature he hosted had serious anger management problems that ALMOST eclipsed his own. This made it difficult sometimes for the man to keep the beast leashed. The last time Talon Constantine lost control, they leveled a good sized town! Granted most of the town had been comprised of wealthy merchants and crooked bureaucrats buried so far up the local Prelaetors ass.... The man strangled the thought as a sinister chuckle rumbled through his mind at the memory. There had been nothing funny about the aftermath. Innocents had died along with the guilty due to his lack of control. This was NOT the first time events like this had happened, and damned his misbegotten soul, it probably would not be the last. Unfortunately, because of this, his superiors kept him as far away from their pristine cities as they could. It was not good P.R. for one of God's Chosen to raze entire towns to the ground in fits of demonic bad temper!

Without Azra being able to recharge in the great temples; the outrider had to make due with energies it gleaned out of their immediate environment. This meant that it was not operating at optimum levels and its host's body took a beating when they rode into battle. There was no rest for the wicked the man thought as he watched the room's other occupant now lazily polishing the bar. He was one of the strongest of his kind. Whenever a problem; be it a Demonae, a re-gen monster or some poor, insane, Tainted soul, threatened the realm, it was Talon Templer Constantine that got called into service. After two long and bloody years, the priest was thankful to be granted even this much of a break!

Constantine was just polishing off the excellent beer when a loud crash from the kitchen shattered the pleasant quiet. The gunman ruthlessly stepped on the ingrained instinct that had him reaching for his holster. Damn... Captain Sig was right. The Wind-Master had eloquently informed Templer that, "...he was wound tighter than a virgin's mainspring," when he dropped the Talon outside town. Templer doubted that a dropped pan of dishes was good reason for pulling iron! The priest forced himself to relax only to second guess the action as the barkeep froze with a panicked expression on his face.

"Damn it Chrysta... get the HELL outta my kitchen!"

There was silence, then a loud thump followed by,

"Crap! Sorry Grant..." The husky voice did not sound at all apologetic to Templer's trained ear.

"Here...just let me fix this!!"

Another loud crash and the bartender flew out from behind the bar. The kitchen door suddenly popped open and a middle aged woman just about ran the big man over. She was laughing as she wrapped what looked to be a huge sandwich up in a napkin.

"This is YOUR fault, Grant. If you hadn't refused to make my lunch, and I quote ...at the butt crack of dawn... unquote. I wouldn't have to fend for myself!"

As she dodged around the living block in her path, Templer noticed that although the woman's movements were quick and oddly fluid, they were marred by a slight limp.

A smile tugged at the other man's wide mouth. It disappeared as he tried to look irate and failed.

"Well, count me as suitably reprimanded." Grant stuck his head through the kitchen door, surveying the damage. "Holy SHIT! How did you create such a mess just making a sandwich?"

The Innkeeper sounded as if he was having a coronary. Templer didn't move. If he had to, he would give the man last rites. The priest suspected this was a scene that played out quite often.

Chrysta caught his eye. She flashed him a raffish smile, then blew the bartender a kiss as she shot out the front door. Grant's shoulders drooped in what looked to be total defeat. Both men listened in silence as the sound of pounding hooves faded into the distance. Templer could not help but feel some sympathy at the other man's sorrowful, much put upon look. The priest knew that his eyes were glowing gold as he looked back at the other man. His outrider had risen to watch the entire scene in fascinated silence. The few friends that Templer had would swear that Talon Constantine possessed no sense of humor... this was not true. He had one, he just did not let it out often to play. The Talon blinked and rose to his full imposing height.

"If you would like, I could go after her. That sandwich looked damned good!"

He did not know whose reaction was more priceless. His demon's utter and complete astonishment or the look on the other man's face. Grant paled a little, then proved he had a backbone. He met the Talon's unearthly gaze straight on with his brow furrowed in concern.

"I wouldn't recommend that course of action. If there is food involved, Chrysta is likely to hand you your ass!"

Templer worked hard to keep the smile that tickled his lips off of his face. Damned if he did not like this man. Returning the empty glass to the bar, the priest surprised himself with a sudden change of heart.

"Do you by chance have any rooms available?"

"I am sorry... Don Ricardo and Chrysta have all of my rooms reserved until after the Festival. You will be lucky to find a room anywhere in town this close to opening day."

Constantine knew that most of his Brothers would not think twice about using their rank to take what they wanted. He could tell by the look on the man's calm face that this is also what Grant expected of him.

An hour later saw Templer astride his Ether-cycle headed out towards the Devil's Anvil. Grant was not mistaken in his assessment of the situation. Once a year, Edgewater re-established its place on the map as a Port with its annual Destria Festival. Breeders, Caravan Masters, and enthusiasts of the elegant animals gathered to buy, sell, and take part in the many competitions involving the rare and useful beasts. The week long festivities would culminate in The Gauntlet. This endurance/speed race covered one hundred miles of tortured terrain through the Devil's Anvil. The winner gained great prestige, and also the choicest caravan routes for the coming year. Templer had arrived in town just a few days before the Festival was slated to start. The crowds had already started to arrive and there was not even a Terra-bird stall available for rent in the next ten days. Grant suggested that he try some of the outlying ranches. Most set aside areas for people to camp for a small fee. The barkeep had been surprised that the Talon was willing to take this option. Templer had assured the man that sleeping in the rough was not a new or unwelcomed experience. As a matter of fact, it would be easier to keep control away from the crowds.

Opening the throttle on his cycle a little wider, Templer leaned into it as he whipped around a turn. This part of the road followed the contours of a convoluted ridgeline. There was a sharp drop off on either side of the narrow dirt track. He enjoyed the surge of adrenaline as the dual front wheels slipped a little then re-gained traction heading into another turn. His friend, Blade, was incredibly talented at riding the powerful bio-machines. The man had spent a lot of time schooling Templer to improve the priest's driving abilities. Constantine did not have the soldier's raw skill but his inhuman strength and enhanced reflexes compensated for this.

Sharp eyes caught movement up ahead. Through the shifting dust, Templer could just make out the large form of a destria stretched out in a full gallop. Its rider was flattened along its shoulder and neck, half buried in the flying mane. The gunslinger eased his big bike over, intending on passing the pair on the left. He wanted to give the notoriously high strung animal plenty of space. Just as he came abreast of the flying pair there was a flash of movement on the destria's right. Seemingly in mid-stride the animal shied sideways, violently fighting its rider's tight hold on the reins. Somehow she managed to stick to her powerful mount's back.

Templer swore as the animal continued its sideways plunging run into the speeding ether-cycle's path. The priest did the only thing he had time to do. He laid the big bike over in a controlled skid. A brief vision of what the heavy machine would do to the destria's fragile looking legs flashed through his mind. There was an impression of misplaced air, and he caught a glimpse of flashing hooves. Somehow the beast made a desperate twisting leap, clearing him along with the sliding cycle. Templer stuck with the bike waiting for the bite that would tell him the dual front wheels had traction again. For a heart pounding second the man thought he had gotten away with it. Then the bottom dropped out from underneath the bike. He had run out of road. The gunman had a micro-second to get clear of the now tumbling machine as they slid off the edge. He experienced a terrifying moment of free fall, then the ground came up with frightening speed. There was a flash of intense pain on impact, followed by darkness. Templer's limp body tumbled down the rock strewn slope until it came to a bloody and broken stop at the bottom.

To Race the Wild Wind Ch. 2

Templer floated in pain laced darkness. Occasionally he would rise towards the surface and awareness would try to worm its way through his brain. One time the sound of a soft curse and strong hands rolling him over brought him up to the brink. The agony of broken bones grinding together dropped him back into the abyss. In another instance he awoke to a warm, spicy smelling hide against his cheek along with hoof beats drumming in rhythm with the pain pulsing through his body. The priest tried to straighten up. This made his outrider sit on him... hard. A rather nasty curse rumbled through his aching head.

"Be still Host! I am having a hard enough time keeping your foolish brains where they belong as it is!"

Heh... that just didn't sound good. The gunman decided it would be much easier to let himself slip back into the comfortable darkness.

"How's he doing?" Grant's rough voice penetrated the darkness, sending a wave of nausea through the priest's aching body. Still, the need to know where he was and who was with him drove Templer towards awareness.

"A lot better than I expected."

This voice sounded vaguely familiar. His muddled brain struggled to put a name or face with it. The words accompanied a pair of cool, calloused hands carefully probing over his sore ribcage and abdomen.

"I have seen self-healing like this once..." The woman's soft voice hesitated, not finishing this interesting statement. A gentle finger gave a light tap on a spot just under his heart.

"All that is left is bruising where there were broken bones. I can only assume that whatever internal injuries he might have had healed just as fast. The head injuries are all I am concerned about now."

Cool fingers traced a very tender spot just over his right eye. Templer could not control the twitch of his eyebrow in nervous reaction to the gentle touch.

The priest lay quiet, keeping his eyes closed. He stretched out his other enhanced senses to take stock of his surroundings. He was laying on a comfortable bed, covered with a soft quilt. Another quick check confirmed that ALL that covered his body was that nice... thick... quilt. The room held a confusing scent of flowers mixed with medical supplies. It was all underlain by the odd spicy smell he had noticed earlier.

The soft touch on his head withdrew. Templer opened his eyes to find himself staring into the concerned gaze of the woman who had been in the bar earlier that day. She sat in a high backed chair placed close to the bed in which he rested. Her eyes, he noticed, were a deep green rimmed in golden brown. Tiny laugh lines radiated out from their corners. These disappeared as her chestnut eyebrows arched in surprise.

"I hope that is your natural eye color. If not... we may have a problem."

The husky voice held a note of concern. Grant leaned forward into the priest's limited field of vision. Templer again wanted to squirm under the other's intent scrutiny. The big man's face relaxed in a slight smile.

"It's okay Chrysta. The glow means his outrider is doing its job."

For a moment, Templer did not know what

was more interesting, the thoughtful but unsurprised expression on his caregiver's face... or Azra's (not to mention, HIS) unadulterated astonishment. The Order held its secrets tight. The Talons even more so. Few outsiders ever got close enough to learn the intimate details of the Priest/Elemental relationship that gave the rank its unearthly abilities. For good reason. It was the official position that the ability to call and control a demon was a gift or a curse. Any soul not Sanctified by the Order, who was Tainted enough to SUMMON an Elemental was an abomination. The Inquisition burnt these poor souls as witches. If the public ever found out that the Talons did not SUMMON their demonic counterparts but instead carried them around in a form of controlled possession... the backlash would be extreme. How the HELL did a small town bartender have that kind of intimate knowledge about outriders?

Feeling very vulnerable, the gunman tried to push himself up. A pair of strong hands pressed into his sore chest, pushing him back down into the pillows.

"WHOA there... let's not be too hasty. How you did not leave half of your brains splattered all over that ridge young man is beyond me."

Those capable hands slid up through his blood matted hair as gentle fingers mapped out his skull. Templer could not help but wince when they lightly pressed on one particularly painful spot.

"I'll bet that is uncomfortable." Chrysta's soft voice was thoughtful. "You had an open depressed skull fracture there when I first got down to you... I swear there were brains and blood everywhere with that and all of your other injuries. All I feel now is a slight ridge where the edges have not finished healing. Do you have a head ache?"

Templer gave a slight nod. Head ache was an understatement. He was certain he could hear his brain swooshing around in his skull with every little movement!

The woman's sympathetic smile made him feel a little better. It should have worried him instead.

"Grant, put that tray over there and give him a hand sitting up."

Before the Templer could object the barkeep set his tray on the nightstand. His strong but gentle blunt fingered hands, eased the priest up while Chrysta positioned some pillows to support his back. Constantine, was too busy checking his skull for leaks to be of much help. The priest did not want to spill any brains out onto the pretty flowered quilt. The woman took one look at his pale face and her deft hands plucked a basin off the night stand to set in his lap.

"Are you experiencing any dizziness or nausea?"

Templer swallowed and relaxed a little when it seemed like his stomach was going to stay where it belonged. He gave a slight shake of his head in answer to her question and lifted a shaky hand, trying to ease her concern.

"I am fine..." He had to stop to clear his throat as his mouth felt as dry as the Western Waste. Chrysta handed him the glass of water that sat on the tray the barkeep had put down.

"Yes... That you are."

These words were so quiet that it took the Talon's enhanced ears to hear them. His caregiver would not look him in the face as she tucked the quilt tighter about his hips. The man had a sudden, awful suspicion it had not been Grant who had undressed him. Glad he rarely blushed the priest sipped his water, then asked.

"Are you the town healer?"
Those odd eyes flashed up to meet his and

Chrysta's tanned face creased in a wicked smile.

"Nooo... although I do fill in for him occasionally. I am more along the lines of the town... vet."

Templer choked on the mouthful of water he had been in the process of swallowing.

The woman's eyes were laughing as she gently thumped him on the back to help clear his airway.

"Really, I fill in for the Doc when he needs some extra hands. I HAVE had some medical training so I had no problem assessing your physical condition. Once I got down to you, it did not take long to figure out that the general medical rules just did not apply. With some of the injuries you had, you should have been quite... dead! By the time I wrestled you out of the ravine it was obvious that a lot of the damage was disappearing. I was planning on taking you straight to the Doc's office but by the time we hit town the worst of the damage seemed to have healed up. Grant and I figured that the fewer people in town who know of your ...modifications... the better." The woman patted the back of his blade-hand drawing his attention to the cybernetic limb.

"I hope it was the right decision. Flesh I can deal with. This is a little beyond my abilities."

Damn, whether sharp metal or punishing rock, something had done a good job of chewing through the tough armor like nano-skin that protected his bio-engineered limb. The woman had wrapped it but the blue and black staining the bandage did not bode well. The Talon hoped the damage was something that his limited skills in field repair could fix.

The woman paused and looked to Grant as if for confirmation. The big man just nodded.

She slanted an odd look back at the man on the bed.

"Let's face it, your particular rank is one that does not inspire love and devotion amongst the masses. This town has factions that would have good reason to make sure you did not take another breath. Leaving you where you might be helpless to defend yourself just did not sit well with either of us. We decided to keep you here."

The trained assassin in him noted that Grant had moved a little closer to Chrysta. He held himself with that peculiar stillness that Templer knew would explode into violence if the big man felt the woman needed protecting. The Innkeeper need not have worried. Kindness in this hard and violent world was rare. The priest was not one to repay it with death.

One side of his mouth lifted in a slight smile as he nodded at them.

"You were wise in this and I thank you for your care."

He did NOT tell them that if he had been placed in the situation they feared and he had not been well enough to control his outrider, things in this little town would have gotten very ugly... very fast!

Chrysta gave his damaged hand a final little pat as she looked toward the window. Templer realized that it was dark outside. He had been out of it almost an entire day.

"Well it looks as though you are well on your way to recovery, I had better be getting my butt back to the ranch." She levered herself out of the chair and walked to the door. Templer noted that the mild limp she had that morning was more pronounced. The woman stopped in the doorway, balancing herself against its frame.

"Grant and I are very aware of some of the "situations" out in the Borderlands that the Talons and those who serve in the Fist are called in to deal with. Most do not realize that along with some of your more unsavory duties there are a few of you out there who put your bodies and your souls on the line to keep the realm safe. That cloak and your weapon..." She nodded toward where the Trinity hung in its holster from the bedpost, "...are a dead giveaway to who and what you are. Grant told me you were here looking for a room this morning. You could have taken what you wanted, and you did not. That tells us more about who and what you are." The woman shifted, wincing a little as she rubbed her thigh. "You are welcome to your share of my room as long as you need it. Be aware that I come and go at some very odd hours. I usually sleep on the duvet." That rubbing hand stopped to pat her bad leg. "It's easier for me to get in and out of then the bed."

Her eyes took on a sudden wicked gleam... "Standing rule is that if YOU can run around nude... then so can I! Grant will run a tab for your meals or anything else you might need. Don Ricardo has agreed to cover it."

Chrysta pushed herself away from the frame, not giving him the option to protest. "Grant, I will be here in the morning with the team and the week's supplies. Talon Constantine, if you are up to it. I can take you out to the accident site as soon as we have the wagon unloaded. I am sure there are things there that you will want to retrieve."

Not waiting for either man to answer, the woman slipped out and shut the door behind her.

Templer glanced over at the silent innkeeper. "Is she always that bossy?"

The gunman's voice was dryly amused. For longer than he cared to remember HE gave the orders. It was odd to have the tables turned. Grant's bushy eyebrows shot up.

"Well no..." The man's voice was deadly serious..."For Chrysta that was pretty tame. You might as well resign yourself to being our guest while you are in Edgewater. It seems that she has adopted you. As you witnessed this morning it does not do you a bit of good to get into a pissing contest with her. That woman inevitably wins!"

Grant ambled over to the door.

"I'll be downstairs closing up. If you need anything, just holler."

With that, the bartender opened the door and stepped out.

Templer listened until the man's heavy tread on the stairs signaled he was heading down to the common room. Then the Talon took stock of the room. It, like the bar earlier, was very clean. There was the bed he currently occupied, plus the duvet Chrysta had mentioned. It was pushed over by a large window that was cracked open to let in the night air. A soft breeze made the curtains rustle as it entered the room. Large glass fronted cases lined the far wall, all of which were filled with what looked like medical supplies. Two high backed chairs and a small table occupied the center of the space. These finished out the rest of the room's furnishings. He noticed another door and wondered where it led.

The priest slid his legs over the edge of the bed. In doing so he noticed the impressive bruising patterned over his chest and stomach. It was slowly fading. Just the fact it had taken so long for the injuries to heal even this much told him that his outrider had earned its keep that day. His clothing he found folded on one of the chairs. It was clean, and small stitches marked where several tears had been neatly mended. Getting dressed, the gunman went over to the other door and turned the knob. To his considerable surprise (and Azra's utter delight) this opened up into a tidy little bathroom. Most of the tastefully decorated space was occupied by a huge claw foot tub complete with hot and cold water tabs. Templer lightly tapped the containment sphere encircling the hot water pipe. The small fire salamander held captive within swirled around and eyed him expectantly. The Priest withdrew his fingers and the elemental settled back down to a spelled sleep. Well, well, well... this was an unlooked for extravagance in a small town inn!

Strolling back over to the window, Templer picked up the Trinity as he passed the bed. It seemed to have survived the fall without a terrible amount of damage. The view from the window opened into a good sized courtyard surrounded by several large holding pens and a stables.

The priest stood at the window, fingers lightly tapping on the high barrel of his gun as he tried to find a reason that these strangers were being so kind. He was uncomfortable with taking advantage of their charity. Because of this, the paranoid assassin that resided within could not help but look for some nefarious purpose behind the generous offer. His tapping fingers froze. This was ridiculous. If the pair had wanted to harm him, they had passed up the perfect opportunity to do so. Besides, Azra notwithstanding, he did not relish the thought of roughing it for the next week. His outrider stayed silent as its host slowly came to a decision. Templer nodded to himself. He rather liked Grant and maybe it would not be half bad sharing a room with Chrysta. He would give it a couple of days. After all, they were on vacation. Still... and this was directed internally.

"One bit of trouble Azra, and I promise by all that is Holy. I will yank our asses out of here and we will spend the next week sand surfing out in the Waste!"

Templer watched the sunrise the next morning from the roof of the Inn. His high vantage point gave the priest an outstanding view of the small town and the surrounding countryside. The town of Edgewater sat in a wide valley created by the Clearwater River. The small river meandered along the center of the valley surrounded by tall trees and almost manicured looking meadows. Constantine understood why the area had become a mecca for breeding destria. The Clearwater had run clean now for generations and the results were evident in the land surrounding this rare, clean water source. The meadows and pastures that bordered it were rich with green grazing. While perfect for the Destria this also fed the meat producing animals that supplemented the dietary needs of the big omnivores.

Sharp eyes picked up a cloud of dust being stirred up on the distance road. This sure sign indicated a caravan on the early morning move, bringing in guests along with supplies for the next week. Only the most powerful and the wealthiest of patrons had the means to arrive via WindClipper as the Talon had. A well maintained landing field for these was well north of the town. The unpredictable winds around the large valley meant NOBODY wanted one of the giant bio-machines landing in their backyard!

The main street of the town measured almost a full two miles. Markets, eating establishments, and several large Inns stood shoulder to shoulder with the inevitable bars and gambling joints. The northeast side of town was occupied by the inevitable small Temple surrounded by the nicer homes of Order officials, sycophants, and the wealthier citizens of the town. As the side streets moved south, smaller and smaller streets branched off at regular intervals. The businesses became seedier the further west of Main Street they got. On the far south side of town was a compound made up of small paddocks each with its own attached barn. These housed the many different beasts of burden that came in with the caravans passing through what was essentially a Port. For the next ten days, they would also accommodate the many destria that would arrive for the festival. Several barns were already occupied by early arrivals. One side of the compound was taken up by the good sized oval track used for shorter speed contests. Beside this were several arenas used for different scheduled events. This track, for the time being, had been set aside for the arriving caravans as a staging area to unload and disband.

The Talon sat up a little as the arriving group moved into town. The part of him that did not recognize the word "vacation" noted whether the mix of animals, people and the occasional rare machine was sanctioned. Smugglers were rife in the more distance Port cities. Edgewater being one of the most remote. Only the valuable clean water source and its importance to the caravans that drove commerce in the Holy cities had drawn the Order's attention to it. A Sanctioned River-witch and strategically placed fire salamander traps provided power for the town. This made the citizen's lives easier along with giving the Hand additional reasons to tax and patrol it. Still, this Port was far removed from the Order's center. The officials here had a reputation for turning a blind eye to smugglers and black marketers.

This caravan was a smaller one. It consisted of the usual mix of heavy laden wagons and pack animals. The wagons were drawn by massive drafters. Numerous tall, wooly pacacams strode amongst them. These grumbled and groaned as they labored under their heavy loads. Standing out in the mix were two ornate coaches drawn by matched teams of uniquines. At the sight of the gentle but spirited beasts of burden, the priest unconsciously relaxed. These marked the caravan as legal. Only the Order had the right to breed and use that particular beast. A number of Fist cavalry rode point and rear guard astride heavy boned battle birds attesting to the fact that at least one individual down there had some political pull.

The low rumble of engines had elegant eyebrows lifting as a several powerful ether-cycles appeared, riding herd on the group. The Cataclysm compounded by the wars and re-gen plagues that followed plunged most of civilization back into the dark ages. Not until the century following the hard won Truce did the Holy Cities began to lead the people back out into the light. The Cataclysm had rendered most machines useless. They had rusted into dust long ago. These had been replaced by semi-living constructs of flesh and metal that only the Demonae could create. Because of the Re-Gen Wars (and what had been created to fight in them) the public looked upon bio-mechs with suspicion. The small Ether-cycles could be mastered by a strong willed individual with some training. The more complicated mechs, such as Wind-Clippers had to be controlled by a Drow. These heavily Tainted humans were sniffed out by the Talons and enslaved as children. They were physically modified to help in controlling the elementals that powered the Sanctioned Bio-mechs. Drows not Sanctioned were rogue. When discovered, they were hunted by the Talons with impunity. This was an automatic death sentence, both physically and spiritually. If, by chance, a person found an ancient machine that still worked, the fuel resources needed to keep them running were exceedingly rare. Any mercenary that could afford to own and operate either type of machine was either very good at what he did, or very crooked!

"HEY, you up there..." Grant's rough voice drew the priest's attention away from the caravan's slow progress. The big man had slipped out the inn's door and now stood with his hands on his hips looking up at the other's dark form. Once he had the Talon's attention, the bartender continued.

"Are you interested in eating some breakfast?"

Templer's outrider provided most of the energy his physical body needed, but breakfast actually sounded good. Better yet, his sensitive nose picked up the smell of something he had not had the luxury of enjoying in a long while... coffee! The gunman stepped off of the roof. He dropped the twenty feet to the ground to land in front of the startled Barkeep. With an easy grace, the priest straightened and settled his cloak. Grant just blinked.

"Well then, you had better come in and eat before it gets cold." The big man stepped aside and held the door open. As Constantine strolled past he wouldn't have sworn to it but the priest was pretty sure he heard the other man mutter... "Show off!"

The priest was just finishing one of the biggest breakfasts he could remember eating when the deep rumble of cycle engines disturbed the morning's quiet. He watched with interest as Grant's warm and pleasant face became cold when a group of five walked through the door. All were young men, dressed in expensive leathers. All had at least one weapon displayed prominently on their bodies. Templer studied the group, his senses going on alert. Something about the boys reminded him of a pack of rogue wolves. The gunman transferred his cup of coffee to his blade-hand, freeing up the other in case it was needed.

"Hey there... old man!" The tallest of the bunch swaggered up to the bar. "My dad wants ta know when yer going to accept the offer he made on this dump ya'all call a bar?"

This boy was tall and lean. He carried himself with the air that he was better than those around him. His long red hair was pulled back from his freckled face in a neat pony tail. Insolent green eyes stared at the older man behind the bar. The rest of the group gathered in silence around their evident leader. Templer noted that all the group had their backs to him. All, that is, except an older blonde who had stopped just inside the door where he could see the entire room. This man bore watching.

Grant met the young man's cold gaze and his lips lifted in a smile that did not reach his eyes.

"Rafe... you can tell your father that if he is interested in buying anything of mine, he can come talk to me himself." The barkeep kept his voice bone chillingly polite. "That way, I can tell him to his face what I always tell you. The Ironwood is not for sale to him, not now... not ever!" The big man set his towel down and placed his broad hands on top the bar.

"Now, if you boys are planning on staying to eat or drink in my establishment, you need to take your weapons outside and leave them there."

The young man's eyes widened then his handsome face twisted into a hateful sneer. "Take and LEAVE our weapons outside? Do you really think you are up to disarming us, OLD man!?"

Rafe stepped back a pace slashing a sideways glance at his friends. They had their hands hovering around or on their choice of weapon. The second the boy's attention shifted off of him, Grant's hands dropped and came up filled with a double barreled shotgun. The gun's nasty looking sawed off muzzle was centered on the redhead's chest. Templer had been content to let the big man handle this, but a blur of motion by the door confirmed his earlier assessment. The stocky blonde's fast draw was impressive. Still, the gunslinger wisely froze when he found himself looking down the triple bores of the Trinity.

Behind the bar, Grant's smile became something scary. "I reckon that between him..." the big man nodded towards Templer, "... and this." He motioned with the shotgun, "We'll have no problem pulling your teeth."

The redhead paled and raised his hands, forcing a dry laugh. The others behind him made a sudden show of empty hands.

"WHOA... Don't be getting your balls all up in a twist... old man! I'm just joking!"

The cold green eyes that met Templer's as the boy turned, were anything but laughing. They widened as the young wolf took note of the hell lit gold staring back at him.

"No harm... no foul... right? We were just playing with ya'all!"

Templer did not answer. He switched his attention back to the man at the door. The muzzle of his gun never wavered off its target. Rafe followed his gaze.

"Come on boys, I can tell we aren't welcome in this genteel establishment."

The blonde gunman lowered his weapon, his blue eyes never leaving Templer's hard face as the redhead led the others towards the door. He stepped back, allowing the pack to exit before him. With a slight nod of respect towards the silent Talon, he switched his icy gaze to look at Grant.

"Don Diego will be livid when he hears of this, you have to know that."

Grant met the hard gaze without wavering. "I know. I just don't care."

The blonde shrugged and slipped out the door. The fact that the man did not holster his side arm or give Constantine his back was silently noted by the gun slinging priest.

Grant released his weapon's dual hammers and replaced the lethal firearm back under the bar. Templer's eyes   tracked the weapon. The Order limited the flow of firearms in the Realm. The fact that he had just witnessed no less than four of them in the possession of civilians was something of interest to a man of his rank. Templer sternly reminded himself he was on vacation as he raised his cup to Grant indicating that he needed a re-fill.

The barman picked up a mug along with the pot of coffee and approached Templer's table. Topping the gunman's drink off, he poured himself a cup of the fragrant liquid and settled into the chair across from the other man. The priest slipped The Trinity back into her holster as he silently watched the bartender take a careful sip of the hot black fluid. Grant swallowed, then leaned back with a sigh.

"Damn, I am getting to old for this kind of crap!" His voice sounded weary. "I cannot thank you enough for backing me. I know by law you aren't supposed to interfere in civil matters."

Templer met the man's honest gaze. "I am on vacation... the rules don't necessarily apply. Besides, I figured you could handle the pup if you did not have to worry about the rest of the dogs."

Grant took another sip and shrugged.

"Yeah... that's the problem when dealing with Rafe. He always stacks the odds in his favor. If you had not been here, I am not sure how this little incident might have turned out. Don Diego owns most of this town. Rafe seems to think that because he is the Don's only son, he is untouchable. And in essence, I guess he is right. If I had shot the boy, even in self-defense, I would not have lived long enough meet the hangman."

Constantine tapped the tabletop lightly with the sharp talons of his blade-hand. With a Talon's enhancements, the rules governing his actions were very specific. Still, if Diego proved to be a radical, those rules could be bent... a little.

"Tell me about Diego."

Grant shrugged his heavy shoulders.

"Don Diego is not happy with Edgewater's slow growth and its small Port designation. He has plans to make it over into a Sin City."

Both of Templer's elegant eyebrows twitched up in surprise. Those were BIG plans. Sin Cities had been created to give the faithful somewhere legal to blow off steam, and as a reward for those that had earned special privileges. Activities illegal in the Holy Cities, were allowed in these Sanctioned Dens of Iniquity. Gambling, pharmaceuticals and fornication were punishable sins even in the rough Bordertowns. The Hand rarely moved to enforce these rules in the rougher Port cities. Without the Order's Sanction there were limits in these places that did not exist in the Devil's playgrounds. (More so if the proprietors were NOT paying the agreed upon kickbacks!)

Grant gave a slight nod, correctly interpreting this subtle sign of surprise.

"The man has the political backing to get this approved. To move his plans along, he has to convert most of the main street to casinos, lotus houses and brothels. There are some of us who don't appreciate Diego's grand dream and refuse to sell out. Rafe has been strong arming the weaker ones in an attempt to remove the opposition. His father has paid the town Peacekeepers to look the other way. The Don is determined to push this down our collective throat, any way he can."

Templer's softly tapping talons stopped, digging a little into the hardwood of the tabletop. Grant was right. Talons had no jurisdiction when it came to civil matters. The Hand would only intervene if the problem adversely impacted the Faithful or the Order's bottom line. As long as the trade (and wealth) continued to flow, his superiors would turn a blind eye up to a point. Especially if the Don was... generous. It was very evident that Diego had money and influence.

Men like the blonde gunslinger did not work for coppers.

"Hnnn..." Templer idly ran a claw along the rim of his almost empty cup. "That blond was fast with a gun. Do you have any idea who he is?"

Grant emptied the pot in the process of refilling the Talon's cup.

"His name is Cal Farraway. Rumor has it that he has training as a Temple guard. Somebody owed the Don BIG and Cal was the payment. When the man isn't tying up, loose ends, for Diego... he earns his keep riding herd on Rafe. I don't envy him the job!"

A heavy rumble from outside and the clatter of hooves on cobblestone interrupted them. Grant jumped up, grabbing the now empty pot of coffee.

"CRAP... that would be Chrysta! I had better get more of this perking. That woman is as evil tempered as one of her destria if she doesn't get her coffee quota filled."
The man's brown eyes pleaded with him from across the table.

"Do you think you could you go out and tell her to take it easy unloading? That will give me the time to get a fresh pot brewed!"

Templer had no reason to refuse what seemed an innocent request.

"No problem, Grant..." the gunman drained his cup and rose, "I can buy you the time you need."

As the lean, shadow wrapped priest stalked past on his way to the kitchen door, the bartender would have sworn he heard the tall man mutter under his breath... "Coward!"

Templer walked through the kitchen and stepped out of the back door into controlled chaos. Chrysta had driven a heavily laden wagon into the courtyard. She was in the process of swinging the team of drafters around so they could back it into the barn. A young man had two other destria on leads and was working at getting the excited animals into a holding pen. Another stable-man had opened the barn's wide double doors. He shouted directions as the woman carefully eased the big, fully loaded wagon in.

As the priest strode up, the animal nearest to him caught his scent and shied sideways into the heavy shoulder of its team mate.

"WHOA... Joshua, you big oaf!" Chrysta yelled and tightened her hold on the reins. The other member of the team pinned the squirrelly beast with one evil eye and snapped blunted, silver capped black fangs at its straining shoulder. Looking suitably reprimanded, the beast settled down. It glanced at the gunman with a remarkably intelligent and reproachful look on its long face. The Talon gave the pair a wide berth as he approached the wagon.

HOLY... the Priest had not realized how truly big the draft animals were. Their withers towered over his six foot five-inch frame by a good seven inches. Powerful, heavy boned bodies rippled with the thick muscling required for pulling loads that could weigh ten tons or more over long distances. The team had heated up on the trip in. Templer realized that the warm, spicy scent he had noticed the night before originated with them.

Chrysta wrapped the thick reins around the brake lever and set it. The two stable-hands began unloading the sacks of feed and the equipment that took up the entire wagon plus some. The woman climbed down from her high seat, grimacing as she put her hands on her hips and stretched. Constantine winced at the sound of several loud pops and cracks as her spine realigned itself.

"Oh... I do hate festival week." Chrysta flashed a tired smile Templer's way. "Why don't we go in and get a cup of coffee while the boys unload this."

For a moment, the gunman thought about throwing Grant back under the proverbial coach. Then, figuring that the other man would be making most, if not all of his meals in the next week, he decided, it would be best if he tried some delaying tactics. The Priest looked towards the two destria confined together in one paddock.

"I have never been up close to one of these guys." He walked over to the fence. Both destria eyed him with suspicious looks from the other side of the enclosure.

"Do they belong to you?"

Chrysta turned towards him with an expression, much like the destria's, on her face. She joined the gunman at the fence.

"The two drafters belong to Don Ricardo. These two are mine."

A soft whistle got an answering whuffle from the smaller of the two beasts who ambled up to the fence. This animal was not as tall as the drafters, much lighter in bone and built with long, clean lines. The bony, cream colored shield on its head was tipped with small white horns. Its' smooth hide was a creamy gold dappled with spots of almost white. A soft feathery mane cascaded down the graceful neck and its gold tipped with white hue was matched in the flowing tail. Sharp cloven hooves peek out from under the feathering that trimmed long, slender legs.

"This is Nuva, she is one of my oldest mares. She is also as close to trustworthy as these creatures come." Chrysta scratched the female's horn ridges as she talked. Nuva leaned into the caress, her blue eyes almost closed in bliss. "You might as well introduce yourself, this is who you will ride later on." The woman stepped back. "Just allow her to smell your hand, and if she wants to taste your breath... let her."

Templer's eyebrows shot up. He hesitated then removed the glove on his gun-hand. He extended it, palm up so that the big animal could inspect it. The pink muzzle brushed lightly over his skin. Nuva tensed, and snorted, wrinkling her lips as if his scent offended her.

"YAH...!" Chrysta's voice was sharp as she placed her hand over his. Templer stiffened at the unwanted touch. The woman ignored him, never breaking her eye contact with the mare.

"You behave yourself, Nuva!" She slid her hand around until it was under his. Nuva's blue eyes studied the woman's face for a long moment, then she looked into the priest's dark eyes. Templer felt his outrider stir uneasily. The mare searched his gaze, as if looking for something deep inside him. He was just about to pull away when the destria relaxed, blew out a long breath and gently lipped at his fingers. When she finished exploring his hand, the long nose came up and nuzzled his cheek. The priest stiffened, very uncomfortable with having those long fangs that close to his undefended face. Remembering what Chrysta had said... he let the breath out he had been holding. The rose colored muzzle brushed his lips. Large nostrils flared as the mare drank it in, then blew it back at him. Her breath was warm and sweet. For a moment the man stood still, sharing his breath and receiving hers in exchange. Nuva whuffled and seemed to come to a decision. She dropped her head to push her nose in between his and Chrysta's hand. Then she rubbed the side of her face along the gunslinger's arm.

Chrysta sighed while stepping back.

"Well, I guess you have made a new friend. She wants you to scratch her ridges."

Templer attentively reached up to scratch along the base of Nuva's small horns. The mare quivered with pleasure and made a soft crooning sound deep in her throat. The texture of her hide was silky and pleasant under his fingers. Without thinking about it, he stretched his blade hand up under that thick mane to gently scratch along her crest. The destria leaned into the caress, her soft pervasive croon deepened, seeming to penetrate to his very bones.

"**Hmmm...**" Deep in his Psyche, the Talon's outrider stirred. Templer tried to tighten his mental defenses, not sure if Azra would interpret the odd sensations as an attack. The tight barrier he tried to weave completely unraveled when the demon... purred?

"**That's NICE!**" The elemental's rough voice sounded almost drugged. The assassin inside tried to tell him that maybe he should be alarmed by his... companion's... reaction to the pleasant sensation, but the Talon found that he just did not care. He blissfully continued scratching along Nuva's head and neck.

"Yes..." He agreed with the presence within. "It IS nice."

"Constantine... Padre... TALON CONSTANTINE!" Chrysta's concerned voice jerked the man back to awareness. He felt so relaxed. "It's Templer... you can call me Templer." It seemed like too much effort to peel the warm comfortable layers from around his brain. The Talon made a serious attempt though when the woman shook him eliciting a soft threatening growl from his outrider.

"Come on... Templer. NUVA back off!"

The gunman blinked as Nuva snorted and gave Chrysta a dirty look. The soothing sensation stopped. With a final pink nosed nudge on his arm, the mare tossed her head and trotted back over to her black companion. She held her head and tail high as if she very pleased with herself.

Templer shook his head... trying to shake off the mental fog.

"What in the seven Hells was THAT?"

Chrysta looked surprised and a little perplexed.

"They do that sometimes. We think it is a throwback to when destria hunted in packs. Now it's used to strengthen herd bonds" The woman studied the cream thoughtfully. The mare met her gaze without flinching as she continued.

"Nuva must like you. They rarely bond with people and it is unheard of for one of them to bond with more than one person at a time." Chrysta shrugged giving the silent pair of animals a final glance. She slanted a sly glance at the priest out of the corner of her eyes.

"Ah well... I guess there is no accounting for taste!"

Before Templer could think of a suitable response, the woman turned on her heel and headed for the Inn. She had not been fooled by his delaying tactics. This was confirmed by the words she threw over her shoulder as she walked away.

"Grant better have that coffee ready by now." The gunman followed behind at a slower pace, surprised by how fast the woman could move with that limping gait. He speeded up to match her... hoping that he would get at least one cup of coffee out of the pot!

Edgewater was filling with festival enthusiasts. As Chrysta and Templer rode out later that morning, they passed people riding destria, Ether-cycles and the occasional freaked out Terra-bird. The priest watched as Chrysta's mount casually reached out and tried to snatch a mouthful of passing Terra-bird. The flightless avian WHONKED and skittered sideways almost dumping its swearing rider. All the big black destria got was a mouthful of fluffy feathers. Chrysta slapped the animal with the flat of one hand, while the other tightened the reins turning him in a small circle. Templer would have sworn that the golden eyes that looked into his face for a moment were laughing as the black shook his head, scattering feathers all around.

As they proceeded out of town, the road cleared out and Chrysta increased their speed. Their mounts went from a smooth four beat walk to a two beat trot. Constantine had ridden Terra-birds before. He found the destria's brisk up and down gait a lot different than the big bird's rolling pace. Pacacams also paced, a motion that was a LOT easier on the ass then this pounding! The priest watched to see how the woman next to him dealt with it. Copying her, he adopted the rocking rise she used. He found this smoothed the ride out a little.

The gunman considered himself to be in excellent shape. This along with the modifications made to his body, as much as he resented them, made it function as efficiently as a machine. Still...
it did not take long and various muscles that he didn't even know existed were protesting. There was a soft snicker from deep in his mind. Azra was awake.

"What are you laughing at?" Templer asked the question already knowing what the reply would be.

"Oh....you are going to regret this!" The demon was laughing now. Templer's answer was a dry,

"No kidding, why don't you tell me something I don't already know!"

"Really Host... I think that even the Inquisition would consider this a form of torture." Azra sounded puzzled. **I must admit that although these creatures are intriguing, I don't see why you humans make such a fuss about them. What makes destria any more special then say... a Terra-bird or even an assoxx... they are all a means to get from point A to point B."**

Nuva shook her head and snorted derisively. Without warning, raw power exploded between the priest's thighs. The first couple of seconds were taken up by a desperate bid just to keep his butt in the saddle. With his outriders help, Templer managed to catch his balance. The edges of the road blurred, as muscles surging, his mount picked up speed.

A movement of black entered his field of vision as Zephyr's head and neck appeared alongside them. The big black matched the cream stride for stride, nostrils flared wide to drink the wind, golden eyes ablaze with a joyous fire. Chrysta flattened out over the black's powerful shoulder and Templer followed suit. Incredibly, both animals put on more speed! They raced knee to knee. Nuva's golden mane streamed out like a living flame, blending with the priest's raven black hair as it lifted to dance in the flying wind. That same wind teased hot tears out of eyes narrowed to mere slits. Templer realized with a start that he was grinning like a mad man. The straining pair's hooves rumbled like thunder on the hard packed road, and for a moment it felt like they were riding on the wings of a storm.

"WAHOOO!" This startling exclamation came from Azra. "**What a RUSH!**"

They flew like this for what seemed an eternity until Chrysta's hands tightened on the reins and Zephyr slowed his flight. Nuva followed the big male's lead slowing until they settled into an easy ground eating lope.

"Wahoo ...?" Templer could not help himself. The priest would never let the elemental live this one down.

"**Oh come ON Host... even you have to admit... that was FUN!**" The demon sounded almost... wistful. "**I cannot remember the last time you unscrewed your ass enough to let us have a little fun! I hereby revise my opinion of destria...!**"

Templer was more than a little disconcerted when Azra's voice took on a childish wheedling tone, "**Come on... Talon of mine... buy me one!**"

Nuva shook her head, jingling her bridle as she chortled something that sounded an awful lot like a laugh.

With the destria's ground covering pace it took no time at all before they arrived at the accident site. Together, Chrysta and Templer peered over the edge while she pointed out the route she had taken to retrieve him. The priest had to search for the remains of his bike crumpled amongst the rocks at the bottom of the ravine. Chrysta wiggled back from the edge and went to get a second rope off of Zephyr's saddle. When she turned back, the woman looked pale and sick.

"Are you okay?" Templer paused in the process of tying his rope into a make shift climbing harness.

"Yep..." Chrysta glanced over to where the ground dropped off into a steep cliff. She looped the other end of the rope around Zephyr's saddle horn to help support the gunman's weight. "As long as I stay way back here, I'll be fine!" She shrugged at the curious look he threw her way.

"Heights and I don t get along."

Templer looked down at the wreck of his bike lying on the distant canyon floor, then back at the woman who fussed with her mount's saddle.

"Don't even ask." Chrysta looked away... embarrassed. "It was scary, it was ugly, and it almost didn't happen! I was sure you were dead. If Inferno hadn't seen you move, you would still be down there. Without the knowledge that you were injured AND still alive..." The woman shuddered, "That climb is NOT something I would be willing to do again."

"I guess that means I had better not fall a second time?" Templer tested his knots.

"You're damned right..." Chrysta grinned, "If you are clumsy enough to fall again, you can just plan on staying down there!"

Templer eased himself over the edge and almost slipped as his concentration was broken.

"Host, we could just fly..."

"NO!" The priest rudely cut the demon off mid-sentence and took a better grip on his rope.

"Give me a break. A quick change, then down and back. It'll only take a few..." Azra moved towards the surface of the gunman's mind.

"I said... NO!" Templer put the brakes on the elemental's stealthy rise. "That's all we need. I do NOT want to have to explain YOU... to Chrysta. Besides Nuva and Zephyr would freak!"

Actually with Zephyr anchoring the rope it took Templer little time or effort to get down to the bike. A quick once over convinced the priest that the bio-machine was not salvageable. He emptied the side bags removing the rest of his gear and rolling it into a tight bundle that could be carried on his back. His last action was to remove the glowing orb that powered the crippled machine. A flick of his mind broke the confinement spell, setting the captive elementals trapped within free. Unlike some... he could see no reason to leave them imprisoned until they destroyed each other or starved. He gave a sharp tug on the rope and Zephyr hauled him back up.

Constantine was surprised when he reached the top. Nuva balanced right on the edge, anxiously looking down at him. If he didn't know better, he would have sworn the expression on that long face was worried. The mare almost knocked him off again as she nosed at him, trying to push him away from the edge.

"HOLY... back off you ninny!" Templer lightly slapped the pink muzzle away from him. The cream got out of his way, all the while giving the priest a look of sad reproach. With a soft whuffle the destria turned her back on him and went to stand by Chrysta. She nuzzled at the woman's shoulder, looking for sympathy.

"I think you might have hurt her feelings."

Constantine ignored the outrider. He refused to feel guilty. Chrysta coiled the rope up and hung it on Zephyr's saddle. She wouldn't look at him, but the gunman could see the woman's lips twitching. As he approached Nuva, the mare gave a big slobbery, heaving sigh and peered up at him from under her eye ridges. Chrysta had to turn away. Although her shoulders were shaking, the woman didn't make a sound.

"Maybe you should apologize?" Azra was believing the whole... poor, pitiful me... routine.

"I refuse to buy into this." Templer was adamant. He tied his bundled belongings behind the saddle.

Chrysta glanced his way, then swung up on Zephyr. The priest put his foot in the stirrup and Nuva's whole body sagged while she gave a pathetic groan.

"I think..."

"AZRA, shut up! I am a Talon for Heaven's sake. WE have the reputation of being the coldest bad asses on the planet to uphold and I am NOT apologizing...OH...MY...GOD!" Templer stared in disbelief. Even the destria's lips were sagging and they twitched piteously as the mare looked back at him with large, sorrowful eyes. The man threw up his hands in defeat. Mother of demons... if this EVER got out he would never live it down!

"OKAY... okay... you win! I give in." Templer laid a hand on the warm shoulder and tried like hell to sound sincere. "I am sorry I slapped you. It was a rude thing to do when you were just showing concern as to my wellbeing." He heard Chrysta choking and spun on his heel to fix her with an evil stare.

"Something wrong?" He asked.

The woman had her hands clamped over her mouth and her eyes sparkled. "Nnooo...." She made a show of clearing her throat. "I seem to have swallowed some dust."

"Humph." Templer gathered his reins and mounted. Nuva pranced around for a moment. She slyly reached around and nipped at his foot.

There was a soft snicker from within... **"For a cold hearted bad ass Host..."** His outrider sounded smug. **"You sure CAVED awfully f..."**

"Azra...shut up!" Templer sighed. He liked the demon better when he had nothing at all to say!

By the time Templer and Nuva rode into town late that evening, the horizon had turned a deep purple and the first stars were twinkling into view. Chrysta and Zephyr split off several miles outside town, heading for Don Ricardo's ranch. This left the other pair to make their own way home alone. There was still a lot of traffic on the main street. All the businesses were gearing up in preparation for the festival. The few individuals dumb enough to get in Nuva's way hastily cleared a path when the mare gave them the evil eye and popped her fangs together, making a sound like a gunshot.

They turned into the alley beside the Inn and were met at the barn door by one of the stable hands. He took hold of Nuva's reins as the gunman dismounted. Templer stretched and winced when his back made the same sounds as Chrysta's had earlier that day. The priest was grateful that Azra was... elsewhere... he would never hear the end of it otherwise. Removing his bundle of belongings from the saddle and giving a final pat to Nuva's crest, he headed into the Ironwood with a hot shower foremost on his mind.

Grant was behind the bar. A couple of waitresses moved amongst the tables in the common room, serving food and drinks. Business was hopping in the small establishment. Chrysta had asked Templer to relay a message to the bartender so he stopped at the bar for a moment, waiting to catch the big man's attention. Grant finished the order he was putting together and ambled over to speak with him.

"SOOO Padre... you survived your first destria ride, and with CHRYSTA to boot... Imagine that!" Grant's smile lit up his whole face. "Are you going to have a meal down here or would you like me to send something up?"

The innocent look that accompanied that smile told Constantine that correcting the man about his rank again would be an act of futility. He gave a small mental shrug. Padre it was. He should count himself lucky that the other man had not settled on one of the other titles that a Talon had to deal with. HOUND was one that instantly came to mind! At this errant thought, the priest's lips twitched up slightly at the corners before he was able to smother the impulse. As he held the others steady gaze, Templer was again struck by how much he liked the man.

"I smell far too much like a destria to eat amongst the public." Templer did his best to ignore the fact that Grant's smile turned into a face splitting grin.

"I may get something later on AFTER I take a shower. I just stopped to relay a message. Chrysta asked me to tell you..." The priest paused, making sure what he relayed was word for word... "Be sure to turn on the electric fence and put out the warning signs... she is bringing El Diablo in tonight after the crowds thin out."

The gunman was concerned when Grant's smile disappeared and his face paled. The other man seemed to sag in on himself.

Templer reached for him with his flesh hand, worried about the bartender's turn of health.

"Are you okay?" His deep voice held a note of concern.

The barman waved his hand away.

"I'm okay, it's just that I hate dealing with

that one. The S.O.B. SHOULD have been named the Anti-Christ!!"

The talons on Templer's blade-hand, which had been tapping lightly on the bar's smooth surface, stopped as the gunman gave his outrider a mental nudge. He studied the other man, noting the increase in blood pressure and respiration that were telltale signs of stress. Just what in the seven Hells was Chrysta bringing into town that could illicit this kind of reaction?

"What is the problem, Grant?"

The big man looked up, his worried brown eyes meeting the gunman's now glowing ones.

"El Diablo is a breeding stallion, this alone in a normal destria would make him difficult to deal with. Add the fact that Diablo is also VERY intelligent. I believe he can out think the average person on any given day. Last but most important... the fucker is unstable. In my humble opinion he is insane. He EARNED the name El Diablo because he is as wicked as they come. I would wager my last copper that one of these days, Chrysta will slip up and that bastard will finish the job he started on her."

The man's quiet voice had real venom in it. Catching Constantine's look of curiosity Grant shook his head.

"You will just have to ask Chrysta. It's not a story I care to repeat. It is bad enough I can't just erase it out of my mind." The man shrugged and gave a heartfelt sigh, "Well, I guess I had better go make sure things are ready for him."

It was a Talon that watched as Grant stomped from behind the bar and headed out through the kitchen door. The man was still mumbling to himself and shaking his head as he disappeared from view. Azra followed Templer's train of thought then interrupted with a savage growl. **"Don't even think about it host. YOU are**

supposed to be on vacation. Call someone else in! WE are not up to handling an exorcism if this is some kind of demonic possession."

Templer thought about it... then ignoring his own vague unease, the man pushed the elemental to the back of his mind.

"Come on Azra... Demonic possession? I am sure our BROTHERS would not be happy to be called in on a case that turns out to be nothing more than us overreacting to a bad tempered stallion."

Ignoring the demon's soft hiss of outrage... Templer gathered up his belongings and headed up the stairs to his room. The long anticipated shower was first on his priority list. Digging in his bags the priest set his Cricket on the table after checking that the quasi-intelligent device was still alive. He felt Azra reach out and feed the insect-like construct some energy out of their depleted reserves. It had no access to light while put away and it was starving. If they had not retrieved the construct, it would have died. As he undressed, the priest listened to the messages he had missed while it had been down in the ravine. The majority of them came from Iniko. This young thief was his go between when Templer had to deal with the Saint. The rather annoying girl operated under the misguided premise that Constantine could not take care of himself. As a result, he spent an inordinate amount of time avoiding her. The fact that the little pest had somehow got her sticky little fingers on his access code... AGAIN... had the man grinding his teeth. Most of her messages followed along the lines of...

"HEY... tall, dark and scary... Where are you?" And... "Come on, pick up you Demon infested prick..." AND... "Answer your damn... Where the HELL are you Temp... answer your damned calls!" The last one proved the girl had lost all control!

"What the FUCK, TALON Templer Constantine! At the risk of sounding like Sig, GET your Gods be damned head outta your tight little ass and at least let me know you are still freakin stalking around in the land of the fricking LIVING!"

The priest was already in the bathroom when that message came on. It was impossible to resist peeking out to make sure the Cricket hadn't burst into flames. The bug WAS glowing a little as the gentle elemental that powered it responded to the outpouring of negative energy.

Templer sighed... if this kept up he would have to change his code again.

As he turned the shower on as hot as he could stand it, Azra stirred and gave him a mental nudge.

"HEY Constantine, look up and to your left!"

His outrider's voice thrummed with suppressed excitement. Templer obliged and noticed a jar sitting on a high shelf. It was filled to the brim with what looked like deep green leaves.

"If that is what I think it is, your sore muscles will soon be a distant memory," Azra was bursting with anticipation. "Take it down and sniff it. Do NOT get any water into it."

"What, you are into bubble baths now?" Templer couldn't help himself. "Oh, how the mighty have fallen!"

"Just do it!" the demon snarled.

The gunman unscrewed the lid and took a tentative whiff. He couldn't control the reflex as his neck muscles jerked his head as far away from the jar as possible without actually decapitating him. He slapped the lid back on, his eyes watering.

Azra howled with laughter at his reaction...

"HAHAHAHA....Serves you right for the bubble-bath comment!"

"HOLY..." Templer prodded the green mash with one talon's sharp tip. "What in the hell is this stuff?"

The Talon was familiar with many herbs and plants, his training as an assassin covered the use of toxic flora and fauna. He had NEVER smelled anything like this innocent looking jar of dried weeds.

"Back in the day... it was called Dreamleaf, or Life's Bane. If it is used the way it's intended, it is a powerful muscle relaxant and pain killer. If you smoke it, dreamleaf is the worst mind-fuck there is!"

"How come I have never heard of it?"

Templer found it hard to imagine how awful the stuff must smell or taste when it burned.

The elemental was silent for a long moment. The priest did not press... Azra's memories were almost as fragmented as his own... the fact that the outrider had dredged up this much information was a surprise. Whenever Azra tried to piece some of these fleeting memories together, Templer tried not to break in on his train of thought. This time... his patience was rewarded.

"I get the impression that dreamleaf cannot be grown on this plane of existence. If this is correct, importing it from Hell would make it very expensive, not to mention highly illegal. A good reason, I think that the Hand has not gotten wind of it. Also, if this drug is mishandled, the results can be quite... lethal... hence its second name... Life's Bane"

Wonderful... as if the realm did not have enough problems as it was!

"And you think I would like to use this...

why?"

Templer was skeptical of the outrider's motives. Altruism was not high on the demon's short list of positive attributes.

"If you dissolve a small amount in a tub of hot water and soak in it, dreamleaf will remove all the stiffness and pain out of your muscles. I just figured you would like to relax." Azra made an effort to sound sincere, which put his partner on instant alert. **"If you are in pain, it carries over to me. I drained our reserves to heal your injuries after the wreck. There is little left to waste on small stuff... like being saddle sore. I have no ulterior motives. I am disappointed that you do not trust me after all we have been through."**

"Yeah...right!" Constantine wasn't buying it. "I think I will pass on trying it this time."

Still, the priest couldn't control his curiosity.

"How do you know so much about it?"

The demon became evasive.

"HMMMM, I think we need to adopt a don't ask don't tell policy about that."

After a long shower... Templer got a glass and a nice bottle of red wine from the bar. He then sat on the roof and watched the crowds coming and going from the different activities in town. It was early morning before the people started to disperse. Knowing he wouldn't sleep that night, the priest laid back and was studying the stars when a guttural scream shattered the early morning quiet. This started out high pitched enough to hurt his sensitive ears then traveled down the scale to end in a deep, rumbling WAH HUH HUH. A massive shadow separated out of the darkness and seemed to flow on to the empty main street.

The destria that appeared out of this shadow glimmered silver in the moonlight. Black striping flowed over his broad shoulders and down his long legs. The stallion's high crested, heavy neck was bowed until his bearded chin almost touched his muscled chest. It was obvious the powerful beast was fighting his rider's control every step of the way. As they came abreast of the Inn, the destria tried to twist sideways. He rose on his hind legs, cloven front hooves clawing at the air. Again that hair raising scream echoed through the night. El Diablo flung his horned head high. His sharp fanged mouth gaped to its widest and his long silver mane swirled in the wind of his passage. Ice cold feral green eyes locked with the Talon's golden ones for a moment. Azra had roared to the surface at the first sight of the mix of hate, rage and insanity that Chrysta called The Devil!

The rider stuck with the animal and made the turn leading into the courtyard. Constantine heard the back door bang open as Grant came out on the run. The battle stallion saw the big man and made an open mouthed lunge at him. Chrysta snatched a double handful of reins and hauled hard, turning that wicked head as she drove her heels into the stud's sensitive sides. El Diablo reluctantly turned and sprang forward, his cloven hooves striking sparks from the cobblestones. She rode the beast hard into the reinforced paddock. As they passed one of the posts, the woman flipped a rope over it, throwing the end to Grant. Its other end was clipped into a thick leather and steel collar that wrapped around El Diablo's neck just behind the horned ridge. The bartender, moving fast for such a burly man, pulled the slack out. The raging stallion ended up with his head locked down close to the post.

Chrysta slid off. She somehow managed to unbuckle the saddle in the same motion. When the stallion lashed out sideways with a sharp hind hoof the woman was already out of range, saddle in hand. She moved to the animal's head and threw the leather over the top rail.

Templer realized with a start that he could see no sign of the woman's former limp. The thick muscle on Grant's arms stood out as the man tightened his hold on the rope when she reached up to remove the bridle. Somehow, even with his head immobilized, the destria stuck forward with a powerful front leg. Chrysta must have had a sixth sense. She twisted away and the strike from the battle stallion's inside claw which should have opened her ribcage just grazed the forearm she threw up as a shield. The Talon was off of the roof and moving towards the paddock as the hot smell of fresh blood filled the night air.

Grant seeing the movement, caught his eye and grimly shook his head. The gunman stopped just outside of the paddock but drew his weapon all the same. Chrysta had spun away from the attack and was heading, bridle in hand, towards the exit. The bartender reached up and unclasped the rope, releasing El Diablo just as the woman stepped through and slammed the bolt closed. The whole fence shuddered as almost two thousand pounds of pissed off destria hit the gate. Grant flipped a switch turning the power back on and the stallion jerked away from the hot fence, voicing his frustration in a deep, hoarse roar.

"Holy..." Azra watched through his silent host's eyes as the massive beast made a fast circuit of his paddock... occasionally testing the electrified fence as he went. "Host... I would rather participate in an exorcism then get our collective ass anywhere near that devil's back. I have changed my mind... I don't want a destria. It is my professional opinion that Ether-cycles are SAFER!"

Chrysta rested her back against the gate, letting it support her. She removed the helmet and ran her shaking hand through her short hair.

"Well wasn't that the most fun we've had in a long while." This statement was dripping with sarcasm. It got a snort of strained laughter from Grant,

"Seems like the last time we indulged in this much Jim Dandy fun was last year about this time."

Templer holstered his weapon, looking from one to the other. He listened to the pounding of heavy hooves as El Diablo made another circuit of his paddock. The angry animal was still snorting and popping his fangs. The Talon decided that being around destria must affect people's sanity, and not in a good way! A small part of his mind told him this was something he needed to report to the Hand. He stomped the errant thought... flat!

The woman stepped away from the gate and the stride that seemed so smooth while dealing with the stallion became a staggered lurch as her leg gave out. The priest's strong hands caught her by the shoulders and provided some support until she could find her balance. Grant, who was walking back towards the kitchen door, turned towards them in alarm. Chrysta waved a hand at him.

"Go ahead Grant, Everything's fine. I'm just sore and tired."

In the dark the bartender could not see the blood dripping from her fingers. He hesitated a moment before heading back into the Inn.

Catching Templer's raised eyebrow the woman gave a small shake of her head.

"It's not that bad." She whispered, "I see no reason to upset him."

She straightened and took a tentative step, testing her leg.

"Let's see if we can make it up to the room without getting blood all over the floor. You have not seen anything until you've seen Grant's M.H.T kick in."

"M.H.T...? I haven't heard of that disorder... is it serious?"

Chrysta smothered a giggle with the hand that was not bleeding at his dry tone. "SHHHH... M.H.T. is short for Mother Hen Tendencies. Poor man doesn't even know he has this dread disease. The symptoms, when they manifest, turn him into a royal pain in my ass!"

She rolled her eyes as she said this bringing a smile twitching to the corner of the gunman's mouth. He could sympathize. Templer was familiar with what it was like to live with a pain in the ass. Azra growled.

"Not funny Host... I could say the same thing about YOU!"

They made it through the darkened kitchen and up the staircase without running into Grant. Chrysta staggered once on the stairs and Templer rested his hand on the small of her back to provide support. He was surprised at the muscle he felt there.

"HMPH," This derisive snort came from his outrider. **"The woman hauled your heavy ass up that ravine by herself! She trains and rides two thousand pound animals that want nothing more than to eat her for dinner and you are surprised that she is muscular. Geez Constantine... where did your Makers put your**

brains when they re-assembled you?"

Templer didn't feel the need to answer that insulting comment, so he ignored the demon. The gunman DID catch himself looking back over his shoulder to make sure they hadn't tracked blood all over Grant's floor.

Once they made it to their room, Chrysta sat down at the table and turned the lamp on. She unbuttoned then rolled up her bloody, torn sleeve. There was a heavy arm guard buckled around her forearm. El Diablo had sliced the tough leather about two inches below the elbow to right above her right wrist. The woman swore softly as she fumbled left handed with buckles made slick with blood.

Templer watched for a moment, then couldn't stand it. "Here, let me help."

With a thought... he elongated one talon on his blade-hand. Slipping the sharp claw underneath the strap she struggled with, he sliced through the blood soaked leather with care. The second and third parted just as easily.

"Thanks..." The woman murmured as she peeled the wet leather off of her arm. She made no comment about what he had just done... but then she had other more important matters on her mind. Blood started to pool at an alarming rate on the table top.

"Shit!" Chrysta's face whitened at the sight of the bleeding gash. "That's a little worse than I expected."

She clamped her left hand above the wound in an attempt to slow the blood flow.

"Would you get the med. kit for me? It's in that cabinet, top shelf, left hand side."

The woman gestured with her chin to give Templer some idea of where to look.

Constantine hesitated... but Azra stopped him before he could say a word.

"Don't offer Host... I am dead serious about the state of our reserves."

Smoothly switching gears, he asked. "Should I be getting the town healer?"

Chrysta just snorted. "Out here... small stuff like this is handled with traditional methods. Doc is at best a Third Tier Healer. It is understood around town that his meager strength is best reserved for when someone has a MAJOR accident. This is something I can handle if you would be so kind as to get me that kit."

The priest searched where she indicated but didn't see the med kit she wanted.

"Hmmm, far back left hand corner just behind the pic..." Azra's rough voice trailed off into shocked silence.

Templer removed the picture, forgetting about the med kit. In the photo, Chrysta stood with another man in front of a destria that could only be El Diablo. Mounted on the beast's back, was one of the most feared men in the realm... Tynan Thranatos... First son of the cursed House Dracul. As surprised as he was at seeing that particular Vamphyrr this far from Hell, this was not what caused the man to spin around. Slamming the photo down in front of the startled woman he growled out,

"Who is that man?!"

Chrysta met his blazing eyes with shadowed green ones.

"I assume that you don't mean Ty. The man on the right is First Tier Healer... Forrest Denia. He served as an acolyte to the Maker's Sect. You might recognize him. He would certainly recognize you."

The priest's breath hissed through his teeth, he did recognize the man in the photo. In the patchwork fabric of his mind the healer had been a lot younger, but Templer definitely remembered seeing him when he suffered under the Maker's knives.

Chrysta sucked in a breath as she watched him struggle to piece together the fragments of memory that the old photo had pulled out of his shadowed past.

"Mother of Demons... you are NOT supposed to be able to remember your Making!"

She was right. He did not remember his original Making. These bits and pieces were coming from the last couple of times the Hand forced him back into the labs for... adjustments. He should not remember these either. The Bindings that the Maker's used to suppress his mind and will, were becoming less and less effective. Holy... if the Hand found out his Vows were not holding; the Maker's table would be the least of his problems! Some of the desperation this thought caused must have shown on his face. Chrysta warily shifted in her chair as if to bolt. Templer dropped his hand... pinning her in place. She wisely froze.

"Please don't judge him harshly, Constantine. Forrest was heavily Tainted. He was lucky his affinity for the healing elements was strong and the Hand didn't cleanse him at the Sorting. He had no choice but to do what was necessary to remain Sanctified. Forrest was not cruel. Like all Acolytes, he was trapped in a situation from which there is little chance of escape."

Chrysta's tired eyes never left Templer's face. They were drawn at the edges and clouded with pain, both emotional and physical. The gunman realized his hand was clamped over her injured arm. Crimson blood oozed between his fingers to drip on to the table top. He drew a shuddering breath and forced himself to release her wrist. Turning, the Talon strode over to the open window absently wiping her blood off of his hand. His spider-silk cloak sucked in what he offered.

"Judge him! How can you sit there and defend him?"

The priest's voice was harsh as he wrestled with torturous images he was not sure were actual memories or the ghosts of old, familiar nightmares. To make matters in his head even more difficult to sort out, Azra was trying to get his attention and Templer was having difficulties stifling the bastard!

"Nobody is so terrible that they don't deserve to be loved. You of all people should understand. Forrest was Tainted. He... had... no... choice!" Chrysta's voice was soft but unapologetic.

Templer spun around to face her.

"WHAT...?" The woman had NO idea what she was talking about. Her lover was given a choice. All Tainted were given a choice... serve or die. This choice had not been offered to Constantine. Death was final and caused no harm. Instead Denia chose a path of blood and pain. By making that choice... he helped to create those who were damned to spend their lives dealing in the same coin... only a hundred fold!

"Where is he?" Without realizing it, his hand dropped to his gun.

"Not anywhere you can find him." Chrysta remained seated her face and body as motionless as stone. The gunslinger drew the Trinity. Damn her soul... if he could not pull the answer from her while she lived. He sure as Hell would get it carried on her last breath. This got a reaction, although not the one the Talon expected. Chrysta seemed to uncoil as she rose. The eyes that met his over the barrels of the big gun were as cold and clear as hard glass. Templer felt Azra's disbelief match his own as the woman turned her back on death and limped heavily towards the bathroom.

"Forrest has gone where nothing can reach him... Templer Constantine... not hatred, not the need for revenge, not even the love of his wife." Chrysta stopped for a moment and a soft sigh escaped her. "You are too late... Reaper. Forrest is already dead."

Her use of that hurtful title shocked Templer into stillness. By the time he recovered the woman disappeared behind the door and he heard her turn the water on in the sink.

Still seething... the gunman took one step towards the door intending to follow when a sharp pain stabbed through his leg making it cramp up. He staggered and just managed to catch himself on the window sill.

"HAH! I'll wager THAT got your attention... didn't it!?"

The outrider had his undivided attention. Templer shuddered at the disconcerting feeling of the demon riffling through his ragged memories. Azra dredged up scene after scene for the priest to see. Acolyte Forest Denia HAD been there during many of the modifications the Maker's performed on his unwilling body. What the demon brought to light was that along with sustaining him during life threatening procedures... the man had tried to help him in any little way he could. If Forrest drew blood or performed a procedure it was handled with care. The healer tried to not cause pain or discomfort as much as possible. There were several times when the kindness was as simple as covering Constantine with a warm blanket when "subject zero" lay strapped to an exam table... exposed, in pain, and so very cold.

"I believe that being indentured to the Maker's was a form of torture for Dr. Denia. The man was screwed at birth. Most healers have an ingrained reverence for life. Some of the things that Forrest was forced to do would have been abhorrent to him. He... had... no... choice. You of all people should know how the Order deals with the disobedient. More so if the poor wretch was Tainted."

The demon kept his rough voice soft.

Templer leaned his aching head against the side of the window allowing the cool night breeze to dry the sweat off of his brow.

"Did he know about you?" A morbid curiosity made him ask.

"Yes... Unfortunately, we had to work together to keep you breathing through some of the more extreme experiments done to your body. As you well know, I have not handled being forced into this union with good grace. I am afraid I frightened him quite badly."

"Hnnn, I'm willing to wager that's an understatement. Let's face it... you are NOT the average, run of the mill Ifrit!"

The priest straightened and turned around as the bathroom door opened and Chrysta came out, her forearm wrapped in a towel. She had removed her torn shirt. He realized that under it the woman wore a matching guard on her left arm and a hard leather vest that protected her upper back, chest and ribs. There was a soft shirt underneath. Glancing at the silent Talon out of the corner of her eye, she went over to the cabinet and retrieved the med kit. The gunman crossed his arms and watched as she dug out bandaging material and an antiseptic.

"That needs to be stitched."

"I know." Templer sighed. He repeated his

outrider's opinion to the woman who was wiping the wound with gauze soaked in antiseptic.

"Yep..." Chrysta flicked her uninjured left hand in his direction.

"I am right handed. I have not been able to train my idiot hand to sew and I am NOT drawing Grant's attention to this." The last part was muttered under her breath.

Templer winced as Azra gave him an ungentle mental nudge and his leg tingled in warning.

"STOP it!" he snarled at the demon. "I can stitch that... if you want?" After his behavior, the priest made the offer with little hope of her accepting.

Chrysta looked at him, her chestnut eyebrows arched in surprise.

"Do I want to ask where you learned to tie a stitch?"

"No..." The woman's quiet acceptance of his unspoken apology went a long way towards easing the sting that being called a Reaper had caused.

Templer sat down opposite her and slipped the towel under her arm.

"Just be satisfied that I learned from the best."

With no warning he poured the antiseptic into the long S shaped gash, flushing it out. The firm grasp of his blade-hand prevented the woman from jerking it away as she smothered a yelp of pain with her left hand

"SHIT...Constantine! At least warn me before you do something like that!" She hissed this in a pained whisper. "The last thing we need is Grant popping in up here to check out the noise!"

The gunman didn't say a word. He knew that

with the way the wound had to be stinging she wouldn't even feel the prick of the curved needle as he started a row of small, neat stitches. He had just placed the last one when he heard Grant coming up the stairwell. Chrysta's head jerked up. She had been resting her chin in her hand watching his agile fingers. Her wide eyes met his. The priest just did not get it. The woman had faced down a cold blooded killer over the barrel of his gun without flinching but the sound of those approaching footsteps had her panicked.

Without thinking Templer swept the medical supplies into his lap and covered them with the towel. He was rewarded with the flash of grateful eyes and a mouthed "Thank you" as the door opened.

Grant stood in the doorway for a moment just looking at them. If the man had any suspicions, they didn't make it to his placid face. He carried a tray with a couple of covered bowls, two small glasses and a slim bottle of an almost electric blue liquid.

"It's late, you should be in bed, and I'd be willing to wager silver you have had nothing but coffee and Anesthetic since this morning."

This was directed at Chrysta. The big man set the tray down on the table and fixed Templer with a stern glare.

"You will NOT let her touch that...," Grant pointed at the blue liquid, "... until she finishes this."

The man set one bowl in front of her and uncovered it. He set the other bowl in front of the startled Talon. Then he made a harrumphing noise and strode out of the room.

Templer cleared his throat.

"Is that what you meant about M.H.T.?"

"UmmHumm." The quiet answer got

Templer's attention.

Chrysta was pale and she looked exhausted. The woman was swirling her spoon through the savory smelling stew, but had yet to take a bite.

Very casually the priest reached over and snagged the bottle of blue liquid, sliding it over to his side of the table. At the woman's startled look... a gentle smile curved his lips.

"Like the man said. You can have this... as soon as you finish that!" He nodded at her bowl.

For a moment... Chrysta just glared at him with narrowed eyes. Templer could almost see the wheels turning in her head as she calculated the odds of being able to take the bottle away from him.

Then she snorted and filled her spoon.

"Anybody ever mention you are a real bastard, Constantine?"

His smile turned smug as he watched her eat.

"Yes... yes they have. Since I can't seem to recall ever having a father... who's to say they aren't right."

Templer watched the woman across from him work her way through her meal. Her face, which had been quite pale, became flushed. Chrysta was spooning her soup using her "idiot" left hand. The right one she cradled in her lap. With a sigh, she finished the last mouthful. Setting her spoon down the woman tilted her bowl to prove it was empty.

Chrysta crooked her right index finger at the bottle.

"Now GIVE!"

The Talon's attention focused on the line of stitches marching down her forearm. The wound was red and had started to swell.

"What the hell?"

Templer reached out, trapping her hand so he could get a closer look.

"This should not have gotten infected that fast."

"It isn't infected."

Chrysta gave her arm an unconcerned look. When she looked back up, the gunman saw that her eyes were slightly glazed, their pupils dilated.

"The inside spur on a destria's front leg is venomous. It is one of the things that makes them lethal hunters. Any time they inflict a wound with those spurs they inject a nerve toxin. It slows prey down and causes mental confusion. Inject enough and it can kill."

Templer's eyebrows just about crawled up into his hairline.

"No worries though." The woman smiled at his astonished look. "I have been poked, scratched, scraped and slashed enough I have developed a partial immunity to the stuff. This will give me a mild fever and some aches and pains, then wear off. NOW..."

The look she gave him was hard and grim.

"If you don't unhand that bottle, I WILL take it from you. If that happens, I will NOT be sharing!"

Bemused, the gunman slid the bottle over to her. The woman uncorked it and poured an equal measure of the brilliant blue liquid into each small glass.

"This is something Grant dreamed up. He calls it... Anesthetic. The cruel bastard makes a small amount each season. When it is gone..."

Chrysta shrugged and handed one glass to Templer while raising the other in a toast.

"May the heavens bless Grant and his magical touch with alcohol."

She downed half the glass in one swallow, and then glanced at him, the look on her face one of total innocence. Templer sniffed the drink. There was a slight sting from the fumes but little odor. Chrysta watched him, one eyebrow cocked. He raised the glass to his lips and meeting her eyes over the rim... drained it. The alcohol also had little taste. It made his mouth tingle on the way down. He became worried when her lips twisted up in a wicked smile.

The Talon set his glass down and froze as what felt like a bomb ignited in his innards. He tried to suck a breath in, but couldn't. Sweet, honey flavored fire scorched up through his throat into his mouth and nose. For a moment the gunman was paralyzed as the flame flashed from fire to ice leaving everything from his lips to his stomach strangely numb. Then it warmed back to a pleasant heat that extended out through his whole body.

"**WOW!**" Azra was impressed

Templer just blinked his watering eyes, not sure of his ability to speak.

Chrysta snickered and finished her drink. She split what remained in the bottle between the two glasses. It was no surprise that the woman wobbled a little when she scooped up a wrap and rose to her feet.

"Well, Talon Constantine. As interesting as this has been, sunrise is almost here. I had better try to get some sleep before festival starts."

She limped back to the bathroom. Templer sipped his drink as he tried to ignore the various bangs and thumps emanating from the small room. When his roommate came back out she was in a long, old fashioned nightgown. She glanced his way as if daring him to make a comment. Chrysta had her leathers and clothes in one hand and her drink balanced in the other, neatly bandaged one. The gunman cocked his head sideways to watch her make her way to the duvet. Along with the limp, the woman was listing. With a quiet sigh, Chrysta collapsed onto her makeshift bed, dropping the clothes, but NOT the drink. She took one last sip then set the half empty glass on the window sill. Once under the old fashioned quilt the woman rolled onto her good side wrapping up like a mummy. Before the gunman reached to turn off the light, she was asleep.

Templer envied his companion that ability. He was tired but not enough to try sleeping. Nightmares haunted his dreams. He slept when his body forced him to.

Quietly strolling to the window, the priest slipped out and made his way to the roof. He spent the remaining part of the night enjoying the cool of the early morning breeze and watching the eerie beauty of El Diablo as the beast prowled and paced around his paddock.

Sunrise was preceded by the sound of feet coming up the stairs and a soft knock on the door. Constantine was just coming back through the window when Grant opened the door and stuck his head in. He seemed quite surprised to see the gunman awake. Chrysta had her head buried under a pillow, her right arm thrown over it. Grant nodded at Templer and came in to lay a bundle of clean clothes and leathers by the duvet. He set two steaming cups on the sill. The Talon caught the murderous look the big man threw El Diablo's way when he saw the thick bandaging. The bartender glanced at the gunman with a questioning look on his face. Templer gave a slight shake of his head and mouthed "Not serious," at him. The barman's face relaxed imperceptibly. He was reaching to shake the sleeping woman awake when a muffled voice emanated from under the pillow.

"GRANT, you better have brought some coffee up with you!"

The woman's hand made random groping motions. Grant slipped one of the cups he had brought up into it and Chrysta's flushed, blurry eyed face popped out from under the pillow. She took a gulp of the hot black liquid before she even sat up,

"Bless you Grant! Mother of Demons... I do HATE festival week."

"Hrmph... then retire so we don't have to hear you whine." Was the barman's unsympathetic answer.

Grant had turned away to hand Templer the

other steaming cup so he did not get the full impact of the dirty look that was thrown his way. Scooping up the untidy pile the woman had left by the duvet, and retrieving the bowls from the night before, the barman headed toward the door.

"I've got breakfast on. You had better hustle if you are bringing in Don Ricardo's bunch for the parade."

As Grant slipped out the door he gave the gunman a cryptic smile.

"Don't turn your back on her where your coffee is concerned."

The big man got the door shut right before her pillow smacked into it.

Chrysta hissed as she rose from the duvet. Her movements were stiff and slow when she straightened up. Templer winced as she poured the half glass of Anesthetic left from the night before into her coffee. He could feel his outrider's internal shudder at the thought of the potent combination. The woman limped to the bathroom taking her clothes and cup with her.

Templer spent a good part of the morning exploring and watching the town prepare for the parade which would signal the start of festival. People appeared out of nowhere until the whole of Main Street was lined with chairs, stands, and large crowds. All the businesses pitched together to set up a four-foot-tall barrier between the street and the crowds. When it got so crowded that Azra became irritable and he became uncomfortable, the priest headed up to the Ironwood's roof to wait for the parade. Grant joined him there, about half an hour before the parade was supposed to start. He brought with him a tray of snacks and a pitcher of the dark brew that Talon Constantine had enjoyed on his first day in town. It was packed in ice. Settling himself on the roof beside the gunman Grant poured them a glass of beer.

"You picked the perfect vantage point to watch... Padre." He gestured with the beer, "We've got a clear view and we don't have to fight the crowds." The big man took a sip and sighed in contentment.

"Just... Perfect."

There was a cheer from the crowds below as the first parade participants came in to view. This consisted of couple of drafters pulling a gaudily decorated wagon filled with the town officials and their various spouses. As the next wagons rumbled through, Grant pointed out different important personages and commented on who decorated the floats and wagons. He leaned forward to applaud and whistle with enthusiasm as one float full of giggling young ladies rolled by. They turned and waved. Templer recognized the big drafter team that Chrysta had been driving the morning before. Grant informed him that most of the draft destria in the parade would participate in a load pulling contest later in the week. Don Ricardo's pair was a favored team.

The priest sat quietly and let Grant's comments wash over him. The barman spoke in such a way that Templer did not feel pressured into carrying a conversation. This was something he was thankful for. The few friends he had would be the first to tell that Talon Constantine was not known for being a social butterfly. He was a dangerous and solitary man... living a dangerous and solitary life. He did not have the time to waste on frivolity. It wasn't that he had not been trained in social etiquette. If it was required of him... Constantine could hold his own in any crowd of elites. Most of the time though, he just did not have the patience for the back stabbing and constant jockeying for social status. (Well, to be honest... the back stabbing he did not mind. The problem being that when he indulged there was usually more than a little blood involved!)

As he watched and listened for the next couple of hours, the priest got an in depth education on how the destria had evolved from re-gen killing machines used as battle mounts, to the very versatile animal it was now. He had the differences between the heavy rump-ed sprinters and the long lean milers pointed out to him. And he learned what it took to be an endurance racer. A group of scarred, thick muscled stallions paraded past, each long lined between two heavily padded leather clothed escorts. Grant explained that some animals were used for pit fighting. The man made it clear that although this was a popular part of the festival, he had nothing to do with it as he felt it was barbaric. Templer heard El Diablo issue a challenge from his paddock. One scarred veteran of the pits veered sideways, rearing and bugling in answer.

These animals caught his outrider's interest.

"I'll bet that would be something to see!"

Templer did not answer. He did not share Azra's taste for bloodletting as a sport. The gunman sipped his beer and watched a large group of destria be being herded down the parade route. The men driving them whooped and yelled, showing off in front of the crowd. He recognized them as the ones who had caused problems for Grant.

Grant leaned forward to study the animals intently.

"Ah... I see that Don Diego's son still hasn't learned that quantity doesn't necessarily equal quality."

There was a smug smile on the man's face, which disappeared as the mass of animals parted. Striding amongst the others was an elegant golden beast that was nothing but quality. The stallion carried his horned, ridged, head proudly with his white mane flowing around his high crested neck. Grant whistled under his breath.

"Now... isn't HE something! Where the HELL did Rafe steal him from? There is no way that came out of the Don's breeding program!"

The next group was pushing through. Grant pointed out last year's winner of the Gauntlet. This turned out to be a smallish animal with crooked front legs. He was a nondescript dusty gray. Templer glanced sideways at the older man to see if he was joking. Grant shook his head earnestly.

"I'm not yanking your chain... the little beggar surprised everyone, he had odds at one hundred to one. I wish I had bet a few silvers on him."

Chrysta led the next herd of animals in. This was Don Ricardo's herd. All of them were slick and shining with good health. Compared to the number of animals that the others had brought in, Ricardo's group was small. Templer counted twenty. Grant pointed out that seven of these were ones that Chrysta bred and owned. She rode Zephyr and one of the stable hands was on Nuva. The old mare pranced and snorted, showing off as if she enjoyed the attention. Grant nudged Templer and pointed out the long legged stallion being led by Chrysta. This animal was a solid unbroken red. He was almost the color of fresh blood. The fierce eyes that flashed under his brow ridges were the hot yellow of an open flame. His stride was as smooth as oil flowing over water.

"That's Inferno! He will be the one to put your silver on in the Gauntlet this year!" Grant grinned, "If that gorgeous bastard runs anything like his sire, nothing here can touch him."

Templer watched in silence as the hot tempered animal tried to take a bite out of Chrysta's leg. The woman doubled up her fist and knocked the fanged mouth away from her.

"She had better NOT pop those stitches!"

Constantine silently agreed as he watched the woman brace herself. The excited stud hit the end of the lead and danced in a tight circle around an increasingly irate Zephyr. The Talon searched for any telltale sign of blood on her right sleeve. There was none yet that he could see.

"Who is Inferno's sire?" He asked, already knowing the answer.

Grant frowned,

"I can almost understand why Chrysta keeps that monster around when that is what you get when you breed to him." The barman sighed,

"His sire is El Diablo."

As his dark eyes followed the group's progress down the parade route, Templer couldn't help but wince at the bartender's choice of words. Monster was a term he was intimate with.

Constantine realized in the first day or two of festival that Chrysta was not joking about keeping odd hours. Between the various competitions she was entered in on Don Ricardo's and her own behalf, plus her unofficial title of town Vet, her visits to the room they shared were sporadic at best. More often than not, when she was there, it was with one of the locals. She spent a great deal of time stitching up a multitude of destria inflicted wounds or bar fight injuries. It seemed the town's people shared Chrysta's views on the high cost and quality of the medical care from the town Healer.

Templer occupied his time attending various events and playing a little poker at one of the smaller, less populated casinos. At Grant's suggestion, he left his cloak and the Trinity in his room. Without these trademarks of rank, the priest found that other than an odd glance or two at his blade-hand, most people treated him as just one of the crowd. The races were scheduled to start on the morning of the festival's third day. Templer realized that both he and his outrider were looking forward to them. It came as a surprise that they were enjoying their time off. He hoped he could pin Chrysta down before the races long enough to pick her brains on which animals he should wager on.

Late the afternoon of the second day, Templer was snagged by Grant as he headed up to the room. He needed a break from the afternoon heat and crowds. The bartender beckoned him over whilst sending one of his girls to the kitchen.

"I don't usually interfere..."

Templer just looked at the man as the word...
liar... came to mind.

Oblivious to the gunman's thoughts, Grant
continued...

"It's just that I KNOW that Chrysta hasn't
eaten since God knows when, and I am willing to
bet you haven't either."

The young woman reappeared. She carried a
tray piled high with sandwiches and other tasty
snacks in one hand, and a frosty pitcher of iced
tea in her other. Grant's face took on a
conspirator's look.

"Now... if I take these up, they will most
likely just go to waste. I am sure if you make it
seem like this was YOUR idea, Chrysta might take
some time to ingest something other than coffee
or Anesthetic."

The man's soft brown eyes and gentle smile
were guileless.

"Hnnn..." (Didn't usually interfere... my ass,
this man was also sneaky, manipulative and very
good at hiding it!) Templer accepted the tray and
pitcher, his stoic expression giving no hint of the
thoughts running through his mind.

Somehow the priest managed to make it up
the stairs and jockey the door open without
dropping either the tray or the tea. Chrysta was
sprawled, fully clothed on the duvet. Her left
arm was thrown over her face shielding it from
the late afternoon sun. Thinking his roommate
was asleep, Templer set his burden down as
quietly as possible. He was taken by surprise
when he heard a soft buack, buack, buack, come
from the duvet. Chrysta looked at him from
under almost closed eyelids, grinning. When she
was sure she had his attention, the obnoxious
woman made another series of mother hen
sounds. This drew a snide snicker from Azra

"I was going to bring this over to you so you didn't have to get up. I've changed my mind." Templer gestured at the table, "You can drag your butt off of there and come eat like a civilized person."

This earned him a snort of laughter as the woman levered herself into a standing position then limped over to join him. Constantine wasn't hungry. His altered metabolism along with Azra's support could make due on very little. He knew from experience that people eat better when someone else is dining with them. The gunman casually picked out a sandwich and took a bite. He was secretly pleased when his psychology worked and Chrysta tucked into her own sandwich with determination if not enthusiasm.

As they ate their meal in companionable silence Templer realized how much he appreciated that both Grant and Chrysta seemed to understand his quiet ways. Neither one of them pressured him in any way to participate in small talk or inane conversation. His friends, were always trying to get him to "open" up. It was like they wanted to change him into something he was not. Granted some were more persistent at this than others. Templer could not remember a time when he had been one for conversation or overt displays of emotion. The Hand's training accentuated these traits. A Talon learned very quickly to hide what he was thinking or feeling. It was just a part of the job.

A soft sigh from Chrysta brought his attention back to the present. With a start he realized that she had been studying him while he was deep in thought. (HOLY... he had to stop doing that! It made him vulnerable.) His companion finished her meal, pushed back from the table, and got up. Limping from cabinet to cabinet she gathered various medical supplies and arranged them neatly in an extensive travel kit. She glanced his way and a small frown wrinkled her brow.

"I hate to ask this." Chrysta looked slightly embarrassed. "Do you have anything planned for tonight?"

"Not really," he answered.

The only events scheduled for that night were a dinner and dance (NOT happening) and the pit fights. He was not attending either. It was his plan to just stay put and make a few belated phone calls. Iniko's last angry message upset his Cricket enough to give it a serious case of the hiccups. The poor thing had chirped intermittently for hours until it calmed down. Templer ignored the little mental nudges Azra gave him. The gunman was justifiably proud of the control he had gained over the sometimes over bearing elemental since their bonding. Because of this, he was caught with his guard down when said demon snatched control for a moment.

"I was hoping you would have some spare time this evening to go over the racing forms with me for tomorrow."

Templer's voice, under Azra's control, came out rougher than his usual silky baritone.

Chrysta's chestnut brows arched in surprise but other than a piercing look sent his way, she didn't comment on the change. Templer choked a little as his rather smug outrider released control back to him.

"Ahhh," Chrysta's smile became a little predatory. "I will make you a deal. If you will come and give me a hand this evening, I will take some time off and attend the races with you tomorrow."

"Aren't you riding in some of the races tomorrow?"

Templer was a bit taken aback when the woman started laughing.

"Bless you... Constantine."

At his confused look she took pity on him, still chuckling.

"I am much too heavy to be a jockey in the speed races." She continued grinning, "But I will thank you for the compliment anyways."

"Hnnn..."

The priest folded his arms, the black talons of his blade-hand tapped a quiet rhythm against the other.

"So what DO you have planned for this evening?" The combination of her and Grant had started to bring out the paranoid side of his personality.

"The stallion pit fights are tonight, so I will be hanging out there."

Chrysta's expression gave nothing away. Templer recoiled a little. The stallion fights were something he had NO interest in attending.

Chrysta gave a small satisfied nod at his reaction.

"I agree... watching two beautiful animals tear each other apart is NOT my idea of a good time. I am not going there to watch. I will be in the barn providing veterinarian care. Sometimes I need another pair of hands or just someone to provide brute strength when putting some of these guys back together. Neither one of my stable hands can stomach the violence or the blood. You seem to have no problem on either account and could even be of help with some of the stitching."

Templer felt Azra perk up at the mention of blood and violence.

"Come ON Constantine, this sounds like a lot more fun than dealing with your obnoxious girlfriend!"

"Iniko is NOT my girlfriend!"

Although to be honest, the demon did have a point. The priest ruthlessly squelched the little stirring of guilt as he agreed to give the hopeful woman in front of him a hand. He would just have to make his calls some other time.

It was very late that night when a much subdued Templer Constantine returned to the Ironwood. Even Azra had seen more blood, rage and death then he could stomach.

"I think I have stitched more tonight than I have in my entire life." The Talon told his quiet outrider. He was a little surprised when he received no answer.

If Chrysta had given any inkling of how traumatic the night would be, he would not have agreed to go. One after another destria had come through the vet barn. Few owners could afford to provide Blessings for their beasts. Chrysta on the other hand, after flashing him a wary look, opened a small case which held several softly glowing Hexes. These Unsanctioned and highly illegal static healing spells were less pricey than the legal Blessings one could purchase from a legit healer. Most could not afford even these black market spells for their loved ones. It was a surprise that Chrysta had a supply of the illegal ones AND that the woman was willing to use them on an animal. When Chrysta produced the first Hex after hastily examining a dying stallion, Templer grimly reminded himself HE was on vacation. The Talon forced himself to look the other way. It was a relief that as soon as they got the screaming beast pieced back together his companion triggered the Hex and the worst of the suffering beast's damage was healed. This was one of lucky few. For those not as badly injured, Chrysta did what she could with traditional techniques. This entailed not only a tremendous amount of cleaning, stitching and bone setting. It also involved a true element of danger. More than once both her and Templer were slashed at, snapped at or thrown into the wall. Once the precious Hexes were gone, those stallions they could do nothing for, had to be put down. Chrysta was the one that eased each one of these into the peaceful sleep of death. As the long night wore on, the woman became more and more quiet. In the end, she sent the gunman off, telling him she could deal with the clean-up. Her expressive eyes were dull with fatigue and dark with tears she did not yet have the time to shed.

When Templer walked into the Ironwood, Grant took a long, hard look at his haggard face and bloodstained clothes. Without saying a word, the bartender poured a brandy snifter full of Anesthetic, forced it into his bloodied hands and sent the priest up to his room. Constantine finished the potent drink in several long swallows. He stripped and stood under the pounding hot water, trying to ignore the crimson stream that ran down the drain in a steady flow. The Talon had no problem with blood. He alone had let loose rivers of it in the line of duty. This was different, this blood had been shed for the sole purpose of entertaining the screaming crowd.

Templer had long come to grips with the fact that in most citizen's eyes... he was a monster. The Talon would be the first to agree with them. Even with his outrider in complete control, those of his rank were highly trained, cold blooded killing machines. The Hand had created his kind in order to bring the devastating Re-gen wars to an end. They had built their own monsters to counteract those the enemy brought into being. With the Truce in place... the soldiers who were extensively modified to battle monsters and survive had been turned to another use. As the most powerful of these... the Talons patrolled the Borderlands dispensing the Hand's harsh justice along with eliminating any threat that invaded from the Wastelands. Their unusual skills were also used to negate other threats to the Order. The "problems" that originated from within, were sniffed out, run to ground and terminated without prejudice. It was acceptable in these circumstances for there to be some collateral damage. It had been drilled into Constantine that all of the atrocities committed in the act of protecting the Realm, were in the end... forgivable. He did not believe it. This night's events had blurred the line dividing what he was from the masses. He was well and truly damned if these blood thirsty souls were an example of what he had become a monster to protect... the priest did not finish this traitorous thought. Instead, he let the hefty dose of Anesthetic temporarily shut his mind down, lifted his face into the hot stream... and tried to convince himself that all of the liquid rolling down his cheeks was water.

The weary priest was standing in front of the open window, watching a storm roll in when Chrysta came into the courtyard. The exhausted woman moved like she was bleeding to death from an unseen wound. She did not seem to notice the underbelly of the storm light up as electricity danced between the clouds. A cold rain started to fall. The rumble of thunder hid the small sound of a gate swinging open from her, but the Talon heard it.

"**Constantine... MOVE!**"

Azra had seen what both Chrysta and Templer had missed in the darkness of the storm. El Diablo's paddock gate was unlocked and swinging in the wind. The tired woman saw it in the same moment that the destria did. She froze as the battle stallion launched himself into a charge. Templer didn't hesitate. He dove through the window at the same time he released control to his outrider. Black shadows spun through the air and what had started out human at the beginning of the leap was something entirely different at the end.

Azra slammed down between the startled human and El Diablo. The elemental's mind was racing. He did not want to kill this beast. Fanning black on crimson wings to their widest span, he spread his arms out... long talons extended, making himself look as large and intimidating as possible. Crouching in a battle stance, the demon met El Diablo's rage and hate with his own.

The startled destria put the brakes on, his cloven hooves sliding on wet flagstones. He came to a shuddering stop just inside the open gate. Snorting, with his neck arched and his regal head held high, the stallion stepped almost daintily over the line then slowly approached the motionless demon.

Azra heard Chrysta's sharp intake of breath as the beast reached out, nostrils flared, to sniff at the tip of one leathery wing. The big animal followed its leading edge until his sharp fanged muzzle was blowing warm breath on the tense outrider's face. The stallion drew back and his jewel-like green eyes studied the demon's gold ones. There was no threat when the soft muzzle gently bumped Azra's shoulder then rested against the demon's bronze cheek. Shocked beyond belief the outrider drew on his host's experience with Nuva. He forced himself to relax and carefully exhaled.

El Diablo whuffled, swinging his flared nostrils in closer to share breaths with him. Azra was overwhelmed with a wave of emotions. These triggered corresponding chords in his mind. Despair, rage, loneliness, and the humiliating feeling of being trapped rolled through him, all of it underscored by a fierce intelligence. It was like taking a savage punch to the guts. Azra jerked back, breaking the contact. The big destria chortled and turned away. With slow, deliberate steps and great dignity, El Diablo returned to his enclosure.

The demon couldn't control the rage he felt as he found himself forced to be the great stallion's jailer. His clawed hands shook as he closed and latched the gate. Spinning, his hot, angry eyes settled on the motionless woman and she became the target for the overpowering emotion.

He was growling as he advanced on her,

"By what right do you keep him captive? He is a sentient being and you are holding him against his will. This is nothing less than slavery!"

Chrysta's eyes widened as the dark demon advanced and she started to back up. At this last statement, those eyes narrowed and her temper exploded to life.

"How DARE you judge me?"

The woman didn't scream or yell. Her normally husky voice deepened to a growl that almost matched Azra's own. Chrysta stalked up until she was right in his face.

"What in the seven Hells do you expect me to do with him? It's not like I can just turn him loose. In case you have forgotten, Destria EAT people! I made a promise a long time ago and I am keeping it to the best of my ability. That silver fucker can try to make me kill him all he wants. It's NOT happening. YOU don't know enough about the situation to be giving me a hard time!"

Azra found himself in a quandary. Human

females (and males for that matter) ALWAYS ran screaming in terror from him. When this didn't happen, it was in battle and they ALWAYS ended up very... very dead. It was a new experience to have a woman standing toe to toe with him. Mother of Demon's... she could not possibly be poking his chest in rhythm with her angry words. The outrider had his own rage barely in hand, and he knew Constantine would make his life a living hell if he harmed this woman.

Azra had heard it said that there was a fine line between anger and passion. Without thinking about it the demon caught the offending hand and jerking Chrysta forward the last couple inches, he silenced her angry words by covering her mouth with his. Being gentle wasn't in his nature and his sharp fangs cut the soft lips, flooding his mouth with the richness of her blood. The taste was amazing; sweet, and smoky with a spiciness that must come from her close association with the destria. For the second time in the space of a few moments the outrider found himself shocked to his ethereal core. Rather than pulling away from his hunger in fear, Chrysta's lips parted and she returned the kiss with an appetite equal to his own. It was not the woman who breathlessly ended it.

They stood still for a moment, face to face, warm breath mingling in the cold night air. Azra did not know what was going on in Chrysta's mind but his was spinning in confusion. His kind was NOT supposed to be able to experience the warm, pleasant, tingly sensations that had accompanied the delectable energy created by that errant kiss. Lust was possible, but that burning, insatiable need was a sweet, empty addiction whose taste he found disgusting once the impulse wore off. It was NOTHING like what he had just experienced.

"Constantine would birth a Terra-bird if he were aware of this."

Azra noticed the red of her blood mingling with the rain at the corner of that sweet mouth. He had a brief savage fight with himself not to lick it off. The woman stepped back wiping it with her bandaged arm. The demon blinked. There was some of his golden blood present there.

Chrysta's eyes were a dark stormy green as she insolently looked him up and then down.

"Yes... I can imagine what Templer's reaction would be. Still, it just might be worth the risk. I am willing to bet my last silver that you would be one HELL of a wild ride!"

Her grin was as wicked as any harpy's as the woman turned and headed for the door. The astounded outrider just stood motionless with the rain dripping slowly off of his wing tips. His mouth worked, savoring the taste of her sweet, spicy blood mixed with his own. A talon-ed hand lifted to lightly brush his lips. DAMN, how the in the hell and more important... WHEN... had she managed to bite his tongue?

Warm spicy breath being huffed into his face greeted Templer when he regained awareness. He experienced a moment of anxiety. Where had Azra deposited him this time? His outrider's warped sense of humor had caused the gunman to awaken in some very interesting places. When he opened his eyes, the priest looked up at Nuva's long, narrow face. The mare was hanging over her stall door trying to nuzzle him awake. Judging from the amount of moist destria slobber adorning his nose, forehead, and cheeks, she had been doing this for quite a while.

"Yuck!"

The man rolled away from the concerned animal, scrubbing at his face. Azra did not make a sound. This was cause for concern. On those occasions the demon pulled a prank he thought was funny, the outrider remained close to the surface to reap his reward of earned chuckles.

Templer regained his feet, groaning as his abused body protested the movement. The transition to his outrider's form still did not come easily. He paid a physical toll whenever it happened. The gunman had no recollection of the events after the transformation. He had a sudden vivid image of a gate swinging open and a lightening lit, wicked devil in full charge. The priest staggered out of the barn and into the dim light of the false dawn. The courtyard was quiet. El Diablo stood in his locked paddock. The big animal, startled awake and grumpy because of it, popped his formidable teeth together as the gunman passed.

"Azra, what happened last night?"

The demon hesitated before answering.

"I... hmmm.... I went storm riding."

The demon flashed him a brief image of flying along the storm's leading edge, racing the wild wind and dancing with the lightening.

.

Templer shuddered. It was almost better NOT knowing how the outrider used his body when they exchanged places. No wonder he hurt! He realized that Azra was trying to distract him from his original question.

"Mother of demons, Azra... What happened HERE?" He waved irritably towards the silver's paddock gate.

The Talon felt his chest tighten as he hurried through the kitchen and up the stairwell. Damn it he LIKED Chrysta. He didn't know what would be worse, that she had been hurt by El Diablo, or frightened to death by his outrider.

"HEY, that's not fair!" The demon sounded genuinely peeved. "I returned the destria to its prison without violence."

Prison? That statement stopped Templer in his tracks. The next had him staggering to lean against the closed door of the room.

"Afterward... I introduced myself to Chrysta." Azra's voice had gone from peeved to smug.

"HOLY!" Was the thought in Templer's head as he opened the door a crack and looked in. He expected Grant to be there with his shotgun loaded and ready. He saw no such thing. The room was quiet in the pre-dawn light. Chrysta was rolled up in her quilt sound asleep on the duvet. She looked unharmed except for a small cut on one side of her generous lower lip

The confused priest slipped in to the room and made a bee line for the bed. Maybe after a couple of hours of much needed sleep, things would be clearer.

"This doesn't get you off of the hook though," he told his head's cohabitant. "I expect a detailed account of what happened out there, in the morning."

"Oh, you will have to get that story from Chrysta." Azra replied. **"A gentleman NEVER kisses and tells!"**

"WHAT?" Templer sat straight up at this comment.

"Hehehe... All kidding aside Host," The demon's teasing tone shifted to deadly serious in a heartbeat. **"You need to find out just how much this woman knows about Talons. More important than this, we need to find out what she knows about you. My relationship to you is not common knowledge outside the Maker's Sept. Even in the Hand only the eldest are familiar with our case. Chrysta's husband was a Maker's Acolyte. He would have a Vow of Silence burned into his mind to insure his obedience in keeping the Order's secrets. As with us... there is NO physical way the man could have talked about what takes place in the labs. Constantine, the thing that stood out the most last night... Chrysta was NOT surprised to see me!"**

"Hnnn..."

Templer lay back down, disturbed more than he cared to admit by the demon's observations. His outrider almost never called him by his given name. Something about their roommate had shaken the ancient being up. On the morrow Talon Constantine would have to see what he could find out. For now, he was overwhelmed with the need to rest.

****
****

Subject zero was aware of darkness, pain, and the terrifying feeling of being trapped. No memories remained of a time before... his life had begun under the agony of the Maker's knives. Not having any experience to draw on made it impossible to put the unending torture into context. He feared it was all he would ever know. The man twisted, struggling against the restraints holding his body tight against the bloodied metal table. Cold so intense that it burned ran through his veins, a residue of the day's experimental treatments.

"I do not know why you struggle so... Priest. You cannot escape. Even if you did, what would you return to?"

His keeper's face twisted into what, for it, served as a nasty smile.

"Your world is forever gone. Even if this was not the case... Who would accept the monster you have become?"

The Demonae's nerve grating voice was full of contempt.

Some part of man's dreaming mind knew that this was not real, but it was buried too far down in sleep to awaken him.

The soft voice urging him to wake up was a familiar torment in this God forsaken hell. Ignoring its insanity was almost a reflex now, the thing that shared his mind was as capable of hurting him as its masters... it could NOT be trusted! The sight of the alien scientist picking up a sharp, torturous looking instrument already stained with his blood had the frantic man arching against the straps holding him down. His breath came in short, panicked gasps.

"Come, come Subject zero... you should be grateful! We are Making you into something greater than what your so called God created. You will be beautiful, you will be powerful and *you will bring the unworthy down like so much chaff in the wind!"*

One of the creature's hands dropped onto the trapped man's shoulder, patting it in almost a friendly gesture. The man caught a scream behind his teeth and struggled harder. Whatever it planned was going to be bad. The creature hissed a sinister laugh as it raised the flashing knife.

"You might as well just lie still and enjoy this... Servant of Fools... I know that I will."

For a second the gunman again thought he heard that other voice calling his name. He disregarded it as the strap that immobilized his right hand and arm parted. He struck at that hated face, the sharp talons of the weapon IT had given him flashing in the sunlight.

In the last instant, that flash jerked the man awake. There had been no sunlight in the pits of Hell. The priest realized the face he was striking at wasn't one of his tormentors and Azra was screaming in his head. It was too late; he couldn't stop the blow from falling.

"CRAP!"

With reflexes honed by years of dodging destria strikes, Chrysta twisted away. As his blade-hand passed just millimeters in front her eyes the woman caught it at the wrist and with incredible strength she yanked... hard! Templer, his reflexes slowed by surprise and sleep, flew out of the bed. He ended up flat on his stomach on the floor. The Talon hit hard enough it drove the air out of his lungs in a whoof. It didn't help that the woman landed on his back with both knees planted just under his rib cage making sure that said lungs were totally emptied. She twisted the deadly bio-engineered hand up behind his back with his palm turned in. If he used the talons, he would only pierce himself.

For a moment they froze there. Templer gagging and gasping, trying to regain his wind and Chrysta leaning hard on his arm, her compact weight interfering with this single minded task.

The woman leaned forward to place her mouth close to his ear,

"Are you AWAKE Constantine? Can I let go?"

Her voice was tight with concern and something else... Pain?

The gunman got enough of his breath back to answer.

"I am awake."

Chrysta released his arm and eased her knees out of his kidneys. She ended up straddling his waist with his stunned body still pinned to the floor.

"Mother of GOD! YOU HAVE GOT TO STOP DOING THAT. One of these days you are going to get us KILLED!"

His outrider sounded like he didn't know whether to laugh or scream.

"YOU are immortal, remember?" Templer answered dryly.

"Not if you succeed in giving me a coronary! HEY... was I imagining things or did that little slip of a woman just take your bad ass DOWN!"

It seemed the urge to laugh had won out. As the demon dissolved into gales of laughter, Templer sighed and turned his attention back to the problem at hand. Namely that he had a member of the opposite sex straddling his hips for the first time in many years. Just because he occasionally slept in a brothel, didn't mean he had been tempted to sample the wares.

He cleared his throat, his wind still wasn't fully back.

"Hey Chrysta?"

She leaned forward a little.

"Yes Templer?"

He kept the tone of his voice conversational.

"I understand the reason you don't ride in the speed races."

Those legs tightened alarmingly on his waist. Damn, but they were strong.

"What did you just say?"

"Oh nothing... you may want to dismount so I can catch my breath."

The gunman's voice was deliberately bland. Again... the friends who had accused him of not having a sense of humor would have been stunned. The prone man wished he was in a different position so he could see the expression on the woman's face as she slid off of him. Her softly muttered "Smart ass" told him all he needed to know.

Templer rolled over and propped himself up against the nightstand. It crossed the priest's mind that he was lucky he hadn't brained himself on the heavy wood in his sudden flight to the floor. Chrysta remained seated with her back against the bed, her arms wrapped around her knees. Concern warred with amusement in her eyes as she studied him. The gunman felt more than a little concern himself. The woman's tanned face was pale. There were tiny lines of pain around her eyes and mouth.

"Holy... I am sorry Chrysta."

The priest was overwhelmed with guilt. He lived with the constant fear of losing control and hurting a friend. This seemed to have finally happened.

"Are you okay?"

Chrysta's face creased into a sudden, warm smile.

"Constantine, you have nothing to apologize for. I am well aware you do NOT disturb someone in the middle of a night terror episode. You seemed so distressed that I ignored what I know and touched you anyways. Technically if there is any fault, it is mine."

The woman shifted position and a fleeting grimace marred her smile.

Templer wasn't willing to release his guilt that easily,

"I hurt you. That is unforgivable."

The smile disappeared to be replaced by a slight frown.

"I am not injured. There is NOTHING to forgive!"

"She is in pain and not admitting it. Templer, be tactful. You do NOT want to trigger her temper. You have NO idea what she might do!"

Azra sounded worried. The gunman again wondered what had happened between the two of them the previous night.

"I can tell you are in pain. Where did I hurt you?"

This earned him a derisive snort.

"You big ninny! In case you haven't noticed, I am ALWAYS in pain. I usually get a chance to warm things up and stretch them out before I start wrestling, then riding personages who are bigger than me!"

Her eyes had a wicked twinkle in them. To his horror, Templer felt a blush creep up his cheeks. Damn it, what was with this woman that she had him blushing more in the last few days than he had in the last eighty years?

"Really Host... you learned to be tactful... WHERE?" His outrider was again consumed by uncontrollable snickers. **"By all that is Holy, Constantine. I am SOOO glad you decided to come here. I cannot remember the last time I have had this much fun!"**

The gunman leaned his head back and closed his eyes. He had decided that this time there was no need for guilt when Chrysta's next words registered on his already bruised ego.

"Maybe I am the one who should apologize? I am afraid I wasn't very gentle, yanking you out of bed that way. Are YOU okay?"

His eyes popped open to look into her totally innocent face.

"OH NO... Too much... THIS IS GOING TO KILL ME!"

Azra sounded like he was choking. Templer entertained the dark thought that MAYBE the demon would laugh himself to death.

"I am fine." the priest's voice was a flat monotone.

"In that case, why don't you get your fine butt off of the floor and help me up."

Chrysta smile softened the sting to his wounded pride. Templer just shook his head. With a much put upon sigh, he got up and extended his hand to his smiling companion. He might as well just give up now. It was evident that between her and Azra, he was well and truly screwed!

The woman took his hand in her strong grip and he steadied her as she levered herself up. The Talon couldn't help but wince in sympathy at the first couple of staggering steps she took. He found it hard to believe that this was the same woman who had just moved with such speed and grace. He finally gave into his curiosity. It should have been impossible for an un-Tainted human to immobilize him that easily.

"Where did you learn that little trick?"

"Hmmm... that?" Chrysta waved her hand in the direction of the bed.

"I make a living working with creatures that outweigh me by a couple of thousand pounds. There are times when speed, surprise, and knowing how to use leverage are all that separate me from being the trainer or becoming a destria's dinner."

She turned to look at him just before entering the washroom,

"Let's just say that it comes with the territory."

Templer's well-trained intuition told him that this was not the whole story and his outrider agreed with him.

"She just told a half truth. There is more to it than that."

The Talon wavered for a moment, caught between wanting to push the point and the sudden fear that somehow the woman was an unregistered Drow. Azra stirred and Templer was surprised when the demon did not automatically test her in reaction to his suspicion. He was again taken aback when the bathroom door opened just enough for Chrysta to stick her head through. The sharp scent of dreamleaf wafted out on the warm, damp air.

"That explanation is not going to satisfy you or the... other... lurking around in your mind, is it?"

She met his glowing gaze without fear or apology.

Stunned, all he could do was shake his head.

"I... Do... NOT... LURK!"

The outrider sounded offended.

"Shut up, Azra."

Templer sat on the demon as Azra sputtered in outrage. He wanted to hear what the woman had to say.

Chrysta gave a small nod.

"Listen, let me finish here, then we can go down and watch the morning workouts. That's where you are going to pick your winners, not off of the racing forms. I have a dressage demonstration this afternoon that you are welcome to watch if you would like. We can meet up this evening and I will truthfully answer whatever questions you might have on the condition that you answer a few of my own."

The smile she gave him seemed a little sad.

"Do we have a deal?"

Templer thought hard about it for a moment. He doubted she would be happy with the arrangement. It was impossible for him to talk about his Making or most of his actions as a Talon. His Vows of Silence were powerful Bindings. They would burn his mind to ash before allowing him to speak of forbidden things. Add to this the occasional forced trip to the labs to have his brains stirred around and you had a recipe for mental goulash. Since he had no reliable memories of before taking his Vows... the priest did not have much of a story he could tell. Azra had even less of a tale. The outrider was bound by Vows even stronger than his host's. An elemental was called into being by a Summons. Whereas Azra was vastly different than any elemental Templer had ever seen... the priest doubted that the energy being even HAD a life before their bonding.

"**I believe Chrysta knows quite a bit about us as it is Constantine, What harm could it do?**"

The outrider did have a point. Their Binding prevented them from telling the woman anything that might put her in jeopardy. Still... some of the atrocities that he had been called upon to commit were public knowledge... no matter how hard the Hand worked to cover them up. Chrysta was smart and very capable of putting two and two together.

"I know Azra, and it shouldn't matter, but I like her and Grant. I do not want to be rejected by them when they realize they are harboring a monster under their roof."

Templer knew that the demon could sense the weight of seldom acknowledged emotion behind his thoughts.

"**Templer, believe it or not, I too would feel... pain if Chrysta chooses to reject us. Have you not considered that she might be experiencing some of these same fears? If she is even slightly Tainted and has not stood to be Tested... she would be taking a deadly risk!**" The outrider's rough voice was thoughtful. "**Besides, I think she might be a little more open minded than you are aware!**"

"Well?"

Chrysta's husky voice jerked him back to awareness. She was watching him, one chestnut brow arched up.

"Sooo, have the two of you come to an agreement, do we have a deal?"

Templer's brows crawled up his forehead like they had a life of their own.

"We have a deal."

The Talon had decided he was going to learn her secrets if it killed him.

"**UMMM, Templer... DO you remember the LAST deal you made with that woman? I seem to recall, stitches, blood, destria bites and kicks...**" *{And one really sweet kiss}* This last thought Azra kept well isolated from the rest.

The gunman stared hard at the now closed bathroom door. CRAP... How did she know just what buttons to push to get him to agree to do these things? HE was a Talon... HE was supposed to be trained to deal with that kind of manipulation! With a sigh, the priest gathered up the shirt he had dropped the night before. He shot the door one more dirty look and then headed down the stairs to see if Grant had any much needed coffee prepared.

Grant had the coffee ready. The big man gave Templer a long, hard look.

"Kind of noisy up there this morning, is everything okay?"

He handed a cup to the waiting gunman and filled it with the steaming black liquid.

The Talon studied the other man's mild face over its rim as he took a much needed drink.

"Morning calisthenics." he answered dryly.

Grant's eyes narrowed but he wisely made no other comment.

Templer made it through his first cup and started on the second when Chrysta made her way down the steps. He noticed that the flowing grace had returned to her limping gait.

"I told you, dreamleaf is miraculous stuff." Azra sounded a little wistful, then sly. **"It has been known to do anal retentive personalities a world of good. You really should try it!"**

"Hnnn...," was the only answer the priest made.

He was busy studying Chrysta as she ambled over to the bar. Instead of the heavy pants and shirt over protective leather gear that she usually wore, she was wearing soft, black suede leather pants and high topped boots that form fitted to her legs. Her loose shirt was white with intricate embroidery on the open collar and cuffs. The simple black leather vest she wore over it accented the fact that this woman was in great physical shape.

Templer usually paid very little attention to

members of the opposite sex. (Unless he was involved in a Hunt!) This was a personal choice. Men of his rank were referred to as priests and indeed they could step into this role if need be. BUT... unlike the secular Priest, Talons were not required to abstain from carnal acts. As a matter of fact, in some of the matters they attended to, sex was an important weapon in their complex arsenal. Many a man or woman had let secrets slip in the heat of passion that could not be torn from them on the Inquisition's bloody rack. Add to this the fact that the elemental creature a Talon hosted could supplement its ethereal needs with the type of energy released during sex. Constantine had been trained almost as extensively in the Art of pleasuring the flesh as he had in the Arts of destroying it! His duties in the last few decades had tended more towards the more mundane tasks of a Talon. Monster hunting, adjudicating border disputes, enforcing Order laws, and Sorting the Tainted did not require the use of bedroom skills in the way espionage did.

The only place that casual fornication was not illegal was at the brothels in a Sin city. Being as how Azra absolutely detested the taste of lust, Templer's outrider actively discouraged any interest his host might have in visiting these places. The truth be told... the demon did not have to work very hard at this. The thought of using one of the poor souls trapped in those godforsaken places made Templer's skin crawl. He would have to be more than desperate! As for pursuing a LOVING relationship with a woman that included marriage, this was forbidden. A Talon's loyalties could not be divided. Those of Constantine's rank were permanently wedded to the Hand. All of this did not matter. Templer was sure there was no woman on this earth who would willingly warm his bed and body once they discovered what being a Talon entailed.

It had been decades since Templer had sampled the flesh. The feel of the warm, strong legs straddling his hips this morning had driven home the fact that whatever else he was, be it priest, Talon or monster... he was still very much a man.

As he covertly watched Chrysta badger the barman about her coffee... the priest couldn't help but compare the woman with the two females he was most familiar with. He was aware that Sig's lover was a lovely young... woman. With her well-toned frame, honey colored eyes, and silky gold hair, the gunman could see why the Wind-master was so protective of her. Add to this Skye's gentle personality and MOST of the time, one could forget that you might find yourself in bed with her alter ego if her control slipped. There was a soft snicker in his mind and Templer hid the slight smile that danced across his lips behind the rim of his cup at the thought. He had oft wondered just how the volatile Captain dealt with those occasions!

The only other woman he had any kind of ongoing relationship with was Iniko. This ward of the Saint's was just a child. At sixteen, the little thief was growing out of the long legged, slender, teen age look. If you could get past her abrasive personality, one could see the beautiful woman she would become... IF she lived to maturity. The Talon and his outrider had an ongoing bet that someone would do her in out of pure aggravation before that day. There was no comparing the young girl to the mature woman before him.

Chrysta carried her tall frame with the confidence created by a lifetime of experience. Her shoulders were broad even for her five foot eight frame. Her arms and long fingered hands had been strengthened and hardened by years of handling destria and her waist was still trim. The priest could attest to the fact that those long slim legs were nothing but muscle and sinew.

Grant handed the woman a small well filled pouch and she glanced Templer's way, flashing him a quick smile before returning to her conversation.

Templer sipped his coffee and continued to covertly watch her. Her face's best features were her large, beautiful eyes. She had high cheekbones, a straight slightly too long nose, a generous mouth, and a strong jaw line. Her soft chestnut hair was clipped very short. This was not the most attractive style but one that made sense when you spent a great deal of time wearing a helmet. No, Chrysta definitely would not meet the standard of what most men would consider beautiful or even pretty. Still... when she smiled at him... it was like the sun breaking through deep shadow to softly warm his tired soul. That, combined with the odd grace she incorporated into almost every move, made the woman down right...

"Hot? Sexy? OH MY GODS, give me some of that... I want to ride it like a monkey!!"

His outrider's sudden intrusion into his thoughts was accompanied by a flood of lurid images.

Chrysta's head snapped around as Templer convulsively jerked in shocked surprise. With a sound like a gunshot, the coffee cup cracked in his hands.

"AZRA... STOP it!"

Templer felt lucky that he hadn't inhaled the coffee that had been in his mouth. Although, the threat of drowning seemed to be the least of his problems as his body reacted in a delighted fashion to the images still rolling through his mind.

"WHAT? You keep telling me I am demon. If

this is true, I am SUPPOSED to have depraved appetites!" His tone was defensive as he snickered. **"You on the other hand don't have that excuse and YOU are the one in control of our body right at the moment."**

The gunman rested his forehead in his gun hand while he forced the other to release the pieces of the cup. Taking deep breaths, he tried to block out Azra's input and get his overly enthusiastic body back under control.

"What the fuck... Azra! You don't like that sort of thing!"

The demon generated images stuttered to a halt.

"WHAT... the... HELL! Your right. I DON'T like that sort... Holy... I think I might be sick!"

"Constantine?" Chrysta was at his side, her face questioning.

"Hmmm, sudden cramp...," was all Templer could think to say, while he silently cussed his IDIOT demon cohort out.

"Ah-hum...," was her unconvinced answer. "If you are okay now, we should be heading to the track."

The woman scooped the pouch off of the bar, blew a kiss to Grant and headed out through the back door. Templer slowly followed her into the early morning sun. He was surprised to see that Nuva and Zephyr were already saddled and waiting. Chrysta attached her pouch to the big black's saddle and lithely mounted up. Zephyr danced in a tight circle waiting for the gunman to follow suit. Nuva chortled in greeting, and when he was seated, swung her heavy ridged head around to lip fondly at his knee. The old girl arched her neck. Stepping high, she followed the black down the alley and out on to the main street.

They covered the couple of miles to the racing compound in relatively quick time as there was not much in the way of festival crowds this early in the morning. The security guards passed them through with no hassles. Chrysta was well known as a trainer and rider. She led them through the maze of barns and paddocks until they came to the stable marked with Don Ricardo's name. The priest was a little surprised that along with the couple of stable-hands who took custody of Nuva and Zephyr, there were also quite a few mercenaries serving as guards. These were posted in and around the stables and on the outside of some of the paddocks. He threw a questioning look at Chrysta and she gave a small shrug.

"There have been problems in the past with suspicious accidents, and animals getting poisoned." The look in her eyes matched the hard edge present in her voice. "This can be a cut throat business."

As she passed in front of a high walled stall a lean, blood red head suddenly struck out over it. Chrysta didn't even blink as black fangs clashed together mere centimeters from of her nose. She did however, protest and slap the slobbery muzzle away when it tried to nuzzle into her shirt.

"Damn it Inferno! You big dope, DON'T mess up the shirt."

Templer could tell by the exasperated affection in her voice that this was an ongoing game the two played.

Inferno dodged the halfhearted slap then danced away snorting in triumph over his obvious victory. The big animal shook out his flame colored mane and minced up to study the gunman with eyes that burned like the heart of a star. The priest carefully stepped back as the stallion showed an inordinate amount of interest in HIS shirt.

Chrysta smiled as she gave the ridged head a final gentle slap then headed toward the exit. As they walked, she pointed out to the Talon the animals in Don Ricardo's barn that were racing that day. She told him which ones were worth betting on.

What followed was one of the most enjoyable days Templer Constantine had experienced in a very long time. They spent the morning wandering the grounds and watching the racer's workouts. When the racing started, Chrysta had V.I.P. seats reserved that afforded them a perfect view of the track. Her pouch had been filled by Grant with a variety of goodies and a small bottle of red wine that they shared throughout the day. With her input, the gunman managed to make a little silver on some of his bets. Even Azra was unusually quiet, content to just observe from the back of his host's mind. The only dark spot in the day was in the third race when a young sprinter had a bad fall in the backstretch. Chrysta started to rise... but settled back down as the sharp crack of a gunshot echoed across the tracks. She sadly explained that with over six thousand pounds per square inch balanced over one fragile leg at a time sometimes the racers strong but thin bones broke from the strain. This type of catastrophic injury could not be healed with conventional methods... the animal was usually put down.

As the races for the day were finishing, they headed back to Don Ricardo's barn. When they arrived Andrew had Zephyr, Nuva and a lovely almost delicate looking filly saddled and bridled. A small crowd had gathered at the adjoining arena, waiting for Chrysta's dressage demonstration. She explained on the walk over that dressage was an ancient style of riding based on the skills that battle mounts were taught before they went into battle. There would be several buyers watching who were interested in purchasing the destria that she would be riding. Chrysta put on her helmet and left Templer at the gate with the Nuva and Zephyr. She mounted the filly, who was a dramatically dappled gray, and entered the arena.

Making a slight bow in the direction of her audience, Chrysta and her mount began their patterns. Templer had ridden Terra-birds many times. The couple of times he had ridden Nuva had driven home the differences in the riding styles needed for each animal. Even so... the priest had never seen anything quite like the display this pair put on. Chrysta seemed as much a part of the destria as the legendary centaurs said to roam West of the Waste. The filly spun and leaped as she performed intricate moves that took incredible precision and control. It was like watching an elegant, dance as the pair floated over the ground. The Talon remembered how El Diablo had battled his rider. He was struck by the amount of training that had to go into producing an animal like this pretty gray.

As the pair came to an easy stop in the center of the arena the small crowd applauded politely. A disturbance attracted the gunman's attention and he recognized Rafe along with several of his cronies making their way to the gate.

"What a waste of time."

Rafe was preening in front of his crowd, showing off as he pushed past Templer to enter the arena.

"Imagine... teaching a destria how to dance!"

The arrogant young man laughed loudly making sure everyone there observed his obvious contempt. His retinue of three laughed with him, but remained on the outside of the arena.

Chrysta turned towards the obnoxious young

man. She motioned to someone behind Constantine. One of the stable-hands took Zephyr's reins and led him into the arena to where the gray and its rider waited. Templer was mildly surprised when five of the mercenary guards entered the arena. They were all heavily padded and more astounding... all were also protected by elemental shields. The priest casually blocked Azra as the outrider instinctively reached out to Test whether the magic was Sanctioned.

"We are on vacation... remember?"

The men began to set up obstacles and very human like manikins. They then positioned themselves in strategic locations around the arena. One of them handed Chrysta a long, sheathed blade. She dismounted from the filly and with a lithe swing, was up on the much larger Zephyr. The stable-hand led the gray over to the side of the arena as the woman rode the black forward to face Rafe. Leaning forward a little Chrysta spoke quietly to the red head. Templer's enhanced hearing had no problem deciphering what she said.

"Little man, you should study your history."

Rafe's face flushed with anger at the contemptuous tone present in her soft voice.

"These dance moves, as you call them, are used to teach destria the Art of War."

As she said this, the rider dropped her reins and drew the sword. Templer saw her legs tighten around the black's sensitive sides and Zephyr spun. As he completed that lightning fast move the black transformed from a quiet beast of burden to a red eyed, screaming weapon of destruction. He launched forward to meet the mercenaries who had also drawn weapons head on. As the beast passed one of the manikins Chrysta's sword drifted out, easily removing its head. Three of the mercenaries tried to close in on the pair. Zephyr cantered in place, turning a tight circle as he lashed out with teeth and hooves. Chrysta parried and slashed with her blade and all three men were forced to fall back.

 The big black broke from his circle into a huge sideways trot. Two of the guards who had been closing on their left side had to scramble to get out of his way. A lightning strike with a front leg shredded a second manikin. One guard charged and Zephyr reared striking out with sharp, cloven front hooves. The reason for the heavy padding became clear as the man was knocked across the sand. Two others tried to get to the destria's unprotected sides but found their way blocked by Chrysta's blade.

 The black, still on his hind legs, hopped forwards. He turned as he came down, knocking both men off of their feet with a swing of his ridged, horned head. Breaking into a gallop Zephyr made a circuit of the arena slashing and kicking as he passed the manikins. He left none of them standing. The mighty beast then turned and charged Rafe. Before he reached the man, Zephyr came to a sliding stop and reared up on quivering haunches. His scream was a guttural challenge, his lips were pulled back to expose black, killing fangs. In the space of a breath he covered the distance to the redhead with three long hops, front legs clawing the air. Rafe back pedaled until he reached the fence.

Chrysta, her point made, snatched up the reins. Zephyr came to a shuddering stop directly in front of the now panicked young man. There was complete silence, then the small crowd was screaming and clapping. They had totally enjoyed the show.

Rafe's face was flushed as he looked up at Chrysta.

"I will pay you whatever you want for him."

He gestured towards the now quiet black.

Chrysta shook her head.

"Zephyr is not for sale at any price."

"Fine, then I will pay twice what your buyer offers for the gray."

The man's avarice was clearly evident in his voice.

Chrysta leaned forward slightly. "You don't understand Rafe." Her voice was quiet. "None of my herd is for sale... to YOU."

It took a moment for her meaning to sink in. Rafe's face twisted and his hand dropped for the gun at his side. Templer's hand also dropped before he remembered that the Trinity was not holstered there. He did not see Chrysta move but Zephyr sprang forward, rearing up. The woman's blade licked out and Rafe's gun flipped into the dirt. The big black's muscled chest struck the staggering man and bore him down to land on his back in the dirt. His deadly cloven hooves slammed down on either side of his pale face. Rafe's three companions all snatched for their weapons. Templer caught the first man's hand before he could clear leather. With a savage twist, he broke the fragile wrist. His blade-hand dropped on the second man's shoulder. Its sharp talons bit deep into muscles and nerves, paralyzing the arm. The priest threw this screaming man away and spun to deal with the third. He froze at the scene that met his eyes.

Nuva had sidestepped and slipped behind the third gunman, who just happened to be the blond temple guard. She had her mouth locked over the back of the man's neck, and was applying just enough pressure that her fangs barely pierced his skin. This man had the presence of mind to freeze and drop his gun.

For a moment everything was still. Then

Chrysta signaled Zephyr, and the black stepped back placing his sharp hooves with care. He snorted his disdain into Rafe's face as he allowed the man to scramble to his feet. Nuva matched his snort as she removed her fangs from her captive's bleeding neck. The mare licked the blood off her lips with evident pleasure while the man scrambled away with a curse. The Don's son didn't say a word as he tried to brush some of the dirt off of his expensive clothes. He turned to gather up his injured group.

As they were leaving, Rafe once more faced Chrysta.

"This isn't over you Tainted bitch!" The words were choked with embarrassment and rage.

Templer heard Chrysta murmur as she watched them leave. "No I imagine it isn't."

The woman looked over at him and a tiny smile crinkled her eyes.

"Why don't you take Nuva and head back to the Ironwood. I'll meet you there when I have finished with this sale."

The gunman just nodded and gathering Nuva's reins he swung up into the saddle. As he was turning to leave, the woman kneed Zephyr up close to him.

"Thank you." was all she said.

Templer was on the roof of the Ironwood when Chrysta and Zephyr came in that evening. The sun dipped behind dark storm clouds gathering on the horizon. The priest had been stopped when he returned with Nuva by security guards now posted in the courtyard. This was one of the items Grant and Chrysta had discussed that morning. El Diablo's gate had been deliberately opened, and Chrysta was taking no chances with the unpredictable animal getting out. These same guards approached her as she dismounted.

The gunman waited as the woman led the big black into the barn, then reappeared to take care of El Diablo's needs. He had noticed that the stable-hands did not deal with the dangerous stallion. Templer also noted that like the night before, while she worked around this particular destria, there was no sign of Chrysta's ever present limp. After making sure the animal had food, and water. The woman checked that the gate was locked. She also confirmed that the electricity to the fence was on. She stood for a long moment watching the beast. El Diablo stopped his eternal prowling and returned her look with a coldly antagonistic one of his own. The Talon heard her soft sigh as she turned and headed towards the door, her graceful stride again marred by a pained limp.

It took Templer a few moments to slip back into the room via the window. He was surprised by a soft knock at the door. When he opened it, Chrysta stood there loaded down with a tray full of food and a pitcher of what looked like tea. She carefully eased her way into the room.

"Grant caught me before I could sneak up the

stairs. He said something about one of us being too skinny."

She glanced at the gunman out of the corner of her eye as she deposited the tray on the table.

"I expect that would be you."

Templer was a little daunted by the amount of food that the barman had sent up.

"I do not need to eat again today."

The woman snorted.

"Neither do I. He made it very clear he doesn't care. If we don't eat, all we get to drink is... Tea!"

Her lip curled in disdain at the thought.

"I don't know about you, but I am NOT divulging my life's deep, dark secrets with nothing in my system but... TEA! You need to either eat your share or help me figure out what else to do with it."

He eyed her hopefully,

"Why don't we go down and tell him we aren't hungry."

The hope died a cruel death when she snickered.

"Yeah, you go ahead and give that a try. Don't forget to let me know how it works out."

"Hnnn..."

Templer wouldn't admit it, but he agreed with her assessment of the situation. "I believe I have seen several stray cats in the area."

"I like the way your mind works Constantine. Although... I think Nuva and Zephyr might enjoy some of this."

Chrysta did a quick perusal of the tray. After selecting several smaller items that could be munched on as needed, she bundled the rest up in a couple of napkins. The larger one was handed to the gunman with instructions on splitting it between the two destria. The smaller one was for the strays.

Templer accepted the bundles while giving her a dark look.

"Why am I the one who gets to disperse this?"

"One, it was your idea. Two, unlike you, I am at least going to eat a little." Chrysta poked him in the chest with a forefinger. "And three, this old lady is NOT climbing out a second story window!"

"Old lady my ass!"

He muttered as he dropped to the courtyard and slipped past the guards. All the gunman needed was for Grant to catch him in the act. If that happened he would be drinking nothing but TEA for the rest of the week, or worse yet, plain water!

It took Constantine the better part of a half hour to get the goodies divided up between the two delighted destria and a hoard of stray cats. Then he had to figure out how to get back in without alerting the sentries.

Chrysta was sitting at the table when he made it back into the room. She had finished some of the munchies and was half halfheartedly sipping a glass of the chilled tea. The woman had taken the opportunity to change into a loose shirt and soft flannel pants while he had been occupied. Templer sat down opposite her and accepted the glass that she had already filled for him. She watched him silently as he made himself comfortable.

"Sooo..." She set her glass down. "Where would you like to begin?"

The priest thought about it for a moment as

he sampled his drink.

"How much did Dr. Denia tell you about me?"

"At first Forrest TOLD me nothing of his service in the Maker's labs." Chrysta shook her head at the Talon's skeptical look. "His Bindings were much the same as yours." The woman ignored the way Templer's brows lifted in surprise and continued. "Initially... the things that I learned were just bits and pieces that I put together listening in on his dreams. He had terrible nightmares, and he talked a lot in his sleep. There were many sleepless nights that I laid by him and listened to the horrible experiments he had witnessed and participated in. I believe that without... outside... help, Forrest eventually would have gone insane."

Templer snorted.

"You will have to pardon me if I can't dredge up any sympathy for him. At least the Maker's did not turn him into an inhuman monster."

"Oh, I wouldn't be so quick to say that. Have you ever wondered what taking a Healer and making him commit acts that are inherently abhorrent over and over again, does to his psyche? Not even the Binding could block the emotional turmoil it caused. By the time Forrest finally got away from the labs, he considered himself a monster in every sense of the term. I almost lost him when the Prince broke his Vows and the true scope of the atrocities he helped commit were revealed. Ty was hard pressed to preserve not only my husband's sanity in those first horrible moments but also his life. We found out the hard way it is quite possible for a Healer to will themselves into death. Forrest came close to achieving this! It took a long time and a lot of help before he found his mental balance and was able to come to terms with it. Rest assured Constantine. Yours isn't the only life the Makers have screwed over!"

Chrysta stopped, sipped her tea then looked hard at the Talon for a moment.

"You don't look like a monster to me, Templer Constantine. Why on earth would you believe you are one?"

The gunman hesitated. The only people who knew the full scope of what a Talon was capable of were his Makers and the poor souls that he was trained to Hunt. As for himself... there were vague memories that he DID retain. They were not clear... and consisted mainly of images of blood and destruction. These were accompanied by feelings of guilt and shame that ran too deep for his Binding to eradicate. He had a paralyzing fear that the differences between what he had been BEFORE his Making and what he had become, were few and dealt mainly in the matter of scale. His Vows... and the tinkering that the Order did in his head on occasion fragmented most of what he could recall. After decades of this... the man truly could not differentiate between memory and what might be just terrible dreams. All of a sudden he realized that this one time he wanted, no... NEEDED to unburden his soul to a sympathetic ear. But that need was tempered by the knowledge that the friendship he had found here with this unusual woman would end because of what he revealed.

Azra stirred.

"Our Vows will not let you do this Host. Please be careful. It won't help your case if you blow us all to hell and back!"

Giving an internal nod to his concerned outrider... the man glanced up, almost afraid to meet his waiting roommate's eyes.

"I do not remember but there is a part of me that feels I was a monster BEFORE my Making. If this is not so... why has God chosen to punish me with this cruel Penance? Do you know what being a Talon entails?"

She held his gaze while nodding slowly.

"Everyone has seen at least one cleansing Templer, and all the Realm's citizens have stood through their own Sorting. It is a Talon's job to dispense justice and deal with those that do not pass the Testing. This is common knowledge."

Common knowledge... Templer did not know whether to scream or sob. He could not number the Tainted children he had burnt into ash... not because of what they were, but because of what they might BECOME. He had faced others not as severely afflicted as Judge and jury, offering the bitter choice of a life given up in service or death. There were many who chose to fight rather than kneel to receive their Markings. To these he was also Executioner. Worse yet, were the rare cases when whole towns refused the Sorting. The Hand had one response to this. When the Reaper walked away, he left nothing but ash rising into a darkening sky and no soul left to grieve the loss.

 Templer dropped his eyes as guilt seared his heart and pain savaged his mind. Just the act of trying to organize his thoughts enough to explain that "common knowledge" did not come close to the true facts was enough to trigger his Binding. He heard Azra's hiss of pain as the outrider got caught in the overflow. The priest ignored it as he attempted to ride the wave... working at finding a way to get what he wanted to say out. For several long moments Templer fought to circumnavigate his Vows. For every new attempt, he was rewarded with a pulse of increased agony. The Talon trapped a scream behind his teeth and tried to drown out Azra's tense warning that if he did not stop he would damage himself! The demon's voice did not break through... the OTHER one did!

"Stop this... Templer... STOP! Mother of

Demons! It's okay. Constantine... you have to LET IT GO!"

There was true pain in the woman's voice, enough so that the Talon's head snapped up in concern.

"Holy!" Chrysta's face as she stared back at him was drawn, and her hands shook as she set her tea glass down.

"Constantine, it truly sucks to be you!"

She tried to smile at him but instead pushed back her chair and staggered into the bathroom. Templer could not drown out the sound of her vomiting.

"Well, that's unexpected."

The outrider sounded concerned.

Templer felt terrible and not just because of the sickening head-ache pounding behind his eyes. He knocked on the door.

"Are you all right in there?"

"It's okay Templer," Chrysta's voice was still a little shaky. "This isn't your fault. Why don't you go and tell Grant we are in desperate need of some Anesthetic up here."

As he descended the stairs, the priest wondered if maybe he shouldn't gather up his things and leave before he caused these good people any more distress. If it made the woman that sick just to look at him... he did not really want to know what she was thinking.

"Don't... you... dare!" Azra was adamant, **"There is something odd going on here and I want some answers. If you try leaving, I will cramp up BOTH of your legs!"**

By the time Templer made it back to the room, Chrysta had moved the chairs over by the open window. The cool night breeze had returned some of the color to her cheeks. The gunman poured two small glasses of the potent blue alcohol then set the bottle on the window sill. The woman quietly contemplated El Diablo as the priest sat back down.

"I can understand..." She started to speak but he cut her off before the sentence was finished.

"NO... you can't understand, not one of you can even come close to understanding how with every day that passes a little more of what makes me human gets stripped away. When it is all gone, WHAT in the seven hells do you think will be left?"

The words came out harsher than he had intended. Chrysta turned from her perusal of the courtyard. The eyes that met his held compassion, and... anger.

"No, YOU don't understand." she smiled and there was something sad and terrible lurking there. "I am more aware than you know of how terrible you feel."

Chrysta sighed and then took a long drink out of her glass.

"During the day, you are just about the most heavily shielded person I have run across in a long time. But, when you were dreaming last night, and as you were struggling just now... your shields shattered. Even knowing that I shouldn't I HAD to wake you this morning. You were broadcasting your nightmare. It was so terrible I couldn't block it out."

She must have noticed the confusion on his face because she snorted a quick humorless laugh.

"My mother and father were both trainers. I guess you can say the career runs in my blood in more ways than one. You may have noticed there are few women who work with destria. If a woman absorbs too much venom it causes lethal mutations in any children she might conceive later on. My mother was aware of this. When she became pregnant with me she fully expected that I would not survive full term. Imagine her surprise when not only did I survive but was born a healthy, seemingly normal child."

She hesitated a moment as it was a Talon that turned to study her with cold, narrowed eyes.

"Oh relax Templer... I stood my Sorting and passed the Test. I am not Tainted. The mutations that occurred before birth do not stem from the Re-Gen Plague. They didn't show up until I hit puberty, about that same time that I took my first hit of destria venom. While I suffered from the poisoning I kept hearing voices in my head. At first I thought it was from the fever. Then I realized that the couple of destria I was working with at the time were talking to me."

Azra had risen and the outrider also studied the woman with suspicion. The woman shot a quick glance Templer's way and seeing the expression of disbelief on his face she stopped talking and her own eyes narrowed.

"OH... you have GOT to be kidding me! What I do is NOT elemental in nature. I would think you of all people..."

Chrysta looked the priest in the eye and softly growled,

"Nuva, come out into your paddock and say hello to Mr. Suspicious here." The woman's eye color shifted until it was bright blue.

Templer watched in amazement as the mare came trotting out, faced the window and gave a whistling call.

His companion smiled a grim smile at the look on the gunman's face.

"It's NOT a result of the Plague. If you need more proof, priest... you go ahead and have your... FRIEND... do his thing!"

Chrysta's eyes hardened and chilled to an ice green. This time she whispered.

"Diablo, you are a mother fucking asshole."

Out in his paddock, the massive silver threw up his head and screamed a hateful challenge back.

"WOW... she is not Tainted host. I don't have to Test her. This tastes of something entirely different!"

As Azra finished, Chrysta's head turned towards him. Templer had a sudden epiphany.

"You can hear my outrider, can't you?" The Talon wasn't surprised when she nodded. He would be the first to admit, he was more than a little freaked out.

"Can you read my mind also?"

"I think Azra must broadcast on the same wave length as the destria. They also "hear" him. I can pick up thoughts from other people's minds if I push hard enough. I have learned to maintain strong shields as it is easy to get overwhelmed. I pick up strong emotions very easily."

The woman smiled at the look that must have crossed Templer's face as the implications of what Chrysta could do with that particular talent sank home.

"You can relax. As I said before, you have some very tight shielding. It is probably an offshoot of having to deal with your internal... guest. I can pick up very little from you and I am not inclined to push where I am not invited. God knows you have had MORE than enough fingers stirring that particular pot!"

This last was quietly muttered and Templer

doubted the woman realized it had been heard. Chrysta smiled and reached out to pat his hand.

"What does get out is mostly emotion. And it only leaks out when it is very strong. So Templer Constantine, having "felt" one of your nightmares and been gut punched by what some sadist has done to your mind... I can honestly say that I do understand some of what you FEEL. I definitely understand what it means to have someone else in your head ALL of the time. Once one of them..." She nodded in the direction of the barn, "...bonds with me, it is very hard to block them without a lot of effort. It can be extremely inconvenient at times."

Templer couldn't help but chuckle at the wry tone this last bit was delivered in. He knew that the term inconvenient was the understatement of the century. Maybe she DID understand more about him than he had realized.

"UHMMM, Templer... Do you think she heard the monkey comment earlier?"

Azra was trying to whisper, not an easy thing for the demon to do.

The priest watched as Chrysta tossed back the last of her Anesthetic and poured each of them a little more. She was biting her lower lip and kept her eyes glued to her task. The woman gave an imperceptible nod of her head.

"OH CRAP!"

Templer got the distinct impression that the demon was looking for a rock to crawl under. He couldn't help himself.

"I thought you said it was okay for demons to have depraved thoughts?"

He made the comment in complete innocence.

"Oh... Shut Up, Constantine!"

They sat for a time, sipping their drinks and watching the storm as it moved in over the valley. It was close enough now the rumble of thunder was disturbing the quiet of the night. The breeze carried in the sweet scent of rain.

Templer was a little startled when his outrider spoke up.

"So Chrysta, I am dying to know how you pulled off that brilliant defensive move this morning. It was most effective, and I for one, found it vastly entertaining."

The priest couldn't help himself.

"Azra, you are such a suck up."

With Chrysta ONLY hearing the elemental's side of the conversation, this deal just might work to his advantage. Very rarely did the Talon win any verbal exchanges with his outrider.

"Hmm," Azra kept his response remarkably polite even though it was delivered in close to a snarl. **"I would still like to hear the answer."**

"The answer to that particular question is a little more complicated."

Chrysta had lifted her glass and was watching the flashes of lightning through the electric blue of her Anesthetic.

"Part of it was the fact that I felt Templer's emotions shift from terror to retribution just before he struck. This gave me a slight advantage in speed. Part of it ties into the differences in my physiology. Honing these mutations day after day working with knuckleheads like him..." One hand gestured in El Diablo's direction. The big silver responded by curling his lips back and popping his fangs.

"... Has made me quite a bit stronger and faster than the average person. Add to this the fact that because of some of the circumstances surrounding my husband's retirement, a mutual... friend... insisted that he be allowed to train both Forrest and myself in combat and defense. I learned how to defend myself from one of the Realm's very best."

The priest remembered the other who had been present in that old photo. He did not even try to hide his astonishment.

"Holy... your FRIEND is Tynan Thranatos?"

Chrysta sighed and set her glass down so she could turn and study the gunman's face.

"As I mentioned before... towards the end of Forrest's service to the Maker's Sect, he became very unstable, both mentally and emotionally. Because he was Tainted, he could not simply quit. I am sure, you know how that works. I don't know who or what Ty threatened... but the end result was that the Order allowed Forrest to retire with the condition that he be bound with a Vow of Silence."

Templer just stared at the woman in shock. Many of his assignments consisted of dealing with indentured Tainted who tried to end their service, prematurely. They were not allowed to just walk away from their duties. These lost souls were considered potential liabilities to the Order and in direct relation, to the Realm itself. It was a Talon's responsibility to REMOVE that threat. The Crown prince of Hell being involved explained a lot. Thranatos was one of the few things on Earth that could stand between a Talon and his prey and still have a chance of walking away from the encounter! The Hand would have been livid at having to look the other way when the Healer left the Order. Templer found he was not surprised at all that man was dead. As a matter of fact, he was rather surprised he had not been the one dispatched to deal with the matter!

Chrysta watched as he mentally put two and two together then she hummed softly.

"Hmmm... Templer Constantine, sadly, I believe I agree with your assessment. Whatever you were before, at present you are well on your way to becoming a monster."

The Talon couldn't meet her thoughtful, assessing gaze. He was surprised when she reached out and cupped his chin in her strong hand, making him look into her face. Her eyes held nothing but compassion and her husky voice was soft.

"I ALSO firmly believe that even with the major changes to your physiology, and the brutal methods that the Order employs to insure your obedience... there is an essential part of you that is still fighting to preserve what humanity you have left. It has fought valiantly in the silent dark, very much alone for a long time... what strength it has is just about spent. If you don't find a way to break the chains that bind and soon... you will be lost."

Just the thought of what Chrysta suggested sent shards of glass through Templer's already aching head. His outrider did what he could to blunt the pain

"Listen as long as you can, Constantine... we just might learn something. This intelligent and insightful woman has some very interesting allies, and no love of the Hand. If you truly want to lose these shackles, I cannot think of a better time or place to start."

Astounded by Azra's quiet, traitorous words Templer was not surprised when they ended in a snarl as the elemental's own Bindings flashed to life... rewarding the demon with a nasty sting.

The priest jerked his chin up.

"How can you consider me still human, knowing what I play host to?"

Chrysta shook her head slightly.

"The key word here is... HOST. Being a vessel for Azra or any other elemental does NOT automatically make you one of them. No more than having several destria personalities popping in and out of my head all the time makes ME a destria. As a matter of fact, I would be willing to bet silver that Azra does not consider himself a demon. He probably feels as screwed by being stuck in you as you feel being saddled with him."

Azra suddenly became very, very quiet. The outrider never had told his host his exact origins. Templer did not know if this was a result of their admittedly antagonistic relationship up to this point... or if the creature was restrained by its Vows. With the shared agony ricocheting around his skull right at the moment, the priest could not find it in himself to blame the demon for keeping his silence.

Chrysta leaned back and collected her glass, pausing to take a fortifying sip. Templer caught a glimpse of the expression that crossed her face. Throwing caution to the wind he tossed back the good amount of potent liqueur left in his glass. The man had a feeling he was going to need it and his companion's next hesitant words did not disappoint.

"I do agree with you on one fact. You ARE a real danger to anyone who gets close to you with the night terrors you suffer. If you are willing... I MIGHT be able to bleed off some of the pressure that is creating such chaos in your mind."

There was no way he was going to let her take a crack at tampering with his Vows. He had seen that happen once. The results had ended up leveling an entire city block. There had been NO survivors.

Chrysta must have caught a whiff of his thoughts.

"SHIT... Templer! Don't even think that! I don't have the raw strength needed for the task or the finesse. Tynan might risk taking a crack at breaking your Vows. HE is a hell of a lot colder than me. I doubt he would care if he burned your mind to ash doing it. Or worse... succeeded and left you a screaming insane wreck. I know better than to try. I am well aware of my limitations."

The woman leaned forward and lightly tapped the Talon's pale brow.

"I don't think all of your memory problems stem from your Binding. The quick glimpse that I got earlier showed evidence that the oldest of your blocks isn't from your Vows. It stems from good old fashioned physical damage that has not been allowed to repair itself. There is evidence there are Hexes in place that are intended to prevent the closing of these gaps."

"Hexes?" Templer was more than alarmed.

"That is the only thing I can think to call them. They are like nothing I have ever seen the Order create. With all the "adjustments" that have been made to your mind... some of these old spells have started to unravel. This is creating instabilities in the rest. The memories that escape are leaking into your sleeping mind. Without anything to bring the information into context, your brain automatically converts it to a form it can understand... namely nightmares! I THINK I can untie this older magic. It has become very weak. I will not be altering your Vows, so this should not trigger any defensive spells. I won't go so far as to say there is no risk. This has the potential to cause some serious harm. Still, it might give you back some recollection of your life before becoming a Talon... IF you are willing to take the chance."

Templer did not answer at first. He silently queried his outrider as to the feasibility of what the woman suggested... AND what the threat to her might be.

Azra was a little slow to respond.

"I do not believe there is any serious threat to Chrysta. I think she is correct in the theory that if she steers clear of our Vows... they should stay quiescent. If her intrusion does trigger a defensive reaction, we should have warning enough to push her out before she gets caught in the backlash." The demon hesitated.

"BUT...?"

"BUT... YOUR mental stability is not the best and my energy reserves are very low. If it comes down to having to restrain you..." Azra gave a slight mental shrug and did not finish the thought.

"Are you absolutely sure that you want to have these memories returned? You might not like what they reveal."

Templer thought about it for several long moments. He did not notice the slight smile that stirred Chrysta's mouth as she watched the talons of his blade-hand beat a nervous tattoo against his other arm. Almost five years had passed since his last visit to the Maker's labs. Not only did the priest expect to get called in soon... he knew it was overdue. Templer doubted there would be much if anything left of who he had originally been if he went there again. It finally came down to the fact that if he were going to do anything to change his destiny, it had to start here and now. He doubted he would get another chance.

"I will agree to this Chrysta... on one condition. If you trigger ANY reaction from my Vows, you get the hell out. If anything else goes south, and it looks as if Azra can't contain the damage... you run as far and as fast as that damaged leg can carry you! Take Grant with you if you can!"

The woman calmly nodded.

"Okay... I need you to do whatever you have to in order to relax your defenses enough that I can slip in."

Templer blew out a tense breath, shut his eyes and tried to force himself to relax. The room was silent for a moment then his companion growled.

"Holy... Constantine. Is that the best you can do?"

Templer could not stop himself. He flinched as she lightly brushed against his inner barriers.

"I am sorry Chrysta. When the Maker's do this, it isn't pleasant."

Chrysta switched tactics.

"Azra, can you do anything inside there to help this along?"

The priest wasn't sure if he should be insulted that the woman had gone over his head. Or grateful when Azra did something internally that caused a wave of euphoria to roll through his mind, drowning any fear he had. He just barely registered Chrysta's...

"Oh... very nice! Thanks Azra that should do the trick."

...along with the gentle caress of an ethereal touch as she rode that wave of pleasure past his psyche's first layers. Once she was inside, Templer expected there to be at least some pain. He was astonished that all he felt was the odd sensation of her carefully sorting through the mess inside his head. The image of someone standing in front of a loom came to mind. The weave in the fabric there was puckered and warped. It might have had a dark beauty at one time. Now it was marred by ragged gaps held together with shimmering patches and large misshapen knots. After studying the whole for a moment, gentle fingers drew a loose end out of the piece and carefully began to unweave a single thread. The priest could feel his outrider hold his breath as the woman untangled the shining silk from a particularly nasty looking series of knots. She followed it to where it had slipped and looped back on itself... leaving a small gap in the fabric. Chrysta took that single thread and carefully teased it straight before weaving it back through its proper place, neatly closing the gap. There was an odd shudder throughout the cloth. The movement put pressure on all the damage, and the shards of pain that accompanied it warned that the knots and patches did not like the change. It was a relief when that small, repaired section rippled as the weave realigned itself easing some of the stress off the tighter sections. Templer felt a lost piece of himself deep inside shift, then settle lightly into place.

"Hey Padre... How's it hanging?"

The coarse voice and crude choice of phrasing sent a surge of anger through the priest. Eyes so deep brown they seemed almost black, lifted to catch the pale, arrogant gaze of the sergeant who worked tonight's security shift. The cleric repressed a soft, long suffering sigh. This one had been trying to get a rise out of him since the day he first applied for clearance to enter the research compound. The guard's baiting had run the gambit from foul language and obscene gestures, to accusations of homosexuality combined with bestiality and pedophilia. If it were up to this simple servant, the Hand of God would exact payment from the ignorant fool.

Fortunately, at least for this heathen, that type of decision was not within the scope of the priest's authority. Tonight of all nights, he could not afford the distraction. His superiors had called in every favor they were owed to gain him entrance to the base. He was, in theory, tending to the spiritual needs of the few faithful who were sequestered here as part of the staff. Hell, he was sure that some of the church's elite now owed favors no amount of penance could negate. Unless the guard actively interfered with the priest's mission... he and his foul mouth would remain safe from harm. Still, it would be rude not to give the man an answer. The cleric cleared all traces of anger from his face as he calmly met the others arrogant blue gaze. Long fingers lifted the heavy cross that weighted the slender gold chain around his neck and a gentle smile curved thin lips as he quietly answered.

"As you can see Paul, everything of mine is... hanging... in its appointed place. As I expect it has been a while since you have actually seen them..."

Here the priest allowed his dark gaze to drift arrogantly down to linger on the man's large, overhung belly.

"Are you quite positive that your... possessions... are still hanging where our good Lord originally placed them?"

The priest patiently waited the few seconds it took for the guard to process the fact he had just been insulted. Satisfied with the anger that flashed across the other man's face, he turned and strode off, intent on returning to the mission at hand. For a moment he truly hoped that the idiot would be foolish enough to jump him. After all, a man has the right to defend himself. Oh... he would not kill the fool, but he would make damned sure that after tonight, Paul would think twice about degrading one of the faith! His stride slowed as he again fingered the crucifix. Then the priest crossed himself with a soft sigh. He would have to do penance when this was done. Such thoughts were not befitting a man of God, even one of the Hand. Although his was an order of death and violence, such thoughts were discouraged. It was not for him to decide who should or who should not feel the retribution of the Lord. When required, he was here only as an instrument of God's will. There should be no enjoyment taken in the execution of the task itself. He knew very well there were many in the elite order who took a perverse delight in what they did. This servant held firmly to the belief one should feel only the satisfaction of a job well done in the eyes of the Lord.

As the priest's dark figure stalked quietly down dim lit halls, his almost black eyes observed everything while seeming to see nothing. This was a skill that had served the Church well in all the centuries that it had meddled in world politics. Many a priest went unnoticed by those in power. This had been especially true in the age of ignorance. In those times, it took little to garner priceless kernels of information that could be used to raise a King to almost Godhood or clip his wings and bring him crashing down. Because of this, all priests were taught this essential ability. It was just carried to the extreme with those that were chosen to enter into his sect. A wry smile twisted the man's thin lips. In his line of work, the small detail that you missed, would be the one that came back to gnaw on your buttocks when you were least expecting it!

His was a familiar figure in the halls of the research facility, so even at this late hour, most ignored him as he silently moved through the almost deserted corridors. Even though he belonged to the Hand, the priest did not enjoy killing. He felt it was his moral obligation to keep the collateral damage down to a minimum. As a result, this had been planned to take place when the staff was stripped down to a skeleton crew. Unfortunately, getting into the reactor building required that he take a life. Although not truly innocent, this death that would weigh against his soul. The security guard was not a willing participant in evil, but ignorance was not an acceptable excuse in the eyes of the Lord. The hapless man's death, and the codes plus I.D. that others in the priest's elite sect had ferreted out, provided access into a long, two story building. This housed the company's huge prototype fusion engine.

The priest studied the hulking machine as he slid into the darkened lab. He gave a slight nod, pleased that things were moving along so smoothly. All he needed now was a few minutes to plant the explosives. He planned to set the timer to go off in a couple of hours during the change of shifts. That would keep any deaths down to a *minimum and give him time to disappear. The company could build another engine but the loss of the elusive Dark Matter nestled in the heart of this one would set the time table back decades. The government had bowed out of the space race years ago and no other in the private sector was even close to getting a long range spacecraft put together anytime soon.*

He did not know why his superiors were so adamantly against the human race reaching the stars. The man really did not care. It was not his place to question why. He was a Hand... strict obedience to God's will had been ruthlessly drilled into him from the time he left the cradle. All in his sect were well aware that the Vatican stealthily apposed the space program from its very infancy during the Kennedy era. The God sworn group of elite assassins had been an active part of the opposition from the beginning.

As the man crouched to place his first package, he froze. Dark ever searching eyes finally picked up on the small detail that he had missed. He hissed, knowing that this mistake was going to bite him in the ass. All across the great machine, small lights flashed in a frenzy of activity. Some shown red but an alarming majority had turned and were changing even as he watched to brilliant green. Fine brows pulled down as the priest straightened, his sharp gaze desperately searching the shadows. This engine was supposed to be non-operational while it was planet side. Its systems were not scheduled to be brought on line until the whole of it had been transported to its cradle. This was currently stationed in space well beyond even the moon's long orbit. The scientist who had developed the theory behind using Dark Matter as a propulsion source had made it very clear that cycling up the Warp Engine while it remained within the planet's powerful energy fields would have catastrophic consequences.

There was a slight movement in the shadows... then the area brightened as some of the auxiliary lighting was turned on.

"What are you doing here...? Father."

The priest did not bother to answer. With the explosives in plain view in his hands, what he was doing here was quite obvious to anyone with average intelligence. The man who was revealed as he stepped into the light was well ahead of the curve when it came to brain power. On the flip side of this as was the case with many whose genius scored in the stratosphere... Doctor Therou's sanity had been questioned on more than one occasion. Sometimes, genius and insanity were kin that walked hand in hand. The priest eased to the side, casually letting his package drop to free his hands up. Even as he did this he had a sinking suspicion that weapons would now be of no use. Guns and knives did no good when dealing with explosives. They were twice as redundant when the opposition controlled the ignition switch on the world's largest bomb. Still... he tried to buy some time...

"I could ask you the same thing, James..."

"Come now, Constantine... I am sure that you have figured that out for yourself. For a clergyman, you are remarkably intelligent. Unfortunately, as is usually the case with your particular caste... you are also terribly naive."

The cleric slid a hand into his trouser pocket, fingers lightly stroking the switch that would electronically detonate his explosives. Suicide was an unforgivable sin... but maybe the all mighty would give him a little leeway considering the circumstances. He tried to keep the scientist talking, there was a chance the man would think he was just reaching for a gun.

"Okay, then answer me this... Why?"

"Ah, again I could ask you the same thing, but

you would not have an answer would you... priest. Blind faith and unquestioning obedience is your sect's specialty is it not? Even so, maybe I can give you a little something to think about. The Church's adversary is not the Devil that you have been led to believe in. That one is naught but a fallen angel. Its true enemy, you poor ignorant fool... is something much worse. The Mother of Demons is not blind to our world. She has been denied entrance for millennium and her time to come again draws nigh. If you believe nothing else, priest, know this. She... does... not... forget, and has no forgiveness. Her kind has no word for... mercy."

The man gave a slight shrug and destroyed the priest's small hope.

"You can kill me or don't kill me, I truly do not care. The future has been set in motion. There is nothing you can do that will change the outcome. Go ahead, set off your explosives. With the Dark Matter only partially shielded, the end result will be much the same. Hell it might even be worse!"

The man's hands dropped, fingers tapping lightly across his keyboard like two long legged spiders.

"I have taken the liberty of disabling all the emergency shutdown sequences. It will take approximately ten minutes for the Warp drive to cycle up. After that..."

The sad, almost gentle smile the scientist sent his way made the cleric's skin crawl across his spine. The man spread his hands, fingers wiggling energetically...

"BOOM! If I were you Templer Constantine, I would be running! Or... if you wish, you are quite welcomed to stay and keep me company here at ground zero. I do believe that I prefer a quick clean end to what I know is coming. Wouldn't you agree?"

The priest's quick mind was scrambling as it tried to find a way to pull a miracle out of this cluster-fuck. He did not think that fervent prayer would be of much help...although he certainly wasn't above trying! The strident howl of an evacuation alarm rang out, shattering the silence. As the cleric turned to run he had a sudden epiphany. Mother of God, he had failed!

The man knew he could not out run Armageddon. He gave it his best shot anyway. He just made it to the small dirt road where he had left his all-terrain transport when an odd tremor in the air spun him around. The priest could not help but watch in morbid fascination as the sky above the labs warped. For a brief moment something truly awesome formed before the peace of the early morning was obliterated. Templer dropped to his knees as the minute star that the unfinished warp drive created collapsed in on itself in spectacular fashion. A split second later it released its primordial energy in an earth shaking explosion. A rippling wave screamed out from the center, shattering reality in its wake. The priest had just a moment to register the monstrous winged forms that rode the fiery whirlwind before the destruction reached him. His last thought was...

"Ah... HELL!"

After that... there was nothing but darkness and pain.

"Mother of darkness...!"

These softly whispered words jerked the Talon back to awareness. He fervently prayed that what had just played through his mind was a particularly nasty dream dredged up by having someone else digging around his skull. The look of stunned shock on Chrysta's face dashed this small hope. Five HUNDRED years... Templer could only stare into the woman's wide eyes as his carefully crafted version of reality started to crumble. Deep in his mind... the damning scene played itself out again, every detail as clear as glass. The Cataclysm had occurred over five centuries ago. How in the seven HELLS could he possibly be remembering this? He turned to Azra... but found no comfort in his outrider's complete and utter silence.

Constantine tried to pull in a breath so he could scream. He had not only been present five hundred years ago, but he directly participated in the events that destroyed civilization. Millions had died in those first horrifying hours. Just as many had perished in the following days as the creatures released began to re-shape the very fabric of life itself on planet Earth. It was only due to mankind's sheer tenacity that human beings still existed at all!

All of this lifetime the priest had let the responsibility for his actions and what he had become rest squarely on the Order he served. This knowledge stripped away his ability to hide from what he was. Centuries ago he had chosen to be a killer. He had allowed his Faith to salve any guilt he might feel and committed atrocities without question because he believed his actions were directed by the will of God. There was only one truth that shone its harsh unyielding light through the dark storm rolling over his soul. Templer Constantine had been a monster LONG before he had gone under the Maker's knives.

The priest's body began to shake as these soul crushing facts slammed against the crumbling foundations of his reality.

"CHRYSTA...!"

This was a growled warning. Azra watched in mounting alarm as the impossible balancing act his host maintained to preserve his fragile sanity shifted. The outrider swore as Templer's mind buckled under the stress and the man started a wild slide into madness.

"HOLY... SHIT!"

Chrysta hissed savagely as she caught the full brunt of the twisted brew of emotions rolling through the priest and got a good glimpse of the stricken look on his pale face.

"What the HELL!! He can't possibly be this fragile!"

This was directed in panic at Azra as the woman knelt down in front of the shaking man. Taking his hands in her own, she tried to siphon off and dissipate the worst of his emotional distress.

"More so than you will ever know!"

The outrider's rough voice was grim as he bolstered Templer's mental barriers with his own formidable strength. If the Talon could not find his balance, the demon would be forced to push him into unconsciousness. He did not know what condition the man would awaken in. IF... he awoke at all! Under normal circumstances the demon wouldn't have hesitated to take advantage of Constantine's lapse. The thought of being trapped in a host who might become cationic for eternity terrified the hell out of the demon.

For several desperate moments they worked in sync, trying to hold the gunman together until he could regain his mental footing. Try as they might they made no progress. It seemed that one little shift in the fabric of his mind had released a series of cascading waterfalls. This torrent wouldn't be stopped until it swept Templer Constantine's sanity off a very steep cliff!

Azra gave a nasty curse and tried to stop his unstable host from pulling the wild elemental energy riding ahead of the coming storm into himself. It was an instinctive reaction from a mind desperate to escape. When the power reached levels the Talon could not contain, it would be released in one massive blast. Templer might not succeed in destroying his physical body, but he sure as hell would level the town!

The outrider was nearing the end of his strength. He desperately gathered what he could spare to try and push Chrysta OUT. There was still a chance for her to get away. He was not surprised when the woman called him something unflattering and resisted. Before Azra could react, another presence joined in the struggle. All three minds were flooded with the sweet rumbling croon of a destria. After a moment a second deeper one also entered through Chrysta's empathic link, and then as if from a distance, a third surprising tenor mental voice bracketed the whole. The deeply soothing, harmonic vibrations had a hypnotic, mind numbing effect. For one long moment they remained balanced on the edge. Then Azra gained a finger hold on the deadly energy his host was accumulating. The outrider managed to build a diversion channel and harmlessly bleed the majority of it back into the storm where it belonged. What remained he painfully absorbed into his depleted reserve. They realized they were making progress when the embattled man managed to unlocked his body enough to take a deep shuddering breath.

Chrysta held the link steady until she was sure that Templer (and Azra) had regained some semblance of control. Then she carefully blocked the three destria out and withdrew. Still glowing, golden eyes flew open as Templer heard the slight hiss of pain that escaped her lips when her leg protested its awkward position. He had regained enough of his equilibrium that he was able to steady her as the woman scooted back into her chair. A brilliant flash of lightening and almost simultaneous crack of thunder made both of them jump. Out in his paddock El Diablo screamed a shrill challenge to the wind. The storm had finally arrived. The wind whipped rain in through the open window and Templer had enough presence of mind to slam it shut before they were both soaked.

The Talon watched the water stream down onto the courtyard as he worked to stabilize his mental balance. When he felt he could speak without screaming, he shakily turned to the still seated woman.

"I can honestly say, that if given the choice to do that again I am not sure I would take the chance." Templer managed a slight smile at the look of concern on his companion's face.

"Holy... Templer, I am sorry! If given the choice, I don't think I would do that again either! I knew the damage was old... that's one of the reasons I thought it would do no harm to repair it. Mother of demons... five hundred years! How is that even possible?"

"I do not know. What you repaired loosened some of the Vows binding me but they are still in place. I remember some of my life before the Cataclysm but nothing much else until the last eighty years. Even though I WANT some answers... I do not think I can stomach learning anything more right at the moment"

 Templer ran his shaking hands through his hair, pulling the raven mass away from his face. It was only then that he noticed the tears that were slowly drying on his cheeks.

"I am not sure if you have given me a gift or a curse tonight Chrysta, but I thank you and your destria for it all the same."

 The priest sighed... "Azra... the same goes for you. I am in your debt. God only knows how this would have turned out without you stuffing your proverbial fingers into the holes to stop the leaks."

"Don't think too much of it Constantine. You have to stay sane so that occasionally I can have someone to talk to. My helping you out was purely an act of self-preservation!"

The demon tried hard to sound unconcerned. HE knew how things would have turned out and he had NO intention of sharing the information!

There was movement out in the courtyard. The Talon realized that Nuva was standing out in the storm her blue gaze trained steadily on the window. If he did not know better, Constantine would have sworn that the mare looked concerned.

"Chrysta, I think I recognized Nuva's voice, just as..."

The priest hesitated. He had come very close to letting go completely and allowing that ebony tide of despair to take him totally under. There was no way he could explain how the trio of destria had spun out a gossamer net. It was made of shimmering threads of forgiveness woven with acceptance all tempered with an incredible strength of will. This caught him as he slipped over the edge. It patiently held his spirit in place until he was able to find the strength needed to reach for the light that Chrysta and his outrider held out against the everlasting night. He cleared his throat...

"Who were the other two that joined her? Do you know why they helped out?"

The woman carefully split the rest of the Anesthetic into their two glasses before she answered.

"Nuva, as you know, took a real liking to you and she could feel your distress through me. The deeper "voice" was Zephyr. He will usually follow where Nuva leads. As intimidating as he looks, Zephyr has a kind heart. The other voice, oddly enough was Inferno. If he had a reason for helping out, he is currently keeping it to himself. He can be a lot like his sire."

Chrysta took a sip of her drink and her tired green eyes studied the priest's face.

"I am truly sorry that I shook things up that much for you Templer. If you would like... we can finish this another time?"

The priest followed her example and took a drink. Her suggestion was a good one. He felt as if the inside of his skull had been trashed by a flock of stampeding Terra-birds. Chrysta did not look much better. The talon-ed fingers of his blade-hand tapped a nervous rhythm against the glass.

"I have just one more question and if I don't ask it... the curiosity is going to kill my outrider."

Azra snarled as one of Chrysta's brows shot up.

"How in the hell did you become friends with Tynan Thranatos, Crown Prince of the House Dracul and only heir to the High Seat of Hell!?"

The woman snorted and set her glass down.

"That's been driving you crazy... hasn't it?"

Templer shrugged.

"The Vamphyrr are not by nature inclined to mingle with the human race." (Unless it was feeding time!)

This dark thought the Talon kept to himself. One of the conditions of the Truce was that the denizens of the darker realms refrain from actively hunting humans. He had been called upon more than once to run a rogue to ground when this happened. The Order did not take it lightly when their citizens were used as involuntary fodder. On the other hand, there was no law preventing the practice of a Vamphyrr feeding from a voluntary... pet. The priest's stomach rolled at the thought that Chrysta might be involved in something along those lines.

If his companion had any idea of what crossed his mind... she made no comment.

"I am sure you are aware that SOME items that come from the Seven Hells are legal to trade. Several times a year the Order sends a WindClipper to make the run to Mictla'n to pick up trade goods. Edgewater is a stopover. Forrest was assigned as company surgeon to the members of the Fist that were sent to protect the transport. The Prince always accompanies the load back from Hell's gate, along with a number of his personal guard."

Her gaze drew Templer's to the cloak that he usually wore. Spider-silk was at the top of that short list, although only the Order could distribute it. The lightweight, bullet proof cloth COULD be purchased on the black market but its high cost was prohibitive. As was any product that was exported from those alien lands. No matter how good the Wind-master was... the risk of encountering pirates along the route would be huge.

Templer's slight nod acknowledged his understanding as she continued.

"During one of these visits, Tynan observed a trainer dealing very harshly with a young stallion. This trainer..."

Here, Chrysta's mouth twisted, as if giving that person that particular title tasted bad.

"...pushed the animal a little too far and the destria decided to push back... hard! In the space of a breath the stallion turned on the man and took him down. He savaged the trainer so badly that by the time we managed to drive him off of his victim, there was not a whole lot left that was recognizable. His owner wanted him destroyed. I interfered, as anyone with half a brain could see that the stallion had been driven to the violence. Forrest then got involved. Things were getting more than a little heated when Prince Thranatos stepped forward and... Just appropriated the stallion. Wow, can that man make an impression!"

Templer nodded slightly. He was not sure that describing the Prince as a man was totally accurate but impressive was a word that fit. Of course other good words would be, powerful... terrifying... DEADLY."

"Let's not forget... Beautiful... charismatic..." Azra interjected.

"Oh yes, that to."

Chrysta agreed. She was idly tracing designs in the condensation on her glass with one long finger.

"The end result of it all was that Tynan and Forrest became friends. The two of them hired me to train Vera's Silver Flame, which was the stallion's name. I was also hired to teach the Prince the difference between riding a Terra-Bird and a destria! Of course with HIM there was very little teaching involved. He took to riding El Diablo like a natural."

The look that crossed Templer's face drew a snicker from the woman.

"It was the Prince's fault... Tynan called him that because the stallion's volatile nature reminded him of his father.

In time, Forrest and I married. When he started showing serious signs of coming apart at the seams, PRINCE Tynan Thranatos pulled some strings and arranged it so that my husband could retire."

Templer interrupted her here. He knew how tenacious the Order was when it came to containing the Tainted who served.

"How did he manage to pull that off?"

The woman snickered darkly.

"From what I could gather, it involved the threat of physically dismembering certain high ranking officials, one or two of the Hand's top Enforcers and several high ranking members of the Fist. I also suspect there might have been a couple of one way trips to Hell bandied about if any harm came to either of us, after the fact. The Hand DID send a watchdog to keep an eye on our behavior though. I bet you can't guess who?"

The Talon thought hard about it for a moment. The memory of a shotgun just seeming to appear in a certain person's capable large hands came to mind.

"Grant was a Temple Guard?"

"Oh you are good!" Chrysta's face hardened for a moment.

"Yes... Grant was a Temple Guard... I guess technically he might still be Ranked! When the man first came here, he seemed a nasty piece of work. I would have told you then, that I would marry El Diablo out there before I would have anything to do with Grant."

She noticed the incredulous look on the gunman's face and gave a bemused little shrug.

"Hey, I will admit to being wrong on rare occasions. We never have figured out if it was the Hand that sent Grant to keep an eye on us and he switched loyalties. Or was he an implanted pawn of Thranatos' that the Prince maneuvered here to make sure there was no funny business against Forrest. To answer the question you asked this morning fully. Tynan worked with me on blades and Grant drills me in hand to hand to this day. With my enhanced reactions I CAN defend myself in most circumstances."

Her fierce expression softened, and she studied Templer with a critical eye.

"Although I have no problem admitting that this morning showed me enough that I would rather not come up against you or Azra in a fair fight."

The outrider's rumbling laughter interrupted her.

"I will bet my wings you in no way, fight fair!"

The woman abruptly straightened up in her chair.

"I was taught you do what it takes to win and worry about the fair part later."

Templer gave a slight nod.

"I was having a hard time picturing Grant as a killer, but that DOES sound like something a Temple Guard would say."

As a matter of fact, the Talon was sure he had heard the same thing a long time ago when he was in training.

The woman across from him leaned forward and the look in her eyes didn't bode well for someone. Waving him close she whispered conspiratorially.

"If you ever want to have some fun and witness something truly impressive, just start a bar fight downstairs. The man is AWESOME in close quarters." She leaned back in her seat and the priest barely heard the softly muttered, "Just don't let him find out it was you who started it!"

Templer just stared at her with one eyebrow arched.

"What?" She sounded defensive. Then her face broke out in that beautiful, wicked smile. "Yeah, I have done it a few times. He is just so damn much fun to watch. If I give the locals notice they will even pay to come. BUT... you didn't hear that from me!"

Laughing quietly, she levered herself to her feet and opened the window back up. The worst part of the storm had passed, and the rain had slowed to a drizzle.

Her dark green eyes glanced down at him.

"Are you planning on trying to sleep tonight?"

His head felt like it was full of hot glass. His body felt like he had gone a round with a dragon. With all of that there was no way in the seven hells he was closing his eyes tonight. He would rather die than dream!

Chrysta just looked at him when his only answer was a slight shake of his head.

"Hmmm, well when you decide you need some rest, let me know. I think I can provide something that will help... IF you are interested. I need to get some sleep so we will have to continue this some other time." The woman sat on the edge of the duvet and wrapped up in her quilt.

Templer watched the rain fall for a moment then silently got up to turn off the light. When he returned to his chair she had laid down.

"Constantine, pardon my asking... but I have heard that a Talon can serve in the capacity of priest in certain circumstances. Do you have to remain celibate?" She sounded sleepy but when he flashed a look her way, the woman's eyes were open and watching him intently.

"No... Talons are not forbidden from partaking of the fruit of the flesh. It is... discouraged... unless absolutely necessary as a part of our duties."

Templer could almost see the wheels turning in her head as she sorted through the implications of that carefully stated answer. He could tell the exact moment when she decided to shelve it for later thought. A small part of him that had tensed up relaxed as there was no disgust evident in her next words.

"So... do you have someone special in your life?"

The gunman knew what she was asking and chose to tiptoe around the answer.

"Yes, I have people whom I consider friends."

The snort that he expected came as if on cue.

"That's not what I meant and you know it! Is there someone special in your life who isn't a... absolute necessity to your duties!? Surely there's a person that regards YOU as someone special?"

"Hnnn,"

Templer did NOT want to be having this particular conversation.

"No, there is no significant... other... in my life. Although I believe there is one who would like to be."

Chrysta seemed to perk up.

"Really... and what about you? You aren't interested in her... or... him?"

"I am too old to be romantically interested in Iniko, she is only nineteen and I am not a pedophile." (Five hundred years too old!) This disturbing thought was hastily shoved to the back of his mind. He did NOT want to wander down that particular path yet!

The gunman was amazed when Chrysta flipped her quilt up over her face and rolled over on her side. For a moment he was confused, then insulted when what sounded suspiciously like muffled laughter reached his ears.

He reached over and poked her lightly in the back.

"That was not intended to be funny."

The sound of laughter stopped but Templer could tell by the way her shoulders were shaking that she must have stuffed something in her mouth to muffle it completely. With a long suffering sigh, he asked.

"Should I leave until you get this out of your system or do you want me to stay and watch you suffocate on your own laughter?"

Chrysta must have realized he was insulted. She rolled over and uncovered her face.

"I am so sorry Constantine; I am not laughing at what you said. I am laughing at the fact it mirrored my thoughts exactly."

At his look of total confusion, she broke out in the giggles again.

"I was watching you when you rose to turn out the lights. The thought crossed my mind that you are incredibly attractive. DON'T give me that look! Just because I am a little older, doesn't mean I am dead! Then right on its heels was... OH MY GOD CHRYSTA... the man LOOKS like he is at least twenty years your junior. YOU are a pedophile!"

Templer felt the corners of his mouth turn up, damn if her giggles weren't infectious.

"Technically, you could not qualify as a pedophile. My actual age NOT including the five centuries is over eighty." The gunman was interrupted by Chaos.

"I am much older than you both. Normally this discussion would turn my stomach. BUT... in this case I can honestly say that being a pedophile would be NO problem at all!"

The priest's smile slipped, and he winced at the thought of having Azra not only aware but actively participating with/in him as part of a sexual tryst.

Chrysta caught his expression and burst out in a new round of laughter. At his wounded look she relented.

"You should count yourself lucky. You have YOUR voyeuristic demon limited to one and HE at least matches your sexual persuasion. I have three, and two of them are MALE. It's bad when

Nuva interrupts by asking; *he wants you to put WHAT... WHERE?* You should try staying focused when the boys are popping up with things like; *tell him he should try it destria style.* Or...*he needs to practice his nibbling.* Or my personal favorite; *WOW... is that all the bigger the dangly bits get?*"

It wasn't her words that finally got him. It was the ridiculous expressions on her face as she imbued each comment with that particular destria's individual personality. All of a sudden, Templer found himself laughing as hard as she was. Both of them continued until their stomachs hurt and all that remained was an occasional giggle or intermittent chuckle. The gunman had forgotten how good a hearty laugh made you feel. It had been a very long time since he had a reason to indulge in one.

Chrysta used a corner of her quilt to wipe her eyes.

"Ahhh Templer, I cannot tell you how much it means to find someone who knows exactly what I have been living with. I truly thought I was the only person in the world with THIS kind of problem."

The woman settled back against her pillows and her eyelids drooped.

Templer watched her silently for a long moment. "Do you?" He asked.

"Do I what?" She looked at him sleepily.

"Do you have someone special in your life?"

Chrysta's expressive face stilled, and the priest thought she wasn't going to answer. Then, she closed her eyes.

"No Constantine, I have let no one into my life since my marriage ended. I have been alone every second of every day, starting from the moment that Forrest died." A small, sad smile curved her lips as she continued.

"Maybe this is how it is supposed to be, being as how I am the one who killed him."

Shaken by her answer and the incredible sadness he heard in her voice, Templer didn't say anymore. He just sat and quietly watched until Chrysta's face smoothed out and her breathing had deepened into a pattern that said she was asleep.

Templer sat with his feet propped on the window sill until the first blush of the false dawn topped the horizon. He spent the long hours turning over all the facts and implications that the night's events had brought up. Contemplation did not make his recovered memories any easier to stomach. After studying them from every possible angle, the priest finally pushed them to the back of his mind. With his Vows intact, it was impossible to bring that horrifying fragment into any kind of context that made sense. His mental balance was shaky enough that if was safer to just let the matter lie. His outrider remained present but thankfully kept his silence, giving his host the space needed to come to terms with his restless thoughts. The gunman was thankful for illusion of privacy but he was also sure it was not entirely for his benefit. The demon just didn't want to disturb their sleeping roommate. Somehow, the seasoned woman sparked a carnal hunger that the demon had NEVER shown in the presence of young, nubile human females. (Or males for that matter!)

Templer glanced over at the duvet. Chrysta had rolled over and kicked one leg out from under the quilt. The soft material of her nightwear rode up, exposing a shapely ankle and slim, well-muscled calf. His thoughts turned to how... arousing... those powerful legs and firm butt had felt straddling his hips when she had him pinned him that morning. Hnnn... Sharp talons drummed a soft rhythm on the arm of the chair. It was possible that the demon was NOT the only one interested!

The sound of someone coming up the stairs brought the priest's attention back to the present. He could tell by the heavy tread that it was Grant. A soft knock on the door and the smell of fresh coffee had Chrysta throwing her cover back. She was blinking herself awake by the time Templer rose to open it.

The big man gave him an apologetic look as he entered.

"Sorry to disturb you at this ungodly hour, but Chrysta wanted to take El Diablo on a good run before the crowds are up and about."

The grim look he sent in the general direction of the duvet showed what he thought of this plan. The barman deftly set his tray down on the table and put the bundle of clean clothes and leathers he was carrying under the other arm next to it.

Chrysta limped over to help herself to a cup of the steaming black coffee. She threw the older man a hard look as she scooped up the bundle of clothes in her other hand and went to shut herself in the bathroom.

"This day is going to be bad enough without you giving me a hard time, Grant."

The man winced at the sharp edge in her voice. For a moment the room was silent, then Temple heard a soft sigh from the other side of the door. Chrysta opened it back up.

"I am sorry. What do you expect me to do? I can't just leave him to rot in a small paddock all of his life. It would make the bastard crazier than he already is."

The softness of her words went a long way towards soothing the sting of the harsh ones.

Templer could see the concern written all over the bartender's face as he relented.

"At least take someone with you."

The respect that Chrysta had for the man showed in the fact that she actually thought about it for a minute. Then she dashed his hopes with a slow shake of her head. "I've got no other mount who can match the pace I can hold him to. Nuva or Zephyr would kill themselves trying to keep up."

She gently smiled at the big man.

"Stop worrying momma hen! I have been doing this for years and MOST of the time I have managed to stay ahead of him. Now, go on downstairs. You can bet I will be hungry when I get back."

She made shooing motions at him and closed the door.

Grant cocked his head at Templer, a silent invitation for the gunman to follow him down to the common room. Once there, it was the gunman's turn to wince when the usually quiet man slammed a fist down on the bar. His voice was a low hiss, pitched so only the Talon could hear it.

"Momma hen my ASS! Damn it... I HATE that S.O.B! It's not Chrysta staying AHEAD of him I am worried about."

He faced Templer and his mild brown eyes were dark with distress.

"Chrysta should NEVER take him out by herself. She was very lucky bringing him in alone the other night."

Grant met the priest's steady gaze and held it.

"I have no right to ask this of you. I know you have rules about what you can and can't do. But for the sake of all that is holy... please don't let her take that monster out alone. I have never seen Chrysta get thrown. If any destria can do it, it's that one. She has told me herself that even the best riders get drilled into the dirt on occasion. If that bastard unloads her while they are out by themselves... Chrysta is as good as dead!"

Azra, who remained quiet during this astonishing speech gave the gunman an ungentle mental nudge.

"Constantine, I can match El Diablo's speed."

Templer was amazed when he seriously considered the demon's offer as he watched Chrysta come down the stairs. She was making minute adjustments to the padded leather vest designed to protect her chest and vulnerable stomach. He kept his voice low so that only Grant could hear him.

"Didn't you mention that the town has had some... incursion... problems from the Waste recently?"

The look the man flashed him was priceless.

"You SNEAKY bastard! Why... YES... I believe I might have mentioned something along those lines."

The bartender's sudden smile included Chrysta as the woman joined them. She flashed the two men a suspicious look and quietly set her empty cup on the bar. Still smiling a rather shark like smile, Grant just as silently filled it for her. With a soft sigh Chrysta took her cup and headed out into the courtyard. As Templer followed, he heard Grant banging around in the kitchen. From the stiff set of Chrysta's shoulders, she could hear him too. The priest was not surprised when the man slipped out the door and joined him in watching her slim form disappear into the barn.

He WAS surprised when she re-appeared and turned Nuva loose into El Diablo's paddock. The old mare immediately started pushing the big silver towards the heavy fence. To Templer's amazement the stallion allowed it. He turned to the other man with a questioning look.

Grant smiled tightly.

"Nuva has been Chrysta's lead mare since El Diablo first came here. No matter how old he gets, he will always defer to her."

Chrysta stood on the outside of the paddock. She had thrown her gear up on the top rail and waited patiently as the two animals circled the enclosure twice. Nuva stayed on the inside slowly pushing the stallion until he was moving right against the fence. As they reached the post where the woman waited, the mare leaned in hard, using her body to pin the male against the fence. He reacted by tossing his head high and trying to back up. Before he succeeded in this, Chrysta reached in and clipped a stout rope to the collar right behind his heavy ridge. The beast gave an unhappy, rumbling cough and popped his fangs. Between having his head snugged to the post and with the mare's considerable weight leaning into his shoulder, El Diablo was effectively immobilized.

Chrysta opened the gate. As she approached, Nuva shifted her body so her chest was against the stallion's shoulder. Her neck and ridged head bridged over his heavy neck. El Diablo would have to go through her to use his mouth or horns on his trainer. It was interesting that as Chrysta worked around the dangerous animal, her limp totally disappeared.

From there it took the competent woman just minutes to get the unhappy animal brushed and saddled. He tried once to kick her while she checked and filed his sharp hooves. An angry rumble and Nuva's sharp fangs on his crest were enough of a warning that the stallion allowed it to be done.

Templer wondered how she would get the bridle on to the dangerous, horned and fanged head. It concerned him when Nuva stepped back and Chrysta unloosed the rope from the post. El Diablo started to swing around, only to freeze, every limb trembling as if it was locked unwillingly in place.

The priest heard Grant mutter behind him,

"Gotcha, you big ugly bastard!"

At Templer's raised eyebrows the big man smiled grimly.

"She is using her link with him to lock him down. It takes a lot of concentration and she can only do it for a few seconds at a time."

Those few seconds were all that the woman needed to get the bridle on and get centered in the saddle. It was easy to tell the second she released her hold. The stallion screamed an angry challenge and reared, twisting and clawing at the sky. Chrysta brought him back down with difficulty. As she wrestled him towards the gate, Templer came to an abrupt decision. He stepped forward, trying to ignore all of his training and experience. The Talon could not believe he was going to do this.

"We have heard that there have been problems in the area which fall within our jurisdiction. I am on vacation but Azra is feeling very restless. He would like to know if you think El Diablo will tolerate him coming along for a fast reconnaissance flight."

Constantine did his best to look innocent. Not an easy feat considering he didn't know who was more astonished... Azra, Chrysta, or himself!

The woman slashed a quick suspicious glance at Grant who immediately raised his hands in defense.

"Hey, don't point that dirty look in my direction! This momma hen doesn't KNOW anyone named Azra!"

This earned him a snort of strained laughter as the woman gave in.

"I don't see as how it would be a problem. Azra... it will be up to you to keep up. I will NOT have the attention to spare to keep track of where you are at."

Her husky voice was a little breathless at the physical effort needed to control the big silver. El Diablo had all four feet jigging in place. His head was bowed tightly against the bit, his fanged muzzle almost touching his chest. The veins and tendons stood out on the backs of Chrysta's hands, a blatant sign of how much strength it was taking to keep stallion from ripping the four reins out of them.

"UNDERSTOOD!"

The outrider could not conceal his anticipation as he pushed forward towards release.

Templer barely had time to warn the demon.

"You had better NOT leave me in the barn again!"

The Talon was not encouraged by the evil snicker that echoed through his mind as Azra pushed his consciousness totally under.

With a quick nod, Chrysta relaxed the reins. El Diablo shot through the gate and disappeared out of the courtyard. Grant backed up against the door as Templer's body dissolved into scarlet mist only to be re-Made into the dark, winged form of Azra. One dismissive, golden eyed glance at the man and the demon took to the air. The innkeeper couldn't help but smile when he heard a couple of startled screams from the street. The few early risers that were out, got a double shock as El Diablo thundered by, followed closely by the embodiment of a black winged, airborne nightmare.

Chrysta kept the stallion in a firmly controlled hand gallop as they made their way through town. From his vantage point above, the demon could tell that El Diablo was not keeping to the slower pace because he wanted to. He had his mouth gaped open trying to duck away from the bit. Every time he tried to slip one way or the other, the woman used the pressure of her strong legs to prevent it. Frustrated, the angry animal snaked his head back trying to take a bite out of one of those legs. Azra noticed for the first time that the saddle had rolled leather guards. These protected her thighs and gave the rider some extra leverage for sudden direction changes. Chrysta thumped the silver's sensitive nose as it came around and the beast hastily put it back out in front... where she could not reach it.

As they cleared the edge of town, Chrysta turned her mount down a beaten track. El Diablo's stride opened up. The demon suddenly understood her warning about having to keep up. He was a high altitude flier. His size and the span of his wings made low level runs tiring, difficult, and in this case... downright dangerous. With a snarl, he pumped his wings harder, catching up to the pair with just enough speed to glide ahead for a moment. As he passed over them, the stallion tossed his head. His flowing mane rippled in the wind like a silver flame. Those feral ice green eyes connected with the outrider's golden ones and a challenge was issued. Before responding to it, Azra spared a glance at the beast's rider. She flashed him a grim smile, flattened out across the stallion's shoulders and loosened the reins another notch.

El Diablo surged ahead. The demon decided to keep the contest purely physical. He knew that he could draw on his otherworldly abilities and win this easily but there would be no challenge in that. He was soon second guessing this decision.

Chrysta proved to be a sneaky individual. She knew this ground and used it to El Diablo's every advantage. The path they were on twisted and turned. Azra's speed was limited because he had to slow and bank to make the corners. The big silver utilized cat like reflexes and flying lead changes to negotiate the turns and switchbacks. They hardly slowed him at all. The rider also tucked the animal in between and around rock outcroppings that the demon had to work to avoid. As they topped the ridge Azra was behind. He gained on the downside as Chrysta had to rein in hard, shifting the destria's center of balance backwards. El Diablo slid down the hill on his striped ass!

As the ground leveled out the stallion stepped it up another notch, covering ground with huge, oily strides. With open air in front of him Azra closed the gap. If the speeding pair made the trees ahead of him he would have to soar up and he would lose ground. The thought crossed his mind as golden eyes tracked the racing pair, that if the destria was to lose his footing at this speed, neither one would get up from the resulting fall.

When the demon pulled even with them, he could see that Chrysta was working hard to slow their headlong pace. The woman had no intentions of letting El Diablo take her into the trees. The stallion was shaking his head and ducking from side to side trying to unbalance his rider. Chrysta stayed centered on him letting her legs, knees and hips absorb the impact of the sudden changes in direction. She managed to turn her mount parallel to the trees. Azra soared and banked to make the turn with them. A soft curse escaped his lips. From his higher vantage point the airborne racer saw what the distracted stallion could not. A massive dead tree had fallen across the speeding animal's path. The demon did not have the time to warn the rider but Chrysta saw it at almost the last minute. She buried her heels in El Diablo's sensitive sides. This got his attention, and she somehow gathered him up before they hit. El Diablo launched himself skyward, front legs tucked, hind legs stretch high and behind. For the first time in his long existence Azra witnessed an earthbound, wingless creature truly fly. The silver soared over the huge log as if he was riding on the wind. He landed lightly on the other side slipping a little in the soft debris.

Using the fact that he was out of balance against him, Chrysta pulled the stallion into a tight circle, slowing the beast until she had him back in a controlled hand gallop. She flashed a tired smile at the hovering demon, guided her mount around the fallen tree and headed back the way they had come.

Azra could not believe the amount of ground they had covered. By the time Chrysta had wrestled the stallion back to just outside of town, a little over an hour had passed and the sun was well above the horizon. She brought him to a halt with difficulty and motioned for Azra to land. He didn't mind doing so as this type of low level flying was tiring. As he approached the pair the outrider was again hit with the same wave of rage, hate, and despair that El Diablo had overwhelmed him with their first meeting. He did not think that his metabolism would allow him to dry heave, but that is what getting hit with the emotional punch made him feel like doing. The demon was thankful when Chrysta put up a shield, blocking the destria's access to his mind.

"Not pleasant, is it?"

The woman was out of breath and her face had the same sick look on it that Azra was sure had been on his face just a moment ago.

"He does that the entire time I am anywhere nearby. It makes working with him twice as unpleasant as it should be."

She glanced towards the town.

"We might cause less of a scene if you go in low and from the back. There are a few towns people just dumb enough to panic and take a shot at you."

The woman started El Diablo forward.

"I will meet you in the courtyard."

It took little time with the help of Azra's strength and speed to get the stallion unsaddled and settled back into his paddock. Nuva remained with him, making the hot, tired male walk in circles until he cooled off. Chrysta balanced herself against the gate. As she rubbed her forehead, Azra reached out and caught her hand gently in his own clawed one. Spreading it open he silently studied her calloused palms and where the reins had run between her fingers. They were red, raw and bruised. She hissed as he traced the red marks with one careful talon.

"Is this the way it is every time you deal with him?" He growled. If looks could kill the destria stud would have rolled belly up..."

"Stop it!" Chrysta drew his attention back to her.

"He wasn't too terribly bad today..."

Her voice trailed off as a motion by the door caused the demon to spin around. Grant was there drying his hands on a towel. He didn't flinch as he steadily met Azra's golden gaze.

"You realize that if you don't let her get up to her bath, she is going to end up in the dirt any minute now?"

Startled, Azra looked back at the woman and realized that she was balanced with all of her weight centered on her good leg. Her movements had been so swift and graceful while dealing with the rogue destria he had forgotten about her crippled leg. Before she could protest, the demon scooped her up. Ignoring her surprised yelp, he took off and hovered at the open window. The outrider helped her crawl through and then followed her in. The frame was a tight fit for his larger form. As he straightened up, Chrysta was already staggering toward the bathroom. The demon caught the smell of dreamleaf as she turned the water on.

When he looked in the small room the woman was sitting on the edge of the tub looking too tired to even get undressed. The demon didn't blame her. He had a feeling that Constantine was going to be in much the same shape when he awoke. At that moment a perfectly wicked thought rolled through his brain. Chrysta's head snapped up at the nasty chuckle that emanated from him. By the time Azra finished explaining what he wanted to do, she was snickering just as evilly. Holy... he LIKED the way this woman's mind worked!

The soft feel of water lapping at his chin jerked Templer into awareness. His first thought was that Azra hadn't left him in the barn. Instead, he was sure the outrider had dumped him into one of tubs that Chrysta kept filled with water for the destria. He struggled to sit up then froze as he registered the fact that the water was very hot. He realized that he was in the huge bathtub in Chrysta's room. What concerned him was the fact that... he was NOT alone! A slender but strong arm was draped across his chest, helping to support him so that he didn't slip down while unconscious and drown. An equally strong leg was curved around his hips, anchoring his lower body so that it stayed submerged. The sharp scent of dreamleaf curled lazily up, entwined in wisps of steam.

The Talon had faced down dangerous men, powerful monsters, and his own overwhelming demons in his long career. None of these caused anything close to the feeling of pure panic that waking up in this particular situation created. Chrysta must have felt his muscles tense in preparation to bail out of the tub. With her uncannily fast reflexes she locked her other arm across his chest, preventing him from getting up. Struggling with her just seemed... undignified. So Templer made a supreme effort and held himself stiffly motionless in the hot water.

"Azra... have I ever told you that you are an ASSHOLE!"

Templer was not surprised when the only answer he received from his outrider was a sinister chuckle. He WAS startled when it was eerily echoed by the woman he was snugly nestled up against.

"Relax..."

This was breathed softly into his ear. That husky voice made the little hairs stand up all of the way down his body. He didn't know this was possible with it entirely submerged in hot water. Other... things... showed interest when the woman slid her toes slowly up the calf of his leg.

"OH... YES!"

Azra's deep voice was a sensual purr.

Templer's whole body jerked. Undignified or not, he was getting the hell out of the tub! He froze as Chrysta clamped down with her considerable strength and made a choking sound.

"I am s-sorry Azra, I just CAN'T. I... I am going to rupture something if I don't stop!'"

Chrysta's sexy voice disintegrated into a severe case of the giggles.

"WOMAN, you sadly disappoint me!"

The demon was having trouble maintaining his stern tone.

"Holy... It sucks that neither of us is in a position that we can see his face!"

Templer again forced himself to relax. Damn it, if he didn't get these two nipped in the bud right now he would be screwed later on.

"What happened to the... I won't run around naked if you don't... rule?"

The priest was inordinately proud of himself when it came out sounding totally unconcerned.

The woman stopped laughing and primly replied,

"Actually, to be totally honest..."

He could hear the wicked smile in the tone of her voice.

"Azra was the one who got naked first!"

"CRAP!"

Templer sank further down into the water. Oh yes, he was SO totally screwed... without the benefit.

Chrysta must have felt sorry for him because she laughed and gently patted his shoulder.

"I am sorry Templer. Even though I knew

teasing you would be fun, this was mostly your outrider's plan. He is familiar with how dreamleaf works and felt you wouldn't try it on your own."

She stretched her bad leg under the water making little waves ripple the length of their bodies.

"He said that you wake up in pain and totally miserable after you shift?"

"Um hum." Templer reluctantly nodded. He found that it was getting easier and easier to relax.

"Well, since I was drawing the bath for myself anyways, we decided to see if this might help you out too. I really couldn't deal with my pain for the time required for you to wake and be submerged long enough to do any good. Besides, Azra felt that if we did give you a choice... you would choose to suffer."

She must have felt his disapproval of the whole thing because the water rippled again as she shrugged.

"Don't be such an idiot. Shifting forms when you are not a naturally born Skin walker has got to be murder on your system... I don't care how enhanced you are. I refuse to stand by and do nothing when your pain upon waking would be a direct result of my actions. Dreamleaf is perfectly safe if used correctly. It has been used as an analgesic for centuries by the Demonae Healers. The hardest part of this decision was figuring the dosage for the two of us together and Azra was surprisingly helpful there. Actually..."

Chrysta was absentmindedly making lazy, feather light circles with her long fingers on his chest. The gunman realized he wasn't feeling so relaxed anymore.

"The getting naked part was really... pretty... easy..."

The words trailed off as Templer caught her fingers in his human hand and guided them down to flatten out across the pale skin of his hard... well-muscled stomach. Unconsciously mimicking what Azra had done earlier. The priest used one elongated talon on his other hand to carefully trace each of her fingers, pausing each time it encountered the bruising on her hands. The man allowed himself a small self-satisfied smile when he saw that all of the fine golden hairs on her forearms were standing at attention.

The smile slipped a little when a warm tongue traced the sensitive outer edge of his ear. She nipped the top of it with gentle teeth drawing a soft hiss of surprise from him. There was no suppressing the hot desire that suddenly wound through his core. The water rippled again as a teasing hand sensually...

A loud knock on the door to their room startled them both. It was followed by Grant's rough voice.

"Hey Chrysta, if you don't get down to eat soon, you won't be able to before the draft competitions start."

"CRAP!"

This soft exclamation was whispered into the gunman's ear as the woman's hand shot up, covering his mouth to muffle his own exclamation of...

"SHIT!"

Luckily Azra's...

"DAMN!" ...was only heard by the two in the bathtub. If Chrysta's destria had anything to say, she was keeping it to herself.

Chrysta kept her hand over Templer's lips and raised her voice to answer the barman.

"Thanks Grant, I will be down in a few."

If the woman had seen the expression that deepened the black of the Talon's dark eyes she would have been worried. Constantine snatched her hand away from his mouth and his own smooth voice answered the innkeeper.

"In case you are wondering Grant... I will be down in a moment also."

As Templer felt the woman's warm body jerk in surprise under him and her whispered "ASSHOLE!" caressed his ear, he indulged in his own sinister laugh. It was time she learned that THREE could play the game that Azra and her had started!

There was no sound what so ever from outside the door for a very long minute and then a stuttered,

"Ummm... okay then... I will see you when you fini... when you both come down." Grant sounded as if he couldn't wait.

The woman beneath him was perfectly still, then she giggled against his shoulder.

"You have no idea what you just did... do you?!"

"WHAT... what did I just do...?"

Templer was suddenly worried.

"Nothing too awful. I am sure you both are going to LOVE being welcomed under the smothering shadow of Momma hen's sheltering wings."

Chrysta broke down into whole hearted laughter as Azra gave his Host a proverbial kick to the rear.

"What the HELL... Constantine. Don't be doing me any more favors!"

The woman choked off her laughter and pushed lightly against him.

"Really, we do need to get out of this bath before we overdose ourselves. Maybe if we hurry he won't have the time to make the heart shaped pancakes!"

"Hnnn... I truly hope you are kidding. I think I would rather suffer the overdose!"

Templer levered himself up, fully prepared to bear the pain that usually overwhelmed him after Azra had used his body. He was astonished when he felt not even a twinge.

Chrysta braced herself on the sides of the tub, drew her good leg under her and then straightened up. Templer reached out to offer a hand only to freeze as he got a clear look at her lithe body. It wasn't the broad, well-shaped shoulders or moderately sized, PERFECT breasts that drew a soft hiss from his lips. It was the scope of the injury that caused her crippled walk. The scar started high on her ribcage just under and to the left of her left breast. It bisected down across her ribs and slanted to the right. Chrysta's ribcage on that side was slightly misaligned. This suggested that the bones had been cut through, along with muscle and flesh. It continued down, cutting deeply across her flat stomach and then curled lazily around her right hip. The muscles had healed but were twisted back on themselves breaking her smooth outline as the scar followed down the outside of the leg then curved back to the front of her ankle. It was obvious that her femur and tibia had been broken at the same time as the flesh had been torn.

The priest had a sudden understanding of Grant's antipathy towards El Diablo. There was no question in his mind that the stallion had been the cause of this devastating injury. He could only assume that it was El Diablo's front inside spur that had done this in a strike much like the one he had tried the night Chrysta had brought him in. Hot anger coiled through Templer's mind as he wondered how the woman was still walking with that kind of muscle and nerve damage. For that matter, how in the hell had she avoided death? This level of injury was not accidental. The big silver beast had struck with the intention to kill!

"CONSTANTINE!"

The savage anger being repressed and something else not as identifiable in Azra's soft exclamation brought Templer's attention back up to Chrysta's face.

The woman had withdrawn from his helping hands when he hesitated. A wary expression flitted through her eyes, only to be hastily covered by sad resignation. The priest was an expert on the fear of rejection and by all he held holy... he wouldn't be the cause of it in someone he cared about! Templer's hands dropped lightly on her very nice shoulders and drew her back towards his naked body. His dark eyes never left those gold and green ones until his lips met hers.

Gentleness WAS in his nature. The man patiently held her mouth until those sweet lips softened and her wonderfully strong arms entwined themselves through his hair to fall around his neck. As Chrysta's wet body pressed firmly up against his own, her mouth opened, allowing the kiss to deepen. She allowed him entry to stroke along her tongue and lips. He was amazed at her spicy, smoky, sweet flavor. When the gunman breathlessly ended the moment, it was to just stand motionless and watch their breath mingling together in the steamy air. Azra had quietly risen and Templer found he did not mind that his outrider had sampled the energy entwined in that kiss. Chrysta also made no objection and when her eyes opened to hold his unearthly golden gaze, they were deep green shot through with blue, gold, and the yellow that burned at the heart of a star.

"Sooo..." A desire like nothing he could remember ever having felt before made Templer's voice deeper, harsher than the norm.

"...how much time do we have before the dreaded heart shaped pancakes appear?"

Something flashed in those unusual eyes. Chrysta's hands gently untangled themselves from his hair to slide down his back and firmly cup his buttocks, pulling him firmly against her.

"Not enough!" she answered. "When we do this, I for one... don't want to be rushed."

One hand left his ass and the man had no time to react as a wicked smile curved the passion swollen lips. Her other hand kept him pinned as she turned the shower faucet on high. Chrysta was grinning like a Harpy as she tucked her head against his chest letting the ice cold water hit them like one of the North land's frigid glaciers. She couldn't decide who screamed louder, the gunman or the demon he hosted. It didn't really matter as she was sure Templer's shocked scream could be heard clear down in the common room.

Ten minutes later, they were seated downstairs being served a large, well-cooked breakfast... complete with the dreaded heart shaped pancakes. Chrysta kept her head down, using her food as an excuse to not directly meet the glowering gold gaze that the Talon pinned her with. Grant opened his mouth once to make a comment about their wet hair... only to be skewered by the same unearthly gaze as the other man's gun hand twitched. He wisely decided to keep his mouth shut.

Chrysta was finishing up her breakfast when Grant ambled over and let her know that the stable hand had the drafters ready to go. She glanced at Templer who had contented himself with only coffee.

"Well," Her smile was warm. "You two have already had a busy morning. Do you feel like riding along today, or do you have other plans?"

The woman's eyes twinkled at him. That immediately put him on his guard. Templer stretched a little, amazed at how GOOD he felt. Normally, after an Azra excursion, he was too wiped to do anything but rest.

"EXACTLY... what are you, or more precisely... we, going to be doing?"

HA... Templer Constantine wasn't born yesterday. The infuriating woman would not get the best of him this time. The priest ignored his outrider's dark chuckle at this thought.

Chrysta turned her cup in her hands absentmindedly.

"The first thing I have planned is the draft competitions. Don Ricardo's team is entered in the weight pulling contest. And I have a team competing in the precision driving." She smiled and glanced over at the Talon.

"The precision driving requires a driver and a passenger. Andrew hates taking the time to just ride along. He has a lot to do just getting everyone primped and hitched. I am SURE he wouldn't mind if you took his place."

"All I have to do is ride along?"

Templer thought hard about it before breaking down and asking Azra's opinion. The demon had a lot more practice when dealing with devious females than he did. (He hoped)

"What do YOU think Azra?"

"HMMM... well, it SOUNDS innocent enough. Although I wonder what she means by getting everyone primped. I assume she means the destria? I don't know... it might be...fun?"

The hesitancy present in his outrider's voice inspired no confidence what so ever in the priest. CRAP... He thought before giving his answer, the woman is making BOTH of us paranoid.

"We don't have anything planned. I can ride along if it helps out."

Constantine flinched when the woman across from him flashed him a shark like smile as she caught the uncertainty in his tone. He had the sinking feeling they had just made a BIG mistake. Templer tried to ignore Azra's uncomfortable squirming in his mind as he followed her out to the courtyard.

"AZRA, stop it! If you were that worried about this, you should have said something when I asked."

"SORRY!"

The demon almost sounded panicked as Chrysta glanced back at them. Her smile got even broader.

True to his word, Andrew had the two huge drafters hitched and waiting patiently for their driver. A smaller, lighter built team was tethered to the back of the wagon. These were covered with soft blankets to keep them clean until their event. Chrysta swung up into the high seat and indicated that Templer should sit next to her. Gathering up the reins, she glanced around as Andrew climbed into the back.

"Constantine here has volunteered for the precision shotgun position today, so you are off the hook."

The look of relief that crossed the young man's face and his heartfelt, "REALLY, that's GREAT!" ... Did nothing for the gunman's worried state of mind.

Chrysta released the brakes.

"Hyup, Jeremy! Hyup Joshua!"

As she called each drafter's name their heads came up, and they moved forward taking the slack out of the traces. Their driver flicked the reins across their broad backs and with a sharp "Get up boys," ... they were rumbling out on to the street.

The drafter barn was a mad house of huge destria, teams of men, and dust. As soon as they pulled in, Andrew took the two smaller drafters and tied them in separate stalls. He then unhooked Jeremy and Joshua from the wagon and led them out to be tied in their designated slot, waiting for the pulls to start. Chrysta went with them and spent quite a bit of time with the young stable hand going over every inch of the two massive animal's harnesses.

Templer concentrated on just observing the remarkably ordered chaos and staying out of the way. As he watched, the gunman realized, although the drafters were known to be much more "sedate" than the average destria, they were far from trustworthy. Hell, their sheer size alone made them very dangerous. Chrysta was called away a couple of times to deal with injuries caused by distracted people getting surprised by unruly destria. One man had his hand crushed and torn wide open when he made the mistake of wrapping a lead rope around it and the big mare he was leading stepped on the end and threw her massive head up. Chrysta expertly cleaned and wrapped it but the tough old man wouldn't agree to go see the town doc until after the competition.

One young man got caught by a surprise blow from a monstrous, cloven hoof. He was carried out, covered by a sheet. His entire chest had been caved in, his death was instantaneous. The priest just shook his head in amazement as Chrysta ducked in and out amongst the big animals, helping out where she was needed. Even the nastiest of the drafters seemed to calm when she was near them. There was more than one envious glance towards Don Ricardo's team. Joshua and Jeremy just stood hip shot and watched the activity with what looked like amusement on their long faces.

A large crowd had gathered by the time the competition started. This was one of the more popular of the festival's events. Chrysta and Andrew gathered Templer up when they took the team out to the arena. Andrew convinced the gunman to wager on Don Ricardo's team even though there were a couple of teams on the lists that were bigger. Chrysta winked at him as she passed,

"Sometimes," she grinned slyly, "Size isn't everything."

The contest rules were simple. Each team was hooked to a sled loaded with large concrete blocks. The pulls started with three thousand pounds of weight. Every team had two tries, at each weight, to pull the sled thirty feet. The weight increased with each round.

At first all the teams had no problems making their pull. As the weight slowly crept up over the five-ton mark some of them started dropping out. By the time the weight rose to ten tons, the field was narrowed down to four teams. There was a huge set of solid blacks, a smaller set of lovely dappled gold destria with black manes and tails and black striping on their legs. Chrysta's team of bays was about midway between those two teams in size and the last team was an evil tempered, massive set of dappled gray twins. These monstrous destria belonged to Don Diego and their handler was none other than the redhead, Rafe.

Eleven tons was the limit for the smaller team and they dropped out after moving the load twenty feet. The judges increased the load to thirteen tons. The Blacks danced and jived at the line. When their stable hand fumbled the lich pin they took off, yanking the driver from his seat and dragging him face first through the dirt a good fifteen feet before he got them stopped. By the time he wrestled them back to the line they were foaming with sweat and frothing at the mouth. This time when the pin dropped they surged forwards but the sled ground to a halt at the halfway mark. Their competition was at an end. Don Diego's team moved the load the full distance with Rafe liberally applying the whip. Chrysta's pair dug in and moved it with little difficulty.

When the judges upped the weight to fifteen tons a murmur swept through the crowd. If either team could make the distance, they would set a record. Chrysta and Andrew had a hushed conversation, and then she walked around her team. She ran her hands over their sweaty necks and haunches. Using her sensitive fingers, she carefully checked each animal's legs. When she finished, Chrysta quietly stood at their heads. Both drafters dropped their muzzles down and seemed to be sharing breathes with her. The woman gave a determined nod, and with a final pat on soft noses she turned to watch Rafe's pull.

The redhead backed his team as far as they

could go. He started flipping their back legs and rumps with his whip while holding them tight with the reins. After few moments of this both animals were dancing in place and bloody foam flew from their mouths. His stable hands dropped the lich pin and Rafe cracked the pair hard. Both beasts launched forward and hit their collars with brutal force. The crowd was remarkably silent. The only sounds were the crack of Rafe's whip, his shouted curses, the harsh grunts of the drafters, and alarming creaks and pops coming from the destria's harnesses and drag chains. With small jerks, the load started to move. The massive grays had their heads down. Their shoulders were low and straining as they moved forward one hard fought step at a time. Even with their supreme effort the sled came to a stop on the eleven-foot mark. Rafe laid the whip on hard leaving long bleeding welts on their steaming hides. The judges frowned but did not interfere. Both red eyed drafters strained in their harnesses, trying to give their handler what he wanted. A wave of blood burst from the off animal's nostrils.

Templer heard Chrysta as she angrily muttered,

"Any time now!"

As she said this, the near animal screamed and violently exploded. Harnessed as he was, the drafter couldn't go anywhere. The beast made his displeasure known by rearing and bucking in place while kicking as hard as he could at the sled and his handler. Rafe baled off as the second animal enthusiastically joined in. The ground shuddered under the team's combined weight as their harness started to come apart. Templer wondered how they would get the two back under control as no one dared approached them. What the two enraged animals were capable of once they fought free was something he did not want to think about.

Chrysta stood quietly and just watched until a judge drew a large caliber pistol. Then the Talon saw her suck in a breath and stiffen. Her eyes flashed to red as she did the impossible and "Locked" down two destria whose minds were unfamiliar to her. Both animals froze, twitching and shaking. They stayed that way as several handlers got them unhitched and positioned between two other big drafters. When Chrysta released her "lock" sagging a little, the exhausted team was dragged reluctantly out of the arena. Rafe exited with the boos and jeers of the audience ringing in his ears.

They gradually quieted as Chrysta led Joshua and Jeremy out to the repositioned sled. All she had to do was get them over the eleven-foot mark to win. If her team could somehow make the full thirty feet, it would be something worth seeing. The woman backed the team in and Andrew dropped the lich pin. She kept backing them until they stood with the traces slack, back heels almost touching the front of the sled. Then she just sat for a moment and Templer could see her mouth moving as she talked to the drafters. The atmosphere was electric in the arena, the silence complete as she tightened her reins. Both destria tensed.

"COME GEE, Joshua!"

The soft words echoed in the quiet, and both drafters surged to the right. The sled jerked sideways a fraction.

"COME HAW, Jeremy!"

Again the drafters shifted, slamming hard to the left. The sled broke free from the dirt holding it. The load was up and moving. Chrysta straightened them out and her voice cracked out as loud as Rafe's whip,

"HYUP! HYUP! HYUP NOW... MOVE IT OUT BOYS!"

Massive rump muscles rolling and rippling, the big beasts dropped their shoulders throwing their considerable weight against the load. Their huge cloven hoofs dug in and with the sound of chains and leather popping under the strain, the sled picked up speed. A murmur of sound rolled through the arena and started to build as they passed the eleven-foot mark. Both Joshua and Jeremy were now foaming along their necks and sides. Froth was gathering around their mouths.

Templer could see Chrysta gathering her reins in preparation to stop the team. She was content with just the win. Jeremy, the oldest of the pair snorted, shook his massive horned head and snatched the bit between his teeth. His partner screamed a challenge, and the team surged in unison as they redoubled their efforts. The crowd roared as the pair continued to pull almost down on their front knees. The noise solidified in to a chant. "GO! GO! GO!"

Templer realized with a start he was hollering with the rest of them. The Drafters passed the twenty-foot mark. Azra was shouting in Templer's mind, GO GO GO. The destria couldn't hear him but Chrysta could. Chrysta shrugged and her HYUP! HYUP! Joined in. The driver knew she was just along for the ride now. They passed the twenty-five-foot line, and the noise was now deafening. As they crossed the thirty-foot mark, the crowd literally came unhinged, clapping screaming and stomping. Hats sailed into the arena as enthusiastic fans threw them.

"WHOA!"

Chrysta hauled back on the reins determined to stop the team and they responded by immediately grinding to a halt. She was off of the high seat in a heartbeat, unbuckling and unsnapping the harnesses from the trembling giants. Their super-heated breath steamed in the air like dragon's breath. Heat rolled off of their bodies in waves, rising from their sweating hides. Templer and Andrew joined the woman in peeling off the leather and collars until the bays wore only their headstalls. Their two handlers got them moving in a staggering walk. Chrysta made the team traverse the arena, allowing them time to cool without seizing up. The crowd came to its feet in a standing ovation. Both drafters responded... arching muscled necks, flagging their cropped tails and high stepping like young colts. Chrysta's face broke in a huge smile as she affectionately slapped Jeremy on his heavy shoulder. Even after they had exited the arena and entered the drafter's barn, the sound of applause still echoed in their ears.

Chrysta turned the team over to a couple other stable hands. Andrew hurriedly departed, muttering something about getting the others ready. The young man handed Templer a neatly wrapped package as he passed, ducking his head to hide the smile playing around his lips. The Talon looked at Chrysta suspiciously.

"What's this?"

The woman had a package of her own, and she snagged the gunman's elbow leading him towards a row of doors.

"Oh... didn't I tell you?" She attempted to sound innocent.

"There is a dress code for the precision driving. Andrew is close to your size so that should fit pretty well."

Templer realized the doors opened to dressing rooms. Before he could react or say another word, Chrysta abandoned him in front of one room and disappeared into another. Her parting words of, "See you in a minute." Came from behind the already closed door and it sounded like she was trying to smother laughter.

The priest stood perfectly still for a full minute trying to think of a way to get out of this.

"Suck it up!" Azra growled, **"We told her we would do this."**

With a sigh the gunman slipped into the dressing room and locked the door. He almost bolted out of it when he opened the package and saw his soon to be attire. It consisted of formal dress from a forgotten age. There were tight pants. Actually, calling them pants was stretching it... they were tights. Knee high close fitting boots of soft leather that laced up the calf fit over these. A white, loose fitting long sleeved blouse with stitched metallic dragons coiling around the wrist cuffs, and a tight, knee length sleeveless overcoat finished the outrageous outfit. The boots and pants were a deep unrelenting crimson. The overcoat was the same deep red. Embroidered, glimmering gold and crimson dragons intertwined and weaved their way over every inch of its surface. There was also a crimson and gold tiara woven into the shape of intertwined dragons. This was meant to be worn on his head.

"Crap, this is bad!" Was all the man could think.

"Hmmm... I think I have seen garments like these before."

Azra sounded thoughtful so Templer held his silence while the outrider tried to access the memory. **"Damn... I can't quite reach it... but I think I have enough..."** The demon sounded confident but there was also a devious note running through his voice.

"Relax Host... let me show you how this is done!"

Chrysta (or Andrew) had gathered a small crowd of stable hands together by the time Templer stepped out of that little room. What started out as anticipatory snickers faded to complete silence except for a couple of indrawn breaths. For a moment, the man just stood as all eyes targeted him. Azra had shown him how to lace, tuck and tweak the odd clothes until they clung to him like they were tailored to his tall form. The blouse and long tunic emphasized his broad shoulders, narrow waist, and well-formed butt. The boots and pants showed every line of his long, hard muscled legs. Azra had suggested that Templer use the tiara to sleek down and hold back his flowing raven hair. Its bright metal caught the light like flames, making the dragons look like a living crown. With his pale skin, coldly regal features, and ebony eyes, the people who watched remembered uneasily that at one time, Dragon-Lords had walked amongst them.

The Talon ignored the crowd, focusing in on Chrysta. She wore a more feminine version of the same outfit. Azra made some minute physiological adjustments causing Templer's dark eyes to flash to gold. The woman stood silent, full lips parted, as he closed the distance between them. Azra had partial control, and he showed the priest how to change his already graceful walk into a sexually charged, flowing prowl. The outrider also released tendrils of sensuality to flow along his and Chrysta's partial link. By the time they reached the motionless woman, her eyes had gotten huge and shifted colors to a stormy green. She seemed to have difficulty swallowing. When they were directly in front of her, Azra took over. The outrider preformed a slow, sensual court bow while he raised Chrysta's limp hand to his mouth for a courtly kiss. She shuddered as his warm breath and soft lips were followed by a sharp nip than a casual sweep of his tongue on her wrist's pulse point. When he looked into her eyes they were glazed and she was swaying slightly. Templer couldn't conceal the self-satisfied smirk that slid across his lips.

"GOTCHA..." Azra purred.

Chrysta stood totally still, seemingly mesmerized by the hand that was nestled in his. The tip of her tongue slipped out to wet dry lips as those stormy green eyes traveled up his chest to meet his flashing golden ones.

"Well... I can't say as that I can recall ANYONE ever filling out that outfit in quite that way before!"

Her words came out husky and were whispered almost against his lips. They were interrupted by wolf whistles and cat calls from the barn crowd. Chrysta staggered hard up against him as she was pushed from behind.

Azra snarled and Templer's head snapped up, intending on giving the rude person the scare of his life. He found himself looking... up... into the glowing amber eyes of two very amused destria. Andrew had brought the precision team up and the beautifully brindled, red striped over gold pair evidently thought the whole scene highly entertaining.

Chrysta hastily stepped back, her cheeks flushing a light pink. HA... Templer thought, we finally made HER blush for a change. Azra snickered evilly and gave him a mental nudge. The man looked up and realized with a stirring of panic that there were more than a few lustful visages in the aisle. SOME of them were NOT female. Constantine was intensely grateful when Chrysta motioned for him to join her. Once up on the driver's seat of the ornate Brougham, they escaped out of the barn.

Later that afternoon they sat in the dimness of the Ironwood having a late lunch. Chrysta was laughing as she laid all the blame for only coming in third in the precision driving at Templer's feet.

"What... you LOST?"

Grant, who had topped off their drinks and was heading back to the bar, swung around in shock.

"Well let's just say it's REALLY hard to concentrate on the course, when you have other... THINGS... on your mind."

Templer grinned into his tea. She could blame Azra for that. Every time the closely seated gunman's arm or shoulder had brushed hers, Chrysta had been unable to control the slight jerk, shiver, or twitch of her hand. It had screwed up her driving completely! She did not actually come out and say this... but the bartender was a smart man. His gaze switched from her to the smiling priest then back as his eyebrows gave crawling right off the top of his head their best shot. Grant snickered and headed back to his bar.

Templer hastily wiped the grin off his face when she glanced his way. He tried like hell to look like he felt sorry for her. Chrysta snorted a laugh at his failed effort.

"It's really no big deal. I only entered the brindled team to show them off and to lure in prospective buyers. Having you..." she nudged the quiet man's arm gently, "...as eye candy drove the bidding up sharply." Her grin turned into a wicked smile.

"You would be AMAZED at some of the offers I got."

"**I wouldn't be!**" Azra was definitely feeling a little smug.

Chrysta's eyes darkened to a smoldering green.

"No... I wasn't surprised by them either. Where did you learn how to play THAT kind of game?"

Azra was so quiet for a moment that they thought he wasn't going to answer, then the demon sighed.

"**I can't remember clearly but I get the**

impression from what fragments I can recall that where ever I originally came from, that kind of game is court protocol. I am pretty sure that if you don't get damn good at it while still young, you don't survive."

"WHERE... you came from?" Templer couldn't hide the surprise in his voice.

He had been told that elementals were called into being by a summons. He had no idea Azra had a life before this.

"OH yes Constantine, I had a life before being bonded to you! I cannot remember much, but it is enough that I grieve what was torn from me. I am shackled to you and in my heart I know I can never return to what was. It is probably a blessing that my Binding prevents me from remembering the full truth. I believe that knowledge might destroy me."

As he spoke the outrider's iron control slipped and Templer's mind was flooded with anger, bitterness, and a terrible sorrow. Chrysta gasped and jerked as she also caught the brunt of it. Seeing her distress, Azra made an effort to rein in the emotional flood.

Templer sat in stunned silence as a terrible guilt overwhelmed him.

"Azra, I am so sorry! I didn't know..."

"And you damned sure didn't ask!"

Anger flashed again, then the outrider sighed. Remembering the man's emotional instability, he took pity on the Talon and relented.

"It's okay Constantine, It's not as if you don't have enough to deal with. When we were first melded I hated all humans equally. I know I did not go out of my way to make your life any easier. In truth much of this is my own fault. In the beginning I was offered a choice... I COULD have refused to keep you alive... then we both would have had the relief that oblivion brings. I am selfish in my own way and my actions took that option from us. I am the one who should apologize for that. You did

not create this mess. Your amazing ability to take what has been handed to you and make it work has helped me to adjust to my own existence... such as it is."

"So... I am responsible for ruining your life also?" The gunman almost whispered the words.

"**YES and no.**" Azra sounded thoughtful. "**Yes... there is no question that because of what was done to you, the life I had is gone. The Maker's did not even give ME the small mercy of remembering my true name! Still... I will not let those that have done this prevail. I have decided that I will live the life that I have now to the best of my abilities. A decision, I will point out Templer Constantine, that you have yet to make!**"

Templer was too stunned to say anything. He glanced at the woman sitting across from him, curious about her reaction to the part of the conversation she could hear.

She blinked and looked directly back at him, chestnut eyebrows arched in amazement.

"I told you before that I was pretty sure HE didn't consider himself a demon."

A sad smile played across her lips when Azra harrumphed in reaction.

"**I hate that term...**" was all the outrider said.

"And... whatever he might be, Azra makes some very valid points, quite eloquently I might add."

The sound of a throat being cleared made them both jump. Grant had returned with a fresh pitcher of iced tea and an extra glass. He had a group of rolled maps tucked under one arm and a couple of pencils stuck haphazardly behind his ears. The gunman stared in astonishment. He found it very hard to believe that the innkeeper had ever been a Temple guard.

The big man smiled amiably.

"I hate to disturb what looks like an intense conversation." He shrugged apologetically, "But if you are leaving this evening, Chrysta, you need to decide the route you are going to take."

The barman slipped smoothly into an empty chair and with a couple of efficient moves had their drinks topped off and the maps spread out on the table. Chrysta picked up her glass, sipped some tea and made an outrageous face at the maps.

"Mother of Demons..." she groaned, "...how I do HATE festival week!"

Grant looked at her without sympathy.

"So retire, at least then we wouldn't have to listen to you whine."

"I do NOT whine!" Was her indignant reply.

Those remarkable eyes narrowed dangerously as Templer choked on his tea. Azra wisely made no comment.

The gunman finally got the tea swallowed and his voice was still a little unsteady as he asked.

"So, you are going somewhere tonight?"

Chrysta nodded to him absentmindedly as she followed a line Grant had drawn on one of the maps.

"Umm Humm. There are several routes you can take to complete the Gauntlet. Some traverse easier terrain, but are longer in distance. Some are quite a bit shorter, but a lot more dangerous in the territory they cover." She met his eyes for a moment. "Sometimes winning is more a matter of strategy than speed. I need to ride the course in advance and decide which way I am going to take Inferno on race day.

"Hold on..." Azra was almost growling, **"There is NO way you can go out and be back by nightfall."**

"Yes, that is true. I will have to rough it tonight and plan on being back tomorrow afternoon."

Chrysta leaned back and the look she gave him had Templer (not for the first time) wishing avidly that he could separate himself from his demon. Her dispassionate tone was dangerously neutral

"Is this a problem?"

"Shut up Azra." Templer was whispering the words in his head.

"I will NOT shut up Constantine! Riding alone at night is just plain STU..."

The words trailed off as the woman leaned forward, her ice cold green eyes trapping the Talon's gold ones.

Grant looked as if he was getting ready to duck and cover as Chrysta smiled. It wasn't a nice smile. As a matter of fact, Templer was pretty sure he had seen nicer smiles on the muzzles of giant Arcanian Dire wolves just before they tried to eat him.

"Well, I guess if you are THAT worried about me doing something as... unwise... as riding out alone, maybe you should..."

"Ride along with you?"

The gunman had never heard the demon sound sheepish before. It was disconcerting to say the least.

"UmmmHumm..."

The woman gave Azra a couple more seconds to squirm under her hard glare, then went back to studying her maps.

Templer, who had been entertaining thoughts of a hot shower, a glass of red wine, and maybe even relaxing with a good book that evening, thought about how sore he had been after just a few hours of riding.

"CRAP! Well thanks a lot Azra. Next time I say Shut Up! SHUT the fuck UP!!"

These words were delivered with a sarcastic sting.

"SORRY Constantine..." The demon was very quiet for a moment. Then... as if he just couldn't help himself... he added. **"This might not be half bad you know. Romantic moonlight, being alone in the dark, big hot bodies moving between your thighs, naked bodies intertwined next to a campfire!"**

Chrysta's head snapped up while Templer

buried his face in his hands.

"**HEY as you keep telling me... IF I am a demon! I am SUPPOSED...**"

Templer cut him off.

"I know, I know! You are supposed to have depraved appetites."

"**AHHH...**" Azra sighed happily. "**You are finally starting to understand me!**"

The evening breeze rustled softly through the overhead branches as Zephyr and Nuva cantered along a narrow path. Chrysta had kept them to the ground eating pace for a couple of hours. Although their mounts were still fresh, Templer was beginning to wonder if they were going to ride the course straight through. Nuva grunted as if in agreement, then stumbled violently, almost flipping her rider over her neck. With difficulty she regained her footing but the next couple of strides were marred by a serious limp. Chrysta brought Zephyr to a sudden halt and slid off of him. Templer was off of Nuva before she came to a complete stop. The woman ran careful hands down both of Nuva's slender front legs then straightened up frowning as the mare held up the left one and looked pitiful.

"Humph," Chrysta eyed the cream suspiciously, and the mare looked back in total innocence.

"Well I don't see anything wrong." The woman glanced up through the trees, calculating how much light they had left. "I hate to stop for the night when there are better places ahead. The old adage, better safe than sorry seems to apply here."

Zephyr stomped impatiently and the woman's eyes shifted to gold for a moment as she conversed with the big black.

"Are you sure?"

The woman sounded doubtful. Zephyr tossed his head and chortled at her. Chrysta's eyebrows arched in reaction to whatever the beast said and she shrugged,

"Okay, it's your back."

With that she turned back to Templer.

"It seems that macho man here." She stabbed a finger at Zephyr,

"... Thinks that he can carry us double until we get to our planned stop. Are you game?"

The gunman looked at the big male who looked right back with an amused, arrogant challenge in his golden eyes.

"I don't see as how it would be a problem."

"Okay, if you males think you are up to it, then who am I to stand in your way?"

She walked over and stripped the saddle and pads off of the black's broad back. The only piece of tack she left on him was the odd harness that encircled the base of Zephyr's neck. It carried the sheathed sword that she had used in her dressage demonstration.

Templer felt Azra stir a little in alarm as Nuva made a noise that sounded suspiciously like a snicker. Chrysta gave both destria a narrow eyed look but didn't say a word as she tied the now spare tack onto the cream's saddle. The priest watched in amazement as heading back to Zephyr, the rider grabbed a handful of his thick black mane, scrambled up his heavy shoulder and perched herself on the animal's bare back.

The gunman was sure he heard her softly mutter,

"I... am getting to old for this CRAP!"

When Chrysta had herself comfortable and was centered, she offered her hand and helped the Talon to swing up behind her. It only took him a moment to figure out that riding in this manner was going to be an interesting proposition at best. As the woman moved the black out into an easy walk, Templer realized that without stirrups there was very little to balance himself with. The gunman had to readjust the Trinity's holster so the big gun wouldn't be poking anybody (most importantly Zephyr) in uncomfortable places. Chrysta had arched an eloquent eyebrow at him when he had insisted upon bringing the triple bored handgun, but had said nothing when Azra had strongly backed him.

The man was also VERY aware that Chrysta's warm, firm butt was cradled snugly between his legs. It was hard to ignore the feel of their thighs rubbing gently where they nestled against each other. The fact that certain portions of his anatomy were pressed tightly against her strong back did not help the situation. The priest tried to wiggle back to a more discrete distance. Zephyr chortled and did SOMETHING with his ass end that scooted him forward, right back into the same disconcerting position. When Templer tried to scoot back again... Nuva, who was pacing quietly beside them snorted and used her big head to push him forwards.

"You might as well give it up and try to enjoy yourself."

Chrysta reached back and guided his hands around her waist. He could tell she was suppressing her laughter.

"They won't give up once they have an idea firmly entrenched in their devious little minds." She slapped the big black male's shoulder in exasperated affection.

"Now, hold on." She warned.

The woman urged Zephyr to increase his pace and Templer tightened his grip, bracing for the jarring trot he knew was coming. He was surprised when Zephyr shifted into a gear that was as fast as the trot but seemed as smooth as silk. Nuva followed suite, and the gunman noticed that there was no trace of a limp in her flowing gait. She caught him looking at her and rewarded him with a cheeky wink.

"This is called a running walk." Chrysta informed him over her shoulder. "It isn't as fast as a canter but it's a lot easier on Zephyr's back when he is carrying this big a load."

Templer took her earlier advice and tried to relax as the big animals flowed along. It wasn't as hard as he thought it would be. Because he didn't have to watch the trail or handle any reins, he could look around and enjoy the scenery. There was a lot here in the way of plants and animals that he had not seen before. The forest in this river valley might have been here since before the Cataclysm. It was deep, and the huge hardwood trees they passed under, had the aura of being very old. These woods didn't have the hostile air that the mountain forests of the Arcanian wilderness had, but there was the feeling that there were ancient dwellers here.

Azra wasn't interested in enjoying the scenery. The outrider was relishing in the wonderful physical sensations that the gunman being pressed up this close to a desirable female was causing. The astounded priest could almost hear the demon humming softly as he inundated himself with pleasurable sensations. This sort of thing usually had Azra hiding himself in the dark corners of Templer's mind. The fact that the demon was actively indulging in it was more than a little disconcerting!

Because of this, neither the outrider nor the man was as alert to danger as they would normally have been. Chrysta had her attention divided between guiding the black and the cream along the twisting path and keeping herself and her passenger mounted. Dusk was darkening the surrounding forest when a flicker in the trees caught the gunman's attention. It was all the warning they had. Two scaly, long necked Terrabirds from hell burst from the trees on their right, two more came in from the left.

Templer quickly realized that these things only shared a Terra-bird's general shape. They stood as tall as a man on two heavily muscled legs. These ended in four strong toes, each well equipped with long, killing talons. Their front limbs sported three nasty hooked claws and their faces were nothing but red eyes and gaping mouths full of long, dagger like teeth. He could feel Chrysta trying to get her reins shifted to one hand to free the other so she could draw her sword. Zephyr started to slow in preparation to fight.

"No!" Templer tightened his legs, driving his heels hard into their mount's sensitive sides. With a surprised grunt the big black exploded into a driving gallop. The Talon's enhanced hearing had picked up on what Chrysta couldn't. There were more of the pack coming up the trail behind them. As one of the creatures on their left launched itself at them, Templer drew the Trinity with one hand whilst pushing Chrysta forward and down with the other.

"Stay down and drive!"

Was all he had time to shout. He fired across and over her back, catching the attacking creature in the face. His second shot caught the thing's partner, breaking its leg and sending it tumbling into the trees. A blur of motion had him shifting to the right and his third shot ruffled through Nuva's mane as he picked off one of the pack that had launched itself at the mare.

A heavy weight slammed into Templer's back almost knocking him off. Hot fire slashed across one thigh as curved talons sliced through skin and muscle. He heard Nuva scream, and the weight disappeared. The enraged mare had reached over and grabbed the beast in her fanged mouth. The gunman heard the cracking of bones as the mare's powerful jaws broke the thrashing creature's back. With a disgusted wrinkle of her lips Nuva dropped it and added insult to injury by trampling the mortally injured killer as she passed over its twitching body.

The Talon reloaded automatically as the monsters behind them started dropping back. He switched the gun to fully automatic bringing all eighteen of its loaded chambers into play. Motion in the trees had him snapping the gun up as different pack members took up the chase. The gunman managed to bring another down but the creatures evidently had some intelligence and they ducked and dodged using the trees as shields. With a sinking sensation Templer realized that the fact that the pack wasn't fast enough to catch them in an all-out, straight race wasn't going to help. The creatures were chasing in relay, hoping to eventually exhaust their prey and bring them down. Nuva had a chance of out running and out lasting them, but she stayed, stretched out at the black's side. Because of the extra load he was carrying, Zephyr was already laboring.

With a curse, Chrysta turned the big male, going off of the trail and

"WHAT THE HELL ARE YOU DOING?"

Azra knew that with the trees slowing them down, they had no hope of out running the beasts. He also knew that with the interlocking branches closing over them that if Templer made the decision to shift forms, he did not have the wing room to get airborne.

"I am heading for the river." Chrysta was breathless, working at threading two large, fast moving animals through the trees without the riders getting scraped or knocked off. "If those misbegotten things are anything like Terra-Birds, they can't SWIM!"

Two of the creatures who were faster than the others jumped from the trees trying to sink wicked talons into Zephyr's heaving rump. The big black squealed and caught one with both hind hooves almost unseating the gunman. It rolled to the ground. Templer slashed the other across its ugly face with his own deadly claws. The thing snarled and twisted away. Before it could jump again, Templer's shot made sure it went down. They broke out of the trees, and the gunman saw they had a clear run to the river. At least ten of the pack had broken off and were flattened out in a deadly race, coming up along the river's bank. The pack was trying to cut the destria off from safety. Chrysta was crooning at the flagging black trying to get just a little more out of him. The gunman took three more of the creatures down but realized that they were going to lose this race. He turned control over to Azra.

Zephyr staggered as the weight on his back suddenly increased. Azra flared his black wings wide. Their forward speed gave him the lift he needed to rise and then dive into the seven pack members who now blocked their path to the river. They went down in a writhing ball of flailing tails, scaly limbs, flashing teeth and slashing claws. The pursuing creatures slid to a stop to join the fray. The outrider's ploy worked, and a path opened for the racing destria to slip through. They pounded to the edge. This was not a good place on the river to cross. The water ran cold, fast, and deep. The black didn't hesitate to leap in. Nuva slowed for a moment, sending a distressed look after Chrysta. She then doubled back and plowed into the battling mess on the bank.

Azra quickly realized he was in deep trouble.

He was badly outnumbered and the sheer weight of his adversaries had him off of his feet, pinned with his wings trapped beneath him and fighting for his life. The demon roared with rage, kicking, slashing and even biting. Even if he had the energy reserves to unleash a small portion of his strength... he had no idea how much distance his companions had put between them. Azra would not risk them getting caught in the blast. He was glad for his restraint when he felt Nuva's massive weight plow into the pile. The battling mare knocked the slavering creatures in all directions with the initial impact. The outrider roared again when she reached down, buried her fangs in his shoulder and yanked him out from under the pile. Kicking and squalling, the destria cleared a way to drag the demon to the river's edge. Once there, she released her grip and leaped into the roiling water.

Azra tried to take off but had not cleared the ground before three of the beasts hit him from behind. Their combined weight dragged him into the icy depths. Chrysta was right, the creatures could not swim. As a matter of fact, they sank like rocks. Unfortunately, because they had attached themselves to various parts of his anatomy, they took the demon with them! As he desperately worked to unlock their death locked jaws, Azra wondered if it were possible for an immortal to drown. He managed to get them off of him, but was too cold and exhausted to fight the vicious current. Even with the icy water, loss of blood and lack of oxygen were taking their toll.

He felt a rush of displaced water and Nuva's big body appeared downstream from him. The mare fought the current making it to his side and turned presenting her tail. He wasn't too proud to take the offer. He tangled his claws in it and with their combined strength they made it to the far bank.

As soon as Nuva cleared the water, Azra released her tail. He dragged himself halfway up the bank then had to stop. The outrider stayed there balanced on his hands and knees. He coughed and choked trying to clear the water out of his lungs. HOLY... it felt like he had inhaled half of the river! With a supreme effort he levered himself up and staggered away from the water. Azra was surprised when Nuva's big warm body appeared to support him on one side and Chrysta ducked under a torn wing to help support him from the other. The woman did not waste any breath with words. Ignoring the demon's protest that he was fine and could walk on his own, she firmly guided his wet, ragged ass away from the river. Azra tried to pull away and was rewarded with a rumble from Nuva plus a nasty look as the mare popped her fangs together. Suitably cowed, the demon let them drag him along. HE knew better than to pick a fight when trapped between two upset females!

They walked until they came to an open clearing. Zephyr was there. The black looked as bad as Azra felt. Chrysta insisted that the demon sit and rest while she stripped the wet tack off of Nuva. He couldn't help but feel grateful that he wasn't a destria, she made them walk slowly until they cooled off. Feeling a little useless, Azra rose and ignoring her dirty look, gathered some wood and ignited it with ether-flame. The sun had set and the breeze that sighed through the trees had a cold bite to it, especially if you were wet. He then carefully settled back by the fire and watched as Chrysta quickly and efficiently spread some type of salve on the animal's various cuts and slashes. He grew a little concerned when she approached him with the open container.

The demon couldn't stop his wings from sucking around his body defensively

"I don't need that!!" He snarled.

"Remember... I am not mortal, there for I heal very quickly!"

Azra was disconcerted when Chrysta just flat ignored his MOST TERRIFYING LOOK and tried to pry his wings open. He pulled them in even tighter.

The woman finally stepped back with her head cocked in exasperation. After all, the demon thought smugly, he WAS stronger than her.

"Yes... I KNOW you heal fast, but it is silly to suffer while you are healing. All this will do is numb up the wounds for a while and prevent any infection." Chrysta looked him dead in the eye, "Don't tell me you are AFRAID of a little salve."

"Harrumph..." was all that the outrider said as he tentatively opened his wings. HE wasn't afraid of anything.

A good half hour later... after many yelps, jerks and "STOP being a baby" comments, Chrysta seemed content with her work. The woman looked down at him. She had ultimately resorted to pinning him on his stomach and sitting on his back to reach the damage to his wings. **"See that wasn't too bad now was it?"**

Azra wondered if this was a trick question. Yes, the stuff numbed things up quite nicely EVENTUALLY. It stung like a son of a bitch when it first hit a wound. Chrysta grinned like a maniac and slid off of her perch. Azra slowly sat up, trying to preserve as much of his dignity as was left. Damn he was glad that Templer had no recollection of the events that occurred when he shifted. He would NEVER let his outrider live this down! A sudden frown marred the demon's aquiline features. He realized that Chrysta's hands were like ice, and she had been shivering while seated up on his back. He snagged her arm as she went by. Mother of Demons, her lips were blue!

"Get undressed," The demon growled.

"WHAT!?" Chrysta stuttered.

Azra couldn't repress a nasty smile... ahhh paybacks WERE such a bitch.

"I did not stutter... STRIP! Or do you need some help?"

He popped the top button of her shirt off with one sharp claw to drive home the fact he was perfectly willing to back up the threat.

Outriders did not BLUFF!

The woman blinked in surprise as a second button followed the first.

"STOP... fine... I can do it myself!" Chrysta hastily peeled the wet clothes off, shivering even worse when the breeze hit her bare skin.

"NOW, come here." Azra purred as he opened his wings. For a moment she froze. Using her indecision against her, the demon caught an arm and pulled her body against his own warm skin. CRAP! It was like hugging an ice queen. He turned her around, sat her on his lap, and then folded his warm wings around them both. He was rewarded a few minutes later when her shivering stopped. Sighing, the woman leaned back against him of her own accord. Azra couldn't help himself. Dropping his head, the outrider inhaled deeply sampling her honest, spicy scent. He jerked back when she stirred, suddenly afraid he had overstepped himself.

A gentle finger traced lightly over the soft skin on the leading edge of his wing.

"Azra... I have been wondering?" For the first time since they had met she sounded uncertain. "Are you able to...?"

The demon, caught flat footed, answered her

with brutal honesty.

"I do not know. Up until now I have never had the desire to sample the delights of the flesh while in physical form. I tend to isolate myself when my host is required to participate in that... type... of activity. The taste of lust is infinitely sweet, but it tends to leave me feeling rather sick. It is not something that I care to feed upon unless hard pressed."

The demon waited for her to pull away at the hard edge in his voice.

That finger stopped its slow tracing and Chrysta arched her head back to look up at him.

"What about the taste of Love... surely you have had opportunity to..."

"My host avoids that sort of thing. Love is a delicacy I have never tasted and most likely never will."

Her face was filled with sadness.

"That must really suck... for the both of you."

It was his turn to blink. Azra could not remember a time when a human had looked at him with anything but fear or hate. It had been even longer since he had held a caring body close to his, or been touched by hands that were gentle and kind, instead of trying to maim or kill.

Azra smiled, a strange thing that his face wasn't use to.

"It is not too terrible. One cannot miss what one has never had. Constantine respects my feelings about lust and only inflicts it upon me when absolutely necessary."

The demon closed his golden eyes enjoying the very physical feel of her warm body pressed against his. **"This is what I miss most in our bleak existence, the physical touch of another given in kindness not violence, the smell of a** female not tainted by fear, greed or hate and the heart of a friend given in trust. It is enough that there is one person on this miserable world who cares for me, no matter my flaws."

Azra opened his wings a little,

"SPEAKING OF Constantine, I really do need to..."

Chrysta turned in his arms, and placed her hands against his chest. Sliding them up around his neck the woman rose until she was kneeling between his legs, her face close to his.

"Yes... but before you go. I just want you to know this. I find I really like Templer, and I also really like you. Each of you are incredible and fascinating beings. Lust is a sweet and empty thing... but sometimes what starts as something purely physical can grow into something quite complex!"

She brushed his lips with a light kiss. "If we humans DO decide to indulge in each other's bodies, please do not hide away. It is not possible for me to make love to Templer without also making love to YOU."

Chrysta stepped away from his arms and moved to add fuel to the fire. Before Azra began his transformation, the outrider indulged himself one last time in the pleasure of watching the firelight play across her naked skin.

Templer's awareness came slowly to him this time. Two transformations in a day was a lot to ask of his body, modified or not. He remembered the harrowing race to the river and the terrible realization that they weren't going to win it. A desperate need to know that everyone was still alive and unharmed had him dragging himself into a sitting position before his body was ready. The priest realized this was a serious mistake as all of his muscles seized up. He helplessly rolled back onto the ground, his entire body caught in seizure like spasm. There was no stopping the gasp of pain that pushed itself past tightly closed lips.

The Talon could not hear or see anything, so caught up was he in the struggle to get his screaming body unlocked enough to draw the next breath. He did feel as strong hands rolled him up against a large warm body that was vibrating strongly. The subliminal rumble of Nuva's sweet, deep croon penetrated the haze of pain, and very slowly dissipated it. Templer realized, as his muscles relaxed enough for him to suck in lungful after lungful of the sweet night air, that he had been propped against the resting mare. She was lying down with her body partially curved around him. The deep rumble gradually quieted and then died away. His pain returned but thankfully at a level that the priest was able to control.

The subtle sound of movement nearby had his eyes snapping open and caused him to reach instinctively for the Trinity. Chrysta materialized out of the darkness and the Talon just managed to stop himself before he triggered another spasm. It only took him a moment to figure out that reaching for the weapon was a wasted effort anyways. The big gun wasn't on his hip. For that matter neither were his pants.

"It seems to be becoming a habit for me to wake up naked when you are around."

Templer was a little surprised by how weak and hoarse his voice was. Chrysta's worried face relaxed into a smile but her green eyes were dark with concern as she untwisted the blanket he had managed to tangle himself up in and tucked it back around his suddenly chilled and aching body.

"Crap Constantine, don't scare me like that!" She sounded a little shaken. "Azra wasn't kidding when he said these changes were hard on you."

The woman very carefully lowered herself down until she was sitting with her back against Nuva next to him. Templer quickly realized that the blanket she was wrapped in was her only attire.

He couldn't help himself.

"Where are your clothes?"

Yes, he would be the first to agree that this was a stupid question. He HAD an excuse though... he was tired, his brain felt like mush and his body felt like it had been joyfully trampled by a team of Chrysta's drafters. Templer believed he was entitled to ask a stupid question or two.

The woman's eyes flicked sideways and the wicked little smile that stirred her lips set all the little alarms off inside his head. She closed her eyes as she tilted her head back to rest it on Nuva's warm hide before answering.

"Azra MADE me take them off."

"WHAT?"

Templer couldn't stop the reflexive jerk of his body as his head snapped around in shock. As everything locked up again in pain, the thought that was foremost in his mind was... ask a stupid question!!

Chrysta swore as she flew to her feet and disappeared into the dark again. This spasm wasn't as bad as the one before. By the time the woman returned, he had managed to prop himself back up. Just this little bit of movement had him breathing hard through clenched teeth.

The woman knelt next to him and held a cup of steaming liquid to his lips.

"Here, drink some of this."

The Talon took a sip and at the look on his face his companion sternly warned him.

"Don't you DARE spit that out! I have had my fill of sitting on top of stubborn males tonight because they don't have the brains to know what is good for them. You WILL swallow that and drink some more!"

As if the grim look she gave him wasn't enough, Nuva rumbled in support of her trainer. The mare curved her ridged head around and gave the gunman an evil look of her own. Templer wisely swallowed the bitter brew. When he had managed to down about half of the cup, Chrysta relented and settled back to sit next to him. He watched in morbid fascination as she drank the rest of the nasty stuff in one go and did not bother to try and hide his satisfaction when she shuddered as she set the cup down.

Those lovely eyes met his gaze and Chrysta shrugged, a slight smile tugging at the corners of her mouth.

"Hey... I never said it tasted good, just that it was GOOD for what ails you."

"What's in it?"

The Talon was curious because he could already feel the pain releasing its razor edged grip on his overtaxed body.

"It is DREAMLEAF..." Azra's deep voice not only held a note of concern, but also one of relief **"...and although this is not the safest way to administer it. I for one, would rather take the risk than deal with any more pain tonight!"**

Chrysta snorted, and in response to Templer's raised eyebrow she added.

"Azra, and by proxy YOU, took one hell of a beating opening a path for us to the river. Add to that a frigid swim in the river along with almost drowning..." She shook her head. "Your outrider was in pretty rough shape by the time he made the shore. He reminded me of a piece of meat that had gone through one of Grant's sausage grinders. When I tried to treat his injuries... He did point out the fact that you have accelerated healing abilities..."

"Like THAT mattered!" This bit was muttered under Azra's breath. Chrysta smiled before continuing...

"He also mentioned that with two transformations so close together YOU were going to need them. After watching you wake up... Let's just say I was pretty sure that without the dreamleaf, neither one of you is going to feel like getting up and RIDING in the morning!"

Nuva chortled her agreement and then settled her nose back into the grass with a sigh.

Chrysta stretched her bad leg and a slight grimace tightened her lips.

"I even gave some to Zephyr, he is going to be very stiff tomorrow."

Templer realized he hadn't seen the big male

since he regained awareness, and he sat up straight to look around for the black. He was pleasantly surprised when the movement was almost pain free. He still could not see Zephyr.

"I wouldn't be too worried about him, he felt well enough that he is taking a trip around the camp to make sure nothing nasty sneaks up on us. I would imagine he is also looking for little sleeping tidbits to snack on. Speaking of which..." Chrysta shifted next to him and slowly climbed to her feet. "Are you hungry?"

As Templer watched his companion limp heavily to the banked fire he felt Azra stir uneasily in the back of his mind.

"What's wrong?" he quietly asked the demon.

The outrider answered with his own question, so softly that his host almost couldn't hear him.

"Are you feeling any pain?"

It took a moment for the point that the demon was trying to make to sink in.

"How long does it take to build up a resistance to dreamleaf?"

Templer knew nothing of the drug but trusted in Azra's knowledge.

The demon kept his reply at an almost subliminal level.

"I am not sure. It is not highly addictive. I believe that developing a substantial resistance to it would take a very long time."

They both watched in silence as the woman made her way back and carefully sat down. She had a bag that Grant had stuffed with bread, cheese, apples and little spicy meat pies. He had also packed a small bottle of red wine that Chrysta regretfully set aside.

"We will have to save that until tomorrow. Drinking alcohol and dreamleaf together would be a big mistake."

Azra made an odd choking sound. Chrysta looked up from cutting the bread and apples. Templer's expression must have caught her attention because she set her knife down and asked,

"What?"

"How long have you been taking dreamleaf?"

The demon saved Templer from being the one to ask.

Chrysta's eyes narrowed a little, but she answered him.

"Six years, every day, twice a day except for one day out of every eight, to clear my system."

"That's DANGEROUS!"

The demon made no attempt hide his shocked reaction.

"I have no choice and you do NOT want to be having this conversation with me."

The woman's voice had taken on an icy edge that Templer had not heard before.

Azra was practically sputtering,

"SOMEBODY needs to have it with you!"

Something shifted in those eyes and the priest tried to intervene. He had a sudden, very bad feeling about this.

"Shut up, Azra."

"I will not shut up... HOST. Taking it like that can have LETHAL consequences!"

His outrider evidently wasn't paying close attention to Chrysta's face because if he had, he would have taken Templer's advice. The gunman saw his companion's face take on an unearthly stillness and her eyes were like dead flat ice. He felt SOMETHING that had been placed between her mind and his suddenly crumble. Nuva jerked, moaning in reaction. Templer had a split second to think "Oh Shit" before a knife of ice and flame buried itself just left of and below his left nipple. It drove deep, through his ribs then down across his stomach and groin. A tendril of flame snaked across his right hip then all the way down his leg. The muscles all along the lethal slash pulled back, jumping and twisting as if trying to remove themselves from the unbearable pain's vicinity. For the third time that night, Templer found himself in the grip of uncontrollable muscle spasms. For one hideous moment he had the fear that somehow he was back under the Maker's scalpel, reliving one of their worst experiments. Then it just STOPPED.

All the man could do was lay there and gasp. He could hear Azra savagely cursing as if from a great distance. Chrysta finally stirred and gently helped him to sit back up.

The woman held his glowing eyes captive with her own. Hers still held that strange, dead ice look.

"Not very pleasant... is it?!"

The green started to leak back in as she sat back and her gaze was almost back to normal when Chrysta looked away with a sigh and went back to slicing bread and apples.

"When you can tell me how to live with that every moment of every day, I will gladly give up the dreamleaf."

Templer couldn't help himself.

"Gods be DAMNED... Azra! When I say shut up... SHUT THE FUCK UP!"

Templer was content to just sit and watch as Chrysta finished preparing their simple meal. His nerves were still jumping from the complete overload the woman had subjected them to. Keeping quiet seemed a good thing right at the moment! Nuva shifted behind him. Humming quietly, the mare nuzzled his shoulder in sympathy. When Chrysta silently handed him his neatly plated portion, the priest realized that her hands were shaking. The woman leaned back against the cream destria's side closing her eyes. Nuva's hum shifted to that deep, soothing croon. Templer was startled when Zephyr's rumbling voice joined in and he realized that the big black had returned to the camp. The small, tense lines of distress around the woman's mouth and eyes gradually smoothed out and disappeared.

Templer felt Azra ease foreword a little in his mind.

"Chrysta, you really need to eat before you sleep."

The Talon winced as the woman's face twitched, but he realized he was as bad as the demon when he joined in.

"Yes... that would probably be a very good idea."

Chrysta's eyelids opened enough he could see they were a kaleidoscopic mix of blue, green and gold. Both males released the collective breath they had been holding when she grinned.

"Isn't that a little like the pot calling the kettle black?"

"Hnnn..." Templer hoped that his abused

body would forgive him. His stomach was still tied into a tense knot. He picked up one of the meat pies as a slight smile twisted his mouth.

"Yes, I guess it would be, except this pot is planning on eating."

The destria's deep croon stopped, and it was Chrysta's turn to get the full impact of Nuva's evil eye. She hastily pulled herself away from the mare's warm side and picked up a slice of apple and some cheese to nibble on.

Surprisingly, between the two of them, they finished what she had prepared. This was if you did not take into account a meat pie and a couple of apples that found their way into Nuva's greedy mouth.

As Templer gathered up and put away the implements from their meal, Chrysta made her way back over to put more wood on the dying fire. When she returned, she had put her shirt back on. She had her blanket draped over her shoulders. The long, loose shirt swayed with her movements, revealing and concealing tantalizing bits of her firm anatomy.

"These are dry." She handed him his warm shirt, "We will have to wait awhile longer on the pants."

The man had straightened out the blanket that Chrysta had initially spread on the ground under them, and she settled back on to it. He was relieved to see that the grace had returned to her movements. Templer stood, turning his back to her as he slipped into his shirt. He knew it was silly. The woman had seen him undressed several times already. What the priest did not realize was although this preserved a little of his dignity, it gave the woman a long uninterrupted view of his strong well-muscled back. Chrysta froze, her gaze lingering on what was a truly impressive behind and her fingers twitched as she ruthlessly stepped on the sudden desire to touch the man's lovely, porcelain like skin. When Templer turned back around, he was modestly re-covered by his blanket. His companion had leaned back and was watching him with stormy, half lidded eyes. His own dark gaze caught her staring as he sat back down. One elegant eyebrow arched as a light tinge of pink touched her cheeks and she looked away.

They both relaxed against their living back rest in companionable silence.

Chrysta when she finally spoke, jerked Templer out of a light doze.

"I am very careful."

The gunman was confused for a moment, had she been talking to him while he was drifting?

"I am sorry?"

His companion shifted a little and her eyes flicked sideways to look at him.

"I am very careful when I figure my dosages on the dreamleaf. I am well aware how dangerous a drug it is."

Templer turned his body so he could see her face. Her mouth gave a wry twist.

"I... apologize... for subjecting you to...." She shrugged

"I tend to get a little short tempered when I am... tired."

The gunman quietly studied the woman's face until she looked away from him in shame. He reached over and using the tip of one talon under her chin, he turned her face back where he could see it.

"You have nothing to apologize for. My... companion... can be overbearing at times."

He felt his outrider twitch indignantly in

response to that, but Azra wisely held his tongue. "And you certainly made your point. Quite clearly I might add!"

Green eyes darkened, then blinked. She reached up to run her fingers along his blade-hand.

"For one who has been so abused by destiny, you have a remarkably forgiving nature, Templer Constantine."

Okay, Azra just couldn't stand it.

"Except when it comes to forgiving himself. Considering he is a man of the cloth... he is abysmal at that!"

Chrysta couldn't quite control the smile that flitted across her face. She looked away as the smile turned sad.

"Sometimes, Azra, even if one CAN forgive one's... self. It brings no sweet comfort."

Her attention jerked back to the gunman's beautiful face when his talon dipped and gently traced the path of her scar through the soft material of her shirt. Chrysta froze, mesmerized by the swirling gold that lit the darkness with-in the Talon's eyes.

The sensitive circuitry in Templer's bio-engineered hand easily picked up the shift in her steady heart rate as the tip of the gleaming talon slipped across her stomach to travel where the old wound sliced across her abdomen and curled around her hip. In passing, the cold organic metal left the material and traveled on to caress soft, warm skin. Its sensitive tip also picked up the slight shudder that traveled over her.

Spreading that hand wide, Constantine braced his weight on the ground next to her hip and rotated himself until he was facing her. This move unintentionally trapped the woman between himself and the solid bulk of the destria behind. They were close enough that the woman's heat carried her warm spicy smell up to him like a rich, sweet perfume. As his head dipped to taste those slightly parted lips, a flash of guilt stopped him.

For her what he was asking was still a punishable sin. She could be whipped or stoned for it if the local magistrate wished to push the point.

"NO, Constantine... this act is allowed if there is truly a need. Your Outrider's reserves are low and, he is insisting that he is very... very... hungry!"

Azra's voice oddly enough... sounded apprehensive and Templer was astounded when instead of retreating to the depths of his host's mind, the demon shifted forward a little.

The Talon felt the soft lips under his curve in a sweet smile. Then, Chrysta's face was all he saw. Pinpoints of blue and gold flashed in and out of the green of her wide eyes as she patiently waited for him to come to a decision. They blazed like brilliant jewels before they closed when Templer finally captured her mouth with his.

"YESSS...!"

Azra rumbled, his rough voice soft and deep. This should have been a distraction. Instead, it was as if the meld between the outrider and the man strengthened. Instead of being two separate individuals... they became the two halves of one.

There was no physical transformation, but Chrysta's eyes flicked open as the shadow of phantom wings arced up, blocking the dim light of the fire. She drew back slightly and Templer slid his human hand under her soft shirt. Slipping his arm around her, the man stroked up his partner's supple spine. The lean, strong fingers that gently touched her... were his. When he curved them at the sensitive spot between the woman's shoulder blades, she arched forward with a smothered hiss at the feel of sharp talons carefully gliding along her skin. Turning that hand, those same ghostly talons sliced through the material covering her warm soft body.

The cloth fluttered to the ground, exposing shimmering skin to the cool night air. Chrysta rose, her lithe body pressed tightly against his chest. Strong arms slid around the gunman's neck and long fingers tangled themselves into his raven hair as Templer deepened the kiss. That sweet mouth opened allowing him entry. It was his outrider that drank her moan when teeth that had elongated into killing fangs nipped gently at her tender tongue and lips.

Chrysta's hands slid under his shirt, stroking along his stomach. A tremor ran through Constantine as the hard muscles there tightened, shivering at the wonderful sensations her cool fingers created. The groan that escaped his lips was an almost harmonic blending of two voices. Moving up, those same amazing hands impatiently removed his shirt. He smiled against her mouth at the soft curse she uttered struggling with the buttons. Spider-silk did not tear easily and, the cloth was suddenly very much in the way!

With a sudden grin against his lips, Chrysta twisted her body hard and Templer found himself on his back with her straddling his hips. His outrider tensed in an instinctive reaction to being in a defenseless position. Templer tempered Azra's response with the sure knowledge that sometimes being on your back wasn't necessarily a bad thing. Chrysta did her best to prove his point. Sliding her hands along his arms until they were palm to palm. The woman started at his mouth. Nibbling, sucking, licking, and even biting, she worked her way over every inch of Templer's smooth skin that she could comfortably reach. The woman shifted her seat when she felt his sudden and intense approval of the stimulation. This brought the demon part of the mix a wonderful new appreciation for being in this particular position.

Shadow wings flaring in long forgotten pleasure arched Templer up. The Talon claimed the woman's now hot hands, pulling her down against his body at the same time. From there it was an easy thing to roll them both over. He pinned her underneath his body with the full length and strength of his lithe form. Between his strong, well trained fingers, gleaming talons, and Azra's phantom touch they stoked and played her passion with a knowledge as old as time.

By the time Templer was positioned to take what was freely offered, Chrysta's eyes glowed like hot young stars. When he finally allowed his partner's body to rise as he entered her, the movement was accompanied by something that sounded suspiciously like a growl. This was eerily blended with the deep rumbles that emanated from both of her destria.

Azra proved to be nothing but endless lustful passion. Templer had learned patience during the long, tortuous years spent under whip and knife. With this he had forged a will of iron. Together they brought their lover up to the trembling brink time and again but did not let her ride over the edge. On the last climb, Templer stopped at the edge and shifted back. Chrysta followed him, her hips lifting with a soft moan.

"Mother of Demons... PLEASE... Templer!"

Black flared to gold and a dangerous smile shifted the gunman's beautiful features. As Constantine thrust forward in one long hard stroke, Azra buried his sharp, unnaturally elongated fangs into the juncture of her shoulder and neck. The taste of her smoky blood flooded his mouth as the woman bowed up hard against him. She muffled her physical scream by sinking her teeth into his shoulder but her mind reached out and locked both man and outrider into her link. Bound together by more than a physical connection they plunged over that edge and raced on the wild wind of savage pleasure that roared through their combined bodies and minds.

When that storm was finished with them, it gently eased them back into the physical world like feathers floating down on the soft breath of a breeze. Templer found himself with his body so totally entwined with hers that it was hard to tell where one left off and the other began. He carefully shifted to the side, knowing she would eventually be in pain with his full weight resting on her. Chrysta hummed softly under her breath and her green eyes opened slightly to see where he was going. They came to full awareness when she realized that he was planning to get up. She quickly re-wrapped her leg around his, effectively immobilizing him.

The gunman relaxed and with his thumb, wiped a little of his blood off of her lips.

"I will need to sleep tonight and I do NOT want to end up on my stomach, with your knees in my back again."

She pushed herself up on one elbow, and her face was serious.

"I can pretty much guarantee that with the dreamleaf in your system, you won't have nightmares tonight. Stay here with me. There is nothing on this side of the river that can sneak up on us. If something does make it over the river, it will have to deal with two destria. If I get any inclination that you are having a night terror, I will go to the other side of the camp and let NUVA wake you up."

Nuva snorted and her head shot around to give her handler an incredible dirty look.

Templer just looked at this incredible woman for a long moment then he lowered himself back down to gather her up with her back spooned against him. One strong arm reached out to snag a blanket and they curled up together under it. He stayed awake for a time, enjoying the simple pleasure of not being alone. Then he let his mind relax and drifted into a deep and dreamless sleep. As the fire slowly died he did not feel the phantom wing curve over the lovers, cocooning them in its soft, protective warmth.

There were still a few stars burning in the early morning sky when a small sound jerked Templer out of a sound sleep. He was squeezed between Chrysta, who had stolen most of the blankets, and what felt like a solid wall. That wall was the reason that he did not feel the morning chill. Zephyr had lain down against him. The destria's broad back radiated heat better than any fire. Nuva was nowhere to be seen. A small panicked squeal, followed by a thrashing rustle outside of camp indicated the mare was prowling nearby, presumably looking for sleeping...tidbits. This was the sound that had disturbed the Talon's sleep.

Constantine slipped out from between his two bed partners. (Now wasn't that an odd thought!) The morning's cold did not bother him but the thought of parading nude around the campsite did, so Templer made the effort to find his discarded shirt. There was a brief tussle as Zephyr made it clear that he preferred to have his soft muzzle resting on the soft fabric rather than the cold, hard ground. When their brief tug of war caused the mound of blankets to stir. The black flashed his adversary a piteous look... which did not work. Templer got his shirt back, but only after it had been worked over by the animal's soft wet lips! The priest wiped at the damp spots this left in the spider-silk material as Zephyr chortled and settled his nose back on the ground. Templer did his best to ignore the beast as he went to retrieve his pants. The man knew when he was being laughed at!

Their pants were as dry as they would get with the heavy morning dew. This made sliding into the supple black leather difficult at best. As the gunman belted them on, he suddenly realized that the Trinity had to have gotten soaked when Azra went into the river. He found the big gun, wrapped in a soft piece of leather, resting on a flat rock. Its holster hung on a branch beside it. They were both situated far enough from the open flame that the heat wouldn't damage the tooled leather. The Talon appreciated the fact that the weapon had been broken open so that the now empty chambers could dry. He found the damp ammunition wrapped in another soft cloth and tucked behind the same rock the gun was on. It only took him a moment to dig his waterproof kit out of his saddle bags and replace the wet rounds stored in the holster with dry ones.

Templer got the fire re-lit and knowing there was no way that Chrysta had left town without coffee, he made a quick search of the other bags. Sure enough, the man found the precious black beans tucked in next to a small bag of dreamleaf. He was pleased that both had been well wrapped and their contents remained totally dry. After getting a pot of coffee brewing, he sat down by the fire and broke the Trinity down. As his talented hands went through the very familiar process of cleaning and oiling the complicated gun, the priest felt Azra stir. Knowing that the energy released during sex usually gave the outrider the equivalent of a massive hangover, Constantine did not press. He continued concentrating on the task at hand, politely giving his "other" some space to deal with the after affects. It was not as if the demon could stagger to the bathroom for a good bout of porcelain worship!

"Ummmm, Constantine...you might want to heat some water."

Templer's hands did not slow in what he was doing as he absentmindedly answered... "I have coffee on already. You KNOW it won't help your headache... right?"

"Yes... that is usually the case." The gunman's fingers paused in their task at the surprise in his outrider's voice. "**I find it hard to believe, but I am not experiencing any ill affects this morning. As a matter of fact, I feel rather pleasantly... sated! That coffee actually sounds good but...**"

Azra was interrupted by a muffled yelp from the blanket's general vicinity. This was followed by...

"Son of a BITCH!" ...a low groan, followed by a softly muttered, "DAMN...I KNOW better than to ride bareback!"

Zephyr snorted and scrambled hastily to his feet. With a cautious look back at the crumpled ball of blankets, the black casually started to amble (sneak) away. He moved faster as that scary ball of cloth shifted slightly and what was contained within released a wicked hiss!

"Nuva... you are FRICKEN lucky I can't get up else I would kick your ass!"

The cream mare had appeared back in camp casually chewing on some little... tidbit... she had found. When the mare heard Chrysta, Nuva's jaws stopped working and she slunk over to join Zephyr in his attempt to hide behind the seated priest. The big black did not help matters when he snorted derisively and bumped Templer with his nose.

"ZEPHYR!"

The woman's head popped out of the blankets as she tried to get herself straightened out.

"What?!" Templer was astounded when it seemed the big animal was going to try to crawl right into his lap! He slapped at the black muzzle to get it out of his way while he hastily reassembled the Trinity and scrambled to his feet. He had not lived for centuries just to end his life crushed underneath TWO anxious destria!

There was a choked sound of laughter mixed with a small moan as Chrysta curled back up under the blankets.

"I was just informed that HE was not the only thing that I rode bareback!"

Templer froze for a moment and heard his outrider quietly murmur...

"He has a point. We did not use the saddles."

The vivid image of what COULD be done with said saddles that Azra played through the Talon's mind WAS not only depraved... Mother of demons help him... it was also very interesting!

The ball of blankets trembled and the woman softly groaned.

"Oh HOLY... somebody shoot me now!"

With a long suffering sigh, the priest went back to the saddle bags and retrieved her bag of dreamleaf along with the small pot the bag was tucked in. He filled the pot with water and set it on the fire to heat. Templer then strode over to the blankets. Without warning, the man scooped up the entire pile, woman included. He instantly felt guilty when he felt her body stiffen and her breath hissed out in a soft curse.

"Sorry." The man whispered in her ear as he carried her over to the fire. Templer settled his armload as gently as he could against the same flat rock that the Trinity had rested on. Chrysta leaned back against its warm surface, her eyes tightly shut in a face made pale by pain. She did manage a smile when he brought her a freshly brewed cup of coffee. The woman quietly sipped it as she watched the Talon strap the now holstered Trinity back into its place on his lean hips. He was not aware of her contemplative gaze as his long fingers systematically tied the straps that kept the big gun secured down to his thigh. When he straightened, all the man saw was her holding out her cup with an entirely TOO innocent look on her face.

Templer snagged the empty cup as the pot of water started to boil. Here he hesitated. The priest realized that he had no clue on how to prepare the dangerous drug. Azra moved forward in his mind.

"Let me do this... Constantine. It is not something you want to play with." The outrider's voice dropped to a whisper. **"You need to ask her what she weighs."**

"Hnnn... I... DON'T... THINK... SO!" The gunman turned all responsibility over to the demon. "I am NOT that stupid!"

"FINE..." Azra sounded put out... it made no difference to Templer... the immortal bastard was on his own with this one!

"Ehem.... If you would please Chrysta, I need to know your exact weight."

The outrider's words were excruciatingly polite.

Templer hid smile behind the rim of his cup. This disappeared when he sneaked a sideways peek and caught the quick look of apprehension that flitted across his companion's quiet face. The Talon could not blame her. He would think twice before allowing another person to mix up a dose of anything for himself. Let alone a drug that could prove lethal if prepared wrong! Chrysta winced as she tried to shift into a more comfortable position and Constantine could see the exact moment she resigned herself to trusting in the demon's knowledge.

"I am one hundred and forty-eight pounds,

give or take an ounce or two."

She pulled her blankets a little tighter about her body and somehow managed to look even more miserable.

"**Constantine... I need the use of your hands.**"

Templer had to ruthlessly quell the instinct that made him automatically fight the demon's request. After a short struggle with himself, the man found he was able to step back in his mind and watch what his outrider did with detached interest. Azra poured a small amount of the crushed herb into the palm of his bio-engineered blade-hand. The priest knew that the demon was using the incredibly sensitive circuitry within the construct as a highly accurate scale.

"**Are you closer to the minimum dose or the max for your physiology?**"

Templer's brows arched up as he silently applauded the stealthy way Azra was working out just exactly how much resistance the woman had built up against the powerful drug.

Chrysta leaned her head back with a sigh.

"I am two grams off of the maximum dose... Azra."

Templer noted that one shaking hand surreptitiously rubbed the spot where that awful scar started as she quietly continued...

"And I don't NEED any lip from either of you!"

The gunman swallowed what he had been about to say and was the only one to hear Azra's soft rumble of displeasure as the demon added a bit more to the small amount nestled in his palm.

Dropping the dried leaves into a slotted metal tea ball, Azra placed it carefully into the cup and poured the boiling water over it. The outrider was just as precise in the time he allowed the leaves too steep as he had been in measuring out the dose. When he finally removed the ball the demon spent a few moments carefully scrutinized the steaming amber fluid. Templer had to ask.

"What are you looking for?"

Using the tip of one elongated talon, Azra flicked a minute piece of leaf that had escaped the ball, out of the cup.

"You should NEVER ingest the actual leaf." The demon relinquished control back over to his host. **"You go ahead and take this on over... I would rather not be the one to hand it to her."**

Templer handed the waiting woman her cup. He had to suppress a shudder as she blew on the vile brew to cool it, then sipped it in careful mouthfuls. The herb tasted as bad as it smelled. The priest had decided the night before that he would rather go back under the Maker's knives then let another mouthful of the stuff pass his lips!

By the time the tonic kicked in and Chrysta got things unlocked enough to get up to get dressed, Constantine had the rest of the camp packed into their saddle bags. The sound of a throat being cleared snapped his attention back to his companion. She stood casually, dressed in her pants, tight fitting riding boots and a pretty, soft pink...

"BRASSIERE!" Azra helpfully interjected.

Templer flinched as she held up what remained of her shirt. It was missing the top two buttons and with the back practically in ribbons, there was not much shirt left! Chrysta grinned and thanked him when the gunman did the gentlemanly thing and removing his black shirt he draped it over her shoulders.

Azra was snickering.

"It's a good thing you don't sunburn!"

"Azra..." Templer was interrupted.

"Yeah, yeah... I know... Shut up!"

Late morning had them breaking out of the forest and climbing a rough path to the top of a narrow ridge line. It had taken Chrysta very little time to saddle the two destria and get ready to move out with Templer helping where he could. The gunman   picked up enough pointers from the competent woman, that if need be, he felt he could saddle a WILLING destria on his own. They started out at an easy walk. Chrysta's prediction that Zephyr would be stiff was proven accurate. Both animals seemed to have no lingering damage and they were now moving along at fast canter.

As they reached the top, Chrysta reined Zephyr in and walked him to where she could overlook the valley. As Nuva came up alongside, Templer took in a scene he did not know still existed on this tired, old world. The land opened up at the base of the ridge in a wide, oval bowl. From one side to the other it was an even mix of old hardwoods and open meadows. Small, shining streams intertwined through it and there was even a small lake at the far end. Chrysta curled her good leg around her saddle horn and just sat looking with envy in her eyes.

"Don Diego owns this. Ten thousand acres of untouched wild land." Her lip curled a little. "He calls it an... investment. I call it paradise." The woman gave a soft sigh and turned Zephyr back to the path. Templer heard her mutter softly, "I wish it were mine and Diego had a feather up his ass!"

"WHAT?"

Azra answered the gunman's confused question.

"She means they would both be tickled."

"Oh..."

The priest did not point out she would have to be a man to bring this about. The Order did not allow women to own land. He wasn't sure how to address her statement, so he chose silence as the wisest course of action and just kept his mouth shut. They eventually came to a place where the path dipped back down. It split into three routes. One dropped into the lovely valley. One followed a winding, switch backed route until it paralleled the river into a dark, narrow canyon and the other continued along the ridge. Chrysta stopped again, seemed to hesitate than took the path along the ridge. At the gunman's questioning look she explained.

"The lower path is the shorter route... BUT... that canyon is called Splatter Canyon for a reason. I would have to be damned desperate to go that way. Winning a race just wouldn't be worth the risk."

They rode on in silence. Templer wondered if the woman was having second thoughts about their intimacy the night before. Even for her, she was being unusually quiet. The Talon was having a few problems with it himself. It did not help that every time he tried to analyze the situation, it stirred up such an unsettling brew of emotions that his mind kept shying away from it.

Azra picked up on the guilt and fear swirling generously in the mix and finally intervened.

"What gives Constantine?"

His gravelly voice was pitched low to keep the conversation private. The priest realized by the tensing in the other rider's shoulders she was probably picking up on some of his emotional storm. He snarled softly to himself as he slowed Nuva, putting a little distance between them. The woman's sensitivity to emotion caused a whole other set of problems in a relationship. With his few friends, Templer could hide his face between the lowered brim of his hat and the high collar of his cloak. His emotions he hid behind a cold mask. With Chrysta, hiding was a little more complicated.

The gunman answered the demon with a question of his own. There was a lot that had been bothering him since Chrysta repaired the rift in the fabric of his mind. This topped the long list and Azra was probably the only being he knew capable of answering it.

"Azra... am I still mortal?"

"No Host... you are not. At least not in the true sense of the word. Your life CAN be wrested from you but whoever attempted this would have to destroy me first. As you well know... that is not an easy thing to accomplish!"

"It is quite possible then that I will outlive every person on the planet?"

This time there was a slight pause before he got an answer.

"Yes... Constantine. Everything that you once knew has already fallen under the iron fist of time. I expect that you again will see all you know and love crumble into dust. There is a good chance this will happen many times before our journey is done."

"I see."

Templer rode in silence as the implications of what his outrider said slowly sank in. A Talon's training prepared him for the fact that being bonded made him very hard to kill. Still, once an elemental had spent its strength, its host was vulnerable. It was proof of their very violent lives that most Talons did not live long enough to retire. The bonding also slowed the aging process but, it did not STOP it. At least this was usually the case. He was different and the Order not only KNEW this... they had been hiding it from him! There were Five centuries he could not recall. Eighty years had passed since he remembered strapping on the Trinity for the first time. The rare times he glanced in a mirror and did not appear a day older, should have raised all kinds of questions in his mind. The fact that his memories BEGAN on the day he took his... Templer winced as some of his deeper Bindings flared into life. Shards of glass tore through his head as his Vows tried to force him away from this train of thought. Ah... so that answered this particular question. Up ahead Chrysta turned towards him with a questioning look on her face. The Talon waved her on as he blinked away hot tears of pain. He reluctantly shunted those questions away for another time.

Constantine's dark gaze again settled on the trim form riding ahead of him. The events of the night before re-played through his head and the priest used all of his iron will to push the images into an internal vault and lock them away. He could not let it happen again. Azra stirred but Templer cut him off before the outrider said a word.

"Don't even try, demon... I do not know how to handle the loss of every man, woman or child I allow myself to get close to. The only way I can keep my sanity is to just... not... care!"

There was a small flash of anger at his use of the D word but this did not stop his outrider from speaking.

"Isn't this something that all living things deal with eventually, be they mortal or not? Even the lowly dove mourns the loss of its mate."

"It's something a NORMAL person would likely deal with a few times in their lives. Azra... I don't think I can face that kind of loss time and time again as death continues to pass me by."

The outrider flinched at the desolation rolling through his host's mind. He was all too familiar with the pain of losing EVERYTHING that one held dear. His sigh was a soft rumble in Templer's mind.

"This is something you will have to work out for yourself. I truly do not know how to help. I will say this Templer Constantine. Eternity is a very long time to be alone!"

Without any direction from her rider, Nuva slowed her pace even more. Chrysta was so preoccupied she didn't seem to notice.

An odd itch developed behind Templer's eyes. As the man absentmindedly reached up to rub his forehead, he was reminded of how he had seen Chrysta do that same thing... many times.

A soft, sweet voice rumbled through him. It was so utterly different from the other voice that usually played in his head that the priest looked around for another person.

"DARKFIRE..."

The words hissing through his mind echoed with age and had a definitely feminine flavor to them.

"Thisss iss what your Lifessstream looksss like now."

A vision of velvet darkness was inserted behind his eyes. A long chain of gold tarnished to brass braided with one of ebony black wove and spun through the emptiness. On one end was a black stone that absorbed the light so completely it looked like nothing more than a dis-embodied shadow.

Nuva stopped and a sky blue eye gleamed as she looked back at him

"Thisss isss what it could be!"

Again there was that velvet black but this
time the chain flowed gleaming in the darkness.
Its golden portion glowed, clean and bright. The
shimmering ebony was braided into it and
together the two seemed as one. The black stone
still anchored the end, but it had been faceted
and polished until it flashed with an unusual
black and gold flame. Interspersed along the
chain where six extraordinary gems. Somehow
Templer just KNEW that each jewel represented
one of the friends that he tried so hard to keep
away from his heart. One glowed a lovely blue.
This was the color of a summer sky. It was as
deep and steady as the strength than ran through
Blade. Chyanne's was a deep velvet red. This one
glowed like the sun shining through a glass of
the rich burgundy wine he loved. Iniko's gem,
much to his surprise, was a steady glimmering
topaz. The clear gold captured the true honesty
that the girl tried so desperately to hide. Skye
was a Sky Queen, so it was a surprise that hers
flowed with the subtle greens of a deep ocean
current. Maybe this had something to do with her
having been raised by a sea wolf? Sig's was a
smooth gleaming silver stone that seemed to
swirl with the mercurial ever flowing fire of
quicksilver. A piece of strong granite the color of
steel streaked through with veins of true gold
and the sharp spark of crystal represented
Sloane. The dwarf was a Son of the Mountain
whose powerful body and sharp wit were
tempered by a heart of gold. Further along in the
ever-dark he could see places on the chain
waiting for him to find and set other priceless
gems.

Templer's heart ached at the thought of
watching these friends leave this world one at a
time... but along with this was the sure
knowledge of how empty his long life would be
without them.

"Yesss... Your Lifessstream MAY flow to eternity. Just imagine what a wonderful thing of beauty it could become, Hmmmm?"

The Talon closed his eyes in order to capture the vision of that lovely chain forever in his mind.

He realized there was a jewel missing. And he asked curiously,

"What does Chrysta's essence look like?"

The sweet voice chuckled and answered slyly.

"AHHH now... That iss sssomething... you... shall have to find out on your own... isssn't it? Darkfire... one lifessstream isss eassy. It sspins out forever empty. It will remain eternally dark. The other includesss pain and ssacrifice but... oh... the beauty you shall achieve! It isss your decision, beloved. Which future will you choose?"

Slowly, the exquisite vision darkened and was replaced by the day's ordinary sunshine. Templer reached forward and ran his fingers through the cream's silky mane.

He had no true way to thank the elegant mare. Nuva's blue eye winked at him and the itch faded. The cream trotted forwards again, neck arched and tail flagged. She was clearly quite pleased with herself.

They caught up with their companions as Chrysta started to turn down an overgrown path and catching herself, doubled back to the main one. She looked around with a slightly bewildered look on her face that cleared as Nuva came alongside the big black.

"There you are!" she flashed a quick smile at him. "I was worried we had lost you there for a moment."

As the woman pushed Zephyr back up into a

canter, she didn't hear Azra murmur.

"That is funny... I was just thinking much the same thing!"

Chrysta stopped a couple of times to check her maps and it soon became clear to the priest she was developing a route that shaved distance while keeping to relatively open terrain. She explained that although Inferno had incredible speed, his agility wasn't the strongest in the field. The rider had to choose her course keeping that in mind. Constantine traced a finger along their path and found the small trail she had almost turned down.

"Where does this lead?" he asked.

Seemingly startled by the question, Chrysta slashed him a quick look and her open face became guarded. The woman folded the map. As she turned Zephyr back to lope along the path she had chosen, she answered in a clipped tone.

"It goes to Forrest's grave."

It took them until midafternoon to make it back to the edge of town. Templer tried very hard to ignore the many contemplative looks they seemed to attract as they rode down the main street. He could not see the attractive contrast they made as they rode along. The tall woman dressed in black, mounted on the dark, golden eyed Zephyr was a perfect foil for his own bare shouldered, dark haired, pale beauty mounted on the elegant cream.

As they turned into the now familiar courtyard, Chrysta called Andrew over to them. She dismounted and was already removing the tired animal's tack.

"I need you to go find the race council and let them know there is a large pack of Rapines hunting along the lower river route. Tell them there are at least twenty left."

Templer watched as the young man silently took in the long cuts on Zephyr and Nuva. His quick gaze flicked over the Trinity resting in its holster on the gunman's hip and noted the fact that Chrysta was wearing the Talon's spider-silk shirt. The young man gave him a quick respectful nod. Then he took to his heels, heading down the alley and out to the street.

The two riders made short work of getting the black and cream cared for and settled into their paddocks. Chrysta was very quiet as they worked. Templer could not help but wonder if her silence resulted from their tryst or if there was another cause. As they passed El Diablo, the stallion rumbled deep in his throat. When Templer looked his way, the beast bared his fangs in what looked like a knowing, nasty smile. Chrysta hesitated at the sound. Without looking at the silver male, she continued on into the Inn. The gunman lagged back a little just catching the worried expression on Grant's face as the woman slipped up the stairs without stopping to see him. It was a Talon who made a point of stopping.

The gunman's black eyes studied the other man's face and Grant looked away with a barely concealed sigh. Templer caught the barman's wrist with his human hand.

"What am I missing?"

He did not release the man when he tried to pull away.

Grant looked up the stairs for a moment.

"I would appreciate it if you could make sure Chrysta comes downstairs for dinner tonight. I would rather she not be alone at all."

Templer let the big man go.

"Would you mind telling me why?"

Grant smiled sadly at him.

"I just like to keep an eye on her on the anniversary of Forrest's death. She doesn't deal with it well at all."

That evening, the priest tried every trick in the book to convince Chrysta to go down to the common room. She resisted to the point that finally in exasperation, Templer snatched her up. He threw her over his shoulder and ignoring her struggles, headed down the stairs. Half way down she hissed "FINE...have it your way!" Templer set her on her feet. Chrysta straightened out her clothes while giving the man the evil eye. Then complying reluctantly with his earlier request, the woman continued down the stairs under her own power.

Grant settled them at a back table. Ignoring her dirty look, the man set a bowl of thick stew in front of her and a beer and small bottle of Anesthetic in front of the silent gunman. He gave Templer a stern look.

"She has to eat first."

Grant transferred his hard gaze to the quiet woman.

"Just to be clear... this is ALL the alcohol I am letting you have."

Her eyes flashed up in anger.

"I can always go to another bar, Grant."

"I think that would be over our very... dead... bodies!"

Azra's deep voice was grim. Elemental fire sparked at the tips of the Talon's blade-hand as the outrider made his point. He could be as stubborn as the best of them.

Chrysta glanced at Templer. He leaned back, crossed his arms and nodded in agreement with his demon. He had to crush the guilt that welled up in his breast as the anger faded, leaving her eyes the same flat dead color the Talon had seen the night before. The look she gave all three of them made it eloquently clear what the woman thought about their ganging up on her.

Grant's ploy worked in that Chrysta finished her meal. Her eyes had at least shifted more to green then gray when Templer poured her a small glass of the potent blue liqueur. The gunman sipped his beer and watched as they greened up a little more when the woman noticed the larger than usual crowd of tourist's.

Grant was preoccupied at the bar when Azra gave his host a slight conspiratorial nudge.

"The guy in the blue is packing."

This got Templer's attention.

"What?"

Azra spoke slowly and there was an odd note in his voice.

"I... said... The guy in the blue is packing iron. The little man in the red shirt has a knife in his boot!"

Chrysta had looked up, and she saw the strange expression that crossed the gunman's face. A small smile played around her mouth.

"If you are really going do this, once it starts, just stay the hell out of his way."

She watched as Templer scooped up her empty bowl along with his beer glass and headed toward the bar. A nudge here, a bump there and eddies of discontent whirled through the crowded room following the general path that the gunman took. He had just reached the bar when with the crash of breaking dishes, all hell broke loose.

Templer just barely managed to step back as Grant came OVER the bar. The big man moved with a speed and grace the belied his size. He was there when the knife came out of the "little man's" boot. Grant caught the man's wrist and twisting it, forced the knife to drop. He used that man as a shield to block a fist from another fighter and kicked that one's feet out from under him. Tossing the knife wielder into a struggling knot of drunken combatants the older man moved on. Grant seemed to flow through the fight. Where ever he paused and applied his fists or feet, men found themselves suddenly sleeping on the hard floor.

Templer leaned back against the bar to watch, impressed in spite of himself. The bartender reached the man with the gun at the same time he was dumb enough to draw it. Blue shirt found his hand, and the gun engulfed in the big man's hard grip. Grant held him effortlessly, waggled his finger in the universal "no you don't" sign and floored the wanna-be gunslinger with a fist between the eyes. Constantine glanced Chrysta's way and saw she had not moved from her seat. The woman watched the big man clear his bar with an appreciative gleam in her now sparkling eyes. Noticing the priest's glowing gaze looking her way, the woman raised her glass of anesthetic in a silent toast.

It took Grant a total of three minutes to get the fight stopped. Those that didn't want their asses handed to them scurried out the door and those that had less intelligence were unceremoniously thrown out. The patron's that were smart enough not to get involved, (mainly locals, Templer noticed) gave the bartender a standing ovation as the last fighter rather forcefully exited the bar!

It took the three of them along with the staff, a good half hour to clean up the resulting mess. Listening to Chrysta's occasional chuckle as she rehashed parts of the fight with the barman and seeing the worried lines relax around the Grant's brown eyes, made having to mop the common room floor TWICE worth it. By the time the Talon finished, Chrysta had gone upstairs to soak in her bath. Grant shooed Templer away, maintaining that he and his staff could manage the rest of the night.

Chrysta was still in her bath when he got up to the room. The sharp smell of dreamleaf floated in the warm air. Templer couldn't help but notice that there was a glass of red wine on the night stand by the bed and a book rested beside it. He was comfortably sprawled across the coverlet, sipping the wine, and working his way through the third chapter of a slow mystery when Chrysta came out of the bathroom. She did not notice that his eyes followed her over the pages of the book as she stood in front of the window and watched El Diablo for a long moment.

"Do you want to tell me about it?"

The man kept his voice soft and nonthreatening.

Chrysta didn't turn away from the window,

"What I would really like, is to not sleep alone tonight."

She turned and gave the prone gunman a hopeful look. He slid over and held the covers up, inviting her in.

Chrysta limped over and slid in next to him. She arranged herself so that she was curled against his left side. Templer carefully slid his blade-hand under her strong shoulders and shifted her closer allowing her to rest her head lightly on his shoulder. The Talon kept his attention on the written page in front of him as her hand slid up to rest lightly on his chest. The woman was so quiet, at first he thought she had fallen asleep. When he glanced down, the gunman realized she was watching his face as he read in the dim light of the room. Her lips twitched up at the corners a little when she realized he was looking at her. She poked him with a stiff finger.

"I have read that one already. Do ya want me to tell you who done it?"

Constantine casually turned the page.

"Only if you want to spend the next night or two out in the barn with Nuva."

He was secretly pleased when this was answered by a quiet chuckle. Marking his spot in the chapter with one talon, the gunman turned a little so he could see his bed-mate's face.

"Speaking of Nuva, we had a short but enlightening conversation today. She is very wise."

Chrysta's eyes widened slightly.

"Well... they do say that great wisdom comes with age. Nuva is quite old."

"Hnnn,"

Templer continued to look at her expectantly.

"How... old... is old?"

The woman squirmed a little. The fingers resting on his chest twisted themselves into the soft fabric of his shirt.

"Nuva was my first mount. She was also my father's first mount, my grandfather's first mount, and my..." She hesitated here and he could feel the fingers do a quick tapping count. "...umm, great, great... great grandfather's favorite mare."

Azra, who had been slumbering lightly in the back of Templer's mind (HE did not like mysteries, he MUCH preferred good old gruesome horror stories) jerked awake.

"Did I hear that right?"

Chrysta shifted away from him and sat up. She punched the pillows into a big ball so she could lean against them.

"Yes, you heard it right. If you tell Nuva I am the one who told you, I will vigorously deny it."

Templer set the book down as an unsettling thought occurred to him.

"Mother of Demons, will El Diablo live that long?"

The priest could see some serious ramifications if this were the case.

The woman glanced in the direction of the window, and Constantine heard her softly mutter.

"Not if HE has anything to say about it."

Then she returned her attention to Templer's face.

"As near as we can tell, the destria trace their bloodlines back to Hell. It is rumored that they evolved from some type of wingless dragon, courtesy of the Re-gen plague. They ALL use to live a very long time but that trait has been bred out. Their average lifespan is now approximately seventy years. One of the things that was also bred out of them is intelligence. A smart destria equals a dangerous destria. Every now and then though, a breeder will get a throwback. These animals are usually dangerously intelligent and if they don't CHOOSE to be with humans, well... let's just say you have a serious problem that lives a very long time!"

Her voice trailed off.

Templer winced. He asked his question already knowing what her answer would be. After all, this sort of thing was a part of his job description.

"Why would ANY intelligent being voluntarily CHOOSE a life of servitude?"

Chrysta snorted,

"I think Nuva does it just for the entertainment factor."

The woman's lips twisted as if her next words tasted foul.

"There is no choice really, the alternative is... terrible."

The gunman's stomach rolled when Azra, his voice a low, soft growl asked,

"And just what is their other... choice?"

Chrysta's voice came out as soft as a breath. Even with his enhanced hearing, the Talon had to lean towards the woman to catch her words.

"They are drugged, abused, and twisted into insanity. Then they are forced to fight in the pits."

Templer had a split second of stunned shock

to process what she had said. Then Azra came completely unhinged. The man couldn't control his muscles sudden recoil as the outrider tried to claw his way out in a howling rage. The Talon ended up clear across the room on his hands and knees, locked in a frightening struggle for dominance.

As Templer's eyes flashed from black to hot gold, Chrysta bailed out of the bed. The struggling man was between her and the door. She hesitated, watching those gleaming black talons dig deep gouges in the hardwood floor as the man fought for control. Chrysta stifled a scream as the mental barriers she maintained started to crumble under the overwhelming emotional onslaught that rolled through the room. She found herself drowning in the waves of hate and rage that poured out of the Talon as his form wavered in a mist of black and red. The woman knew she had been lucky the first time she had dealt with outrider's savage temper. She did the wise thing and took the only other way out of the room.

Templer didn't know how long they struggled. When he was finally able to push Azra into retreat, the very air around his body was white hot and pulsing with unreleased energy. There was no safe outlet for the powerful surge. If he did the easy thing and just let it go, the blast would level the building... possibly even the entire block. The Talon's nervous system screamed as he took precious seconds to buffer the elemental power. Once he felt he had some control, he pulled it back, allowing the molten tide to return to its vessel. His vision sheeted to red in agony. Azra was designed to absorb this kind of energy... Templer was not. The priest had never attempted to do anything like this without his outrider's direct participation. He doubted he would ever attempt it again!

When he could finally see again Templer

remained where he was. The priest drew in harsh, shuddering breaths as he rested on his hands and knees between the bed and door. He heard footsteps flying up the stairs and the door blasted open as Grant just about kicked it off of its hinges. Constantine found himself in the unenviable position of staring down the double barrels of a sawed off shotgun. Not sure if even Azra could repair a head splattered all over the wall, the gunman wisely froze. Grant took in the shredded floor, the scorched wood and the other man's weary features. The barman's voice was eerily calm

"What in the seven HELLS is going on?!!"

Templer noticed with approval that the shotgun never wavered.

"I apologize for the damage. Azra and I had a slight... disagreement."

He remained very still as Grant's eyes surveyed the rest of the room. The priest tensed when the man's finger tightened imperceptibly on the trigger.

The big man's voice came out in a growl.

"Where is Chrysta?"

Templer realized that the woman was not in the room.

"I am sure I frightened her." The priest felt a sharp stab of guilt.

"She probably did the smart thing and got the hell out of here."

Grant frowned and the shotgun dipped a little.

"That's odd, I didn't see her pass me on the stairs."

Constantine had been waiting. When the shotgun dipped, he shot forward, flesh hand closing in such a way that the hammer on the lethal weapon couldn't fall. As good as Grant was, the Talon got possession of the shotgun. He had the big man's arm twisted behind him, before the Grant could draw his next breath. The wide open window caught Templer's attention.

He carefully applied pressure, causing the captive man to give in such a way that he turned to where he could see it too.

"I believe she went through the window." Templer kept his voice calm.

Grant sagged a little in relief. Then jerked in the gunman's tight grip.

"Wait!" The bartender was almost whispering. "You FRIGHTENED her badly enough that she felt she HAD to go out a second story window... SHIT!"

Grant twisted suddenly and broke the Talon's hold. He practically flew to the window. Templer followed more slowly, a little confused. He had been in and out of the window many times. He knew, even with her fear of heights, Chrysta could negotiate the climb easily.

"Damn!" Grant was panicked. Templer didn't understand why.

"It's too dark, I can't see her." The Talon stepped closer to the window. His enhanced sight had no problem with the dark. He could see Chrysta. She was unharmed and evidently had stopped just as she reached the barn door. He could also see El Diablo safely locked in his paddock, stalking along the fence towards her. There was no way for the big silver to get out. Templer was just about to tell the other man that he could relax, when the woman turned and started back. He noticed there was something odd in the way she moved. All of the woman's easy grace was gone. As she limped along the fence line, El Diablo followed, maintaining his distance. A serious shudder of unease passed over the Talon as he caught a glimpse of Chrysta's face. It was deathly pale. Her lips were pressed together so tightly that they were white. The unease flashed to fear as he realized that her eyes were glowing the same feral ice green as the eyes of the battle stallion ghosting along behind her.

"What the hell!?"

This slipped past the gunman's lips in a whisper.

"WHAT?" Grant finally caught a glimpse of what was going on.

"SHIT!"

The man turned and went flying out the door. That was enough for Templer. He dropped out of the window, landing lightly in the courtyard below just as the woman reached slowly for the lock on the gate. Constantine realized that even with his speed he wasn't going to reach her in time. Every action seemed to slow. His unnatural eyesight clearly saw her hand open the latch. El Diablo reared behind the electrified gate, his guttural, anticipatory WAH WAH WAH echoing in the darkness. Templer remembered how Zephyr had taken that position in preparation for a killing strike. Chrysta had called it Levade. The gunman had covered three quarters of the distance when the electric circuit was broken. The gate swung open. Chrysta just stood passively and watched as her death towered over her. Templer could see one of the guards come running from the barn but the man didn't have a clear shot. He knew he couldn't risk using the shotgun with her that close to the target.

"Mother of Demons..." The priest tried to move faster but knew deep down he was not going to reach her in time.

There was a sound like thunder and he

caught a flash of white as fury incarnate came sailing over her paddock fence. Nuva landed hard. She slid past Templer in a shower of sparks. As she reached the woman, the mare spun. A hind leg lashed out to catch the gate, slamming it closed on the startled stallion. El Diablo's frustrated scream echoed through the courtyard. The beast twisted away as he tried to avoid a painful shock. Nuva placed her big body between her trainer and the re-imprisoned stallion. She snaked her head around in a threat display, her vivid eyes glowing gem bright.

Templer heard Grant run up behind as the gunman managed to slip past the furious mare and re-lock the gate. He turned and saw Chrysta's eyes flicker between feral green and sky blue. Nuva seemed to win the mental tug of war as they flashed blue once more than faded to their normal green and gold. A look of anguish crossed the woman's face as she lifted a shaking hand to rub her forehead. Templer saw her eyelashes flutter queerly and that is all the warning he got. Chrysta's eyes rolled to white and her body dropped. The Talon's inhumanly fast reflexes saved her from hitting the hard flagstones. Easing her limp form to the ground. Templer ran a careful hand over it, trying to see if there was any physical damage. The gunman could feel her heart hammering away through the sensors in his hand. Her skin felt clammy and cold.

Grant knelt next to him. His face was worried when he checked the pulse in her wrist. Templer gathered the woman up in his arms, lifting her with ease.

"I believe she is in shock. We need to get her inside."

It took him little time to get her back up the stairs. It took even less to strip and tuck her still form into the warm bed. Templer was relieved when he felt that frighteningly rapid heart rate ease back to a more normal rhythm. Grant followed him up a little more slowly. The barman took a moment to stop and grab a bottle of good brandy and some glasses from the bar.

When the he came through the door, Templer turned from the bed, crossed his arms, and pinned the man with a fierce glare.

"Would you mind telling me, what the HELL just happened?"

The Talon's deceptively soft, grim voice made it clear he expected some answers... NOW!

Grant set the brandy and glasses on the table and slipped past the gunman to satisfy himself that Chrysta was okay. Templer watched him intently, but didn't say a word. The barman returned to sit at the table and he poured the amber liqueur with hands that were shaking. The Talon walked over and settled one hip on the window sill. In the shadowed room, all that Grant could see of the man was his tall, dark silhouette, and the subdued gleam of that wicked blade-hand. More disconcerting was the glimmer of eyes that glowed like the coals of a banked fire.

Taking a drink from his glass, the barman hesitated before answering.

"THAT... Was almost a repeat of what happened six years ago. I don't understand the mechanics of it. Chrysta could explain better than I, but if he..." One blunt fingered hand waved toward El Diablo's paddock. "...can catch her while she is emotionally agitated, with her guard down. He can follow the fear or anger into her head and force a link. If she can't get her shields up in time. The fucker can lock HER down in much the same way that Chrysta does it to him."

The shadowed man's glowing eyes dimmed a little and his talons tapped a restless tattoo on his folded arm.

"So... when I frightened her enough to make her escape out the window, El Diablo took advantage of her distraction?"

This was murmured in a tone loaded with self-loathing.

Azra stirred from the sleep that Templer had forced him into.

"What have I missed?"

The rage from earlier had burnt itself out and the demon sounded infinitely weary.

"WE... were responsible for almost causing another tragedy."

The gunman's words were short and clipped.

Templer "felt" the Outrider ruffle through his recent memories. Azra flinched as he took in the damaged floor, Grant's troubled face and the woman lying pale and still on the bed.

"I am truly sorry Constantine."

This was a soft whisper. The priest didn't answer. He had no forgiveness in him, either for Azra, or for himself.

"There is no need to apologize, Azra." This came from the bed.

Chrysta had her eyes closed, but Templer could tell from the increase in her heart rate that she was fully awake. She sighed and those exotic green eyes opened.

"You can't fault a living being that is only being TRUE to its nature." She slanted a sly glance at Grant and the brandy. "I HOPE you intended some of that for me?"

Grant managed a smile and poured some into the glass that Templer had ignored. He was startled when the other man, moving so quickly and quietly that he just seemed to appear, scooped up the drink... and carried it over to Chrysta. Templer knelt and helped her to take a drink of the rich warm, alcohol. The woman let her fingers linger for a moment on his hand. She didn't try to prevent it when he withdrew.

It was a Talon rose and stepped back. His stern

face was as cold as alabaster.

"So, do you want to give me an official explanation as to why something as dangerous as El Diablo is still walking in the land of the living?"

Chrysta pushed herself up a little on the pillows. She was clearly uncomfortable with having him stand over her. The priest relented to the extent that he retrieved a chair and sat down next to the bed.

"I am sure you realize that El Diablo is one of the "throw backs" that we were discussing earlier. He did NOT choose to submit to human control and was well on his way to the Pits when he killed his trainer."

Chrysta watched the Talon's reaction carefully. Azra twitched a little but stayed subdued.

"I interfered when his original owner wanted to euthanize him. The stallion became my responsibility at this point. He HATES me with a passion that only an old line destria can achieve. In El Diablo's eyes, I prevented him from being released from a life he finds unbearable. Nuva convinced me to keep trying with him, as he is very, very young in her eyes. She felt he could be recovered. I actually trusted in her judgment when Silver Flame CHOSE to serve Thranatos. HOLY... those two were MADE for each other."

Chrysta paused, pressing her fingers tight against her temples. Templer wordlessly handed her the glass of brandy.

She took a sip and continued.

"It seemed like we had the problem solved. Silver Flame worshiped Tynan. He was content to have Forrest work with him and even tolerated me to an extent. Then the Prince started visiting us less and less. It was okay at first, a young stallion needs time to grow and mature before he is asked to do much. Silver Flame seemed to be content with seeing his chosen sporadically. The last couple of times he came, Thranatos was DIFFERENT. He had always been aloof and more than a little cold. But now he became downright fey. He seemed very unstable.

On his last visit, I went out to the barn to take care of the evening chores and found him with one of the barmaids. Mother of Demons Templer... I am pretty sure what he was doing wasn't rape. The girl seemed to be enjoying herself. But pleasure or not, I am positive that if I had not intervened she would have surely died. As it was, her blood loss was life threatening. When I disturbed them, Tynan left her and had me against the wall before I could even blink."

Chrysta took a long swallow of her brandy and the look she gave Templer was full of questions.

"I KNOW that Tynan is Vamphyrr. This in itself makes him very dangerous. Still up until this point, he had always treated the women at the Ironwood with nothing but polite courtesy. This time... when he looked at me, there was nothing human in his eyes. All I could see was lust and hunger."

Templer picked up Grant's bottle and refilled her drink.

"That sounds like he was in Rut."

At her look of confusion, Templer leaned forward and tilted her glass with a gentle finger, making the woman take another drink. He was glad to see a little color returning to her face.

"You and the maid were very lucky to get out of that barn alive. Once every few years vamphyrr, be they male or female, go into Rut. It can come on very sudden and with little warning. The first time or two can make or break them. It takes an iron will to overcome their dragon legacy. If they fail, it will strip any humanity left and replace it with a mindless need for blood and sex. Thranatos is young for a vamphyrr. This may have been his first one. Tynan might not have recognized the signs in time to leave. During the Rut, the hunger for blood and desire for sex become... difficult... to control. Another of their kind can deal with them in this heightened state... most human's don't have the strength required. If they are in the wrong place at the wrong time... they simply die."

The Talon shrugged as he sat back. This was putting it nicely. More than once he had been called in to deal with rogue vamphyrr. The victims he had seen who had died from simple blood loss had been the lucky ones. A vamphyrr's body could continue long past the point that a human would die from exhaustion. Add to this the fact that many of the breed were NOT gentle lovers... Templer shunted the gruesome memories aside.

"This is one of the reasons that casual mingling within the two races is highly discouraged!"

Chrysta snorted at this dry disclaimer but could not quite bring herself to laugh outright.

"I got lucky. Nuva and Zephyr realized that I was in trouble and they tried to tear the barn down. Forrest and a couple of the prince's guard came out to investigate. It took all three of them to pull him off of me. Tynan departed that night and has not been back since. When he left, the prince broke his bond. El Diablo did not understand and felt he had been betrayed. He quietly went from being just unstable to being completely insane. He does NOT want to live his life under any human's control and constantly searches for a way OUT. Not only is he looking to suicide, but because he knows I had something to do with his bond-mates disappearance, El Diablo would LOVE to drag me into death with him!"

Azra rumbled softly,

"If he is insane and suffering, why do you not... accommodate... him? That would be the humane thing to do."

Chrysta closed her eyes for a long moment. She absentmindedly turned the glass around and around in her hands. When she glanced back at the still gunman. Her eyes were dark, her face haunted.

"Yes... well... that decision was taken out of our hands six years ago." She hesitated before continuing.

"El Diablo is only twenty years old. For an old bloodline, he is still considered a baby. Even so he is probably one of the most intelligent destria I have run across. No... He doesn't have the WISDOM that Nuva has, but it would come in time. Now it is just an ability to think and plan. And the bastard DOES plan."

Grant gave a short humorless laugh. He had finished one glass of brandy and poured a second. He raised an eyebrow at Chrysta and lifted the bottle. She shook her head and handed her empty glass to Templer.

"For a couple of months we thought it was going to work out all right. You had to be careful around him, but no more so than when you are around any breeding stallion. Forrest had gone in to his paddock to deal with routine care and I was out in the courtyard. Standing rule was, no one dealt with him alone."

Grant stirred.

"I... unfortunately, had stepped out for a little while. A fact I am sure El Diablo was aware of."

Chrysta nodded her agreement.

"Oh yes, HE had been planning this attack probably since the day Thranatos rejected him. El Diablo gave himself enough time he was able to change the chemical composition of his venom."

Templer's eyebrows arched up.

"They can do that?"

Chrysta flicked a quick look his way.

"Only the old line can. Thank God!" She shuddered. "El Diablo, like Nuva, is well aware of my immunity to regular destria venom. So... he changed his. Forrest never had a chance. He had just finished and was walking towards the gate when El Diablo struck. He hit Forrest with one spur, precisely placed along the full length of his spine, instantly immobilizing him. Then he looked right at me and purposely crushed his victim's leg.

When Forrest screamed, I went right OVER the paddock fence... no gun... no sword. Pure instinct drove me and it was as stupid a move as one could make! Of course... that's what El Diablo intended. He picked up on my anger and fear. Then the bastard followed it right in. He FORCED a link..."

Chrysta's face was as pale as death.

"It is like mental rape. I could not stop him and once he was inside, I could NOT get him out. He... LOCKED... and held me. Then systematically broke every bone in Forrest's body."

Templer was pinned and held by eyes the color of dead ice.

"Do you remember that little trick that Nuva pulled the other day when she immobilized that man in Rafe's group?"

The priest nodded slowly. Chrysta closed

those terrible eyes, thankfully releasing him.

"Be well aware they CAN remove someone's head that way."

Tears were tracing silent trails down the woman's face when she turned it away from the frozen Talon.

Grant's rough voice picked up the tale where she had to stop.

"I returned to the Inn and came out the back door just as he was rearing over her like he did tonight. In the space of time it took me to get to my gun, he laid her open like he was filleting a fish. By the time I got a shot off the bastard had already done lethal damage to Chrysta."

Templer's brow furrowed in a sudden dark frown.

"You're a Temple guard. If you shot him, he should be dead!"

Chrysta snorted and turned her head back to look fondly at the older man.

"It was one hell of a good shot. Grant "creased" him. That's where you shoot the third spine along a stallion's neck ridge. The shock of the bullet shattering the spine knocks them out."

Grant solemnly shook his head.

"No it wasn't a good shot. I MISSED my target. I was TRYING to blow his bloody head off. I thought he was dead when I retrieved Chrysta. Thank the Gods I had hexes stock piled as they are scarce in this small town. I couldn't do any kind of real healing because she needed to be surgically put back together. I took stop gap measures. Between that, Nuva, and Dr. Whitet we held her together until I could get hold of one of my contacts and he could get a medical team air lifted to us."

Grant stopped here, noticing Templer's

incredulous look. The big man shrugged self-consciously.

"Hey, I was owed a few favors."

Azra had been silent through the entire tale. When he did speak up, all the human's in the room flinched at the repressed anger they felt roiling through the still air of the room.

"This still does not explain why that son of a bitch IS... NOT...DEAD!"

Grant's face was grim.

"The High Lord of Hell made it very clear when he arranged the air lift that if anything happened to El Diablo there would be... consequences."

Temple could only look in astonishment from the big man back to the woman whose fingers were nervously plucking at the edge of the quilt that covered her. He had wrongly assumed the man had called in favors owed by the Order. Chrysta met his eyes squarely.

"The surgeons who were charged with saving my life had their hands full. El Diablo's altered venom stripped the outer sheath off of the nerves along the wound. There was no way to alleviate the pain this caused. Add to that the emotional trauma and I just really didn't WANT to live. It is really hard to keep someone alive when they keep pulling out all the tubes, wires and stitches. After the third time in surgery to repair the damage I caused to myself, I got a visit from the Crown Prince's father. HE made it very clear he felt El Diablo was my responsibility. If I died, there would be no one to care for him."

For a moment her eyes gleamed impishly.

"I proceeded to tell the insufferable bastard that he could go fuck himself sideways!"

The priest's lips twitched involuntarily. He

could just imagine the powerful Vamphyrr-Lord's response to that.

She saw his reaction.

"Yes... it was almost worth it to see the look on his face."

The gleam faded.

"Then he informed me of the consequences if I died, or if something "unnatural" were to happen to Silver Flame."

The look that Chrysta gave the gunman was perplexed.

"My head couldn't believe that he would go through with the threat, but my heart told me he was deadly serious. I worked VERY hard at staying alive after his visit."

Templer felt a chill run through him.

"What where these... consequences?"

Grant got up and gathered the brandy bottle and empty glasses.

"He said, he would raze the town of Edgewater to the ground."

Chrysta watched silently as Grant slipped out of the door then turned questioning eyes on the quiet Talon.

"Would he have?"

Templer winced. He remembered what history taught about the Head of House Dracul... before the Cataclysm. He told her the truth.

"Yes... rest assured that if you or El Diablo had died, Lord Vlad would have brought all that he is down on this town. The High Lord of Hell does not bluff!"

Templer rose and went to stand by the window. He watched as El Diablo prowled the perimeter of his paddock and thought about what had almost happened this night.

"I cannot believe you have dealt with this for six years!"

She answered the unspoken question that she heard in his voice.

"Hmmm... well...Grant would still kill him in a heartbeat if he thought he could get away with it. I have learned that you can't fault a creature for being true to its nature. I have also begun to understand why he is the way he is. There are fewer and fewer of the old bloodlines cropping up. I see and understand Nuva's fear of losing her heritage entirely. It is my hope to someday be able to somehow... acquire... enough land that I can just turn him out with a few old blood mares to keep him in line and let them live their lives in peace. With age comes wisdom and if we could give him a chance to not HATE and rage all the time, he might still come around."

Chrysta studied the priest for a moment sharp eyes noting the tenseness in his lines. She smiled and patted the bed next to her in a silent invitation.

"I am sorry Chrysta," Templer's deep voice was no more than a soft whisper.

"I need to be alone... to think."

Something flickered in her eyes and the smile saddened a little. She wiggled herself down into the quilt before closing her eyes.

"It's okay Constantine. I understand."

Templer sat in perfect stillness. His black eyes watched until Chrysta's even breathing pattern told him she was deeply asleep. He then slipped quietly out the window and up to the roof. The priest spent the rest of the long night slowly rebuilding the walls around his heart that the woman had managed to tear down in the five short days he had known her.

"Templer..."

Azra tried to intrude, and the Talon patently ignored him.

The man watched the bright silver form of El Diablo prowling his fence line restlessly and added another layer to the wall. Chrysta had her hands full dealing with one monster. She did not need another around to distract her. The almost fatal events of that night had driven that particular point home.

Constantine silently chastised himself for ever letting his guard down enough to care. He was a mortal danger to ANY that got close to him. He could not even blame the Order for this. It rested squarely on his own shoulders. HE had been the one who had chosen to serve, blindly following orders because of a misguided faith. This servant had begun to scratch at the truth, he was blind no longer. The Order might have changed its name, but Templer instinctively knew it and the... Church... he served in the distant past were one and the same.

He had been a willing killer and a fool before the Cataclysm. The five centuries between then and now had only served to twist him into something much darker. Nuva's beautiful chain of jewels was an illusion. He DESERVED that tarnished gold and black, empty chain stretching into eternity.

"Constantine..." His outrider spoke in a low, sad growl.

"Shut up, Azra."

Was the only response he received and to Templer's grateful surprise, the demon silently retreated to the back of his mind.

The sun slowly broke the horizon in a dazzling display of reds, pinks, and gold. The Talon took no pleasure in the sight. It was just another dawn, in a string of empty days that would march on forever. The silent man used this thought to add another layer of nothingness around his aching heart. He knew that once that wall was thick enough, although the pain would still be there, he wouldn't be able to feel it.

The priest shifted position as his acute hearing picked up the sound of Grant knocking at the door of the room. He could smell the inevitable coffee followed by Chrysta's usual grumble.

"Holy... I HATE festival week."

The gunman felt his lips quirk at Grant's ready response.

"So retire, then I wouldn't have to hear you whine."

Templer ruthlessly schooled his features back to the cold visage that the people he knew, would have recognized.

He listened as Grant left the room and heard Chrysta come to the window.

"Constantine, are you up there?"

The words were softly spoken. He did not answer. The priest stayed silent, watching the courtyard without really seeing it. He heard

Chrysta's soft sigh as she turned to get ready for the day.

The smell of dreamleaf wafted up, and the man was amazed at how familiar a smell could become in such a short time. He waited, allowing the morning to flow around him without touching him. This was a trick Templer had used many times to stay disassociated from people and events. He tried to convince himself that this would become easy again... in time.

The gunman watched as Andrew brought Nuva out. The mare was groomed and tacked up for a ride. He was proud of himself when Chrysta came out the door and he was able to observe that odd, flowing limp as she joined the pair in the courtyard, without feeling attachment. He had a harder time squelching the flare of jealousy that rose in his breast as she mounted then gave the young man a hand up to ride behind her. Templer's body reminded him of how pleasant riding that way had been. He ruthlessly crushed those feelings. One could not be jealous if one... did... NOT... care!

Ebony eyes caught the flash of green as Chrysta looked up towards him and lifted her hand in a half wave. He made no move to return it. The woman dropped the hand and slowly gathered her reins. Templer saw a fleeting smile cross her lips, then she turned Nuva and, they headed out of the courtyard.

The priest remained on the roof, wrapped up in his own dark thoughts. When the sun was hot overhead and the noon crowds were wandering in the street, he rose. Templer stretched the kinks out of his lanky frame and returned to the room. It took little time to pack his belongings. He strapped the Trinity on his hip and settled the heavy black cloak over his shoulders. He was threading the last buckle when Azra stirred.

"SO... we are leaving?"

This was a soft whisper in the dark recesses of his mind.

"Hnnn..." was the only answer the outrider received as tucking his chin behind the tall collar of a Talon's signature cloak, Templer strode out the door.

Grant looked up from wiping the bar when the priest came down the stairs. His expressive eyes narrowed as he saw the gunman's bag. They scanned the slender man's pale face and skipped away from whatever they saw in those flat ebony eyes. Templer nodded in the man's direction as he continued through the common room. Grant opened his mouth to say something but the soft chirp of his Cricket interrupted him. The sound of a panicked voice erupted out of it when the barman answered.

Grant spoke in a quiet voice.

"Calm down Andrew, I can't understand you."

Templer's hearing easily picked up the voice on the other end of the phone as the stable hand was practically screaming.

"Grant, ya gotta clear the street..."

There was a loud thump followed by what sounded like the pained grunt of a destria.

This was a civil matter. It was NONE of his business. The Talon continued toward the door. The blood curdling, guttural scream of an enraged battle stallion that came from the bio-construct, had him stopping and reversing his course in one motion. Grant caught his eye and turned the agitated Bug so that the gunman could better hear what was going on. It was upset so the connection was faulty. What they heard was fragmented at best. Templer heard Chrysta breathlessly cursing. Then faintly...

"INFERNO... No, No, No... SHIT!"

Again there came a loud thump. This time it was accompanied by a squeal from Nuva. Andrew came back on and what came through sounded completely panicked.

"Ya gotta clear the street! ... Can't stop him ... CRAZY!"

There was another chilling scream.

Andrew sounded like he was in tears.

"We got about two minutes before... hit town... IF... can stay on him! She... can't stop... have to SHOOT...!"

Grant was over the bar and heading for the door as he shouted into the device.

"WHAT?!"

There was another heavy thump.

"...CLEAR THE STREET... Inferno... insane...!"

Templer was a step ahead of the big man as they flew out the door. His nimble fingers changed the rounds in the Trinity to armor piercing bullets as he ran. He felt Azra grimly adjusting the load. The outrider hardened the lead while stoking the chambers with static demonic fire. Charged this way... the ammo was safe until it hit a target. Backed by the outrider's power, they could punch through thick dragon-steel.

Most of the people on the main street were concentrated beyond the Ironwood. Templer knew that if they were going to stop the stallion, it would have to be there. No one in the street paid any attention to Grant's shouting. People scattered like sand crabs when an ebony cloaked shadow strode out to the center of the street and raised its hand. Fire and thunder shattered the air as the Talon released a controlled blast of elemental power straight up.

There was a rumble like an approaching

storm and the crimson destria appeared at the end of the street. The Talon waited silently, feet carefully braced, the big gun pointed down in what looked like a relaxed stance. Inferno was covered in sweat. Bloody foam flew from his mouth as he ran. The beast was ducking and dodging as he tried to escape Chrysta's iron control. Nuva ran shoulder to shoulder with him. She was using her big body like a battering ram, trying to slow the raging male down.

As the astonished gunman watched, Inferno skittered sideways trying to reach a child pressed against the front of a building. Chrysta jerked his massive head around but couldn't stop their sideways drift. Nuva fell back and came up on that side, blocking his run. The stallion screamed as they thudded together and his fangs slashed long, bloody furrows along the straining mare's side. She gave a grunting cough of pain but held her ground. The red male twisted violently, almost unseating his rider and reached for Andrew with his deadly mouth gaped wide. Chrysta recovered her seat and her fist drove down hard on the animal's sensitive muzzle forcing it away from the young man. They were covering ground at an alarming rate.

"CONSTANTINE..." Azra prompted the Talon.

Templer set the gun for a single shot but continued to hold his fire. The priest did not want to kill the beautiful crimson beast. He was giving Chrysta every opportunity to get him back under control. When the pounding destria were close enough that Templer could see Inferno's blazing red eyes, the Trinity snapped up. He still did not fire as Nuva remained tight against the stallion's side. The male's heavily armored head was dropped like a shield over his vulnerable front.

With a strangled shout, Andrew peeled the

cream off to the left. Chrysta braced one hand on the stallion's neck. Reaching forwards, she wrapped her other hand in the rein up close to Inferno's armored head. Burying her feet in the stirrups, the rider used all the muscles in her body to drag that head up and twist it to the side. For a split second, the gunman had a clear shot at Inferno's broad chest. The Trinity SPOKE once. The bullet caught the destria dead center at the base of his heavy neck. It took out his windpipe along with the big arteries that ran on either side. Then the eldritch power with-in... exploded. This shattered the stallion's shoulders and spine.

All control lost, the doomed animal's front end dropped. Inferno's ravaged chest plowed into the street, and Temper watched in horror as sheer momentum caused two thousand pounds of fast moving muscle and bone to somersault. Chrysta was locked in the saddle and she had no choice but to ride him down. At the last second she tucked herself tight against the foaming neck, trying to avoid being crushed. The hurtling body slid a good twenty feet before coming to a ground shaking stop at the Talon's feet.

Templer didn't holster his gun as he came around to the side, desperately looking for the woman. He jerked back as Inferno's head came up like a snake, still snapping at whatever he could see with dull red eyes. The Trinity swung up to target him but somehow the rider appeared on the stallions off side.

Chrysta grabbed the long muzzle. Strong hands forced that deadly mouth closed. She then trapped Inferno's head under her arm and held it tight against her leather chest guard. The woman locked her other hand around the offside horn and pressed her face against the bloody foam streaked head. The woman was speaking softly. As the Talon watched, Inferno s eyes faded from that terrible shade of red to the deep yellow that burned at the heart of a star. There was confusion in those fading eyes as the male tried to chortle at the woman who held him. She gently rocked the massive head when the soft sound turned to a cough. The stallion was drowning in his own blood. Chrysta scratched at the stallion's bloodied ridges giving him what comfort she could.

Templer knelt by Inferno's neck. He slowly stroked the silky mane with his talon-ed hand and felt amazement when the dying beast softly crooned. It started low... strengthened... then slowly faded as the fire that burned at the heart of a star dimmed, turned cold and went... out.

The Talon's hand paused as the sensitive pads ran over something that didn't feel quite right. Elongating the sharp tips, Templer followed the odd signal down. In the space of a few seconds he plucked out three crystalline hollow needles. Chrysta settled the great head on the ground with a couple of final pats on the soft muzzle. Before she could rise, the priest silently opened his hand, allowing her to see what he held.

Her chestnut brows furrowed in a frown.

"What in the hell are those?"

The woman reached to take them but Templer hastily grabbed her hand... preventing it.

"They are an assassin's weapons. Hypodermic darts that will dissolve in the victim's body within a half hour. They leave no trace."

Templer's ebony eyes silently followed the tear that traced down her pale face. Then flashed up to see the terrible anger that flared in those odd eyes as she realized what he had said.

Before she could speak, Andrew's panicked voice

broke in.

"CHRYSTA!"

Both of their heads snapped around to see Nuva staggering. The mare was covered in red foam from front to back and her usually bright eyes were glazed. The stallion had slashed her to bloody ribbons down both sides.

Chrysta levered herself off of the ground with a groan, freezing for a moment when she saw Templer's crimson lined cloak. Then she turned on her heel and ran to the mare. As the woman reached the cream she snapped orders at the young stable hand.

"Andrew, CAREFULLY... take those..." she nodded at the slowly dissolving needles in Templer's hand. "Find the race council. I want to know what was in those. Then find Don Ricardo, he is going to want to know why his prize stallion..." Her voice broke here,

"... is dead."

She glanced at Temper.

"Damn it... I haven't had the chance to replace my Hexes. I know you were leaving, but I could use your stitching skills."

The gunman flinched away from the hurt in her eyes, but nodded. He would stay and help. Andrew took off running. Between Chrysta, Templer, and Grant... they coaxed and cajoled the old mare to the barn... one slow trembling step at a time.

With Chrysta working on one side and Templer working on the other it took nearly three hours to get the long, deep slashes stitched up. The Talon did not reprimand his outrider when Azra dipped in to their limited reserves to support the mare while they worked. He could not provide enough energy for a full healing. The beautiful cream would have some terrible scars.

When they had finished, Chrysta took the time to slowly clean all the foam and blood off of the mare's soft hide. Nuva stood through it all. Her proud head stayed down. Her body continued to shake while her breath came in long soft moans.

Azra stayed silent as they stitched, not wanting to distract them from the delicate work they were doing. Templer finished his side and then stepped back to clean up the mounds of bloody cloths and gauze. The outrider's deep voice rumbled out.

"I have done what I can for her body but her mind is terribly distressed."

Chrysta looked up from where she was cleaning blood off of one slender white leg. She stood and ran her hands over the mare's soft muzzle.

"Yes, I imagine she will be... distressed... for a long while. Inferno was her only son."

The barn door banged open startling them all. One of the girls that worked for Grant ran in... Wringing her hands.

Chrysta looked at her in surprise. This girl in particular NEVER came to the barn. It did not help that she was crying.

"Chrysta, you have to come now... it's Grant."

The woman laid her head against Nuva's sleek neck for a minute. The priest barely heard her whisper.

"Mother of Demons... can this day GET any better!"

They followed the little waitress to the common room. Andrew had just made it in and a heavy set man with silver hair was pouring a couple of drinks at the bar. Chrysta nodded at him as she entered. Grant was seated at a table staring blurry eyed at a sheet of paper in front of him. On the table was an empty bottle of Anesthetic and another that was almost empty. The man was quite drunk. He reached for the second bottle to drink the rest only to have Chrysta's quick hand plucked it away. Her face was worried.

"What gives Grant?"

The man blinked owlishly as silver hair slipped a cup of coffee in front of him. Grant stabbed a blunt finger on the paper and looked at Templer.

"Please don't let her kill me." The words were slurred but very understandable. "Or maybe you should... you know, just LET her kill me."

The Talon looked at Chrysta in astonishment. She glanced down at the paper and froze.

"OH HOLY... Grant... what have you done!?"

Chrysta seemed to sag, the piece of paper fluttered out of suddenly boneless fingers. The anger on her face had Grant pushing back from the table. The silver haired stranger snagged the offending paper before it reached the floor. He met Templer's unearthly eyes without flinching and offered a soft hand.

"Talon Constantine... I presume."

The Don had a mild tenor voice.

"I am pleased to finally make your acquaintance. I am Don Ricardo."

Templer's gaze flicked down to the hand then back to the calm face. He did not extend his own hand. The pale gray eyes blinked sedately and with a slight shrug, the man went to studying the paper.

"Hmmm... It seems Mr. Brenaan here was confident enough in Chrysta's abilities that he put the Ironwood up as collateral in a legally binding wager with Don Diego. Along with a substantial amount of silver I might add. He wagered that she would win the Gauntlet tomorrow."

That quiet face tilted towards Grant who had his eyes closed. The bartender's big body loosely sagged in his chair. Chrysta had turned her back to him but the gunman could tell by the stiffness in her shoulders she was livid. Her breathing had developed an occasional odd hitch.

Don Ricardo set the paper on the table and chose his next words delicately.

"Since we no longer have an entry in said race..." He gave a sad nod at Grant, "I see no way to prevent the Ironwood from changing ownership."

Andrew cleared his throat nervously and coming forward he tapped Chrysta on the shoulder.

"Umm... the stuff in the needles... it was Thearazine."

The boy back pedaled as Chrysta turned. Don Ricardo sucked in a breath and his quiet face hardened in anger.

"What's Thearazine?"

Templer had already figured out the answer but wanted it verified.

"It's a hallucinogen and a stimulant. They use it on the pit stallions to make them more aggressive."

Chrysta's face tightened with a flash of pain and she hugged her arms around her ribcage miserably.

"If you are holding any guilt about putting Inferno down, LOSE it. That amount was an overdose and he would have died a horrible death if you hadn't." She turned a stricken face to the inebriated barman. "Grant what were you THINKING? Forrest loved this bar... and you were his best friend! That's why he deeded it to you in his will."

The big man stirred and his brown eyes sluggishly opened.

"Did it for you..."

The woman returned his gaze with a bewildered one of her own.

"What!!?"

Azra had been listening intently,

"Hold on... Constantine... May I see that

contract?"

Templer reached out and slid the contract over to where his outrider could peruse it.

After a short minute, there was a soft rumbling.

"Ummm... CHRYSTA... Did you see what Don Diego wagered?"

The woman tiredly shook her head. Her eyes were still studying Grant, who had laid his head down on crossed arms.

"Diego put up the ten thousand acres between Dragon back ridge and Flattop Mountain as his wager."

Azra hummed thoughtfully then clarified the location for the confused priest.

"That is the valley Chrysta called... paradise!"

Don Ricardo sat back with a low whistle of astonishment. Chrysta just blinked, too stunned to say anything. Andrew slipped by the Don, he needed to get out to the barn and check on Nuva. As he passed, the young man laid another small piece of paper on the table.

Ricardo smiled and shook his head. He smoothed the paper out.

"The council has decided that since foul play was proven in this case they will allow a substitution for the race tomorrow."

Templer sat forward as a sudden thought slipped through his mind. He re-studied the contract in front of him.

"This is worded in such a way that Grant bet that CHRYSTA would win the race, NOT Inferno."

The gray eyed man's fingers drummed a soft tattoo on the table, but that isn't what caught and held the gunman's attention. Chrysta's face had become very still and... Thoughtful.

Don Ricardo pursed his lips as if he had bitten a lemon.

"It is no good. I have no other destria of the same caliber as Inferno. Really, I have none that even come close."

"No... You don't...But I do."

Chrysta sounded a little breathless as she whispered this. The woman ran her hand down the right side of her chest guard and gave it a small tug. She looked long at Grant, slid her gaze past him and let it linger on Templer for a moment. A nasty little smile twisted her lips. She turned and headed for the stairs tossing words over her shoulder as she went.

"Go ahead and fill out a substitute entry Don Ricardo. I WILL be ride the Gauntlet tomorrow."

Don Ricardo gathered himself up and looking perplexed he asked.

"What destria am I entering?"

Chrysta paused for a moment on the stairs, and both men winced as a name floated down.

"Vera's Silver Flame."

Don Ricardo hesitated for a moment. He rose with a nod at the silent gunman, picked up that little piece of paper and strode out the door.

The Talon's head snapped around as a horrendous noise emanated from the bartender. The man was snoring.

Azra shifted as Constantine glared at the other man. The outrider's voice was dark.

"Do you think Chrysta would mind if I killed him now?"

"Hnnn..." was the gunman's answer.

It took Templer a few minutes to locate his

travel bag. Grant had tucked it behind the bar for safe keeping. Azra broke into his thoughts as the priest was contemplating what he should do next.

"I think you should follow Chrysta."

The Talon hardened the walls around his heart.

"I said I would stay and help with Nuva. I promised nothing more."

Azra shredded those walls and froze his heart with his next growled words.

"Use your head HOST! Do you really think that an un-Tainted human can have a two-thousand-pound animal roll over the top of them and come out of it completely unscathed? Something is not right here. You... need... to follow Chrysta!"

The gunman took the stairs two at a time and slammed the door open. He could hear the tub being filled and smell dreamleaf. Chrysta was standing with her back to him, watching from the window as Andrew did the evening chores. She had slipped out of her boots. The woman seemed fine as she turned towards the door, and Templer could have KILLED Azra when the outrider snickered.

"For someone who does not... CARE... You sure came up those stairs awfully..."

In the next moment, the Talon grimly told the demon... "Shut up!" as he strode towards the woman. Even from the door he could see Chrysta's lips had taken on a bluish tinge. She was pulling at the chest protector, desperately trying to get it off.

As Templer reached her, the woman sagged against him. She panted in shallow... panicked breaths.

"I... CAN'T... breathe!"

Easing both of them down, Constantine didn't even bother with the buckles and straps on the leather guard. He sliced through all of them and the shirt underneath with careful talons. Even fighting for breath, Chrysta managed a strangled laugh.

"DAMN... Constantine, you are HELL on shirts."

Templer sucked a breath in through his teeth as he saw the extensive bruising that covered the right side of her rib cage.

Azra vented a savage curse...

"I don't care how precious they are here... THAT needs a Blessing!"

The man felt as Azra again drew on their reserves but stopped the outrider when Chrysta grabbed his wrist to get his attention.

The woman shook her head... as she wheezed,

"I can't use any magic within twenty-four hours of the race... no Blessings... no Hexes! Just get me to the tub... oh...HOLY... not the PANTS!"

This last was in response to Templer cutting her pants off. Scooping her naked body up, the Talon carried her bridal style and carefully set her in the steaming tub. For several LONG minutes the priest knelt and watched while Chrysta struggled to breath. He couldn't stand it. He rose to his feet and was telling Azra to power up (race be damned!) when things started to ease up. Chrysta sank down deeper into the water with a relieved groan. Even though the breaths she drew in were shallow and careful, her face had better color and her lips pinked up.

The woman opened one eye, quietly taking in the tall, ebony cloaked man standing tensely over the tub.

"I think I just cracked some ribs. If it will make you feel better, you can check them when I get out."

Templer stood silent, gleaming talons tapping on his crossed arm. Without a word, he exited the room, leaving her to soak. Going down into the empty common room, the priest checked on Grant who was still snoring. Then he raided the bar. Templer found where the Innkeeper kept the Anesthetic (even with the dreamleaf, this would be unpleasant) and then he went looking for linens. He found some very nice quality ones upstairs. It was a shame to use these, he thought as returning to the room he tore them into long, wide strips.

Templer was ready when he heard her struggling to get to her feet. Slipping into the bathroom, he plucked Chrysta out of the tub, and wrapped her in a towel. He deposited the surprised woman onto one of the straight backed chairs in the room. She sat gasping while she looked at the supplies he had laid out in astonishment. He stepped behind her, carefully peeled the towel down to expose her upper body, and sternly reminded her...

"You SAID I could check you out."

She gave him an apprehensive look,

"Well... yes... that I did."

Chrysta flinched when the priest ran careful fingers over the bruised area. It started at her right shoulder and covered most of that half of the woman's ribcage. Traveling around her side, the damage extended over the sternum and into her left side also. Templer's touch was as gentle as he could make it, but checking her ribs took a little poking and prodding. He elicited more than a few gasps, a couple of yelps and several interesting swear words that even impressed

Azra.

When he was finished, the Talon held an internal conference with his outrider to compare notes. Then he poured and handed the woman a large glass full of Anesthetic.

"Drink all of that!"

Her brows flew up, and she started to protest.

"Shut up and drink it Chrysta!"

This was a terse growl. Azra did not like mixing the hefty dose of potent alcohol with the dreamleaf but he also knew she was going to need it!

Templer sat in the chair opposite her and watched solemnly as she did as they demanded.

"From what Azra and I can tell, you have at least three cracked ribs on the right. One rib on the left has an open fracture and you have a badly bruised sternum. There is also a lot of soft tissue damage. I am going to wrap you tight. It will make it easier for you to breathe."

Templer's glowing eyes held her green ones for a moment. The man noticed that hers were already starting to glaze. Dreamleaf and alcohol were a VERY potent mix.

"I truly apologize for this beforehand. I... AM... going to hurt you."

"UmmHumm..." Chrysta tilted her head. He did not have the heart to smile as he assessed the wasted look she gave him. Her eyes were most definitely glazed! She blinked and reached out to catch the edge of his spider-silk cloak. Rubbing it between two fingers, she smiled sweetly.

"Ahh... Constantine... at least you are honest about it."

Templer tried to work as quickly as possible. He had steeled himself to be emotionless. He knew from experience that having those ribs and muscles compressed would be excruciatingly painful. The priest couldn't ignore Chrysta's soft hiss of pain as he tightened the first wrap. Azra stopped him before he went to the next. Outrider and Host had a short, very nasty argument before the demon made him untie the knot and wind the wrap tighter.

The second time this happened, the woman growled softly.

"AZRA... If you do that again, I will follow you, FIND you, and kick your black, bat winged BUTT to HELL and back!"

The outrider was quiet for a moment, but he did not relent. He could... SEE... things that Constantine could not. Azra knew there was a little more damage than just a few cracked and broken ribs. The demon growled. Normally he loved being the bad ass but right at this moment it... SUCKED! His anger at the situation made him snarl back.

"If you are feeling froggy WOMAN... go ahead and JUMP!" Then he rumbled at Constantine. **"I can't believe I am saying this. YOU... are being too soft. Step aside and let me do it!"**

Templer gladly gave the outrider control of his hands. This way he could tell himself... HE... was not the one doing the hurting. Azra worked fast, wrapping the bindings one at a time. Each supporting bandage was pulled almost cruelly tight before the demon tied it off.

Chrysta gasped out one strangled... "SON OF

A BITCH!!"... Then kept as quiet and still as possible. At one point Templer heard the outrider harshly admonished her.

"DON'T you pass out Chrysta... I need you conscious so I can judge how tight..." This ended in a savage curse as the demon moved on to the next wrapping. **"I am sorry. Just hold on. We are almost there!"**

When the Azra tied off the last knot, he slipped around in front of the shaking woman where she could see his unhappy eyes glowing muted gold. Chrysta's face was deadly pale. She was right on the edge of passing out. Her pupils were so dilated that her eyes looked almost black. Azra slid back, returning control to his host. Constantine knelt so the woman could rest her head against his black shirted chest. He stayed this way, providing support and balance until she could gain a degree of control. The priest listened as her breathing gradually settled into a steadier rhythm. He shared Azra's satisfaction that each breath was deeper, stronger and less pained than before.

Templer gently ruffled his fingers through her short hair and murmured in her ear.

"Better?"

At her slight nod, he continued... "At least we did not SIT on you."

The Talon was rewarded with a soft chuckle, followed by a careful cough.

Chrysta stayed still, content to just sit and rest against him. Templer maintained his position. This was something he could do forever... if need be.

His companion's fingers slid over the soft black material of his cloak. When she spoke, her words were muffled and sad.

"You weren't even going to say good bye?"

She tightened her grip on the man as she felt him stiffen, not letting him pull away.

Constantine's deep voice was rough and strained as he tried to articulate the raw emotions that roiled through him.

"Chrysta... don't... I can't..."

Azra stayed silent as he felt the woman ride the emotional storm in. He watched as she carefully opened herself to the longing, anger, anguish, self-loathing mess that WAS Templer Constantine. Most of all she tasted the underlying damage caused by decisions in a first life gone TERRIBLY wrong. The man was consumed by ravaging guilt, and a deep, paralyzing fear that the same thing was happening again.

Withdrawing her mind, Chrysta slid her hands around his strong shoulders and back. She rocked them both of them... slowly and gently.

"It's okay Constantine." she whispered, "I know better than to try and take what you are unable or unwilling to give. That would be as... futile... as trying to race the wind."

Azra did not interrupt, although the outrider knew from experience that racing the wild wind was a lot of fun. Sometimes... once in a great while... you could actually catch it for a moment. Then... oh HOLY... it would reward you with the ride of your life!

Chrysta lifted her head and pushed the gunman back a little so she could look at his distressed face. She gently poked him in the breast with a stiff finger.

"Just... don't... be LEAVING... without saying good bye. That would be unforgivably rude!"

Templer stood up and backed away. A small look of confusion mixed with relief crossed his pale features. Her calm acceptance and understanding was not what he had expected. This was not the clingy, teary reaction he had been slipping away to avoid. He was... oddly enough... disappointed!

Chrysta must have been able to read a little of what he was thinking because she snorted.

"WHAT... Did you think that after living as long as I have, that I couldn't possibly survive without a man in my life? P-L-L-LEASE!"

Her gentle smile took any sting out of the words. In his relief, Templer did not notice that her easy to read expression was shuttered tight.

The woman carefully levered herself up and passed her hands over the mummy like bindings on her chest.

"Thanks, this is really helping a lot."

Slipping past the motionless man, Chrysta snatched up the neatly folded shirt he had placed on the table. Then she headed for the door.

A couple of quick, gliding steps had the Talon blocking her path.

"Where do you think you are going? When the alcohol and dreamleaf wear off, you will find it hard to walk."

Chrysta sighed.

"Truth be told, walking isn't THAT much fun right now. It doesn't change the fact that I need to go check on Nuva." Seeing the look that crossed his face, she hastily put up a hand and stepped back. "Being carried hurts almost as bad as walking so... DON'T..."

As he carried her down the stairs... Templer did his best to ignore her annoyed glare.

The woman insisted that the he stop and set her on her feet when they reached the back door.

Templer watched in fascination as she buttoned her shirt to hide the damage and closed her eyes in concentration for a moment. When Chrysta raised her head and opened the door, she glanced casually in El Diablo's direction. He stared balefully back. There was not a sign of any pain or discomfort as she strolled across the courtyard and into the barn. As Constantine followed behind he felt the big silver's hot gaze tracking him. The waves of hate and rage that emanated off of the beast made his gun hand twitch out of instinct.

In contrast the inside of the barn was quiet and calm. Templer stood for a moment letting his eyes adjust to the dimness. He could hear Chrysta running her hands slowly over Nuva as she checked the mare out. She spent a few minutes stroking Zephyr's long black nose. Her eyes flashed between blue and the gold as the woman "talked" to them both.

She gave each a final pat and walked back over to the door.

"I won't have any time to visit them in the morning."

Was all she said as she passed the gunman on her way back out into the cool evening air. This time, as she walked by El Diablo, she stopped. For a long time, she stood watching the stallion. Chrysta was so still that Templer laid a hand on her back. He was worried that she was in the silver's thrall.

"I wish you would reconsider this. Even with dreamleaf, you will not be able to walk tomorrow."

The woman flashed a tired smile at him,

"Well... it is a good thing I am RIDING the Gauntlet, not WALKING it. I think I am going to just go up and try to get some rest. Would you mind seeing that Grant doesn't spend the night at that table?"

"Hnnn..." was all the Talon said as he watched her go back inside.

It was dark by the time Templer had the big bartender wrestled up to his room. He left the big man sprawled loosely across his bed. When the priest returned to their room he found that Chrysta had stolen most of the pillows off of the bed. She had wedged them around herself on the duvet so she could sleep half way sitting up. He stood and watched for a time as the woman drifted in and out of a light doze.

"She probably cannot breathe lying flat." Azra observed unhappily.

Templer brought a chair over to where he could sit and observe the woman's restless sleep. The outrider's wrappings had helped, but it was easy to see that she was still very uncomfortable. The gunman sat for a couple of hours, hoping she would settle into a deeper sleep where her body could find some relief.

He finally couldn't stand it any longer.

"So... do you have any ideas on how are we going to stop her?"

"I don't think we can. With the way that wager is worded it has to be CHYSTA that wins the race." Azra sounded as miserable with that particular answer as he was. **"She evidently feels acquiring this land is worth the considerable risk. Nothing you or I can do or say will make a difference."**

Templer growled,

"We could tie her to the bed."

Azra gave a low, dark chuckle.

"Whereas that sounds like it might be fun if she were up to it. I would not want to be around when she managed to free herself."

The outrider's voice turned thoughtful. **"It seems to me there is another whose fate is tied up in how this turns out. We just need to find a way to get through to him. Listen... I think I might have a plan!"**

That was how Templer found himself outside of El Diablo's paddock, holding his cloak loosely in one hand, with the Trinity on his hip instead of being snugly nestled in the other. The man winced as the big silver, who stood at the far side of the enclosure, slowly curled his lips back and popped his nasty, LARGE, sharp edged fangs together with a sound like a gunshot.

"I can't believe I let you talk me into doing this." The outrider could hear the apprehension in his host's voice.

Azra couldn't help himself.

"I can't believe you LET me talk you into doing this!"

That startled a chuckle out of the Talon followed by a quiet,

"Azra, you are such an ASSHOLE... Here we go!!"

The priest vaulted over the fence. He made it to the center of the pen before the massive destria even twitched. It seemed that El Diablo just couldn't believe his eyes. That couple of seconds was all they got. With a low rumbling moan... the stallion charged. Templer held his ground until the last second. He spun away, dodging hooves and teeth as he flicked the cloak in front of the lurid green eyes, disrupting the animal's flow. The Talon knew El Diablo was intelligent. He would only get one shot at this. Again the stallion charged, and again at the last second Templer melted away from in front of him, flipping the scarlet lined cloak in front of those insane eyes.

The third time the stallion charged, Templer didn't dodge. The animal ducked sideways as if expecting him to. As he did this, the Talon stepped forward, sucking himself up on his toes as the wicked black horns sliced through his shirt barely scoring his stomach. He turned with the stallion and tucked himself behind the heavy ridge where teeth and horns couldn't reach. Reaching over the thick neck with his blade-hand, he locked onto the long horn as he threw his cloak over the silver's face. He slammed his gun hand hard digging his fingers into the heavy bone of El Diablo's long nose. The beast's momentum had his boots sliding along beside the flashing hooves. Using ALL of his enhanced strength Templer twisted... hard. He could FEEL El Diablo's astonishment as his massive head was twisted up and back. The whiplash that traveled along the animal's spine took him right off of his hooves and he crashed onto his side into the dirt. Moving like nothing more than shadowed lightening, the Talon buried his knees on that high crested neck. He tightened the cloak around the ice green eyes, blinding the silver. At the same time, he tightened his talons around the big arteries and windpipe under the heavy jaw.

"BE STILL!" He hissed.

The big animal started to thrash, then caught Constantine's scent. Evidently there was enough of Azra in it to confuse the beast. El Diablo snorted and lay still.

Azra slipped forwards and together the gunman and the demon, painted a picture of that high isolated valley. They explained what Chrysta wanted to do, although the low angry moan that rumbled through the body under them at mention of her name did not bode well. Azra rumbled right back.

"LISTEN... ASSHOLE, (Templer smothered the slightly hysterical snicker that tried to pass his lips) **"You are in a win... win here. If you finish first in the race with Chrysta alive and well, you get paradise. You lose with Chrysta still alive and I will personally grant your heart's desire and take... you...out... the Prince of Darkness be damned! On the Flip side... If you HURT, the woman in any way... WE shall make it our life's mission to ensure you live a very long and unhappy life!"**

The stallion released another long, shuddering angry moan.

Azra stepped back into the shadow. Templer did a quick calculation.

"Okay, oh brilliant one. How do we make it to the damned fence?"

The Outrider answered nonchalantly.

"WELL Constantine... as one asshole to another, my suggestion is... How fast can you RUN!"

Templer was up in a flash. He was amazed at how fast something as large El Diablo could move! The Talon could feel the battle stallion's angry breath and snapping teeth right on his ass as he flew over the fence. The outrider and his host stood and watched as the enraged stallion circled the paddock looking for a way to get to them.

Templer dusted his pants off and checked the long shallow slashes dug across his stomach.

"That went over well, don't you think?" His words dripped with sarcasm.

"SHUT UP...Constantine!"

Chrysta was still fitfully sleeping when the Talon slipped back into the room. He studied her white face silently noting the light sheen of sweat on it. Setting his cloak and gun down, Templer went in to take a quick shower. He was pretty sure that the heavy scent of El Diablo that surrounded him would disturb the resting woman. As he stepped out wrapped in a towel, he realized her green eyes were open and tracking him.

When she saw she had his attention, Chrysta smiled slightly.

"I have been laying here trying to levitate that bottle of Anesthetic over to myself. I haven't succeeded yet."

Tucking the towel around his waist the priest poured a small glass and took it over to her. She hissed through her teeth and coughed softly as she carefully reached for it. One finger drifted out to trace across the already healing slashes on his pale stomach.

Templer looked away from the question on her face.

"It is nothing. At Azra's suggestion, I got in to an argument with one of the barn... cats."

One chestnut brow rose as Chrysta sipped the drink.

"UmmmHumm..."

The Talon winced as his outrider, not one to be willingly thrown under the bus, piped up.

"HEY... my idea was better than his!"

The gentle finger stopped moving.

"And just what was his idea?"

Templer hastily removed portions of his anatomy from out of her reach as Azra smugly answered.

"HE was going to tie you to the bed!"

Templer spent the rest of the long night watching Chrysta slip restlessly in and out of sleep. He helped where he could when the pain drove her awake. This consisted of him getting ice packs from the bar and slipping them around her body where he knew the bruising was particularly bad. He had just returned from downstairs when a noise out in the courtyard had him drifting silently over to the window. The barest hint of predawn light revealed Andrew setting up supplies in the courtyard. The stable hand was preparing El Diablo's tack for the day. As the gunman watched, Grant came out and had a short conversation with the young man. He must NOT have liked what he heard because he shot back into the bar.

Constantine was already moving. By the time the bartender made it up the stairs, the priest was standing in front of the door blocking his entry.

"Move!"

The big man made the mistake of giving the Talon what sounded like an order.

Anger slammed through the usually stoic priest. He uncoiled like a serpent. Templer had the bartender off of his feet and pinned to the opposite wall before the other man could twitch. His hand blurred and the Trinity came up in it. The sound of multiple triggers being cocked was loud as the big gun settled at the stunned man's temple. Grant stared into the Talon's hard, pale face and those hot gold eyes and wisely froze. He knew he was outmatched and looking at his death. Templer also froze, caught in a savage fight with his own temper.

Azra rose in his mind, but oddly the outrider

had his own rage in check.

"Constantine... she will hate you if you kill him!"

Templer blinked but his grip didn't slacken and his gun hand remained deathly still.

"This is YOUR fault... Grant! Give me a reason NOT to blow your fool head off."

Brown eyes closed for a moment and when they opened they held the Talon's unearthly gaze without flinching.

"I missed my shot six years ago. Because of ME that S.O.B is still alive." Grant's face twisted, "I thought the slight chance of losing the Inn was worth the risk, if she gained that piece of property for El Diablo. I didn't realize the risk would become so great."

The Innkeeper looked totally miserable. "You might as well go ahead and shoot me. If he kills her today, I will do it myself."

Azra kept his words calm and quiet. The outrider was all for blood and violence but he didn't want his host to do something THEY would later regret.

"He is deadly serious Constantine. You cannot punish him anymore than he is punishing himself!"

"Hnnn..."

This came out as a slow growl. Templer let the man drop. He backed off of his anger enough to ease the hammers on the Trinity down and get the big gun re-holstered. The Talon's tall, shadow cloaked frame continued to block the door.

"Chrysta just got back to sleep. I do NOT want her woken up."

Grant straightened his clothes and cleared

his throat. He eyed the closed door.

"Is she okay?"

The hopeful look that accompanied this question, quelled whatever anger was left in the priest. He dashed that hope when he answered truthfully.

"No, she most definitely is not... okay."

The big man flinched and ducked his head for a moment.

"Well... then... is there anything I can do to make this easier?"

Constantine managed a slight smile and pushed the bigger man lightly towards the stairs.

"I would imagine that Chrysta will be looking forward to some of your excellent coffee when she wakes up."

Slipping back into the room, Templer checked on the still sleeping woman then went back to watching Andrew polish and check every inch of that harness. El Diablo had ghosted over to the gate and he also watched the young man with avid interest. A short time had passed when Talon's vigil was interrupted by a soft scratch at the door. Opening it, Templer observed Grant. The man had returned with a tray balanced in one hand, and a long black duffel in the other. Constantine stepped back. With a finger admonishing silence raised to his lips, he allowed the man in. The bartender set the tray on the table and Chrysta stirred a little then settled as the smell of coffee permeated the room.

Grant glanced her way and his expressive face stilled as he took in the tight wrapping on Chrysta's upper torso. He gestured at the duffel bag.

"She will want to go over this before the race." He kept the words pitched low as he headed back out the door. "I am going down to boil some water. She is going to want more than just coffee."

He stopped as a soft voice murmured from the duvet.

"Maximum dose, Grant." ... Was all Chrysta said. The big man's shoulders hunched a little, but he said nothing as he nodded and left the room.

Curious, Templer opened the big leather bag. On top he found a box. The Talon looked towards Chrysta who made a motion with one finger indicating he should open it.

"I would appreciate it if you would make sure those are in perfect working condition."

Nestled on the soft cloth inside was a beautiful handgun. Azra rumbled softly in appreciation. He could tell it had been made specifically for Chrysta by a gunsmith with an eye for detail. Its bore peeked evilly out from between the black fangs and long, lean muzzle of a stylized destria's head. An ebony horned ridge flared to form a protective shield over the hand when it was held. The horns on this were sharp, it could be used as a slashing weapon if need be. The grip was shaped into an elegant arched neck which was a little small for his hand, but he guessed would be a perfect fit for hers. The whole piece gleamed a shadowed black and fiery crimson. A soft tooled leather holster accompanied it. The gunman took a moment to flip open the six round chamber and verify that it was very clean and well oiled. The gun's mechanism operated as smoothly as the Trinity's ever had.

Templer glanced over at the resting woman but she had leaned her head back and her eyes were closed. Chrysta looked like she was concentrating on just breathing... slowly and carefully.

The next item in the bag was the reason it was so long. Resting in a black and red enameled sheath was a long, slender ebony sword. Holding it up to the dawn's soft light the priest could see the ripples of color where the metal had been folded, beaten and folded again. This was light, strong, dragon-steel. It seemed too long to be wielded by Chrysta comfortably but the Talon realized it was the perfect length for use when mounted on a destria.

Underneath these unique, beautiful weapons laid a chest and back guard. This was not made of hard leather. It looked like nothing more than a reptile's scales made out of glinting black and crimson metal. The scales were linked together in such a way that the whole thing flowed as supple as a serpent' skin but hard as dragon scales. There were pieces designed to protect the arms and legs with it. Templer's brow furrowed, he felt he was missing something here. This did not look like protective riding gear. It looked like...

"Battle armor!" the outrider softly finished the thought.

There was a quiet snort from the bed. Templer looked up to meet shadowed green eyes.

"It's called the... GAUNTLET... for a very good reason!"

Seeing his confused look the woman clarified.

"There are probably six real contenders in the race. The other twenty give or take, are ringers. These are entered by the big money owners in order to interfere and stack the... odds... in their rider's favor. Violence and death are part of the game."

Azra's vicious snarl matched the gunman's.

"There will BE no Gauntlet if WE go in and clear the field."

The subdued thunder in their angry tone made it very clear... Azra WASN'T joking and his Talon was backing him!

Chrysta flinched as she had a sudden, vivid mental vision of the blood bath that could ensue. The woman stifled a groan as she shifted. It was evident that she was carefully testing to see just how painful moving would be.

"NO! Any help ON the course by someone who is not entered in the race is grounds for immediate disqualification. You CANNOT interfere in any way."

They just growled in response.

A soft knock interrupted and Grant came in carrying a steaming mug. The sharp smell of dreamleaf preceded him.

Chrysta went to sit up and froze. What little color was she had... slowly drained out of her face.

Templer felt too badly for her to be smug... but he still let her know how he felt about the whole thing.

"I TOLD you that you wouldn't feel like walking."

Grant slashed a hard look his way and started towards the bed. The Talon met him there. Between the two of them they got the woman sitting up. Grant supported her while the gunman steadied her hands so she could drink the bitter brew.

Chrysta shuddered when she finished,

"HOLY... That is... NASTY!"

She hissed softly as they helped her lean back against the pillows. Her eyes were closed.

"Mother of Demons, I do... HATE... festival week!"

Grant's face twisted, and he looked away. Templer elbowed him sharply in the ribs. The barman grunted with the impact,

"Then you should retire... so we don't have to listen to you whine."

The Talon nodded a little in satisfaction when Chrysta's lips twitched up in a smile. After a short while the woman coughed carefully and sat up. Her movements were a little slower and stiffer than usual but the dreamleaf had worked its magic. She suggested that Grant go down and scrounge up some breakfast. As soon as he left, she made her way over to one of the chairs and slanted a meaningful look at the Talon.

"I hate to ask it of you, but some of these..." Chrysta passed her hands over the wrap.

"...need to be re-tied. I have to have some support all the way to my hips."

Templer steeled himself, lifted the edge of her shirt and could not hide his wince as he saw that the bruising had extended down to her right flank. What followed was a miserable fifteen minutes for the both of them. Still, when Azra was done, the woman was wrapped tightly enough for support but not so tight as to interfere with her mobility. Chrysta managed her pants and shirt alone but needed help to lace up the tall riding boots. Running her hands over the dragon mail she shuddered.

"I am not putting this on until the last minute. I don't want to bear the weight until I have to."

A little later they sat down in the common room. Constantine watched as Chrysta picked halfheartedly at the breakfast that Grant provided. She actually ate very little, being more interested in the coffee than anything else. After pushing her food around on her plate for a while the woman glanced at the sunlight outside and sighed.

"Well, I guess we had better go out and get HIM ready."

Grant sat down.

"Hold on a moment, we need to know if you will be keeping to the planned route?"

Chrysta shook her head.

"No, El Diablo hasn't had the conditioning necessary for that kind of distance. I will take him through Splatter canyon. It is the shortest most direct path."

Grant winced but nodded. The three of them then made their way out to the courtyard.

Chrysta checked over the tack that Andrew had been working on so diligently and nodded her satisfaction. She looked at the stallion standing in the center of his paddock. Those feral green eyes glared balefully back.

Glancing sideways at the ebony cloaked priest, the woman smiled slyly.

"Well... Nuva is too injured to help hold him for saddling. Anyone here got any bright ideas?"

"I could shoot him and we could saddle his corpse!"

Grant drawled this with no hint of humor.

Andrew snickered as Chrysta pinned the barman with a hard look.

"THAT is NOT an option, Grant!"

The big man just shrugged.

In the end they all four entered the paddock. Chrysta helpfully mentioned that with four targets to choose from at least ONE of them had a chance of getting a rope on the rogue.

Andrew flashed the woman a dirty look.

"That is NOT funny Chrysta!"

El Diablo just stood and watched the woman as Templer walked up and clipped the rope to the animal's heavy collar. If his stomach hadn't been roiling in nervous reaction, the gunman would have laughed at the stunned look on the woman's face. The Talon didn't feel like laughing a moment later when he was tightening the cinch on the saddle and the wicked head whipped around. The beast's nasty fanged mouth closed on the shoulder of his gun arm. Templer felt a slight tug on his hip and Chrysta had the Trinity drawn and the triple bores buried under the stallion's jaw. Constantine grunted as those massive jaws tightened painfully. The man flinched at the triple clicks as the woman pulled back the master lock that primed all three hammers on the big gun. Her hand was as steady as a rock. A ... I could do this if I wanted to... look passed through the feral green eye closest to him before El Diablo released his arm. Templer reached over and took the big gun out of Chrysta's hand. He carefully dropped the hammers back into the safe position and re-holstered it.

He glanced sideways at her.

"The recoil would have shattered your wrist if you had fired her from that position."

His companion shrugged.

"I know that, and you know that." She grinned. "HE... didn't know that."

When they finished, El Diablo stood resplendent in black and crimson. Not only was the saddle and bridle these intense colors, but the stallion also had dragon mail that glittered over his shoulders, rump, high crested neck and wide chest. Andrew tied him to stand and wait. The stallion arched his neck checking himself over. He seemed very aware of the impression he made.

Chrysta snorted a short laugh.

"No modesty in his family I guess."

They could hear the fanfare as preparation got under way for parade to post.

She turned toward the street.

"Well that's my cue to go get ready."

The woman headed for the door.

"Give me a few minutes please then clear the entrance to the street."

Grant watched her until she disappeared inside than turned and grabbed Templer's wrist. He had a small map in his other hand.

"How long does it take you to recover from one of your shifts?"

The Talon frowned but answered.

"Twenty minutes if someone is pushing me to wake. Why?"

The barman spread out the map.

"You will have to head back this way when they hit this mark. Chrysta will need you here when she makes the finish line."

Grant saw Constantine's confusion.

"Listen I don't trust Diego! You can't help her out while she is ON the course... but... there is no rule saying you can't keep an eye on her from ABOVE the race."

Azra surged forward as they both realized what he was suggesting. The Inn keeper handed him a small Spy-Bug.

"You will be able to communicate with her

using this. DON'T distract her! DON'T interfere on the course!"

Templer scooped up the little construct and was already shifting as he moved. People screamed... scattering as Azra flowed down the alley sending a wave of elemental power ahead of him. Grant followed at his heels. They cleared the alley and held it open to the street as they waited for Chrysta to bring the Devil out.

People were gathered along each side of the street. The noise level of the shouting and clapping rose as the big racers were paraded to the starting line. More than one rider had their hands full as the intelligent animals responded to the noise and excitement. Two stallions rose on their hind legs, screaming and striking at each other. They battled until the race handlers drove them apart. The beautiful golden stallion of Don Diego's crow hopped in a circle trying to dump the Don's red headed son. Azra was VERY disappointed when Rafe managed to stay mounted.

The riders were trying to get the high strung beasts to line up and had just succeeded when an angry scream echoed out from the alleyway. It started impossibly high, making the hair stand up on the back of everyone's neck. Then it traveled down the scale ending in a deep, rumbling WAH WAH WAH. Every destria on the line spun, not wanting to have their ass ends to the monster coming down the alley.

Grant snickered.

"Bet they didn't take the... I am a bigger bad ass than you... factor into account when they agreed to let that bastard race!"

The ground seemed to tremble as the big silver stallion thundered out onto the street.

Chrysta had him collected in a tight canter and she just managed to bring the impressive beast to a sliding, rearing stop. The black and crimson dragon-scale glittered in the sunlight. When seen against his gleaming silver hide, this armor accented the black striping that extended over El Diablo's massive shoulders and down his powerful legs. His white mane and trimmings flowed in the wind of his movements as if they were living things.

The difference between the destria bred as racers and this throw back to a battle stallion were stunningly apparent. The runners were sleek, powerful looking beasts. Even so they did not have the massive high crested neck, or the thick rippling muscle that made El Diablo look like a primordial force of nature. The only stallion that came close to him in size was the dappled golden beast of Diego's. This destria was confident enough in his virility that he reared, screaming his answer the rogue's challenge.

Chrysta tightened her grip on the four reins and turned the great beast in a circle while he cantered in place. This kept the stallion occupied while they got Rafe's animal back under control. The woman had put on her dragon-mail. It rippled, glimmering like solidified ebony fire over her trim form. Crimson gauntlets adorned her forearms. These matched the greaves strapped to her lower legs. All were equipped with sharp dagger like blades that pointed out. The black and red almost delicate looking sword strapped to El Diablo's shoulder, the beautiful gun holstered at the woman's hip, and the living, breathing, INSANE weapon that she rode drew the attention of every person on the street.

Even some of the hardened riders looked as if they would rather be elsewhere! It was very obvious that this pair was a force to be reckoned with. As the stallion slowly turned in place picking up and pounding down those big cloven hooves, Azra noticed that there was a large sheathed dagger and a small black pouch on Chrysta's other hip. She moved easily with the stallion, her body alive with that odd, lithe grace that always seemed a part of her every move.

Azra shifted uneasily as he watched. The

dreamleaf had not eased ALL the woman's pain that morning and she should not have been able to move that smoothly. When she glanced his way, the woman's mouth was pulled into a tight, predatory, tooth baring smile. Her eyes were shimmering, jewel bright, in her lightly flushed face. Noticing the outrider's dark frown, the woman gave him a cheeky wink.

Chrysta held the stallion back from the line. She nodded to the stewards, making it clear that she did not mind starting from behind the pack. The crowd quieted in anticipation as the competitors lined up again. They roared as the starting shot echoed out. The tightly packed racers surged down the course with a sound like rolling thunder. Chrysta had El Diablo so tightly in check that his body looked almost compressed. His massive head was bowed to his chest and most of his weight was shifted back on his dancing hind legs. She held him there, waiting for the main group to clear the confines of the street.

As he watched his competition move out, the stallion's body stilled, holding like a quivering statue. One ice green eye rolled in Azra's direction and those black lips peeled back in an evil, fang toothed smile. That wicked anticipatory expression jerked the outrider out of the crouch he had assumed before taking off. Before Azra could react in any way, Chrysta rocked her center of gravity forward. She loosened her hold on the reins at the same time. El Diablo uncoiled, launching himself down the street like a thrown spear.

Azra's golden eyes narrowed. All the alarms in his head went off as he watched the rider use her whole body to keep the savage animal away from all of those tempting human "morsels" lining the street.

"GRANT!"

The outrider crooked a black talon in a come hither gesture. Azra's respect for the man recovered a notch when the bartender came forward without hesitation. The Innkeeper listened intensely to the demon's gravelly voice, quietly nodding to indicate his understanding of the instructions. He backed away as the demon strode out into the street to give himself wing room.

Azra growled back over his shoulder as he crouched to take off.

"If either of them give you... ANY... flack, you tell them that Constantine is not the one they will have to account to if they refuse what I demand!"

In a flurry of black on crimson wings and wind the outrider sprang up. He shot along the street, causing the crowd to scream and clap again thinking it was all a part of the show.

It only took a few minutes for Azra to catch up to the racing pair. Chrysta was following the path that led to the river route they had traveled before. The other riders were avoiding it, proof that the news of the pack of rapines had been passed along. The woman was cutting every corner she could before they reached the forest. She often directed the galloping stallion off of the path to cut across open ground. This was shaving distance but it made the rider work harder. Azra could see her body making constant and minute adjustments in its balance as she used her skill and experience to steady the big animal as they traveled over the rougher ground.

Azra slipped the little Spy Bug in his ear, wincing as it set its claws so it would not fall out. The demon dropped his altitude, picking up speed so he could ride over the pair. He leveled off high enough it wouldn't distract her but low enough that his black shadow passed over them. This alerted the rider that he was there. He saw

Chrysta's head move slightly as a flick of her fingers acknowledged her awareness of him.

He mentally nudged the Bug to transmit knowing now it wouldn't startle her.

"I won't be able to see you once you are in the trees. Contact me every couple of minutes so I can follow where you are at!"

Chrysta must have set hers to transmit a constant feed. She did not physically answer him. Instead Azra suddenly heard El Diablo's pounding hooves. He was also privy to Chrysta's occasional murmur as she encouraged the stallion. More often than these were the hissed curses as she swore at the beast when he fought her control.

She flashed a quick, narrow eyed look up at Azra's dark winged form as they entered the shadow of the forest.

"No matter what you hear, Azra. DON'T interfere!"

The winged one gave a slight nod as he dropped a little lower to just skim over the trees. She would be traveling where he couldn't see her for a long while and he wasn't PROMISING anything.

Azra found that if he flew at just the right height he could get fleeting glimpses of silver and crimson. This made the pair a little easier to track. He almost dropped into the trees when a loud thump and crack came over the link.

"Damn it...you FUCKER! Do that again and I WILL put a bullet in you."

The radio did a fairly good job of picking up the fury in Chrysta's voice.

"Are you okay?"

He heard her grunt as she fought the silver for control before she breathlessly answered.

"I'm fine... fricken ASSHOLE just tried to scrape me off on a tree."

The only sound for a while was the muffled rumble of hooves. Azra relaxed a little. Maybe the stallion had worked it out of his system.

A sound came over the radio that the demon was very familiar with... the double click of a gun being cocked.

"We have company."

Was all Chrysta had time for.

El Diablo screamed hoarsely. Three sharp CRACKS echoed through the forest as Chrysta's gun voiced its own challenge. The sound of the stallion's grunt of pain at twin impacts came over the feed. A screech of talons skittering over dragon-mail made the demon's skin crawl. The racing pair broke into a slight clearing. Azra had a glimpse of a rapine hanging on to the stallion's shoulder. The creature dug its talons in while trying to reach the rider. Chrysta swung her elegant gun up and over, literally putting her hand in the dagger toothed mouth as she pulled the trigger. The ugly head disintegrated. El Diablo's flying back hooves caught another attacker that had launched itself at his rump. As the trees closed back around them the pair was pulling away from the pursuing animals. The pack slowed down. They had lost five members in the same amount of seconds. They knew they were hopelessly outmatched when it came to keeping up with the destria's speed. The rest turned off, looking for easier prey.

Azra listened carefully. El Diablo's hoof beats never faltered and Chrysta's breathing settled back into a steady rhythm. It sounded as if neither had come to any real harm. With the noise of the rapines crashing through the undergrowth, the demon lost track of the pair for a moment. He gained altitude trying to get a glimpse of them. As a result, the outrider was high, a little behind and to their left when the pair broke out of the trees.

They were heading for the ridge overlooking Paradise valley when El Diablo slipped sideways while in full stride. He twisted and spun in one fluid motion. Chrysta's injured muscles could not compensate for the combination of three different direction changes in the space of a breath. The rider was pitched off over the silver shoulder on the right. Azra watched as she tucked into a ball and hit the ground rolling. Chrysta must have known what El Diablo was thinking because she continued to roll, just vacating the spot where all four of the stallion's sharp cloven hooves viciously landed. The stallion followed, trying to crush her under his hooves. Luckily, sheer momentum carried him past her rolling body.

The outrider cursed, gaining speed and losing altitude faster than was safe as he tried to make it there in time. He snarled another as Chrysta gasped harshly over the radio.

"AZRA... do NOT interfere!"

Flaring his wings wide, the demon shot over the two as the woman rolled gracefully to her feet. Her eyes never left the stallion who had made his turn and was charging back. Chrysta crouched slightly and sidestepped as the beast reached her, barely avoiding those snapping jaws. As El Diablo's speed carried him past, she stepped forward. One hand buried itself in the flying white mane and one hand caught the harness that held her sword. The stallion's forward momentum jerked her off of her feet and up. With a quick twist of her hips, the rider landed back in the saddle. El Diablo screamed his frustration as she wrestled him around and put him back on the path.

As they topped the ridge, Azra made a pass

that put him close enough to feel the heat coming off of the stallion. He could see that Chrysta's mail seemed to have protected her a little but the sound of her breathing in the transmitter was ragged. Her movements as she kept up with her mount's constant antics had lost some of their fluidity. The outrider lifted, then dropped in a slow curving glide over the valley. There were three riders far enough ahead on the course that the dust of their passing was just starting to settle. A couple of driving thrusts with his wings and the demon gained some altitude. He turned back just as El Diablo shook his head violently and slid to a stop. Chrysta stuck with him this time. Her hiss of pain ended in a sharp, gurgling cough. Azra was hurtling back when he realized that the silver was just standing, nostrils flared as his sides heaved for breath, looking over Paradise Valley.

The demon heard Chrysta murmur.

"There... you dumb ass. THAT is what you are well on your way to losing."

Shifting all four reins to one hand, the rider worked at getting the pouch at her side open with the other. Azra folded his wings and rolled so he was moving backwards through the air. When his speed dropped to almost zero, his wings opened so he could hover. Chrysta had her hand over her mouth, her body slightly doubled while she coughed again. As her green eyes lifted to catch the demon's concerned gold ones, she shook her head slightly and smiled.

The woman re-arranged the reins in her hands and tried to turn the big silver back to the path. El Diablo resisted for a moment, his intelligent green eyes studying the valley. That icy gaze drifted over to the hovering form of the outrider. Then the stallion's head twisted back to analyze the woman on his back. Chrysta stared him down. If she was worried about her ability to stick with the big animal, she didn't show it. His head snaked back around and El Diablo suddenly reared. His guttural challenge echoed over the peaceful valley. Those mighty front hoofs didn't even return to earth before the beast twisted and launched himself into a driving gallop.

Azra shot ahead of the pair. The other riders had stayed on the longer, easier path. None it seemed, wanted to risk the unknown in Splatter canyon. Gliding back the outrider realized that El Diablo's gallop had changed. The stallion wasn't fighting his rider's hands every step of the way. As a result, his stride had become longer... Each movement more fluid. Some of the true speed that the stallion was capable of was coming through. With each huge, oily stride the rogue covered a little more ground. Chrysta was still holding him back, trying to make sure he had the stamina to finish strong. She had been given a bit of a respite. The sound if her breathing settled back to a more normal rhythm.

The woman turned the silver down the lower path. After a couple of strides, her head snapped up.

"Azra, something's not right at the entrance to the canyon."

The outrider raced ahead gaining altitude. The extra height gave him a clear view of a small group of racers blocking the path. It looked like they had found some of the ringers.

The demon snarled softly.

"Someone has planned an ambush for you and El Diablo."

Chrysta slowed the stallion.

"SHIT!" This was followed by a softer. "How many are there?"

The demon took a quick head count.

"It looks like there are six of them. All seem to be carrying small arms."

"REALLY... you don't see any rifles?"

The woman actually smiled. It was a wicked, nasty smile. It reminded Azra of the evil grin that El Diablo had sent his way at the start of the race.

"Well... it sucks to be them now... doesn't it?"

The woman drew her sidearm. With a quick flip of her wrist, she opened the chamber, checking that the weapon was fully loaded.

She then flipped it closed.

"Let's hope this bad boy remembers the battle training Thranatos gave him!"

Azra flinched as Chrysta dropped all four reins across the stallion's thick neck. This meant she was controlling the silver with her legs and body alone. El Diablo knew something was up. His deep, rumbling moan promised violence. The black and crimson sword whispered out of its sheath and seemed to become an extension of Chrysta's right hand. Now the outrider understood why she had trained herself to shoot with her offhand.

The woman shot a glance up at the winged shadow above her.

"You know... the rules state that you can't PHYSICALLY interfere with the race. It says nothing about not scaring the shit out of them."

Azra's grin was just as wicked as hers as he shot up, climbing hard and fast. When he was far enough up that he wouldn't alarm the group, the demon banked to travel parallel to the bluff that the canyon split. The demon could see the other riders drawing their weapons as Chrysta and El Diablo broke out of cover and roared down the path. They held their fire, waiting for the pair to come into range. Azra rolled and folded his wings, leaving just enough surface for control. Then he dropped into a steep dive, picking up speed as he started his run along the bluff.

One minute, the waiting men were confidently watching the silver stallion's charge, knowing that they had the advantage in numbers. In the next, a savage roar from their left had them looking then screaming, as they jockeyed positions, trying to get away from the black winged nightmare that rocketed towards them on the wind. The ploy worked. Instead of running into the fire of six guns, the silver was fired upon by only two. The others frantically turned their weapons on Azra. He cursed as he felt the tug and pain of a couple of bullets finding their mark. Flaring his wings with a sharp CRACK, the outrider rolled over the ambushers. His speed along with the maneuver caused the rest of the flying lead to miss.

El Diablo held his ridged, horned head low as he charged. The heavy bone served as a shield, protecting his vulnerable neck and chest. He came in fast, ducking and dodging, responding to Chrysta's signals like a well-trained battle mount. Her beautiful sword licked out like black edged flame. In a move reminiscent of one of the Forsaken's legendary shadow-dancers, the woman deflected the other shots that the men had time to fire. Her gun sang out three times. The shots were deadly accurate even though she aimed on the run. Two bodies flipped off of their mounts and another destria reared. Twisting and screaming, the animal unseated its rider. The others had no time to re-group as a screaming, slashing juggernaut plowed into their midst.

One destria went down, the impact taking the animal clean off of its feet. Its unlucky rider had the misfortune of his having his face meet El Diablo's front hoof. He did not get up. The second rider turned his mount and brought his hand gun slamming down at Chrysta's head. She caught the blow on the muzzle of her gun. Using the same motion, she slashed sideways with the blades that were on her gun hand's gauntlet. Her attacker's throat opened, and he twisted away trying to staunch the flowing blood with his hands. Chrysta also lashed out with her foot driving the sharp edges there into the side of the man's destria. This animal had slammed against El Diablo, snapping and slashing with long black fangs. Squalling the injured beast fell back. The third stallion made the unwise mistake of engaging the enraged silver in battle.

Both animals reared shoulder to shoulder. Each tried to unbalance the other as their fang filled mouths snapped at soft throats and muzzles. El Diablo ducked sideways. The other beast staggered as he overbalanced. His rider whipped his gun around trying to get a bead on the vulnerable soft neck behind the silver's ridge and Chrysta's gun cracked one more time. The bullet peeled the man out of the saddle. The other stallion tried to disengage but El Diablo was relentless. His black horns hooked under the doomed beast's soft jaw, ripping through muscles and arteries. The silver lifted the entire front half of the other animal high into the air then he slammed the bleeding body into the dust. El Diablo tried to savage the fallen destria but Chrysta drove her heels into his sides. Her strong legs forced him off of his victim. With a frustrated scream he continued on into the canyon.

Splatter canyon was aptly named. Sheer rock walls rose up on either side of the rolling river. Its current ran swift and deep. There was a narrow path that had been cut into the cliff on the right, providing a treacherous passage along the gorge.

Azra soared, trying to find some lift. He did not like the narrow claustrophobic confines of this place. The racing pair was climbing as he passed. Chrysta sheathed the sword. The demon admired the skill it took to slide the slender blade home while the sheath and the rider were moving. She also holstered the gun as she directed the running stallion up the path.

"You NEED to re-load!"

Azra had been with his host long enough to know this was a basic gunslinger's rule.

"I need to watch were we are going more!"

Was the breathless response that came over the transmitter. The pair was moving at a ground eating pace, fifty feet above the rolling river. Chrysta had the four reins gathered back in both hands. Her upper body was positioned forward over the thick silver shoulders, helping to brace and balance the big animal on the rough path. She kept her gaze firmly ahead, looking for obstacles. The demon did not see her glance even once at the river below.

They came around a bend only to have the path disappear. Chrysta had time to shout "Son of a BITCH!" as she tried to rein El Diablo in. The silver shook his head and grabbed the dual bit between black fangs. He continued on without slackening his pace. Azra would have sworn the animal was part mountain goat as he flowed from ledge to rock to bare bump across the rock face. His cloven hooves slipped and slid as he scrambled for purchase, sending rocks rolling into the river below.

Chrysta kept up a panicked litany of curse words all the way across until the silver made it back to a solid path. El Diablo smiled a wicked Destria smile and pounded on.

The woman became very quiet. The only sound coming through the transmitter was her harsh gasps and an occasional grunt as she shifted with her mount. Azra passed almost level with them when they were one hundred feet above the river and she spared him a quick glance. Those green eyes were dark with fear, her jaws tightly clenched. The outrider remembered that Chrysta had a real fear of heights. The path leveled out a little allowing El Diablo's stride to open up again and the outrider had to work to keep up.

The path had started to drop back towards the roiling water when a rock shattered at head level with the woman. She flinched sideways in reaction.

"What in the hell was that?"

El Diablo grunted and jerked as something impacted on the dragon-mail covering his thick neck. Sparks flew as it ricocheted.

"SNIPER!"

Azra was looking but couldn't see anything on the opposite cliff. They couldn't hear any gunshots. Evidently the hidden gunner figured out that the mail would stop a regular round. When the next bullet came the armor across the silver's rump jumped, then split. A red furrow streaked across the thick muscle. The stallion screamed in angry protest.

"HOLY! Those are armor piercing rounds!! AZRA... that side is NOT part of the course. FIND him!"

The woman knew that they had no way to hide.

The outrider had been scanning the cliffs, but still couldn't pinpoint the sniper's location. His head snapped around as Chrysta grunted and jerked back. The mail along her ribs rippled.

"SHIT!"

Without hesitation, the woman jerked the big stallion's head around. Riding like all the hounds of hell were on their ass she drove El Diablo right off the cliff. The silver dropped. Hitting the water hard he promptly sank. Azra dropped with them, pulling up at the last moment. The demon ignored the threat from above, desperately looking for the pair. He saw that long silver head break the surface. The stallion's panicked green eyes looked into his own for a moment then the beast went under again. El Diablo was heavy boned. Destria were not designed as great swimmers. Add to this the weight of saddle plus armor and you had a perfect recipe for drowned devil!

Pain shot through Azra's left wing, dangerously close to the bone. He snarled and pumped to gain altitude as another bullet skimmed across his back.

"THERE!"

This time he was at the right angle to see the flash of a silenced rifle.

Azra headed for the spot, picking up speed with every powerful wing stroke. He shot along the river then soared up. As he passed the gunner on the cliff, the winged nightmare reached out and plucked him off with little effort. He continued to climb out of the canyon. The man screamed once as they shot over the flat tops of the bluff. When the outrider reached the peak of his climb he drew his victim up to where the man could get a good look at the golden eyed face of death.

It was the blond Temple Guard. The man had enough steel in his spine he tried to talk his way out of the situation.

"Oh man, Oh man, it's nothing personal. I am just doing my job. DON'T kill me. I was just following orders. Constantine is a Talon. HE would understand... it's nothing personal... you know.... I was JUST following orders!"

Azra hissed softly.

"Hmmm.... Yes, Templer would totally understand your predicament." The words deepened to an angry growl. **"YOUR problem is... I...am NOT Constantine!!"**

The outrider rolled, dropping into a steep dive. His strong arms turned the blonde so he could see the ground coming at them. At the last moment Azra released the screaming man while snapping his wings open with a sound like a cracked whip. The man continued on his trip to the ground while the demon's winged form shot up. The laws of momentum along with gravity gave the body a very satisfying crunch when it drilled into the hard ground.

Azra glided fast over the ground bleeding off some airspeed. He dropped over the edge back into the canyon. Golden eyes searched frantically for any trace of silver or crimson. They filled with relief when he finally spotted the stallion struggling in the rough water. Chrysta's head popped up alongside the destria and there was a flash of sunlight on wet metal. She was cutting every bit of armor off of the drowning beast, trying to lighten the load.

The struggling pair finally made it to where the path dipped down low enough that El Diablo could pull himself out. The woman held tight to the sword harness as he dragged her with him. Once out of the water Chrysta let go. She curled up on the damp bank. The sound of her coughing and retching was clear over the transmitter.

Azra was still too far away to help when El Diablo swung his massive head down hooking sideways with those wicked horns. He caught the woman just below the waist, twisted a little and lifted. Chrysta cursed breathlessly as the painful pressure made her body expel a lot of the water that her cracked ribs prevented her from coughing out. The silver ignored her protest, scooping her up so she could get her feet under her to lean against his warm side. The woman was still coughing as the stallion pushed her with his nose towards the stirrup. HE was ready to get back under way. The woman dragged herself back into the saddle and glanced up as Azra winged by. She pumped her fist once, and the battle stallion surged forward again in a hard gallop. The pair reached the end of the canyon, turning for home. There were only two other racers in sight. Azra realized they were at the point that he needed break off and return to the town. He dropped low over the flying beast.

"I have got to leave now. Are you okay?!"

He was more than a little concerned that Chrysta didn't seem to have the breath to answer. She just lifted one hand and twirled it before pointing towards home... letting the outrider know she had heard him. With a savage snarl the demon shot up and rocketed towards the town. He wanted to give Constantine the time he would need to be fully awake when she finished this run.

"Templer..."

One deep rumbling voice worried at him.

"Constantine... Come on... You have to wake up!"

Grant's lighter baritone also intruded along with sharp stabbing pain. They both took turns annoying him. The voices came from inside and out, forcing him towards reluctant awareness. Realization flooded back, and the priest jerked himself awake, blinking in the bright sun. Azra had deposited him on the roof of the Ironwood. Grant was crouched next to him. The Innkeeper was using painful pressure points to force him awake. The big man helped him to sit up.

Constantine could not suppress the groan as his abused body protested violently.

"Damn it... Azra what did you do this time?"

"I am sorry... Constantine. We ran into some... difficulties not to mention... a couple of bullets."

The outrider sounded infinitely weary.

The gunman frowned and levered himself to his feet. Grant was searching the distance outside of town with a long range scanner. Smiling nervously, Andrew handed the Talon a small Spy-Bug.

"She should be back into range any minute now."

Templer listened but heard nothing but static. He joined the two in intently scanning the race course.

"There they are!"

Grant handed the viewer to the gunman. He could just make out a group of three riders at its maximum range. They were still too far out to decipher any detail when the transmitter crackled to life.

"Is anybody out there?"

The signal was faint, but Chrysta's exhaustion carried through. What had Templer's dark eyes narrowing was the soft bubbling cough that followed.

"We can hear and see you."

The Talon kept physically calm on the outside but inside was another story.

"WHAT in the seven hells happened out there Azra?"

The outrider answered, giving his host a terse, abbreviated description of the long day's events. He finished with...

"I took the liberty of having Grant call a couple of your friends. I believe we are going to need them."

The three racing destria were now close enough that the priest could see that Diego's gold was in the lead. The scruffy gray winner of last year's race struggled gamely in second and El Diablo was a little further back. Each huge stride was closing the distance on the other two. Chrysta could hardly be seen. She was buried in her mount's flying white mane. Even as they watched, El Diablo pulled up alongside the gray. The storm colored animal lengthened his stride and for a minute they ran side by side, nose to nose. The gray had won the previous year for a reason! He was not one to easily give up.

Templer heard a solid thump through the transmitter. Chrysta cursed harshly as the two stallions slammed together... hard. Both riders struggled to keep their seats. El Diablo peeled foaming lips back from long black fangs. Twisting his massive head, he pinned the gray with one ice green feral eye. The Talon did not know what the other beast saw in there. But it was enough that he slowed and veered violently sideways, visibly fighting his rider's control. The big silver pulled ahead into second place.

Constantine listened silently to the rider's quick uneven gasps. Her words of encouragement as she egged the tired stallion on... were frighteningly breathless.

The woman cleared her throat with another wet, bubbling, cough. This seemed to help. When she spoke again, her voice sounded a little stronger.

"Tell Andrew that El Diablo is dangerously overheated. He needs to have Joshua and Jeremy ready the minute we get there."

Templer relayed the message and Andrew went scrambling off the roof. After a couple of minutes, the boy hollered up at them.

"Come on, we have to meet her at the paddocks."

The gunman looked over the edge. The stable hand was mounted on one drafter, with Zephyr, Nuva and the other big boy in tow. Grant jumped down behind Andrew, and Zephyr lined himself up so that the Talon could drop down on him. No sooner was he settled and Andrew had them moving down the street to the destria compound where the race would end. They could see the full length of the two-mile main street from the large enclosure that had been designated for Chrysta's mount. The sound of the crowd swelled as the tired racers came into sight.

Don Diego's gold was ahead. Chrysta flattened down a little more and Templer could see her hands moving in time to El Diablo's huge stride. They were finally working as a team and the battle stallion was flying low. The pair pulled alongside the leader. Rafe struck out, catching the silver across the face with his whip. El Diablo ducked away.

The crowd screamed as the gold and the silver pounded together along the street. Their white manes and tails billowed and flowed, mingling together in the wind of their passing. Both stallions were close to their limits, their strides at full stretch. Steam rolled off of their super-heated bodies. Foam flew from both as El Diablo closed until they were neck to neck.

Constantine suddenly understood why Chrysta believed the beast's descended from dragons. Little flickers of flame had started to appear. These snorted out of flaring nostrils with each animal's straining breath. It also sparked on the hard pack underneath the pounding hooves. Rafe stuck at the face of the silver stallion again causing El Diablo to cough out an angry scream. The third time the man struck, Chrysta's sword whispered from its sheath and was there to block the blow.

The two animals slammed together, and the silver faltered. Templer's twist of fear joined Azra's as Chrysta lost her seat for a split second. The stallion gave a funny twist as he recovered his balance that put his rider back in the saddle. Rafe struck back at Chrysta causing her to twist painfully to block the whip. El Diablo fell back a fraction. His fanged mouth reached out, grabbing the red head by the thigh. The battle beast jerked. It forced the screaming Rafe to drop his whip. The man desperately grabbed on to his mount's mane. The silver couldn't hold on. That mouthful of leg was interfering with his breathing and he had to spit it out.

The silver pulled even, matching the gold stride for stride. They were one hundred yards from the finish line when the golden beast suddenly faltered... then recovered. Rafe was slashing him with sharp spurs, driving him on. Blood had started to stain the foam flying from the lovely destria's mouth. Templer saw Chrysta's green eyes slash sideways, and she did something that caused her mount to drift out a little. The gold nosed ahead for a moment. Then the beautiful dappled stallion gave an odd stumble as something inside of him gave under the pressure. Blood flooded from his nostrils. This time when he faltered, he didn't recover.

The racer pancaked, front legs stretched forward, back legs stuck behind. He slid along the street on his chest and belly. His weight and momentum dug a furrow in the dirt. As the golden body came to a stop his rider baled off with a curse. The heat from the animal seemed to concentrate... compress. With a muted whump, the dying beast spontaneously burst into flame. Chrysta had El Diablo past the burning corpse and over the finish line in the next few strides.

The crowd was yelling and applauding but they stayed well back. El Diablo slowed as he approached the paddock. His rider was sliding off even before he stopped. They had won, but the stallion had severely overextended himself. He staggered a couple of feet and dropped to his front knees. His nose was almost buried in the dirt as his sides heaved. Templer could feel the heat rolling off of the stressed animal. Chrysta was gasping almost as bad, but she didn't rest. She was stripping tack off as Andrew threw buckets of water over the steaming beast.

"Come on!!! GET up! Joshua... Jeremy... GET HIM UP!"

The woman sounded desperate. Templer had a sudden fear that Chrysta may have killed the beast in trying to save him!

The two drafters rolled forward, positioning themselves on either side of the stallion's trembling body. Dropping their massive heads, they hooked their blunted horns together under the stallion's foaming neck and chest like a basket. Using the incredible strength in their thick necks and muscled shoulders they heaved him up. Pinning the staggering stallion between their heavy bodies, the pair of drafters forced El Diablo to take one step...then two. Andrew was pouring water over all three, trying to bring that terrible heat under control.

Chrysta remained in front, coaxing and cajoling the silver as he took one shaky step at a time. Templer and Grant formed a united front keeping the crowd away from the paddock. Don Ricardo finally showed up and managed to get most of the crowd to disperse to the victory celebration. In a short time, the only sound was El Diablo's whistling breaths along with Chrysta's quietly murmured encouragements and her occasional soft cough. As the stallion became steadier, she signaled Andrew to stop the water and took the bridle off of El Diablo's head.

The exhausted woman backed away, letting Nuva and Zephyr come in to help the drafters keep the stallion walking. She bent forward at the waist coughing violently. When Chrysta turned towards Templer, her white skin combined with the blood around her mouth had both men running towards her. They didn't reach her before her strength gave out and she collapsed into the dirt.

The priest reached her first. Chrysta fought him as he tried to roll her on her back. He growled in surprise.

"Damn it Chrysta... be STILL! I need to check the damage."

She continued to struggle.

Azra snapped out.

"CONSTANTINE... She can't breathe laying

like that!"

Templer shifted her body up so that she was half sitting against his bent leg. Her breathing eased a little. The priest hastily cut her armor off... Only to hesitate at the woman's slight snicker. Her eyes flicked open.

"Holy... Constantine. What is with you and CUTTING off my clothes?!"

The Talon managed a slight smile and brushed a knuckle along her cheek. Then... he reached to cut the dirtied, bloodied shirt and wrappings off.

Grant put out a hand to stop him.

"Don't... I think that might be the only thing holding her together right now."

Constantine gave a terse nod and let Azra come forward as he gently checked over the damage. Some of her cracked ribs had that grinding feel that meant they had definitely splintered. There was a good chance this had caused some internal damage. The fact that Chrysta kept coughing up small amounts of blood verified this. There was also a bleeding hole on her lower left side where the sniper's round had penetrated her dragon-mail. Azra breathed a silent sigh of relief,

"There is nothing here that I can... see... that a good Healer can't deal with. You need to call your wind riding friend and find out how far out he is."

The gunman pulled out his Cricket and coded in Sig. The pilot picked up on the first ring and Chrysta's eyes popped open in surprise at the language that poured out of the device. Templer winced and held the agitated Bug away from his ear.

"Damn it Spooky... where in the Fricken HELL have you been? Iniko has been up my Fucking ass because NOBODY has heard from your sorry, skinny BUTT for a freakin WEEK!"

The man hardly paused for breath.

"Then some JACK ASS calls, demanding I make a GODS BE DAMNED special delivery! DO I look like a flippin delivery BOY? AND... he has the mother Fucking set of brass balls to THREATEN me with that bat winged fucker from HELL that lurks inside you."

Azra growled.

"I... DO... NOT... LURK!"

"Shut up Sig!"

Amazingly, there was silence on the other end. Something in the Talon's voice brought the tirade to an end. Templer continued, knowing he had the Captain's complete attention.

"Tell me how much longer until your arrival time?"

The Wind-master was silent a moment,

"Approximately one hour. We are fighting one HELL of a head wind and my gals are NOT happy infringing on a wild Tengshe's territory!"

There was a slight hesitation. The voice on the other end was filled with concern.

"Yer DAMNED lucky we weren't completely outta range. The Saint packed my med bay with a shitload of high end equipment I can't possibly afford. Then he told me to kick this pig to her max, even if I have to fricken burn her up getting there. Temp... are you shitten okay?"

"I am fine, Sig, but someone I care about... is not."

The priest spoke in almost a whisper.

He heard the rough pilot swear at someone, admonishing them that he didn't fucking care what concerns they had. Then he came back on.

"Give me Forty-five minutes TOPS... Constantine."

As he hung up the phone Chrysta reached up and tapped his chest. She kept her eyes shut. Templer slipped her cold hand into his flesh one.

"It's okay Chrysta. We have help on the way. Everything is going to be fine."

She coughed softly and tugged again on his shirt. He had to drop his head to hear her quiet words.

"Do you want to hear the good news first or the bad?"

Templer had a sudden feeling of dread.

"Hnnn... good news is always appreciated."

The woman smiled at him and Templer's heart stopped at the sadness he saw reflected in her eyes.

"I started chewing dreamleaf at the beginning of the race. Right at this moment, I really don't hurt at all."

Azra hissed.

"I KNEW you were moving to easily. This... is NOT good news!"

She flinched at the anger present in the deep rumbling voice,

"Well... it is better than the bad news."

Templer looked into her green eyes. Their pupils had shrunk down to pin points.

"What is the bad news?"

She sighed.

"I swallowed a whole mouth full of it back there... along with half of the river."

"You... what...?"

This came out a stunned whisper. Templer remembered Azra being very clear you NEVER actually ingest the leaf. If the dead silence from the darkness within didn't fill him with foreboding. The stricken look on Grant's face did.

The priest dug at his outrider. Azra became very quiet and very still.

"Azra... how do you treat an overdose?"

The demon growled unhappily.

"You... DON'T!"

The Talon's heart froze.

"Grant, maybe you should get Dr. Whitet?"

The big bartender shook his head slowly,

"He won't be any help. By now he is plastered. He would have to sedate her into a coma to avoid what's coming. The man does not have the strength or the equipment that type of support requires."

The gunman glanced down at the quiet, pale woman he had cradled against his chest.

"Azra, what are we dealing with?"

The outrider rumbled quietly,

"Any time now, Chrysta will start seizing. It will get progressively worse until something, most likely her heart, gives out. Given the condition she is in..." Azra hummed softly in misery. **"Ah Constantine... your friend will not make it in time."**

Templer didn't have a chance to respond in any way. He felt an odd tremor pass through

Chrysta and her eyes flickered open.

"Oh HOLY..." She whimpered. "Any of you can shoot me now."

Her pupils blew until they covered the green, making the woman's eyes seem solid black. Then Chrysta's body arched against his, muscles jumping and quivering. This first one only lasted a few seconds but the priest could feel her heart hammering and stuttering against his chest when it ended.

As she slowly relaxed, Azra gently prompted the gunman.

"HOST... you need to make sure she does not swallow her tongue."

The Talon nodded. He used sharp talons to slice a strip off the thick leather of the gun belt that held her beautiful gun. Chrysta's eyelids fluttered open at the sound and he knew the woman was at least partially aware of her surroundings when her brow arched up and her lips quirked as if to say... what... now you are cutting my clothes into PIECES?

Templer gently pried her jaw open. Her green eyes widened a little at the strange feel of his fingers in her mouth. He pushed her tongue down, slipped the strap in and closed her teeth on the leather. The priest cupped his flesh hand firmly under the woman's chin, holding her mouth shut so she could not spit it out.

Again the only warning Templer got was Azra's terse...

"GET READY..." And that odd tremor. This time the seizure lasted longer. When it was finished, Templer had to roll the woman to the side. Grant worked to clear the frothy blood from her airway before she choked.

When the gunman braced Chrysta back against his chest, she was unresponsive.

"There has got to be SOMETHING we can do to help her."

Templer did not like being in the position of total helplessness.

Azra rumbled a deep sigh,

"Constantine... You will not like this. There is only one way for this to end. We could make it easier on Chrysta and help her out of this world."

Templer realized what his outrider was suggesting. His arms unconsciously tightened around the woman's still form.

"It's okay... Host. Of all the times we have removed innocent souls from this world, this would be the time it would be forgivable."

Templer knew in his heart that Azra was right. All of the Tainted souls that they had removed from this world in the course of following orders against this single one... it should have been easy. Constantine realized that even one more soul was one to many. Especially this particular one. He was tired to death of being a Reaper.

"I can't do it Azra!"

"I know you can't." The demon's voice was very soft. **"But I... can. Let me out Templer... you need not have any part in this."**

Without warning, the third seizure hit. This time there was little break in between. Templer could feel Chrysta's ribs grinding as Grant helped while the priest struggled to hold her. As Chrysta's body slowly relaxed, her racing heart faltered and skipped. Templer watched the barman gently clear her airway again. He silently accepted the fact she couldn't last the remaining half hour it would take for Sig to reach them. He steeled his heart and prepared to release his outrider. He would not let his selfish soul be the cause of any more pain. A soft nose bumped him hard enough to stop the process. The gunman felt Nuva lay down behind him. Both her and Zephyr were loudly crooning. Chrysta's heart rate responded by becoming stronger. The thready rhythm steadied.

A familiar itch built behind Templer's eyes.

"Darkfire... we hold her essence here! We do not have the strength to alssso shelter her." Nuva sounded... strained. *"One must ssstay and hold... the other must join with usss."*

Templer hesitated in confusion. He gave a quick rundown of what the mare was saying to an even more confused Grant.

Andrew overheard and came forward. The young man was in tears.

"I think Nuva means that you need to change. When you become that... demon thing, your consciousness goes somewhere else. They want YOU to go with them and leave the demon form here."

Nuva nudged the Talon's shoulder.

"The shadow... knowsss... his heart. He MUST be the anchor. The flame shall be her shield."

Constantine felt the odd tremor that preceded a seizure and didn't hesitate. He faded back as Azra pushed forward. Before the Talon gave up total control, he snarled a warning.

"AZRA... You need to let this play out to the end. Don't you do anything... PERMANENT. No matter what happens!"

"UNDERSTOOD!" The outrider growled. **"Now HURRY!"**

As he finished the change, Azra was hard pressed to hold Chrysta's convulsing body without hurting her. He wrapped his wings around her like a full length blanket and used their strength to help keep her from tearing herself up inside.

This seizure did not want to let up. The destria's croon picked up a desperate note. The demon snarled softly.

"Come ON... Constantine! Whatever you are going to do... you need to do it NOW!"

Azra suddenly realized for the first time since he had been implanted, he could not feel his human host at all. Templer Constantine was totally gone.

Templer floated in the velvet dark as he had before when Nuva had spoken to him. The same blackened chain twisted and spun before him. He noticed that the tarnished strand was gone. Looking back, he could see the glowing gem forming the anchor at the end of the chain. All the darkness that had been held within the stone now flowed around him like living shadows. The Talon realized that instead of having a body here, he was nothing but ebony flame.

Up ahead, the darkness was lit by a gentle glow. This light pulsed with all the colors of life. There were images held within of a beautiful place. These shifted and disappeared. They seemed tantalizingly close yet at the same time were impossibly far away. Voices wove through the brightness in an eerie song. They promised joy. They promised glory. They promised peace.

The essence that was Chrysta was trying to reach this glorious place. This was being prevented by a wall of woven blue on gold energy. Time and again she came against it and every time it gently pushed her back. As the Talon approached, Chrysta was under attack by what looked like nothing more than a carpet of crackling lightening. This hostile force rolled over her diamond-like essence. Energy tendrils flashed and burned as it covered her. These knocked loose small wisps of sparkling light and vaporized them. Templer realized that because her destria were preventing her life force from leaving, the woman's soul was being torn apart a piece at a time. He and Azra had done much the same thing many, many times. When they destroyed a Tainted, body and soul... they prevented it from reaching this final peace.

Templer increased his speed. Like hell if he would stand by while someone he cared for was destroyed in this way! He slid his essence between hers and the lightning. With the first strike he realized that the licking bolts were made out of intense, fiery pain. He felt Chrysta roll underneath him, trying to break for the light again. The priest tightened his energy until it formed a shield of ebony strength that she couldn't escape. The fiery bolts still penetrated and passed through him, but his energy insulated hers. He absorbed a lot of the terrible pain before it could reach its mark.

The Talon's time spent under the cruel hands of his Maker's had taught him all he would ever need to know about... enduring. He closed his mind and hunkered down. Templer would ride this out and protect her until either Sig made it or they BOTH burned down to nothingness.

Azra breathed a small sigh of relief when the woman he cradled in his arms and wings stopped convulsively thrashing. Small tremors still ran through her body, but whatever his host and her destria were doing, it was helping. Grant cleared Chrysta's airway again and wiped the blood off of her face. When the big man went to return the leather to her mouth, the demon stopped him.

"I don't think we need that now. She will breathe easier without it."

Andrew came forward to give the bartender a clean towel and a new strip of leather. Just in case. He flinched when the outrider shot him a cold, gold eyed glare.

"This... DEMON thing... has a name. It is Azra. You do not have any excuse after this to call me by anything other than that!"

The young man swallowed hard and nodded. Grant gave the boy a sympathetic look and glanced sideways at the dark form next him.

Azra growled softly and looked away.

"I HATE that title. I may not remember exactly WHAT I am... but I am NOT a demon!"

They sat in silence as the dark of night descended. The two destria, the two men, and one large dark demon cradling the quiet woman did not know what a... odd... sight they made. Twenty minutes passed when Templer's Cricket chirped.

Azra could hear the roaring scream of Tengshe pushed to their limits underscored by the crude mouth of the Wind-Master, along with the sounds of alarms.

"Devil be DAMNED! I don't care WHAT the fuck is causing it... Just fricken FIX IT!" Then... "We are just outside of the shit-hole you call a town. Give me some kinda damned signal so I can find your sorry asses!"

Azra had already calculated that IF the pilot was as good as he maintained, he should be able to set his ship down on the field that held the race track. It would be a tight fit, but it was close to where they were. Pumping one closed fist into the air the outrider released a short bolt of energy. This gave the pilot a flare of sorts. A few seconds later the roar of the enslaved elementals that powered the great WindClipper filled the air.

The Captain's voice came over the Cricket.

"Holy SHIT! Why don't ya just give me a shitten postage stamp to land on!?"

The outrider motioned at the Bug and Grant

held it up for him,

"Shut UP Wind-rider! Retrieve your balls from where ever they are hiding and land that thing. We are running out of time!"

There was absolute silence on the other end. Then...

"Uh... shit! Temp?"

Azra snarled.

"It is Templer... not Temp! And NO... this is the bat winged fucker from HELL!"

"Oh... well... where the hell is Temp... um... ler?" The pilot was delicately maneuvering the ship down as he spoke.

"Constantine is... occupied... at the moment. Now shut UP and pay attention to what you are doing!"

Azra had real concerns for the buildings at the far end of the track. Even El Diablo raised his weary head to watch with interest.

As the ship settled, the outrider had to give the foul mouthed, brash human a degree of respect. He set the big WindClipper down without touching any of the structures that were just inches away in a couple of places. The demon sighed, Templer would NEVER hear the end of it from the obnoxious man.

"There is a damned medical bay set up in my forward cargo hold. The doc's that the Saint sent are already heading out."

Yep, the man's cannabis coarsened voice was definitely sounding smug.

The small group met the medics halfway. Again, the outrider had to admit that some humans seemed to have more than their share of courage. (or foolishness) The physician in the lead paled, but didn't flinch as Azra laid the woman's still body on the stretcher. It was with reluctance that he stepped back releasing responsibility to them. He had to remind himself that the Saint would send no one that reported to the Hand. Of the Captain he had no doubts. That one would burn with his ship before he betrayed his friends.

The stars caught Azra's golden eyes as he stepped back. The sound of Grant explaining what was going on deadened as the demon realized he was looking at his freedom. All he had to do was break the chain that tethered Constantine to his body. Azra's Bindings would not stop him; the host had abandoned this vessel willingly. The Talon would not die but with his other in sole possession of his body... the man's soul would be forever trapped in limbo. Azra rationalized that Templer would prefer this to the life he had. The human would have his heart's desire and he would be free.

"A-Azra?"

A soft hesitant voice along with a warm hand stroking his wing, pulled the dark one out of his thoughts. Andrew was beside him. The boy tried to push him to follow as the medical group made their way to the ship. The doctors were already pumping sedatives into Chrysta and were inserting an airway for her on the run.

Azra slashed a hard golden eyed glare at the young man while lifting his lips in a savage snarl.

The man paled but held his ground.

"You need to go with her. Chrysta will need you when she wakes up."

Whether he knew it or not, Andrew's hand was slowly stoking that dark soft wing. (OH MY GODS! His reputation was ruined when young men were so unafraid that they dared to PET him!)

The fire died in the golden eyes that stared into the young man's face. Azra realized that the courageous youth was right. Nuva had KNOWN what she was talking about. This shadow knew his heart... he WAS the anchor.

Azra sent his consciousness spinning down that fragile black chain. As he intertwined with it... Azra could feel that his host was nearing the end of his strength. Although the storm he defended against was losing its hold, Templer did not have the reserves to return. The outrider sent a tendril of strength to the Talon's essence. For a moment the smooth shield would not let him in. Then it recognized its partner. The ebony fire sluggishly contracted. Wavering... it linked up and weakly allowed Azra to tow it home.

The outrider noticed as they withdrew, that the destria's wall was fading. Nuva and Zephyr were also retreating, their strength almost spent. The subdued gleaming essence that was Chrysta did not stir towards Heaven's Gate. Her brilliant scintillating colors were gone, the gem barely lit. She was held to life by artificial means now. Azra reached the medical bay just as the doctors whisked the comatose woman off to surgery. Infinite weariness filled the outrider's limbs. Before he allowed the shift, he turned to the young man at his side.

His golden eyes held Andrew's with a stern gaze.

"Constantine will be in rough shape when he awakens. Do NOT under ANY circumstances allow the white coats to... handle... him. That could get very messy, very fast! Do you understand?"

Andrew, his eyes wide just nodded.

With a sigh of relief, Azra triggered his shift. Grant and Andrew gently caught the limp body of Templer Constantine as he collapsed into their arms.

Templer woke to darkness. More frightening than this, he woke to the terrifying smells of the Healer's Sect. He was lying on a bed in a small curtained off alcove. The Talon could hear the sound of people arguing. As he listened he forced his tired body to relax. He had to work to suppress the natural instinct that was telling him to get the hell out of there!

He could identify Andrew's voice. The young stable hand sounded angry but was attempting to keep his volume down.

"I don't care who you are... I don't CARE about the Saint. I have... ORDERS... to not let ANY Doctors mess with him." Templer heard the young man mutter, "And the person who gave me that order is a HELL of a lot scarier than you!"

Constantine levered his protesting body out of the bed. If the boy knew anything about the Saint, he might think differently. The Talon picked the Trinity out of its holster. Staggering over, he silently stuck his head through the curtain. Andrew had his back to him. Andrew was preventing a medic from passing. The medic had two burly interns (thugs) with him and was threatening to have them remove the young man.

The Talon was quietly amused when Andrew snorted derisively and his body took on a fighting stance. He looked and sounded fierce enough that the orderly's hesitated.

"Listen, asshole! I deal with two thousand pound, hoofed, horned, and let's not forget FANGED, meat eating devils with poisonous spurs EVERY day. I am still here to tell you about it! If you THINK you can get by me... bring it on!"

Templer silently lifted the big gun and aimed it in their direction. Both interns paled when they got a good look down its triple bores. The gunman put his finger to his lips and motioned slightly with the long barrels, indicating that they should leave. The men complied with haste. Andrew relaxed his aggressive stance with a soft, tired sigh.

The exhausted priest had managed to make his shaky way halfway back to the bed when Andrew appeared at his side. Wrapping a strong arm around him the boy helped Templer the rest of the way. He eased the gunman back down on the bed. The stable hand admonished him the entire time that Constantine should in no way be trying to get up until he got some rest. The Talon's lips quirked. What was with Chrysta that she attracted men with the dreaded M.H. T's? At this thought, his memory of the past day's events flooded in and the man struggled to sit back up against Andrew's remarkably strong hands.

The gunman was a little surprised to find he was so weak that the young man managed to pin him on the bed.

"Damn it! Constantine... listen! Chrysta isn't even out of surgery yet. Azra said that you need to REST."

Templer was exhausted. He was in no small amount of pain and heavily stressed by being even this close to a medical bay. He reacted to being restrained mostly out of instinct. Andrew froze, sucking in a breath as the Trinity's cold muzzle pressed against the soft skin under his jaw.

"WHOA... Constantine... back OFF! I LIKE this boy. He has... Spunk! Damn it HOST... STAND DOWN!!"

Azra realized what was happening and he

managed to freeze his overwrought host's muscles before the man did anything... permanent. His deep growl softened.

"I am weary; your strength is totally spent. PLEASE Templer... go... to... sleep!"

Andrew saw uncertainty flicker in the Talon's eyes. He slowly reached up and sliding his hand down the barrels of the big gun. He just as slowly eased it away from his throat. The boy just caught the heavy weapon as Templer let his suddenly limp hand fall. The stable hand could tell that the priest was fighting the overwhelming need to sleep. He patted the lean, long fingered hand laying on the blanket.

"It's OKAY! Between Grant, Captain Sig, and myself... NOBODY is going to disturb you. I will personally make sure you are awake when they bring Chrysta out."

The young man's eyes never left the tired, pale face. He breathed a silent prayer of thanks when Templer's long black eyelashes fluttered down to cover his unearthly black and gold eyes. The man was finally asleep.

It was eight hours before the surgery team finished. It was another two before they considered the injured woman stable enough to allow anyone to see her. Andrew ignored his exhaustion, staying so he could be with the Windrider when they cautiously woke Templer up.

The head of the surgery team met them before they reached the curtained partition that held Chrysta's bed. The space was crowded with a myriad of life support machines. The healers that were linked to both her and the bio-machines were nothing but faceless shadows in the dark. Grant rather belatedly joined them.

The physician cleared his throat nervously.

"We repaired most of the internal damage. The patient lost a rather large amount of blood because of it. With our support, her system seems to be handling this without too much difficulty. If it were all we are dealing with our acolytes could perform a Blessing and everyone could go home. Unfortunately, we have run into a problem. The substance that the patient overdosed on has insinuated itself into her nerve cells. It is over stimulating them and causing excruciating pain. At the same time this has stripped her body's ability to protect itself against the pain."

Templer did not like the way the Healer referred to Chrysta as... the patient... rather than using her name. He growled,

"And this means?"

The physician flinched at the dislike in the deep voice. He rubbed a tired hand over his face. He was NOT telling this frightening man how close they had come to losing the woman the first time they had tried to bring her up out of the drug induced coma.

"We are NOT dealing with an earthly substance. None of us is willing to try a Sanctioned healing while she has a product from Hell infiltrating her system. It is taking all our acolytes can give to keep her pain levels bearable... WHILE SHE IS DRUGGED!

Every time we try to reduce the sedation and wake her, these levels increase until her body tries to seize again. We can't think of any way to purge the toxin from her system. All we can do is keep her sedated with the hope that, if given sometime and support, her body will flush the drug out itself."

The Healer hastily left with instructions to get him if there was ANY change. Grant silently visited the bedside for a few moments. He could not stay he quickly explained. The man had been late because Don Ricardo had called a town meeting. It seemed that Don Diego was trying to squirm his way out of paying up on the bet by insisting that his son had overstepped his authority in making the wager in the first place. Templer had to figuratively "SIT" on Azra as the outrider's rage combined with his own rolled like a tide through his mind. Templer knew that his body could NOT deal with another Shift this soon.

Seeing the look on Constantine's usually inexpressive face, Grant hastily grabbed his shoulder.

"No... She needs BOTH of you to HERE! The Don's don't take lightly when one of their own acts without honor. Chrysta has many people in this town who care for her and WE will make sure Diego doesn't get away with this."

After he left, Templer settled one hip on the edge of the bed. He slid his hand under Chrysta's, which was lying cold and still on the covers. The Talon tried very hard to ignore the wires and invasive tubes that were keeping her alive. He refused to look at the silent forms of the Acolytes whose Tainted abilities provided the strength her body lacked. It did not help to tell himself over and over that this had NOTHING in common with the experiences in his life. She was not being tortured.

"Azra, what are the chances that her body can purge itself?"

The outrider took a long time to answer and Templer knew before he did, he would not like it.

"I told you before Constantine. There is only one way for this to end. You should have allowed me to do something... permanent... while you were unawares." The words were hard... in contrast to the demon's voice which was infinitely gentle. **"I am sorry... Templer."**

It was just... too... much! Constantine surged off of the bed, savagely shoving Azra... DOWN... as far as he could. The Talon strode out of the medical bay. He needed to get away from the oppressive machines. He needed to escape his fear of being there. Most of all, he needed to outrun the overwhelming emotions that crashed against the crumbling walls he maintained around his heart. Templer staggered off of the ship into bright sunshine. He winced at the sudden itching, burning head ache that slammed him behind the eyes. Azra tried to claw his way up but even this faded under the piercing pain and the dull buzzing that accompanied it. Together... it flat shut his mind down.

A little while later, Sig stepped out of the shadowed hatch. He had seen Templer blow by, visibly upset. The Windrider was surprised that the man had controlled his extreme dislike of anything related to Sanctioned Medicine as long as he had. It said something about how the introverted Talon must feel towards the injured woman his... companion... had called them in for. The Captain gave him some time to collect himself then went out to check on his friend.

As he lit his ever present smoke, the man's sharp eyes traveled over the animal pens that his Clipper was parked amongst. He burnt his fingers when he saw where Constantine was. Sig had been warned to stay away from the paddock that housed a massive silver, black striped beast. He hadn't needed the warning. Any dumb ass could see the sharp black fangs and evil eye the animal possessed. That is why it horrified him to see the shadow clad form of his friend INSIDE the paddock. The Talon was kneeling in front of the animal's dangerous sharp spurred front legs. Its heavy ridged, horned head was level with the man's, the dagger fanged mouth almost touching his pale cheek.

"SHIT...!"

Sig moved slowly towards the fence. He did not want to startle anyone, but maybe he could distract the creature from its intended victim.

Blood on shadows. This strange thought looped over and over again in the Talon's sluggish mind.

"HOST..." a sharp hiss penetrated the fog he couldn't seem to shake from his head.

The gunman muttered.

"It's TEMPLER..." Then his malfunctioning brain registered the ice green eye starring into his along with the black on silver striped legs he was kneeling in front of.

Oh SHIT... was his first immediate thought.

It was chased away by Azra's,

"Do... you... THINK! Don't make any fast moves... keep everything calm."

Templer realized that his gun hand was around the base of El Diablo's very sharp spur. A drop of blood red venom had gathered on its razor tip. As he watched, the shimmering liquid solidified in the warm, dry air. It dropped to join three identical ruby "gems" nestled in his blade-hand's black palm. It looked just like four drops of blood caught against a midnight shadow.

A voice like the kiss of thunder, echoed through his mind.

"HAVE THE WOMAN... INGEST... ONE OF THESE."

The cadence of the words sounded... young. But the Talon had the sudden impression of a granite mountain that was being up thrust. One day, if given the chance, this creature would be a force to be reckoned with. As El Diablo acquired age he would become like that massive granite peak. He would never yield. Like the mountain he would be powerful enough that mighty storms would run up against him and stop in their tracks! Constantine understood why Nuva had been so insistent on saving this one.

The Talon realized he did not have full control of his body yet. Those feral eyes flashed with... amusement... and SOMETHING forced his flesh hand up. He found himself vigorously scratching the soft skin under the collar that rode behind that solid, horned ridge. El Diablo sighed in pleasure and closed his eyes. Then he released his "lock" letting Templer go. The priest slowly eased up and staggered back. Strong hands reached through the gate and YANKED him out of the paddock.

"Mother of FUCKING demons! What the SHIT do you think you're doing? Have you gone Fricken INSANE in the week you've been here?"

The excitable pilot had the spider-silk cloak bunched in his fists and was shaking the Talon as he shouted. This did not help his splitting head ache at all. He managed to close his hand over those precious drops so as not to lose them.

Templer freed himself from the Captain's rough grasp.

"It's okay Sig and yes... I think I have probably gone insane over the course of this week."

The man held an internal conference with Azra as they studied the gleaming little drops.

"What do you think, we know there is no love lost between him and Chrysta?"

His headache spiked,

"I DO NOT DO THIS FOR... HER," There was still dislike in the feelings that accompanied these words. The ice green eyes glinted wickedly at them from

"I DO NOT DO IT FOR THE FLAME! IT IS DONE FOR THE SHADOW WITHIN... THE ONE WHO IS MY BROTHER IN SPIRIT."

Azra cursed.

"I am NOT a demon!"

El Diablo shook his head and chortled.

"THIS IS TRUE... YOU ARE A SHADOW OF WHAT YOU ONCE WERE."

Templer could feel his outrider's utter surprise.

"Do you know what... ARRHH!"

The forbidden question triggered Azra's bindings.

"Whoa... SHIT!"

Sig's strong arms supported him as Templer sank to his knees. Both of the priest's hands clenched against his head as Constantine shared in the agony that blasted through his partner.

A deep croon intruded, pushing the pain down to bearable levels.

"I CANNOT BE THE ONE TO BREAK YOUR CHAINS. FIND MY BONDMATE...HE WILL KNOW HOW TO HELP."

The silver's soft croon died out... his last words when he withdrew seemed almost wistful.

"PLEASE... WHEN YOU FIND HIM. TELL HIM... I STILL WAIT."

With Sig's help, Templer regained his feet. The Windrider stirred the ruby gems with a careful finger when his friend recovered enough to explain what had happened.

"Hell... Temp. My strength lies within the air and wind. I can't fricken tell ya if these are the poison or the cure. What does Batly think?"

Azra flinched at the new nickname... but did not complain. It was better than... demon.

"I cannot see as how it could hurt. Chrysta WILL die if we do nothing."

Templer sent Andrew to get Grant. If this did not work the bartender would want to say his good byes. They found themselves a few minutes later trying to explain to the doctor why he needed to bring his... patient... up out of the coma. It was important to remove the ventilator so she could swallow. The physician argued with them for a good ten minutes before Azra lost ALL patience and snatched control for a moment. The Trinity appeared in Templer's hand. With hot golden eyes he stared the frightened man down as he pulled back the hammers.

"DO IT!"

"Fine... anything that happens is on YOUR head..." The healer muttered. "I should at least have a crash team here if this doesn't work."

Azra moved back but before he did he murmured,

"IF this does not work... no crash team will be necessary."

Templer didn't contradict him.

The physician hastily made some adjustments on the blinking machines that helped to keep Chrysta comatose. He then nodded at one of the motionless Acolytes. This man must have been highly ranked to be aware enough to communicate. The linked healers moved close enough lay hands on the motionless woman. They would serve as buffers as long as they could ride out the pain. All watched tensely as her pain levels started to rise. It was not long and she blinked. Chrysta's eyes opened then narrowed as her discomfort grew. The shadowed gaze drifted over to the silent form of the waiting Talon. He responded to the bewilderment in them by kneeling next to her. Templer ran his fingers through the short, chestnut hair and spoke quietly in her ear.

"I know you hurt. Be still if you can. We need you to keep some control if only for a little while."

One by one the healers dropped out of the link... unable to bear the increasing agony. Before the healer was ready to pull the ventilator, only the highest ranked Acolyte still held his position. He reached the end of his strength too soon... collapsing as tremors traveled over Chrysta in waves. The woman held on to the gunman's hand and silently fought her body's desire to seize up with all of her iron will. A stern look from golden eyes had the surgeon pulling the tube before he really wanted to. As soon as Chrysta quit gagging and coughing, Templer pressed on her chin to open her mouth and dropped one blood red jewel in. The Talon was glad he held that lovely mouth closed when he saw the expression that crossed her face. He was pretty sure if he hadn't, Chrysta would have spit it right out.

A corner of his mouth twitched up as Azra spoke out.

"Don't make us sit on you... woman!"

Somehow she swallowed the bitter pill.

For too long the only sounds were the frantic beeping of the monitors, Chrysta's pained gasps, and a softly hummed... lullaby? Templer couldn't believe what he was hearing. This last came from AZRA! If forced to admit it... Templer would agree that the gentle tune... WAS soothing. Chrysta closed her eyes and seemed to get a little relief from it. After what seemed an eternity, the woman released a long sigh. The frightening tremors backed off. The outrider let his humming trail off as the red lined monitors changed to green.

Chrysta tiredly opened her eyes. Her words were hoarse but like music to the Talon's ears.

"GODS! That tasted NASTY! Worse than dreamleaf. I really hope you brought some coffee to wash it..." She shifted a little and winced. Her eyelids were already drooping.

"Hey...!" She murmured, "Azra... don't stop. That was... nice." The outrider picked up his tune and continued until she was asleep.

His superiors were pushing Constantine to end his vacation and return to duty. There were a couple of nasty problems that had cropped up that needed his particular... talents. Sig agreed to stay and give the Talon a lift whenever he was ready. The Captain had found the casinos. The Windrider wouldn't admit it but he was having a great time.

It didn't take Templer long to figure out he needed to stay a few days longer. Chrysta was a TERRIBLE patient. She didn't like the healer (although the gunman couldn't find it in his heart to blame her.) and would NOT follow his instructions. The physician refused to use a Blessing for fear of some weird cross dimensional interaction. On the morning of day two SOMEHOW... the woman convinced Grant to do it. The Talon made it very clear when he found the bartender helping her to sit up afterward, that he would NOT be leaving the two of them ALONE together again.

Although the Blessing worked as it should, Chrysta was still sore not to mention weak from blood loss. This was something only time would heal. The healer demanded she stay in bed. By the evening of the second day, she had used everything in her arsenal trying to convince the Constantine to let her leave and rest in her OWN room. He disregarded the grumbling. He pretended he didn't hear the cajoling and acted as though he was asleep through the badgering. In the end she resorted to WHINING.

Azra was absolutely NO help. He suggested that Chrysta would PROBABLY rest easier in her own bed. As the gunman carried her back to the Ironwood, (tubes needles and all!) the Talon did his best to ignore Grant's "HAH, she got to you too!" look along with the smug little smile on Chrysta's face.

Grant came up later that night. He grinned when he saw the woman curled up asleep against Templer's side on the bed. The priest put down the book he was reading when he saw the look on the barman's face. The finger he put to his lips admonished silence. Grant got his grin under control. The big man set a glass of red wine and one of water (Oh...Chrysta will LOVE that!) on the night stand and dropped a long sheet of paper in front of the book in Templer's hand. Then he very quietly gathered up the Talon's dirty clothing and slipped back out of the room.

The priest took a moment to study the paper and contemplated waking the woman to show it to her. It seemed the other Don's had made Diego see the light. Grant was now the sole owner of Paradise Valley. He studied the face of the peacefully sleeping hellion next to him and then shot a glance at the glass of wine and his book. The pleasant silence won out. Templer let the woman sleep.

The next morning the Talon got the woman to drink the whole glass of water by promising to remove the needles that she (and he) detested. Chrysta drank it with NO complaints and sipped her coffee while he kept his end of the bargain. When he came out from taking a quick shower the woman was standing at the window watching the courtyard. She had the folded deed dangling out of one hand. Azra assured him that, although still a little shaky, she was fine.

Grant had returned his clothing. They were clean and folded neatly. Where the spider-silk had been repaired with neat tiny stitches... the fabric was slowly weaving itself whole.

"You would be surprised at how neatly Grant can tie a stitch. He is almost as good at it as you."

Chrysta had left the window and settled herself carefully on the duvet. She watched him dress, her face quiet and still.

"You are planning on leaving, aren't you?"

Templer hesitated as he buckled the last strap on his cloak. The priest didn't realize he had tucked his chin down behind its high collar, hiding his face as conflicting emotions caused his stomach to roll.

Chrysta's sharp eyes noticed though. They shuttered themselves and she casually turned to look back out of the window.

"I understand Constantine. Just be sure to remember your promise and at least come to say good bye."

"Hnnnn... I would tell you that now. Just in case I don't have time to come by later."

Templer flinched, hating himself when her head dropped a little.

Then those strong shoulders straightened and Chrysta looked back at him with a slight smile.

"Do you think you will come back through this way?"

The Talon shrugged awkwardly,

"It is... possible."

The woman slowly stood and came to stand in front of him. She pulled his collar down revealing his face and softly kissed him on the lips.

"Well then... good-bye Templer Constantine."

Her green eyes stared deep into his.

"And good-bye Azra.... it has truly been an honor to meet you."

The outrider did not utter a word until they were halfway down the stairs, then he growled very softly.

"Constantine... You are such a coward!"

Templer froze in his tracks and savagely snarled.

"Azra... what in the seven Hells do you think will happen to Chrysta and her destria when I go back on the Maker's table? She might not be Tainted by the re-gen virus... but they will consider her a threat just the same. Mother of Demons... El Diablo is going to scare the living SHIT out of them. Add to this that woman's connections, no matter HOW tenuous, to the House Dracul..."

Azra hissed,

"HOLY... Templer... they will give Chrysta to the Inquisition and will turn her valley and everything in it to smoke and ASH!"

"BINGO... and just WHO do you think will get assigned this pleasant task?!"

When the outrider answered... it was in a sick whisper.

"What are we going to do?"

Constantine continued down the stairs.

"WE... are going to get as far away from here as possible. WE... are going to keep our heads down and do WHAT we are told, when we are told to do it. WE are going to pray to whatever deity will listen that I can keep our asses out of the Maker's labs. Last but not least... WE... are going to try and FORGET about Chrysta until we can figure out a viable excuse to pay a visit to the Crown Prince of HELL."

Foul weather moving in that afternoon took their departure time out of their hands. Sig wanted to get his Clipper out of the area before it hit. The storms this close to the Waste were known for abundant lightening and their unpredictably wild winds. The wild elementals contained within the massive front would make the Tengshe under the Wind-Masters control squirrely at best. Templer did find a quick moment to make it back to the Ironwood. When he opened the door, Chrysta was sound asleep on the duvet. Templer slipped into the room and stood for a long moment just watching her sleep. Then... the man knelt down, ruffled his fingers ever so carefully through her hair and lightly brushed her lips with his.

"Good-bye Chrysta."

He whispered softly against her mouth.

The woman stirred but did not wake. Grant watched him come down the stairs for the last time with understanding on his open face. The man lifted a hand and the Templer nodded in farewell.

Ugly black clouds were building on the horizon when Sig   delicately lifted his WindClipper out of town.

They were about ten miles out when Constantine couldn't stand it anymore. If Azra didn't quit radiating unhappiness, his host just might have to get creative in finding a way to kill himself!

"AZRA... do you want to go back and say good-bye in person?"

"YES... very much so... I just hesitated to ask as your physical condition is not the best right now. Your body has been through a lot this past week."

The Talon groaned softly,

"Go ahead, one more time will not hurt."

His outrider chuckled darkly,

"Yes... it will! Tell the Windrider I will catch up."

Azra winged back towards Edgewater at almost his top speed. He suspected Chrysta was a lot more upset by their leaving then she let on. He didn't trust that Grant could keep her from over extending herself too quickly. The sight that presented itself in the courtyard confirmed one of his suspicions. Chrysta had somehow gotten by Grant and was standing outside with Nuva, talking to another person. The outrider's sharp eyes picked up on the fact that she was wearing one of her leather riding vests.

With a shock, Azra recognized the person she was arguing with. It was the redheaded son of Diego. The outrider picked up speed. He was too far away to react when the woman lashed out, planting a fist upside the man's face. Rafe staggered back and clawed at his sidearm. Azra dropped fast but knew he wouldn't be able to beat the man's shot.

He need not have worried. Nuva reached the fool as he brought the gun up and buried her long black fangs in the redhead's shoulder. She yanked him up, flipping his body across the courtyard like a doll. When the man landed, he lost the gun. Azra landed lightly beside the woman as Nuva STALKED her victim, following him intently as he tried to crawl away.

"DON'T kill him Nuva."

The woman murmured this quietly as she watched the mare clinically study Rafe. Almost casually Nuva snapped a fore hoof down, breaking his leg. At the redhead's scream, Azra slashed a look at the woman standing quietly beside him. She made no move to stop the destria. Her eyes gleamed rich blue and a nasty smile curled her lips. The outrider realized that she was not only sharing in the old mare's vicious retribution. She was ENJOYING it! HOLY...

He loved this woman. Constantine was a FOOL to let a gem like this get away. No matter the logic! Azra's initial plan changed then and there. Trying to deny this piece of his heart would tear what was left of Templer's sanity apart.
Somehow they would find a way to protect what both of them loved. Another scream from the redhead drew his attention and Azra saw that the mare had nipped a good size chunk out of the boy's ass.

Chrysta snickered evilly,

"I'll bet that leaves a scar!"

Nuva plucked the man up by the collar and hoisted him over the fence and into El Diablo's paddock.

This time Chrysta moved.

"CRAP! NUVA... what part of... DON'T kill him didn't you get?"

Nuva snaked her head at her lifelong trainer and popped black fangs together.

Chrysta stopped in her tracks.

"Damn it... if El Diablo kills him, we will end up with a blood bath on our hands." She turned with a sigh... and walked back to the outrider.

"On the flip side, Nuva is right. Inferno was El Diablo's son too."

They watched as the big silver flowed towards Rafe. The man was pushing himself backwards on his bleeding ass but wasn't making much headway due his other injuries. El Diablo stopped and dropped his head to look the redhead right in the eye. Whatever Diego's son saw there, it had him screaming and begging. With a deep guttural moan, the stallion reared, striking that terrifying killing pose. He slashed down with both front legs. His spurs opened Rafe's face in two deep slashes that traveled down his cheeks from his eyes to his chin. The man curled up in a weeping ball. El Diablo nosed him once in contempt and then walked away.

Grant came running out when he heard all the screaming. Chrysta sighed and turned towards him.

"Guess we had better get him out of there and over to Dr. Whitet's office."

The bartender just curled his lip.

Azra shifted, his golden eyes hot.

"OH... PLEASE... let me do the honors."

The woman eyed the winged one narrowly.

"We REALLY don't need a range war Azra. Promise me you won't kill him."

The outrider cleared the fence and scooped the bleeding, broken man up.

"I will PROMISE no such thing when it comes to this stinking piece of offal!"

He pointed a sharp black talon at Chrysta.

"You...though. I promise to kick your lovely little ass if you don't STAY... RIGHT... THERE!"

The woman sputtered but Azra did not stick around to see that she obeyed. He shot up until the town appeared very small and lifted the arrogant young man so they were face to face. The redhead just stared at him in terror, eyes already glazing as he slipped into venom induced shock. The Outrider gave the man a light shake to make sure he had his attention.

"If YOU or your useless sire even consider causing Chrysta any more harm... or even just a little grief... you had better pray that her destria kill you. If they don't... I promise on the Vows that Bind me, no matter where you hide, my host and I will run you to ground. Be you on Earth or in Hell... WE... WILL... find

you!"

Azra dropped his distasteful burden at the town Healer's office, slightly amused by both doctor Whitet and his receptionist trying to hide under the office desk.

When the outrider landed back in the courtyard, Chrysta was quietly checking that the long slashes down Nuva's sides were healing well. The sound of the approaching storm's thunder ALMOST drowned out his rumbling growl. She turned to eye him cautiously. One hand reached out and casually tapped her hard leather chest guard with a sharp claw.

"SOOO..." He snarled, **"Were you planning on going... RIDING!?"**

His gold eyes glinted wickedly.

A slight flush rose up her high cheeks.

"NO... Grant made me put this on before he would let me come out."

"HUMMMM...Is it laced up nice and tight?"

Was it possible for a demon to sound innocent? Azra gave it his best shot.

Chrysta gave the vest a light tug,

"Grant laced it himself, so yes...It is VERY tight."

"GOOD...!"

The outrider gave her no warning. He just picked her up and took off.

"OH... SHIT!"

Chrysta wrapped her arms around the outrider's neck in a death grip. She buried her face, eyes closed, under his chin. Azra climbed hard, covering ground at a tremendous rate of speed. He leveled out on the topside of the storm. He knew he couldn't stay here long, there was not enough oxygen but he needed the height to gain the speed for what he wanted to do.

"**Chrysta...**" Azra murmured softly in her ear.

"**Do you TRUST me?**"

The question startled her enough that Chrysta unburied her face and looked up at him.

"Of course I trust you!"

The woman in his arms looked down... and froze. This was not fear though. She was stunned by the eerie beauty of the black roiling clouds below them being lit from within by the fires of hell...or heaven.

"Oh..." She whispered.

Azra could not help himself. He breathed in her intoxicating spicy scent and ran a tongue along the edge of her ear.

"**Know this then... I will... NEVER... let you fall!**"

The outrider shifted the woman until her back was held firmly against his chest. He crossed his arms so he was holding her tight across the hard chest guard. He was glad for that piece of leather. If she hadn't had it on he couldn't do this. Hooking a leg over hers... he dove.

The wind snatched her scream as they dropped into a canyon created by the clouds. Azra dodged the lightening. Dipping from one side to the other he compensated for some of the turbulence that wracked these storms. For a moment... one of the wild Tengshe dancing in the wind partnered with them. The elemental dragon gaped its mighty mouth in a joyful grin then gave the outrider a needed boost of speed as it sent them along. Leveling out a little, he raced for the wild wind at the head of the storm. They lifted right before they reached the great horizontal vortex that the massive front was pushing along. Azra timed it perfectly, riding the crest then inserted himself neatly into the wave.

He could hear the woman screaming but it wasn't the scent of feat that he smelled on her. It was pure exhilaration. They surfed the curl, picking up even more speed as the powerful wind helped push them along. Azra tightened his wings in. Skating on the edge of control he shot along the tunnel created within the wave. Smaller Tengshe danced and twisted around them, gleefully drafting in their wake. All too soon they reached the end of the vortex. With the storm threatening to crash over them, Azra came rocketing out of the clouds to soar into a rain filled sky.

The outrider could feel Chrysta shaking against him and he again shifted his hold until the woman was cradled bridal style in his arms.

She looked up at him, her green eyes wild and sparkling.

"HOLY... WOW... Can we do that again?"

His deep laughter rumbled against her,

"I think once is enough for tonight!"

At her disappointed look the outrider gave her a little squeeze.

"There is nothing to say we cannot do it again... some other time."

Azra landed and gently set her on her feet at the Ironwood's back door. She stepped into him and pressed her warm wet body tight against his. Her strong arms laced behind his back. Azra dropped his wings around her sheltering them from the rain.

"Chrysta..." This was almost a whisper.

"Racing the wild wind is... NOT... futile. There is always the chance that you will catch

it. When you do... it will give you the ride of your life!"

The woman pushed back and looked at him, her beautiful face still and thoughtful. Azra caught her lips with his, he didn't draw blood even though the desire to... TASTE... her was strong. She couldn't afford to lose even a little right now. They were still engaged in a slow, delicious kiss when the door popped open. Azra raised his eyes in time to see a grown man... POOF... up like a broody hen.

"CHRYSTA... What in the HELL are you doing out in the rain?"

Grant pinned Azra with a hard look.

"And YOU... you should know better!"

Chrysta released her hold and backed up smiling sheepishly.

The outrider opened his wings while running a careful talon down her cheek,

"You will think about what I said?"

She flashed him a wicked smile.

"Oh yes, Azra. You can count on it."

As the outrider raced to catch up to the airship, he smiled wickedly thinking of the evil look that had crossed her face when he said good-bye. Constantine was totally screwed.

Chyanne wiped down the bar while surreptitiously watching the shadowed presence sitting in her bar. She, like everyone else, had been happy to see Templer after the week he disappeared while on vacation.

Where ever he had gone, it seemed to have done him a world of good. Yes... the priest came back exhausted but he had also been more relaxed, less closed down. The Talon had even taken the tongue lashing that Iniko dished out with unusually good grace. Constantine had spent a lot of the last three months, when he wasn't on a mission, here at the Den rather than holing up at the Order's local Sanctuary. This was something that his friend's thought was a good sign.

About a week ago though, the quiet man had gotten positively... silent. The woman set the glass down with a sigh. It was very evident to her experienced eye that the introverted priest had met "someone" while he had been away. The Talon answered his Cricket (will wonders ever cease) a couple of times at the bar. Whoever it was he talked to, had made his unreadable face light up, and his dark eyes glimmer like gold in ebony gems. Speaking of which... Chyanne saw a flash of gold and hastily looked away. Templer was depressed enough as it was. He didn't need people staring at him. Something had happened and it was really bothering the man. Chyanne nodded her dark head slightly. Whoever was breaking Constantine's heart was going to get their ass handed to them by yours truly! If ever the chance arose.

"Templer..."

Azra stirred unhappily.

"Shut up... Azra."

The Talon unconsciously traced a finger over the rim of his almost empty wine glass. He glanced up, catching Chyanne watching him. He was relieved when the woman hurriedly glanced away. Templer needed to forget... her. This could not happen if people kept asking him if he wanted to TALK about it.

"Why has she quit calling?"

Constantine silently asked his outrider.

Azra sighed as and bit back the first answer that came to mind. (I can't answer that AND shut up at the same time!) He only said,

"I don't know Constantine."

The man pushed him back a little, leaving the demon to his own depressed thoughts. Azra was proud of the way Chrysta whole heartily implemented his advice. She stalked Templer like a superb, intelligent predator. There was nothing overt or aggressive. The woman used silent, SNEAKY tactics designed to not frighten off a wary prey.

At first she just called every couple of days. Sometimes Templer answered his Cricket, more often he didn't. When Chrysta couldn't reach him she did nothing that would seem... pushy. She left innocuous messages about working in Paradise valley to get it ready for the destria, or how well Nuva had healed. Once she was laughing hysterically as she warned him to make the Anesthetic she had sent to him on the first month he was home, last. It seemed that Grant accidentally blew up the still. That was the first time the Talon returned her call, rationalizing to himself that he wanted to make sure NO ONE was injured.

After that, Constantine made it a point to pick up when she called. Azra kept his laughter to himself. Gradually the man became uncomfortable sleeping in his lonely cell at the Sanctuary. The priest started spending more time at Chyanne's Inn, but even that was lacking what the man was unconsciously looking for. The outrider did not fail to register the fact that Templer seemed unhappiest about where he was AFTER talking to Chrysta on the phone for a while.

Most recently, the wily woman started sending pictures and short videos. These usually coaxed a smile from reluctant lips. They were usually accompanied by... interesting... language as she tried to figure out how the cricket's video function operated. One in particular was memorable.

This video showed Paradise Valley flaming with the rich reds, yellows, and golds of the hardwood trees in autumn. Chrysta appeared, riding Zephyr as they came up the river path. Nuva was galloping parallel to the pair with Andrew not so much riding her as seeming a part of her. Bracketed between the two, El Diablo strode. The stallion was unencumbered by any tack, his head thrown high, moving in total freedom. Behind him poured a river of gleaming hides, flowing manes and tossing horned heads. Templer stared in amazement. There must have been thirty old line mares and stallions in that herd. Chrysta and Andrew stopped as they topped the ridge and surprisingly, so did the big silver stallion. They watched as the beasts thundered up and over the ridge, heading down into their new sanctuary. The destria looked like nothing more than an extension of the flaming forest. The sun glimmered off of the reds, gold's, silvers, blacks, and grays as they poured over the rim towards the freedom that Chrysta and El Diablo had risked so much to acquire.

As the last young male passed, El Diablo brushed up against Zephyr. His long muzzle bumped Chrysta hard on the shoulder. Turning away, the old line stallion rose slowly into that beautifully classic Levade. He held this for a long minute, his white mane and tail tossing in the wind. His triumphant bugle rang out, echoing off of the hillsides. Then he launched himself without a backwards glance to follow his "family" down the path to the destiny that awaited them.

Chrysta called shortly after explaining in a voice that could hardly contain her pleasure that many of the Don's had turned over any destria that showed signs of being old line blood into her care. Nuva no longer had to worry about losing the destria's legacy.

They had received one more call after that. The woman sounded tired, but happy. She also sent a picture of a beautiful little log cabin nestled in a picturesque clearing. The lake that occupied one end of Paradise Valley was in the back ground. A one-word message accompanied it. This simply said...HOME.

That had been ten days ago. They had heard nothing since. No one called. No one answered when Templer broke down and tried to call. Azra very much wanted to physically go and check on things, but his host kept shutting him down whenever he tried to suggest it.

The deep roar of an Ether-cycle penetrated the Talon's dark depression. He realized that it must be getting late if Blade was back already. Chyanne would be closing soon. With a soft sigh, he rose intending on heading up to his room. Unfortunately, he was intercepted as Iniko came thundering down the stairs. The Talon couldn't help but wonder how someone so small and slim could be so loud.

She grinned impishly at him,

"Hey long, tall and scary... why don't you quit being so moody, broody and come out to the club with me."

She didn't even flinch at the dark frown he threw her way,

"It is Templer...and No thank you, I am heading up to bed."

The girl snorted,

"Come on... EVERYONE knows you don't need to sleep! It'll be fun."

Azra rumbled quietly,

"I will raise my wager ten to one that the annoying chit doesn't make it to maturity... any takers?"

Templer's lips quirked involuntarily at the irritation in the outrider's tone. Azra had maintained for years that someone would do the little thief in out of sheer annoyance before she had a chance to mature.

"No thank you Iniko. If you are intent on pickling yourself tonight..." He stepped aside. "Be my guest."

"Your loss Temp." She blew him a kiss, "HEY... if I hurry, maybe Blade will give me a ride!"

Templer vaguely registered the fact that the soldier had not made it inside yet.

He was halfway up the stairs when there was a shout from outside, followed by the shimmering ring of steel on steel. Iniko's scream had the priest flying down the stairs. The young woman's voice held a note of true terror. As he passed the bar... Chyanne joined him. The sound that came next made his blood run cold and had the Trinity practically leaping into his hand. It was the coughing scream of an enraged destria. The two of them came sliding out of the door, into the dark of night. The scene that the street lamps illuminated froze them both.

Iniko was down, pinned to the ground by the front hoof of a lovely black and red brindled destria. This beast had her black fanged muzzle in the woman's face and was systematically slobbering, licking and whuffling into it. She did a good job of ignoring the frantic shrieks of, "GROSS... Yuck... that's DISGUSTING!"

Evidently the young woman had come running out of the door right under the mare's feet and had startled her. The destria had reacted with remarkable restraint by just restraining the girl and not harming her.

Blade, thinking Iniko was under attack had struck with his sword only to have Zephyr surge forward. The slender black sword of Chrysta's deflected the blow but as Blade's heavier sword slid by, it had cut a long shallow slice across the stallion's heavy black shoulder. Zephyr was up in a battle stance, totally pissed and Chrysta was trying to get him wrestled to the ground. Before the redheaded swordsman could strike again, Templer's deep voice cracked out like a whip.

"EVERYBODY... FREEZE!"

True to his Fist discipline, Blade froze. Chrysta finally got her mount to come back to earth with a shuddering thump. The brindle gave Iniko's face a last swipe and carefully backed off of her so she could get up. The young woman scooted back on her butt until she was against Blade's legs. She stayed there, scrubbing at her face. The soldier glanced uncertainly at the ebony cloaked Talon. Templer didn't return his look. His eyes never left the rider who sheathed her sword and was carefully examining the stallion's injury.

The Talon holstered his gun and was standing quietly with his arms folded, when Chrysta, satisfied that the wound was nothing serious, looked up.

"Hey there... Padre."

The words were soft and accompanied by a smile.

Templer's black talons tapped a tattoo on his arm.

"You quit calling." Was all he said.

Chrysta blinked.

"I am sorry Templer, Vortex..." She stabbed a finger at the brindled mare, "...ate my Cricket a couple of days into the trip."

Said mare looked the gunman in the eye and grinned a wicked destria smile.

Constantine's heart skipped a beat when he looked up into deep yellow eyes that glowed with the fire that burned at the heart of a star.

The woman grinned,

"You would be AMAZED at how people just seem to disappear when you are traveling with three of these guys. Even though I tried... I couldn't borrow a Cricket either. Besides, Nuva REALLY wanted to surprise you. Although in retrospect that probably wasn't the brightest idea she has ever had."

The cream's head popped up from behind Zephyr's bulk. She seemed amused.

"Hold ON... Did I hear that correctly? You traveled all the way from Paradise Valley... ALONE?!"

This was a deep growl.

Templer saw the woman's eyes narrow.

"Shut up Azra!"

"I will not..."

She was tired and dusty but when Chrysta's smile turned wicked, she was absolutely beautiful in the Talon's eyes. Her husky voice was soft.

"Shut... up... Azra"

Miracle of miracles, the outrider shut up.

Chyanne had been watching the woman unconsciously control the huge animal she rode with her legs alone. Maybe she would just hold off on that ass kicking for a little while.

The woman slid out of the saddle with a groan,

"HOLY, I have been in that saddle so long I was beginning to think that my ass had grown a destria."

She stretched, rubbed the offending piece of her anatomy and shot the priest a contemplative look.

"The Dons are financing an exploratory run through the Western Waste. They are going to take a crack at setting up a Trade Route connecting the Realm to the Golden lands in the West. As winner of the Gauntlet... I have the honor of Commanding this little adventure." Her shadowed eyes never left his face. "Since we are going to be passing through Mictla'n I am here to requisition the Hand for a Rank of the Fist's best and one Talon... to augment our own guards."

Templer's brows flew up. These Don's had balls... they were going to try and establish a silk road that included HELL. Chrysta smiled as she watched him put the pieces together.

"SOOOO... Constantine, what do you think? Do you and that ancient reprobate you host feel like coming with us to race the desert wind?"

The priest froze as he was overcome by conflicting emotion. Azra gave him a gentle mental nudge.

"Come on... Templer. You were willing to

die for her... Why are you not willing to LIVE for her?!"

Templer's friends couldn't believe it when the priest covered the distance to the woman in the space of a breath. He enfolded her in his cloak, strong arms pressing her against his lean body. For a moment, it seemed as if both were wrapped in warm, dark wings. Chrysta looked up, her green eyes searching Templer's gold ones.

Azra's exultant,

"YES...!!" rolled through them both as the woman found what she was looking for. Her lips curved in a slow, contented smile as the Talon's mouth gently traced her jaw and his warm lips closed over hers. His outrider was included when Templer Constantine finally opened his heart and claimed the one that they loved.

Printed in Great Britain
by Amazon